The Darkness Within Saga:
Fallen Sepulchre

by JD Franx

The Darkness Within Saga: Book 3

Fallen Sepulchre

Author JD Franx

Copyright (c) JD Franx

Registered Copyright 2018

Cover Illustration and Design (c) Amalia Chitulescu
www.amaliach.com

Editing by A.S. Winchester Editing Services

Kindle design and formatting by Rachel Bostwick

All rights reserved

ISBN 978-0-9953363-2-2

For My Children,

It has been a very long few years for our family and I doubt I would be able to do this without you both. Whether it is bouncing ideas around or help with proof reading, or dragging you both with me to wander through old buildings and castles in Europe, I want you both to know I am forever grateful to be your dad and I appreciate all the support you have both given me since I started this journey in becoming an author five years ago. As this third book ends this part of the story that has been a part of our lives for so many years, I want you both to know that it is for the two of you.

Table of Contents

Chapter One

ZADDYK LAUREN'S FINAL JOURNAL ENTRY, 5025 PC
TRANSCRIBED BY BROTHER DONIS KINCAID
Words of original prophecy seen by
Prophet Zaddyk Lauren
as written in entirety by the hand of Brother Donis.
Dated the day of Kael Symes' death, 5025 PC.

Common people believe the gods give nothing without taking something in return. Wizards and magic users call it the cost paid for when a god uses magic in the mortal world — the balance of magic. Me? As one touched by a god, I call it a curse. The prophet's curse. The curse of seeing what may happen. In reality, it matters not. It matters only in that it is irrelevant... Sorry, Brother Donis. The effects of the madness have begun.

All that matters is that, while a prophet can see the future, the more we do so, the less able we are able to explain or describe what we have seen. This takes time to seep into the waking mind of a prophet. The sleeping mind fares no better. The madness takes complete control at some point, and that point is within a year or perhaps less. I can no longer explain what I see with any clarity when in a prophet's dream. This will likely be my last official journal entry. Perhaps, at the least, the last one any mortal mind will understand, for already I feel the insipid approach of madness while in the waking world. A heavy price by most standards. It is a price well worth paying. I have finally seen what I have tried so hard to see many times: **Black's poured blood.** *My apologies, Brother Donis. I meant to say... the death of Talohna's only DeathWizard.*

It is the trigger event that will change the course of this world's future forever. In the coming few years, Talohna will suffer wars unlike any other era in history. Ancient gods will walk among mortal man, and something far beyond a god will rise from the realm of the blackest nightmares, a being unlike anything a mortal mind can imagine. I cannot find the words to explain what I have seen beyond — the madness ensures it even as my mind struggles to comprehend it. Factors beyond anything anyone could have imagined have made it so. I have seen the links — put the pieces together.

Kael Symes was born here in Talohna, banished as the feared DeathWizard of dark legend, but then returned home by those swarmed by evil — all three events caused by magic. As if it could be any other way. A DeathWizard born of Giddeon and Aravae's prodigal blood, of the gods-blessed Elderblood and from one of the old Dyrannai Elvehn bloodlines. The odds of such a thing... Only the gods' hands could have guaranteed such a birth. For what purpose? To live for only twenty years? To die young? I think not. Then, why so many powerful magical bloodlines in one man? Why the DeathWizard's magic of life and death? All that magical power, the like of which our modern world has never seen. I cannot begin to fathom the workings of a god's mind, but I have seen what will rise from the darkness they have created. I know not whether to weep for Talohna or to smile and fall into my coming madness content in the fact I have done all I can to help those who will defend all we care about. I am at peace with either because I have already seen it in frightening detail. The darkness will bring changes to the world of Talohna unlike any other time in our history. I have seen it... I do see it... I feel it... I have felt it. If... if... if...I...

If I could only find the words to make you understand what I saw within the visions of my scrambled mind then you, too, would join me in madness. With all I hope, my prophecy will have to do. The Last Light Prophecy must be revealed in full. One piece handed to each of three prophets scattered through time. I sincerely hope they help, for my piece of the Last Light… The final piece of three is what I see:

"Dark towers rule over fallen cities. From the sea, from slavery, from magic and death, and from the oldest blood the dogs cry for war. Only if united by the birth of blackness will the dogs of war push back against the darkest power. Pray the dogs welcome the blackness before they, too, fall to the darkness as men and gods alike wage war on creation and the darkness it hides beneath soaring towers.

With darkness covering Talohna, the dogs of war howl as innocent blood flows from mountain

rivers. Can a god really die? Pray, Talohna. Pray the blackest god never dies."

REALM OF DEATH
FOREST OF ABANDONED SOULS, 5025 PC.

The Arkangel of the underworld's Paradise Realms tore Kael free of the Void's grasp. It would be several minutes before he became conscious and even longer before he finished falling to the forest floor. The Void's warmth protected him for only minutes before the hissing and fighting for his soul began. Perdition's vilest and most powerful demon lords — along with hordes of their minions — clashed with the angels of Paradise. The fighting started just seconds after Kael's death. The soul of a DeathWizard was the largest prize in the underworld's demented halls of Hell as well as in the hallowed halls of Heaven. Every ounce of the Arkangel's influence could not keep the angels of Paradise from joining in the disastrous fray. Souls were power in the war hundreds of millennia old, and a DeathWizard's soul was the most powerful of all.

Seraphina — better known as the Arkangel Seraphi — had used an obscene amount of her magical energy to pull Kael through the Void early. What she had done was against the laws of magic and the decree of the gods. The Void should have delivered Kael's soul to Paradise via the Tree of Life — he was marked for the second realm of heaven, but the demonic Lower Brethren had other ideas. Demons followed no laws, gods, or otherwise, and every creature of the afterlife knew Seraphi refused to permit another power-filled innocent soul to be stolen by the demon hordes of Perdition. It had always been the Arkangel and the Archdemon's responsibility to make sure souls went to the hall the gods had marked them for. But, the Archdemon had been gone for many millennia, and the Arkangel had been fighting a losing war because of it.

The crisp snap of wings made her turn.

"Narhia, thank you for coming," Seraphi said, bowing to the lesser angel. A loud crack rolled over the forest as a small black tear in reality formed to her right. A small demon hopped through the tear, and with a twist of his wrist, the rift closed.

"Kaseem? You came," Seraphi said. Shock marked her features. Only three feet tall and fat, the scaly demon looked up at her and snorted.

"Not every demon wants to see the mortal world in flames, Arkangel. I am tired of fighting."

Seraphi nodded, and her mood darkened. "You are both sure you want to do this?" she asked.

"If we are," Kaseem growled, "we go now. Garz'x was minutes behind me. Your brothers and sisters are losing, Seraphi. Rajazeye's hordes joined with Arreal's heretics to slow him, but it won't be long before he joins us. Widening the barrier will only give you a few minutes to help the boy. Do not let Garz'x get him." Narhia nodded her agreement and took the demon's hand. Her wings lifted them both from the grass, and the angel glided to the right, dropping Kaseem at the border on the Perdition side of the forest. Flying toward the Paradise side, she banked to the left, swerving around a black tree riddled with pulsing, purple veins. She dropped back to the forest floor fifty feet from Kaseem and drew a golden dagger.

"Ready, sweetheart?" Kaseem shouted across the neutral ground. Getting a nod, he blew her a kiss, smiled, and pulled a jagged dagger from his hip. *"To reinforce the neutral zone and strengthen the barriers, I offer my life willingly, to be taken by the hand of Paradise."*

Narhia smiled as if admiring the demon's dedication. *"To reinforce the neutral zone and to strengthen the barriers, I offer my life willingly, to be taken by the hand of Perdition."*

Seraphi bowed to both as demon and angel each used magic to levitate their daggers. With a rush of power, both weapons shot away only to be buried into the chest of the other a split second later. Demon and angel fell together, still alive. Gold and black blood sprayed from the wounds as dark tentacles sprung from the forest floor. Purple thorns snapped out of the vines and snared the angel and demon, dragging them across the neutral zone to the giant tree. With a sickening crunch, the vines retreated into the earth and took the pair with. The Tree of Life pulsated, and the neutral zone widened by fifty feet on each side. The barrier between Paradise and Perdition shimmered with waves of renewed energy. The bodies and souls of the angel and demon were sacrificed to strengthen the barrier between the afterlife dimensions.

The Arkangel sighed. It was a sacrifice worth making. Not all the Brethren wanted to be part of the domination or the destruction of the mortal world. There were even a few demons whom Seraphi had come to call friends over the past several millennia. Kaseem was one.

Kael's scream of terror snapped the Arkangel from her thoughts.

As he smacked the first branches of the monstrous trees, she barked a spell in the Brethren's ancient language. The two words slowed Kael's descent, so he crashed into the leaf mold unharmed — or as unharmed as a coveted soul in the afterlife could be.

It took several seconds for Kael to realize he was not dead from the plummet. In fact, there was no pain at all. His body had slowed just before impact. More magic.

That meant someone had helped him. He looked up to see who his benefactor was.

"Thank you?" he asked. The stunning creature smiling down at him was unlike anything he had ever seen. Her pale skin radiated a soft glow to match her long blonde hair and golden eyes, both shining with the power of the benevolent gods. The goodness inside her washed over him as if it were a living entity.

"Yes. I pulled you through the Void. That is why you fell," she said, kneeling beside him gracefully. Without hesitating, he scrambled back and panic set in.

"Where the hell am I?" he demanded. "What the hell is going on? How did I get here? Who are you?" The urgent need to draw a breath halted his inquiries.

"My name is Seraphi," the creature said. "I will tell you what I can and then we must leave. This forest will absorb our souls if we stay too long, but I cannot protect you outside of this neutral zone."

"No," he replied. "I'm not going anywhere with you until I get some answers first, and then I still won't."

"We do not have time for this, Kael. We are not safe here long."

"How do you know my name?" he demanded. "Who exactly are you?"

Stepping forward, she bent at the knees, snatched his chin, and held it tight. "You are dead, Kael. This is the underworld, the afterlife. When you died, your soul passed into the Void, and the fight to possess it began. It was the only thing that gave me the time I needed to bring you here. Had I waited for the Void to bring you through the Tree of Life, you would be in the hands of some demon or angel, and you'd be standing in one of the Nine Hells or Three Heavens. You would be nothing more than a puppet or a conduit for power instead of being here with me."

"I... I... I remember dying," he said. "So, how the hell am I here?"

"Listen to me, Kael!" she barked. "You died. You are a soul. Now, listen to me so we can leave before—"

"Uh... okay." He interrupted her and climbed to his feet. "Why do I not feel like a soul? Shouldn't I be see-through or something if my body is back in Talohna?" Looking down, he saw his clothing and Orotaq cloak had come with him but not his weapons. Of course, they had not. Finally, he touched his arms and pinched his cheek. "I feel... real."

"You are real, dammit. You can feel pain here just as in life. In some circumstances, you may even die—but die here and you will cease to exist." Pointing to the sky, she added, "The soul becomes whole upon exiting the Void, and your soul is in great demand on either side of this neutral ground. The fighting hasn't reached us yet, but it will soon. They will breach the barrier if I have to keep explaining every little detail."

"Tough," he growled. "Trust is earned, not... wait..." It finally dawned on him what she was saying. He shook his head in disbelief. "What the hell would anyone want my soul for? I've been here for a whole sixty seconds. Even when I'm dead, someone wants me for something. Christ in Heaven, don't I ever get a break?"

"You should have, Kael. Your soul was bound for the Heavens of Paradise. You did nothing in your life to warrant going to Perdition."

"That's a matter of opinion," he answered. He knew his voice held an edge, but he no longer cared. The peace and quiet of death had lasted a whole of two minutes. All the stress and worry of life came storming back even though he was dead.

"Not opinion, Kael." Seraphi sighed. "Fact. To fight or kill evil does not condemn you to Hell. Your soul was marked for Paradise by the gods of Talohna." She waved her hand over his chest, and a white glow lit up his deathflower and the vines that had spent months growing across his body. As she removed her hand, the light subsided and disappeared. "Your magical soul shines with the purity of your physical self. Only the pure may enter Heaven, but the pure can easily be pulled into Hell. The Lower Brethren—the demon guardians of Perdition—don't always play by the rules, and there is no Archdemon to stop them. They wanted—still want—your soul. The angels of Paradise are often no better. I commanded them to stand down and to treat you as a guest when you arrived, but clearly, some disobeyed. That is all that matters here. As an Arkangel and the only ArchBrethren left, I had the power to bring you here while they fought over you."

"Why?" he asked, standing to listen to her.

"You are a creature of pure magic. You may even be the first true Kai'Sar ever born. Your deathflower vines have grown to mortal completion. That has never happened in history. It means your magic is nearly whole. If you were to gain access to the rest, your possibilities are endless. That has never happened before, either. Both demons and some angels want that power. Your suffering would be a bonus for the Lower Brethren."

"Why? I haven't suffered enough already? I need more, huh?"

"They are demons, Kael. It is what they do."

Overwhelmed by the information, too many thoughts and questions tumbled through his mind. Only one finally jumped to the forefront.

"Take me to Paradise, Seraphi. My wife has to be there, and my friend, Max."

"It's not as simple as that, Kael."

"Of course, it's not," he retorted. "Because even Talohna's afterlife is also plagued by magic and greed. What do you want from me? What's it gonna cost for me to see them, again?"

"Nothing. I only want you to finish what you were born to do." He frowned but said nothing as she continued. "You misunderstand me. Your wife and friend are not in Paradise."

"What do you mean? They have to be. They've never harmed any—"

"Listen, Kael, please. We have little time. They are not in Paradise because they are not dead or else they did not die within the barrier marking Talohna's dimension."

"How? I saw..."

"You saw them die, yes. And what you saw could have been a reality or perhaps the twisted hallucinations caused by the distortions inside the dimensional bridge. It is also possible they died within your own dimension. I do not deal with the living or with souls of the dead from a dimension other than this one, Kael. I do not know whether your wife and friend are alive or if they even made it to Talohna."

"Christ, will I ever get a straight answer?" The reality he was dead and that he would never see them again hit home. His knees buckled from the weight of despair, and he dropped to the grass.

Seraphi knelt beside him. "Kael? Look at me," she said, lifting his chin and looking into his eyes. "I am giving you as straight an answer as I am able. I know not if they live, but if you want to find out, then you must listen to me. You are a very unique creature. A true Kai'Sar. If ever in all of time there is one who transcends death, it is you. But to do so, you must first defeat death. There are twelve dimensions in Talohna's underworld, and you must master each one to walk away from death and back into the living world. Once there, you can find the truth of what happened to them."

Thoroughly confused, he shook his head. "How do I master death? What does that even mean?"

"Every underworld dimension has an overlord — nine demons and three angels — all of whom must surrender control of his or her dimension to you. Whether you make an agreement or alliance for control or whether you kill them or force them to surrender it in battle is up to you. Unlike in the mortal world, demons and angels can die here, they will surrender first. Once this happens, they will give you a token of their realm. You must have all twelve tokens for the Tree of Life to open the doorway back to Talohna. Only then can you return to the mortal world, we believe."

"You don't know?" he asked.

She shook her head. "No one has ever done it."

He rubbed his aching head. "There's no way nine demons are gonna surrender their realms to me. How do I fight? How do I hurt something in the underworld? What the hell am I sup— "

A thunderous crack of energy shook the ground under him and cut him off. Twenty feet away the air ripped open, and two sets of vicious claws shoved their way through, pulling the tear apart wider. Hooves followed as the massive creature stepped from between the underworld realities.

"It is too late," Seraphi whispered. "We are out of time."

Her words hit Kael's ears as the demon passed through the torn veil. Kael got his first look at one of the rulers of

Talohna's Nine Hells and recognized the demon lord. The towering abomination wasted no time announcing his presence.

"He is mine, Seraphi," the demon stated, his voice heavy with malice.

"You can't have him, Garz'x. Not yet, you know the rules. He will enter your realm when the Ladies of Fate decide."

The Lord of the Nine Hells shook his head in disagreement. Chains hanging from his massive horns rattled and clicked against the spikes lining his chin.

"You have been unchallenged too long, angel. I will take him. Now." Turning to Kael, the demon laughed. "Your days of controlling demons are over, little wizard. You belong to me in this world."

Kael's mouth went dry.

"You may try, Garz'x," Seraphi snapped, "but you will find out the why the gods made me far superior to you. You may have tricked Salotan into banishing himself from our realm, but I am not that stupid, and drawing power from all the souls in Hell cannot make you an Archdemon."

"Perhaps not, angel. But you are weakened, and that makes me stronger than you," he roared.

Two long bolts of crackling white energy formed in Seraphi's hands. The demon lord roared a second time, lunging at the Arkangel while Kael stumbled backwards. Both celestial bolts slammed into Garz'x, hammering him deep into the dirt and grass of the forest floor. Dark smoke rose from the scorch marks creasing the demon's hide as he struggled to rise.

Seraphi spun to face Kael. "You need to run! I won't be able to hold him for long. He has all the power of Hell behind him, and I used most of my magic getting you here," she shouted. Long whips of white energy formed in her hands.

"Where?" Kael cried, terrified. "What am I supposed to do?"

She cracked the whip in her hand. "Run!" she screamed and leapt into the air to meet the charging demon once more. Kael watched in horror as Seraphi's wings unfolded from her back with a savage snap and thunder rolled through the forest. Her whips lashed out, but the laughing demon caught both. Even as they burned and blackened his flesh, he was not deterred. With no other choice, Kael turned, scrambled through the dirt, and ran.

He glanced back for only a second and saw the demon lord drag the angel to the ground at his feet, using her own whips against her. With no other choice, he focused on where he was running and plunged headfirst into darkness.

DWARVEN MOUNTAIN RANGE
ARKUM ZUL.
10 DAYS AFTER KAEL'S DEATH, 5025 PC

"You broke our deal!" Voranna Talavyr barked when she entered Arkum Zul's long forgotten throne room.

"That is a matter of opinion, my dear, I assure you," Sythrnax said. He remained calm but watched the Dead Sister closely as he sat on the marble throne. Even though she was bruised and weak, she was still extremely dangerous. "In fact, I imagine I'll be having a very similar conversation with your Cardessa when she arrives."

"Did you kill Kael?"

"No, I did not. King Bale's assassin did."

"Did you organize it?" she shrieked.

"Most assuredly, my dear." Sythrnax smiled, and he quickly ducked as a bolt of green energy snapped past him and tore a chunk of granite from the wall the size of his head.

His head tilted to the side. "This is the thanks I get for saving your life, and those of your fellow Sisters? For helping you when you were on the brink of death? Beyond death for some of you. Kael was quite thorough in that mountain glade."

"You killed our savior!" Another sizzling arc of energy forced Sythrnax from the throne, and it exploded behind him.

"Merely a means to an end, witch," he snarled while debris from the old throne pelted the back of his neck. "Nothing more than that."

"Nothing?"

Sythrnax nodded to the two guards at the throne room's entrance. Voranna frowned as they made a move to stop her. Muttered words tumbled from her lips, and both guards fell dead with putrid green froth foaming from their mouths.

Sythrnax grunted but knew he could not help his men. The corruption of the witch's demonic magic was too effective for even an Ancient of his power to counter. The effort would have exhausted him, or even overwhelmed him.

"If the Cardessa is only minutes behind me, Sythrnax, she will kill you."

"And why are you here?" he demanded. "To what end? To show me how easily you can kill two mortal guards? You waste my time, witch. Leave now, and your life may go with you. Stay, and you will die along with your Cardessa. I do not give second warnings."

"You betrayed us!" Voranna snapped.

Sythrnax rolled through more blasts of energy. The third bolt scoured his side.

"You insignificant little pest!" he roared and dropped to a knee as she approached.

"You will pay severely," she hissed. "Even if I have to drag you through the gates of the 9th Hell myself."

Rising from the stone floor, his eyes blazed a violent purple. "The audacity of you, mortal dosa, is staggering in its arrogance. The Ancients *will* walk Talohna again, regardless of the cost. One dead Kai'Sar is a small price to pay for my people to be free. If you disagree, then continue your attack. You will quickly come to understand what my people are capable of. Ella the White learned the hard way. So will you."

Voranna snorted and laughed. "Ella didn't have all the power of Hell behind her when she faced your Vikress. It cost me everything I held dear and every last shred of my humanity, but I have the favor of all nine demon lords. Your magic wasn't the only thing that helped to bring me back from death's door. Even you cannot stand against the power I have access to, and your pathetic pendants do not work against demonic magic."

"Enough talk, dosa!" Sythrnax hissed. His staff appeared in his hand, freezing vapor rose steadily from the blades at each end. He spun the staff, forcing Voranna to step back. The blades missed her throat by a hair.

She spat out the words to the black web hex. The caustic webbing leapt from her left hand and wrapped itself around Sythrnax's fingers and staff.

"Witch," he growled as the staff vanished, taking the webbing with it. "Hex magic? You had better be able to do more than that." Sythrnax's left hand shot out, the black stone in his glove pulsating with dark energy. It cut through Voranna, and she evaporated into mist. Only when it was too late did he realize his mistake.

"Much more power," Voranna whispered from behind him. Sythrnax felt a sharp jab in his neck as the witch's words washed over him. "I did say *all* nine demon lords. Did I not?" Voranna breathed out, appearing behind him. "Everyone forgets about the queen of suffering and her unique magic."

Sythrnax stumbled as the demon queen's venom surged through his body. Colours flashed before his eyes, and he tripped. The torches inside the chamber blurred, and his hold on reality weakened. The image of his long-dead daughter wavered in front of him. He shook his head, trying to dispel the image and knowing in mere moments reality would be a forgotten concept. He had mere seconds to save his life.

Falling to his knees while the dizziness overwhelmed him, Sythrnax giggled with madness. "You forget how long the Ancients have been around, dosa. *Asravan hasek oulai*," he hissed. In seconds, the spell cleared the ichor, and he regained his footing. "The Fae studied Reetha's ichor for centuries, looking for a cure back in the days when demons walked this world. Where they failed, we succeeded." He turned as the witch's curved daggers sought out his heart. His tresa snaked out from under his hood and coiled around her blades and hands.

"You came closer than most, Dead Sister," he complemented while the witch pushed hard against her blades to no avail. "Perhaps with another thousand years of experience, you'd have succeeded in killing an Ancient." Voranna tried to pull away, but his silver-scaled appendages tightened, holding her fast as he called his staff back to hand.

He saw no fear in her eyes while she grinned. "Someday, Ancient, one of my kind will kill you, and on that day, I'll be waiting for you in the 9th Hell."

Laughing, Sythrnax placed the blade of his staff over her stomach. "You'll be waiting forever. My soul will never grace your afterlife—" Agony tore into his back, cutting his words short. His arm jerked with the pain, and his staff slid into Voranna. His tresa retreated, slithering down his back to protect against a second attack.

"Release my Sister, traitor," the Cardessa demanded. Her rational, emotionless tone reminded him of the Vikress Illara.

Spinning, Sythrnax pulled his bladed staff from Voranna, and she fell to the floor. "She has been released, my dear Cardessa. You attack without provocation. Does this mean we are in a state of disagreement?"

"Only until your death, liar."

"Come now, Mydea. You don't really want to do this. We don't have to do this. There is another way."

"Dead Sisters don't negotiate with traitors." Sythrnax smiled, but for the first time in longer than he could remember, real fear crept into his stomach. He was already injured and quite severely by the way his tresa refused to leave his back. The pain tugged at his attention, making it a struggle to focus. "Very well. After you, my dear," he said.

The Cardessa wasted no time. Round sparks of green energy jumped from her hand one after another as the old woman moved slowly and chanted. The stone inside Sythrnax's glove pulsed in tandem with his staff, powering his shield as spark after spark ricocheted around him. Chunks of stone exploded from the granite walls. With his focus split between his pain and the attack, he nearly missed the fan of spines unfolding on her forearm and rushing from her right hand. The demon spines stitched the floor and arched away from his body while he pulled more magic from the stone in his glove. More spines snapped his way as the Cardessa chanted faster, alternating between the two demonic spells.

Sythrnax noted the Cardessa's cadence shift. It slowed for a mere second before picking back up. She was timing her chants for a third spell, and he was running out of time. Intense pressure assaulted his senses then pulled away, dragging something from his body. Falling to one knee, he realized the witch was grasping at his soul with her magic. His heart hammered with fear, and his anger flared at the audacity. The Dead Sisters' leader was far more powerful than he had guessed, but he grinned anyway. Using three offensive spells at once left her with little or no defense as she tried to overpower him.

"You lose, witch," he mumbled between clenched teeth as he reached for more power. His staff pulled deep from the stone in his right glove. "*Kin Atoll Frosai,*" he barked. The savage spell rolled out from his staff while he slammed the bottom blade into the granite floor. A wall of frost rolled from his staff and blanketed everything, freezing anything in its path. The Cardessa froze as well. As the mist subsided, her body remained still, a demented statue of iced flesh.

"Foolish old woman." He approached the Cardessa and frowned. "Well, you are stubborn," he whispered and leaned in for a closer look.

Power poured into the old woman from several demonic hellscapes, keeping her alive. It would do so until her body thawed.

"That is impressive," he added. "But statues break when they are knocked over." He slowly pressed a single finger to her chest. He smiled and shoved. Her frozen body tilted backwards as the frost and ice cracked, freeing the Cardessa's right hand. The old woman reached out and clawed his left arm above his glove.

"Dosa witch," he snarled while the Cardessa toppled, and her body shattered on the floor. Sythrnax released a deep breath, but it was cut short by a surge of pain where she scratched him. Glancing down, he gasped as a black corruption spread along his skin from the three scratches. "Vile wench. *Asravan hasek oulai*," he muttered but stumbled as dizziness swarmed his mind.

The spell did nothing to clear the filth from his blood, and for a moment, he panicked. It distracted him. He realized it too late as a blade punctured his throat, and a kick to the back of his leg brought him to his knees.

"That is not poison, fool," Voranna whispered. "It is the physical essence of demonic magic drawn from the dead body of a blasphemer. You will need to know from which hell it came and what race the dead was if you want to purge it from your blood. Never assume a Cardessa is harmless, and certainly do not turn your back on a Dead Sister unless you are sure she is dead."

"Surely, we can," he began and tried to stand. The blade in his neck sank deeper, and blood ran down his neck to his shoulder.

"Do not move, snake," Voranna hissed. "This blade is a breath away from ending your miserable existence."

"There is another way!" He gasped.

The knife slid deeper and hit a nerve. Sparks raced down his arm. As if sensing the pain, the Dead Sister twisted the blade and caused the sensation to triple with intensity. "You killed my Cardessa." She spat. "The only way forward starts with your death. Good bye, traitor."

The blade moved in his neck as he tried one more time. "There's another DeathWizard!" he said quickly. The blade faltered.

"You lie to save your life?" she asked. Disbelief rode every word. "I thought you were a warrior? Not a lying coward."

"It's true, or at least it will be," he said calmly. "Let me explain."

"For sparing your life? Our Cardessa is dead. Your life is forfeit for that."

"Someone has to pay for it," Sythrnax offered. "It does not have to be me. You and I are the only two here, Voranna. Tell your coven the guards attacked her from behind the moment she entered. Naturally, you killed them. Then, you can go wait for your new savior."

"Two mortals cannot kill a Cardessa, fool."

"Then make it six guards and four wizards! I do not care. But kill me, and the information I have dies with me."

"If you are lying—"

"Why would I lie? Do you believe I have not thought that far ahead? Sacrificing Kael was no loss because I knew there would be another of his kind—one young enough for the Dead Sisters to teach your beliefs to this time. Or it will be when it's born. My people have access to knowledge you cannot begin to understand. Some of our Syddic priests can touch the strings of time... prophecy, I believe you call it. Only their minds do not melt under the touch of the godly power because it does not come from your pathetic gods. What do you say, Voranna?"

The blade slid somewhat from his throat. "If you speak the truth, then we have a deal," she said.

"I do."

The blade left his flesh. "Speak, and do not make me regret it."

Sythrnax turned and smiled as the throne room door opened behind him. "You won't... Cardessa. Kael's death at my hand will be nothing but an insignificant memory within a year."

"Tyr's bloody blades!" Dominique Havarrow barked. "You better not have said what I think you did, Ancient."

"Captain? What matter is it to you?"

"You killed Kael?" the Northman asked.

"I did. I hope I didn't rob you of a revenge oath, did I?"

Havarrow's hand dropped to his newly forged obsidian scimitar, and he grabbed the haft of a Reaver axe at his waist. "No. I owe my daughter's life to Kael. He is a brother to my clan."

"Of course, he is." Sythrnax sighed, slowly sitting on the ruined throne. "You do have a dilemma then, don't you? Your honor will demand my death, yet you gave me your word, you would return my people to their homeland and never turn those floating fortresses against my people. I did help you build them after all. Northman honor is a tricky entity, is it not?"

Sythrnax watched the pirate struggle with the desire to kill him. If Havarrow decided to attack, he would be hard pressed to defend himself. The stone in his glove was spent after killing the Cardessa.

"Captain, for bringing my people to their homeland, you may stay there with us and enjoy the benefits of the Ancients second rise to power. Or, you can stand by your honor, fulfill our deal, and then gather your pirates to leave my people's kingdom — if you do *that*, you'll never be able to return to the far side of the Kasym or to our kingdom, again."

Dominique stared for only a few seconds. "I will return you home," he said. "The rest will be a decision for another day." Bowing, he turned and walked out of the throne room.

"That was bracing." Voranna smiled. "Perhaps you should tell me where my soon-to-be-born DeathWizard is? Before you end up spitting blood on the end of a Northman war axe."

Sythrnax sighed heavily. "Very well. One of your fellow Sisters will have the child with her in about a year, whether it was born to her or not. The Syddic priests were not sure if it is a new birth line, or Kael's, or perhaps even—"

"That mangy mongrel the Cardessa has been force breeding," Voranna growled. "The one born at the same time as Kael? He's a simpleton, scarred by the magic that created him." Sythrnax nodded as she continued. "Three years go by, and now, he possibly impregnates a Sister? I do not believe it, and that is not good enough, Sythrnax. That inbred dog will only spawn another simpleton." Magic flared bright green in Voranna's hands.

"It won't be the only one," Sythrnax sputtered quickly and made a futile effort to protect himself but failed.

"Speak! The truth, or you will die a slow and miserable death," the new Cardessa demanded. Agitated by her anger, the magic sizzled violently in her hands.

"Fine," Sythrnax growled, holding out his hand. "Before the snows fall in just over a year, there will be at least three DeathWizards in Talohna — possibly more. One or two will be born to the Black Sun approaching — by your Sisters or others, we do not know. The few priests in our Syddic Order who have been freed cannot tell us more. With Giddeon Zirakus imprisoned by the DragonKin, I would imagine several could survive their births during the Black Sun coming in less than eight months. There is no one left to track them down and kill them. Find them all, and you'll have everything you have ever wanted. There should be at least three of them born."

The new Cardessa scoffed, whirled, and headed for the door.

"Voranna?" Sythrnax barked.

She turned, raising an eyebrow.

"The filth in my blood?" He reminded her.

The Dead Sister snorted. "Can't help you, Sythrnax. The only person who could," she glanced to her left and down at the remains of the Cardessa, "is in too many pieces to tell you."

"How long, witch?" he snarled.

Voranna bobbed her head back and forth in a mockery of thought. "If the stories about the Ancient's ability to heal themselves rapidly is true, I imagine you'll stay ahead of it for a year before the initial effects return and you die. Slowly. And hopefully painfully."

"There has to be another answer, Voranna." He persisted as panic re-asserted itself. It was a feeling he disliked immensely.

The new Cardessa smiled at him. "You know of anyone who has enough control over demonic magic that they can draw it from your blood without killing you?" she asked.

His eyes went wide as the answer came to him, but Voranna said it first. "Yes. He could have, but you killed him, too, didn't you? There were many reasons why Kael was our savior, Sythrnax. Freeing us from the dependency of demons was only one of many. His control over the magics of the afterlife was another." She turned on her heel and left the throne room without another word.

Sythrnax relaxed, finally. "You were listening?" he asked as the Vikress entered the throne room from behind a curtain at the back of the destroyed throne. She paused at his side.

"I did." She grabbed his arm and stared at where Mydea had scratched him. Its progression had drastically slowed once his natural healing kicked in. "You have grown slow in battle, brother. I suggest you correct that problem."

"The warriors of this world have produced no significant battle challenges. Yet, the Dead Sisters magic is a vile, putrid filth. They are unlike any foe we have encountered before. Nothing like them existed in our time."

"Because they would have been executed for even thinking about demonic magic, let alone using it. This world and the dosa within it are soft as if all we accomplished was for nothing. The magic here is pathetic and weak. The Dead Sisters will fall in line if they have their savior — in whatever form that takes — and if not, we will wipe them from existence and purge them from all of history. I do not believe it will come to that. We will watch the Sisters closely. But, the Kai'Sar. Three of these DeathWizards, as they are now known, are halfway to a very serious problem."

"Yet we will need four of them in the coming years," Sythrnax added.

The Vikress rubbed her forehead in frustration. "True, and six would be ideal. But forget that for now. It is a matter that does not require our attention currently. The pirate, however, does. He will not fall in line."

Sythrnax shrugged. "Once the Sepulchre is destroyed, the remaining seals will open, and he can take us home. We will destroy Havarrow and his new ships before they leave the beaches of our homeland unless he swears fealty to you."

The Vikress nodded. "It begins again, brother. When the blood of the Lost enters this world, we can begin. I would never have thought being exiled for so many millennia would get us closer to freeing what was stolen from us so very long ago."

"The magic granted to us by the true gods of Talohna," Sythrnax said and smiled. "I have not felt our magic for so long I have nearly forgotten it."

"Soon, brother. But after we free our people and return to our beloved homeland," the Vikress said as a frown marred her forehead.

Chapter Two

"My decision to stay in Stillwater permanently has finally paid off. Hidden away in an alcove in the library is a journal from what I believe to be a true Ancient being. It has taken months to translate just a few pages, but I have discovered that this Ancient was a member of a religious faction of their governing body — a high ranking… priest, of what was called the Syddic Order. I will devote most of my research and personal time to translating the rest of this journal. If only Giddeon and that young red-haired… Ember, that was her name. If they were here, this would be much faster. I have sent word to Giddeon and will wait for his arrival, but they have only been gone for a few months. No word has reached us about his mission.

I hope this priest will have much more to tell me by the time they return to Stillwater. They will be so excited to learn of this Ancient priest who my fellow scholars have taken to calling the ghoul. I have tried to tell them repeatedly the name is spelled Ghul, but they are young and their mirth helps lighten the day…"

Salabriel Aranasse.
Stillwater Dig, 5025 PC

DYRANNAI FOREST
FIELD OF THE FALLEN 5025 PC

Agony assaulted every sense Ember could recognize. Her brain sparked as if it were a sleeping limb trying to wake from numbness. Moving was a mistake, and pain sliced through her arms and legs. Slowly opening her eyes, she struggled to place where she was.

A massive forest surrounded her and those she had jumped with. Directly in front of her stood the granite pillars of a large mausoleum, and just like Yrlissa had described, black vines were etched into the surfaces. They covered every inch of the pillars. A heavy set of polished gray and white doors kept the crypts below secured. The weight in her lap dragged her attention back to their immediate situation, and she stared down at Kael dead in her arms. Their last few days came rushing back on her.

All the running, the fighting, and the death bombarded her.

"No, Kael," she cried. Pulling him closer, she held him tight and buried her face in his heavy cloak. Her heart ached as the odors ingrained in the cloak wafted up her nose. Blood, smoke, magic, and death was all she could smell. The body in her lap did not even smell like Kael, and her tears continued while panic nearly overwhelmed her entire being. "This can't happen. Please, God, help me." She prayed, already knowing no answer was coming.

A scuff of feet in the grass and a moan made her glance over her shoulder. She saw everyone she had realm jumped with from the Animus Seal below Kazzador Mountain were unconscious. Everyone except a young blond-haired girl no older than twelve. Ember recalled the concussive shock from activating the jump spell and the agony that had torn through her head. The little girl stared at her with startling, all too familiar yellow eyes before turning to the forest and bolting.

Ember suddenly understood what had happened to her jump magic, and why.

The young girl had hitched a ride on her spell, throwing the power needed out of balance. The last second correction to her magic had saved everyone, even if she did black out upon arriving. When the little girl reached the tree line of the forest, she stopped.

She turned to Ember and pointed at Max. "He will die soon," she said and rushed away, disappearing into the forest.

Ember wiped her eyes and focused on Max.

Grabbing her alchemy pack, she eased Kael off her lap and scooted to Max's side. As she did, she desperately tried to pull herself together. She needed to be able to help him. The sword wound caused by one of Sythrnax's warriors was deep, and his punctured side bled heavily. She dropped the useless pack and closed her eyes, forcing her senses into Max's body and attempting to follow the swathe of destruction caused by the enemy's weapon. Ember searched the shattered remnants of her mind for a spell to heal a mortal wound. More of the magical wall holding back her Fae genetic memory collapsed, and a trickle of Fae knowledge entered her mind, accompanied by something else—something different.

She felt... different. Her entire body became unknown, and she gasped as the pain and aches caused by her injuries and her fatigue from travel melted away as if they were never there. The rumors and stories Yrlissa had told her about the Fae became a reality as her Fae accelerated healing magic kicked in. More importantly, a myriad of spells came with the change, including one to save Max. The words throbbed against her mind and gave her a headache.

"*Sianas Afaney,*" she said aloud. The spell slipped off her tongue without any conscious thought. Her side split open when the spell activated. Ember bit her bottom lip to suppress a scream and waited for her new accelerated healing to ease the pain, understanding the purpose of the spell. It had transferred Max's wound onto her body so her accelerating healing would mend the wound at a quickened pace.

She tried once more as her side began to heal.

"*Sianas Afaney,*" she spat out through clenched teeth. Grabbing her bleeding side, Ember clung to the magic and forced her senses deep into Max's body to the point where the enemy's sword had stopped doing damage. She released the magic, and it shifted the deepest part of his wound to her own insides.

Ember screamed. She was unable to move all the damage at once. Even with her accelerated healing, the transfer of damaged tissue, nerves, and organs was overwhelming. Ember struggled to keep the magic active and to concentrate through the agony.

It was a vicious cycle. As the wound and pain would fade with one spell cycle, she was forced to repeat it to fully heal Max's body. The longer she pushed, the more unbearable it became. The misery increased dramatically, and her consciousness wavered until she nearly slipped away. Pushing the magic harder one last time, she fell backwards while the wound in Max's side closed, but it was only partially healed. Pain radiated from Ember's lacerated insides, and she stared into the blue sky, sobbing as she waited for her magic to offer up relief.

Slowly dragging herself upright, she checked on Max. His breathing was slow but steady. She could feel how much blood he had lost, and he was far from fully healed. The spell had closed the wound, stopped the bleeding, and mended muscle and nerve, but rushing the process had left the wound extremely fragile. It would take weeks for him to recover, but he would get better if he did not push himself.

Ember eased her way back to Kael's body and snuggled into him. Something crunched under her knee so she glanced down. A broken glass vial lay on the ground between them. Picking up the chunk of glass, she carefully examined it before realizing it must have been Kael's. The label was partially missing, but she could still make out some of the letters: *.B. urge.* Holding it tight in her palm, she she cuddled back into Kael and passed out with her head on his chest.

DYRANNAI FOREST
DAY AND A HALF LATER

"Please, Max. Go talk to her. She hasn't moved since yesterday."

Wincing, he struggled to sit against the fallen logs surrounding their campsite. "What am I supposed to do, Yrlissa? Pry her off Kael's dead body? I don't know what to do for her... Fuck, Yrlissa. I barely know what to do for myself. Kael was the closest friend I had," Working to stand, he grimaced as a wave of pain rolled through his body. Ember had yet to leave Kael's side. He stared at the Elvehn assassin. Swollen and blood-shot amber eyes stared back.

"Leave her be," Aravae said softly. "We have several hours left. Ember knows what must be done."

"She won't even speak to me."

"She is hurt and angry, Yrlissa," Aravae said. The Elvehn woman's control over her emotions was not surprising. Like most Elvehn, Max guessed Aravae's mourning would be done privately during a time called the Commune, and it would only begin after more important matters were taken care of. "You lied. We are the first people to stand on this land, in this forest, for over five thousand years. My family has not lived here for thousands of years before that, and yet, you have been here before. You knew the area well enough for Ember to transport us here safely, and you withheld valuable knowledge from the one person who could have used it to save my son — to save the man she loved. She may never forgive you."

"Speaking of which," Max snapped. "If you knew Ember could jump us like that, why the fuck didn't we jump to Kael sooner?"

"Because," Yrlissa retorted. "She wasn't exactly in the condition to jump us, was she?"

"Don't you dare play semantics with me," he growled. "There were plenty of chances before she saved that bastard Northman's life."

"When, Max?" Yrlissa challenged. "After the jump to Corynth when her heart failed? Or maybe after she healed that child in Dasal? I did what I had to. It saved our lives in Kazzador City. It was fraught with risk, and the jump nearly killed us all."

"That's bullshit, Yrlissa," he snarled. "You were protecting your secrets. Again! At some point, we could have jumped. Ember would have, I know it, and she's a hell of a lot tougher than you give her credit for. Kael might still be alive had we..." He pressed his left palm to his forehead. "Fuck. We didn't have to lose... We lost him... I can't... Goddammit."

"Easy," Aravae said as she put a hand on Max's arm. "He has a point, Yrlissa, and Ember may never forgive you. I do not know. However, we have other concerns right now. When the time draws closer, I will talk to her and help her prepare Kael for the afterlife. It is a mother's... it is my duty."

Yrlissa sighed with frustration. "I understand, but we need to do it soon so that I can preserve his body before the sun disappears from the sky. I need Mylla's rays of light for the spell. Our only other option is to cremate him, and I will not allow that to happen."

Aravae nodded her agreement.

DormaSai's king, Nekrosa Kohl, and his queen, Sephi, overheard their conversation.

"You are quite concerned about preserving his body," the King said. "Why?"

"I... it is safer," Yrlissa said.

Nekrosa frowned and glanced at his wife. "So, the scrolls were right?" He smiled, and he turned back to Yrlissa. "Why didn't you tell her?"

"Tell her what?" Max demanded.

Yrlissa sighed with frustration again but ignored Max as she spoke to Nekrosa. "The little I could have told her could have been tortured out of her. I know firsthand what Dead

Sisters can do to make you talk. Even now, it is *still* knowledge that can be used against us should Sythrnax get his hands on it."

"Told her what?" Max growled, his temper flaring. "I won't ask a third time without busting your fuckin' head, Nekrosa."

Sephi stepped in front of Max but looked to Yrlissa. "May I? Tell him what we know?" she asked. Max calmed visibly as if her voice had a soothing effect.

"Fine. I suspect you two know more than most anyway," Yrlissa replied.

Sephi nodded and faced Max. "From what we discovered hidden inside the catacombs below the library in Drae'Kahn during the rebellion, Kael's kind were created by the gods to help Talohna's races fight a war—one that they were badly losing. We assumed, like most people, that it was for the DemonKind Wars."

Max scoffed, but it was Yrlissa who interrupted as she frowned. "Created by the gods and the Lesser races, and with far too much magic. For a war, yes, but not that war."

Sephi nodded at the corrections and continued, "We found one scroll that told us about the Guardians. How every wizard like Kael had a Guardian, and that person had a wide array of responsibilities. Most of the documents were faded and unreadable, so we never learned all the Guardian's tasks, but we did learn one. It said should their charge die, they had to do everything in their power to lay the wizard to rest, bound by a stasis-preservation hybrid spell. It had to be done before the second day of death had passed. We assumed it was to avoid releasing the DeathWizard's chaotic magic back into the world, or to avoid growing black deathflowers perhaps. The normal coloured flowers are dangerous enough. The rest of the info was lost, but we have scholars searching the catacombs every day." Looking over her shoulder, she stated, "You should have told Ember what you are. She had a right to know."

Yrlissa frowned, and her nose turned up with disgust. "It is not as simple as that. The magics that combined to make wizards like Kael were flawed, volatile, and wildly unpredictable from the very beginning of their creation. Seven lives were sacrificed — one of a god — so their magic could be taken and used for the ritual." Yrlissa shook her head as if trying hard to control her anger. "Magic is not designed to create living weapons. At times, it took everything we had just to keep a DeathWizard under control, to stop the corruption from eating their souls, and when we couldn't? We had to kill our life-long charges... our friends... our family... I didn't want Ember to watch me do that if Kael had succumbed." Yrlissa covered her mouth with her hand and walked away.

Having listened to the entire conversation in awe, Nekrosa finally spoke. "You were a Guardian. Weren't you? "

Nodding her head, the assassin returned slowly. "I *am* a Guardian, the very first initiated into the Guardian Pact. I am the only one left alive today. I was present over ten thousand years ago during the rituals that created the Black Suns, the Guardian Pact, and the first six DeathWizards."

"Incredible. Do you know where the magic failed? Or why?" Nekrosa asked, his eyebrows furrowed by the depth of his thoughts.

Before Yrlissa could answer him, Sephi added, "I know what you're thinking, luv. Yrlissa, no one alive knows more about death and the other side than Nekrosa. Perhaps he can help you figure it out."

"You don't understand!" Yrlissa snapped. "There's nothing to figure out. The magic is broken. It's not balanced! It's chaotic and extremely dangerous. God-magic mixed with Elvehn and Human magic, Demon, Fae, and Dragon... it was a disaster, and it was wrong to even try. We could never figure out if it was the corruption of death or if the people born with the magic didn't have the strength to handle magic from another dimension — from the afterlife. I'm talking about the magic of all the Lesser races combined with that only the gods can use. All of it handed to a mere mortal being...."

"Jesus," Max said, frowning, but Yrlissa never slowed.

"We had the first-hand help of all the gods, Sephi. I stood and had this same conversation in this very field with the gods of life and death after we buried the first three DeathWizards to fall to the corruption. Of the first six born, only two survived, and they barely managed to hold the corruption off. At times, even they couldn't hold back. So, we directed their madness, their destructive force of chaos against the Ri'Tek. If *we* couldn't... if Mylla and Dathac—if the gods—could not figure it out then, well, I'm sorry if this sounds rude, but what chance would a mere necromancer have now?"

"You don't think it's worth a try? I can pull a spirit from the afterlife and get answers," Nekrosa offered.

Yrlissa whirled and grabbed the King by his throat. She felt the frozen touch of Sephi's ice blade on her throat the moment she touched him, but it did not stop her. "If you ever pull a soul from the afterlife in my presence, I will kill you, Nekrosa Kohl, and your wife will be miles too slow to stop me. Do you understand me?" Nekrosa nodded and flashed a grin as she continued, "Pulling a soul from the afterlife leaves them up for grabs by the demon hordes of Perdition upon their return. It upsets the natural balance of power in the afterlife. Leave the souls of the dead at peace, they've earned it."

"Fair enough," he said. His voice was steady, and his eyes were void of fear. "It was just an offer. We need all the help we can get, do we not?" Yrlissa released him, and the flat side of the cold dagger slid harmlessly across her throat. The warning from Sephi was clear.

"Ember still needs to know these things," she added, spinning her dagger back into its sheath.

"I will tell her everything," Yrlissa said. "After Kael is safely interred."

Max nodded, and a sigh of relief slid from his lips as he sat back down to hold his side. He watched Ember. She was only fifty feet away, but she might as well have been back on Earth as she showed no signs of recognition of those around her. He could not believe Kael was gone. Ember would never be the same and neither would he.

"Fine." He finally agreed. "Tell her later, but what do we do after that? Kael is dead, and, in my opinion, there's only one thing that needs to be done now. A Northman and two Cethosian wizards need to join him on the other side. Preferably after they suffer first. A lot."

"No," Yrlissa said, shaking her head. "Believe it or not, we will need Kasik, Giddeon, and Saleece before we're done. We should stay here for a month or more. Let Ember mourn Kael while you heal. She needs to be able to say goodbye and to deal with her loss, and you will need to be battle ready. The hectic life we're going to have once we leave this forest won't allow for it. After a wound like that, you are months away from being fight ready, and Ember must be mentally sound and physically whole for what is to come. We all do, and we have the time. An Animus seal is open now, and you all need to know what's coming. We must prepare. There are those of us who have spent our entire lives trying to avoid this day. The Luhnee and their Keepers will already know about Kael and will be here to help with his internment."

"Bullshit," Max quipped. "The only need I have for those three will be to die."

"Max," Yrlissa said. "Do not worry about Giddeon. I have a feeling he's getting far worse than you could ever give him. The traces of magic lingering in the Animus room when we arrived were familiar. I've felt it before, but it has been a very long time."

DRAGON ISLES,
VER KARMOT, 5025 PC

Talohna's only living ArchWizard, Giddeon Zirakus, had been alone in his cell for what he guessed to be a couple of days. After the assassination of his son, Kael, Giddeon had been so shocked and disoriented that he had been completely unprepared for the sudden arrival of the DragonKin's Queen Superior and her group of warriors and mystics. Believing them guilty of Kael's death, Queen WhiteScale and those accompanying her apprehended Giddeon, his daughter, Saleece, Kasik, and a priestess of Mylla named Sister Nikki. Somehow, they were all transported back to the DragonKin home island of Ver Karmot. Though he didn't know for sure, Giddeon strongly suspected at least one of the women with the Queen was a true mature Fae. They had jumped to the Dragon Isles using the same Fae transportation spell Ember had used to save their lives from Bauro BlackSpawn and his pirates many months earlier. However, the jump had almost killed Ember. The massive use of magic had drained her life force and left her on the brink of death. Only Max's ingenuity had restarted her heart and saved her life.

This Fae, an older woman with blazing red hair, had jumped twice as many people ten times the distance and never showed so much as the slightest bit of discomfort. Giddeon grinned at the memory of how the magical transport had felt. That was real Fae power — magic not seen in Talohna in over ten thousand years. It was unlike anything he had ever experienced, and he was elated to have had the chance, even given the dire circumstances surrounding their capture. The fact he had seen a living Fae other than Ember gave his heart real hope for the first time in many years.

His smile quickly faded, though, as the reality of his situation returned to the forefront of his mind. He was in a lot of trouble, and the DragonKin rarely felt the desire to explain themselves. As ArchWizard, he would demand an explanation. Nobles, royalty, and high-ranking wizards were entitled to a tribunal when dealing with inter-race crimes. Being shoved into a dungeon prison without an explanation was insulting and he was sure it was illegal based on Talohna's political treaties.

Giddeon had not seen Saleece or Kasik since being tossed in his cell. Queen WhiteScale's only words at the time sent shivers up his spine.

"You will answer for your crimes, Giddeon Zirakus. Pray your punishment is left in my hands and not the hands of the very angry Fae mother who still has access to Darklings."

Darklings. Giddeon shivered with a groan. He had always assumed the myths were just that. Myths, stories, or nightmare imaginings and nothing more. Some historical documents even stated as much, that they were stories merely used to frighten young Fae children into behaving. Other myths about Darklings were better off not being thought about. The hairs on the back of Giddeon's neck stood on end at the thought of an emotionless Fae poking and prodding the tender parts of his brain with long-forgotten magic he could not begin to understand.

The sensation quickly passed. Queen WhiteScale would not dare subject him to such appalling debasement, not while Joran Bale was still king of Cethos and the royal fleet was in the waters of Talohna. It would take King Bale time to mobilize and perhaps even more time to find him, so Giddeon shook his head to focus on his immediate situation.

The whole time he had been in the cell, he had been offered no food. A bucket of drinking water had shown up while he slept the first night, but that was it. Having not eaten since the day before Kael's death, intense hunger pangs gnawed at his stomach, and he was nauseous all the time. The water only helped a little. Tired and sore, he drifted off into an uneasy sleep and was plagued by nightmares yet again. Morbid dreams tore at his emotions as he watched, helplessly, while Kael died again and again.

Heightened emotions from the effects of the near-lucid dreams overwhelmed Giddeon. The images shifted to the moment he, Saleece, Kasik, and Sister Nikki had betrayed Ember, Max, and the others by darting them with tribal sleep poison. His wife, Aravae, had been among those whom he betrayed. Her eyes, clouded by the haze of death, stared up at him accusingly. The words of the prophet, Zaddyk, bombarded his mind and visions of the young man's destruction-filled prophecies rolled through Giddeon's sleeping mind over and over.

The city of Corynth fell, burning under the claws of creatures he did not recognize. The cities of Dra'Kahn,

Kyll'Darhen, and even Avalera City in the Southern Kingdom country of Ellorya joined Corynth's fall. All were destroyed by waves of dark invaders with no real form.

Like his other dreams, it haunted him every time he closed his eyes. The hungrier he became, the harder it was to stay awake. The more time he spent locked in his distorted dream reality, the more horrific its impact was on his psyche. The nightmares weighed on his conscience, and his soul ached with guilt and regret. During his few waking moments, he prayed to every god in the pantheon for the dreams to stop.

But they continued unabated into the fourth day. Though few people had his mental discipline, the insipid approach of insanity crawled into the dark recesses of his mind, and Giddeon feared the time he could hold out was lessening.

Angering a creature like the Fae was a stupid thing to do. Especially when they had the magical ability to walk in dreams, enhance emotions, and rip at memories. Giddeon knew what was happening even though he was powerless to stop it.

He smiled in his growing exhaustion. When King Bale arrived, the DragonKin would pay for their arrogance in believing they could treat him like that. If a Darkling really did take over, things would quickly get worse. As the fifth day approached, there was a violent change to his dreams as he realized it might take much longer for King Bale to find him. It scared him because he had no doubts the games were over.

The possibility of a Darkling entering his mind was becoming a terrifying reality. Not understanding his fear had been a reality for almost two days, Giddeon's body shook with stress while he suffered hours of emotional torment under the power of a Darkling.

BLOODKIN CASTLE
VER KARMOT

Queen Shelaryx WhiteScale watched her friend and the Fae High Monarch, Eva Thornwing, emerge from the magic of her dreamwalk spell. It had taken her and a Dark Fae deep into Giddeon's mind as the ArchWizard sat cross-legged and unconscious on the floor before them. Carved from the island's bedrock an aeon ago, the sparse room produced a chill that slowly seeped into a prisoner's bones and added to the stress of questioning.

"Any answers?" Shelaryx asked as the Fae Matriarch untangled her fingers from the Dark Fae's hands. The DragonKin Queen immediately bent over and slid a heavy set of enchanted wooden manacles over the Darkling's wrists. They took every precaution possible when it came to the powers of mind manipulation wielded by the Dark Fae. An older female DragonKin Zephyr slipped a similar collar around the Darkling's neck before attaching a wooden chain to the manacles. Made from the inner bark of the enchanted Dyrannai tree, countless magical symbols had been burnt into the wood aeons ago. The tree's resin cured the shackles and locked the magic inside. A matching gnarled wooden key, activated by the Fae Matriarch's power, sealed the Darkling's collar tight and cut off the creature's frightening powers.

Eva stood and answered the Queen. "Yes. With Dar'Tan's help, I have pulled and twisted the events of that day from Giddeon's mind at least a dozen times. We used memories and fears to manipulate his mind until we found the answers we were looking for. Giddeon and those following him used a sleep poison to render Ember and those loyal to her unconscious before they went after Kael on their own."

The Darkling chuckled lightly. "I'd be happy to go in again, my dears. His memories are tantalizing and delicious," Dar'Tan crooned.

Shelaryx ignored the Dark Fae's taunting, knowing Eva would not allow the Darkling to feed on Giddeon's most active emotions. It was a bluff and bluster, the kind of mind game that made the Dark Fae so dangerous.

"What about the assassin who murdered Kael?" Shelaryx asked. "Was Giddeon aware of him?"

"I cannot be sure," Eva said, shaking her head. "I do not believe so, but I could be wrong. Even with a Darkling's help, there is a difference between watching the events through the memory of his dreams and knowing what Giddeon had real knowledge of. Dreams are only an interpretation of what happened, and memories deteriorate, regardless of one's mental prowess. If I push further into his raw memories, he might not survive the emotional distress."

"I don't mind if the wizard dies. In fact, let's call him guilty, and I will happily help him along—end his horrible suffering at the hands of these half-breed lizards," the Darkling offered. A high-pitched cackle crawled from his throat.

"Gods-forsaken animal," Commander Zatassa said. Yanking the wooden chain, he lashed out with his claws. Eva stepped in front of Dar'Tan and the DragonKin commander's sharp claws stopped mere inches from her face, nearly peeling it from her skull.

"I cannot allow you to hurt him, Commander," Eva stated, her Fae empathy overruling her common sense.

"Well then." The Dragonkin's Queen nodded for Zatassa to stand down. "I guess we'll have to find out what Giddeon knows another way." Her light chuckle echoed through the throne room.

Eva agreed. "I will leave you to it then. I cannot be here when you… question him. I know from his dreams he meant my daughter no real harm, and I suspect he did *not* plan what happened to Kael. If I stay, I will be compelled to stop you from getting the answers we desperately need."

"I assumed as much. Stay in touch, my dear. It's been good to see you, again."

"We have missed the DragonKin, Shel, but we will be side-by-side again. Soon, if things continue to go so badly."

"They will," Zatassa offered. "Giddeon and his witless followers have perpetrated the first seal opening. The Ri'Tek are already moving on the Dwarven seal. The Elvehn Animus Seal is still unprotected, and we can do nothing to help the Dwarven Host. The Ri'Tek do not know where the Human seal is located. If the Dwarven seal falls, my Queen and the Kin will help defend the Human seal. We cannot let it fall. Most of the Ri'Tek Syphoners are there. Cracking that seal might very well destroy the Sepulchre."

"Perhaps I can help the Dwarves," Eva said. "I cannot jump with warriors and mages that close to the Kasym's breach, but I can use our ancient obelisks to get myself and several enchanted weapons there. I just need some added precautions before jumping to Dal Dagore."

"It has been over twenty years since you were last there, and you only made it because of Ella. The tunnels from the Animus room have been collapsed. It would take years to excavate them. I know of no other way to get to the Dwarven stronghold."

Eva shook her head. "I need our witch of the White again, or else a certain Elderblood Wizard."

"I understand the witch can get you there, but you honestly believe Seifer Locke is powerful enough to safely shield you from the chaotic magics of the Kasym breach?" Shelaryx asked, the doubt in her voice heavy. "With some of the Ri'Tek already free, the Kasym will be highly active."

"Our Fae scholars believe the Locke's line of Elderblood is untainted. With my help, he may be able to help jump to my — to the Dwarven brothers' location. If he knows where to find Ella the White, then all the better."

Queen WhiteScale nodded. "Then, I wish you well, my dear friend. We will need every advantage we can create at every turn."

"They are going to open all the Animus Seals, are they not?" the Fae Matriarch questioned.

"I do not see a way to stop them without Kael. The seals were always a temporary measure, Eva, we knew that. To have Talohna free of the Ri'Tek for over ten thousand years was a blessing we knew would never last. It is time for us all to stand up and fight."

"And, thanks to this fool," she said, motioning to Giddeon. "We are going into war having lost the only real weapon we had against them."

"It matters not now. If the second or third seal opens, I'll drop the shield that protects the Dragon Isles to concentrate on defending the Human Animus seal in DormaSai. They cannot get to yours, and ours is far beyond being any help to them. Even the Ri'Tek cannot tunnel through a hundred feet of melted stone, and they only have the numbers to attack one seal at a time. They will find us waiting at the third. After the Dwarves, the Human seal is their only option. We'll fight to protect it with everything we have. The Sepulchre must stay intact for as long as possible."

"And the Elvehn seal?" Eva prompted.

"They will never safely move a force through the Forsaken Lands. Jasala's creations will attack the moment any Ri'Tek steps across the bridge. You must remember her original goal was to build an army to help fight the enemy when the seals opened. None of us believed she would ever conjure the power needed to create the Sepulchre. The Ri'Tek do not have the time to go after the seal below Jasala's tower."

Eva nodded her agreement. "You are right, but my Fae must be extremely careful in this realm. Should the enemy capture even one of us, our blood will destroy the Sepulchre, and the remaining seals will all open at once. Thankfully, the magical races are not what they once were, and Ember is far from recovering her full genetic memory. With her so far from maturity, her blood will not contain what they need for centuries."

"I will only call on you when it is imperative that we do not fail."

"You have my thanks. We remain few in numbers even after so many years. Living off-phase from Talohna has not been easy, especially for those trying to have children," Eva said, bowing with respect. "Before I leave, have you decided what to do with the priestess?"

"Sister Nikki? She is free to go if you have no objections. She is not important, and it will serve us better the less she is told."

"I agree," Eva said. "Even Giddeon feels she is insignificant. A temple-sheltered priestess does not belong mixed within these events. It merely means another lost life. I will return her to wherever she wants before I jump back to Vaenaria."

"Once word spreads of what happened to her, she will be hunted—especially by the Dead Sisters. Perhaps she will be safer here on Ver Karmot?"

"It will be her choice," Eva stated.

"Should she leave, I will offer her a blade of marked soul for her protection. If any Dead Sister, witch, or debased fanatic should go after the girl, the blade will send souls killed by it to Kael in the underworld. It will give him the strength he needs and may help him understand."

"Jasala came the closest, but even with nineteen years and the best Guardian to ever live, she couldn't figure it out."

"Kael is not Jasala, Eva. Have hope. Now, take care, my dear," Shelaryx said and turned, signaling for her guards to follow. A bright flash and crisp snap of power at her back let her know her oldest and dearest friend had returned to the Fae Realm, taking the shackled Darkling with her.

Queen WhiteScale, followed by two Talon guards and one Zephyr wizard, headed for the dungeon deep below BloodKin Castle in Cyrstalis City, dragging Giddeon with them. It was time for the ArchWizard to answer for the death of his own son. Though she did not have to, the Queen walked. It would help cool down the dragon-fire temper roaring in her heart and in her blood. If she did not, Giddeon would not survive the interrogation.

Chapter Three

THE AFTERLIFE
1st DIMENSION OF HELL, YEAR 1

The sensation of falling overwhelmed Kael. He swung his arms as he tried to grasp onto something, anything. The fall lasted several seconds before he hit the ground, hard. Rolling as best he could to reduce the damage from the sudden stop, he slammed against a wall of red rock. He looked up, and he saw fire and brimstone everywhere. The air reeked of sulfur and death. A high-pitched squeal of a laugh reached his ears, drowning out the wailing of suffering souls. He shook the stars from his pounding head. Blinking finally helped to clear his vision, and he opened his eyes. A short demon stood in front of him. It laughed a second time.

"Great," Kael mumbled. "Out of the frying pan and straight into the fires of Hell."

"You have no idea, my boy." The demon cackled. "You lucky you land here first. The others would already have you tied to a rack."

"I'm lucky," Kael muttered sarcastically. "Says the demon who finds the DeathWizard. Wouldn't that make you the lucky one?" The small demon smiled, flashing rows of razor-sharp teeth. He reminded Kael of the gargoyle statues adorning the most expensive hotel back home in Sam's Bay. It was even complete with wings, claws, and a forked tail.

"Me? Only if could keep you, I cannot."

"You don't want me for yourself." He repeated the sentiment, not quite sure he had heard the demon right.

"No. Would love you," the demon said, licking his sharp teeth. "But, no. Other plan. Salo big plan."

"Lucky me," Kael grumbled. He had no idea what the gargoyle meant.

"Yes. *You* lucky, yes. I am Rajazeye, ruler of First Hell and second most powerful demon in Perdition." Kael shook his head at the boastful statement.

"You rule the lowest level of Hell, and you are the second strongest demon lord? I guess math isn't your strong suit or the truth, for that matter." The demon laughed, and again, the high-pitch cackle hurt Kael's ears.

"Lesson one, DumDum DeathWizard. Souls equal power for afterlife, not torment level. 1st Hell draws more souls than others, except 9th. Souls are power. Not forget. Now, I do little to help, but offer my realm in exchange for deal."

Kael snorted and stood. "A deal with a demon?" Glancing down at his feet, he shook his head. "I'm not standing at a crossroads, am I? It's a little cliched don't you think? What do you want? My soul in return for your realm? But let me guess, you don't collect for ten years."

"Nonsense, boy. I give you two totems of Rajazeye realm, one for door back home. Second, you wear until back Talohna. Then, you take to Salo RedMaw. No questions, no failure, no change mind. Deal?"

"Lycori's vampire clan? Yeah, I know where they are, kind of."

"Queen Reetha not playing well with others. Getting artifacts to your realm... difficult now. This easier for both, you and Rajazeye. Agreed?"

Kael nodded.

"Good," Rajazeye said, grinning. The rows upon rows of teeth made the smile appear more like a grimace.

"So, just like that. Easy, no fighting, no dying? Is there some kind of ritual or something?" Kael asked, stunned as he took the twin totem necklaces from Rajazeye. He put one around his neck and slid the second deep into the inside pocket of his Orotaq cloak.

"No want soul. Just favor. You may spend centuries fighting way out of afterlife, Kael. Less time here means back sooner. You need return Talohna sooner. I slow you not. One more can do help. Push you to 8th Hell... I think you land there... should, yes. Perhaps land in Heaven... ew, hope not," he said, shivering. "Either way, you fight... you kill, but in 8th you find Kin to help." Magic flared in the demon's hands.

"Wait, for Christ sake!" Kael cursed. "I don't even have a weapon!"

The demon cackled, again. "You are weapon, DeathWizard. Good luck, boy, and be wary. Seldom what you see in lair of Kroa be real. Beware Reetha's Ichor." With a pop of magic, a rift opened behind Kael. Rajazeye jumped forward and shoved him into the black, rippling doorway.

Again, Kael fell through darkness for seconds on end before he came to a jarring halt.

He opened his eyes and stared around. He struggled to comprehend what he saw. A meadow of colourful flowers stretched for as far as his eyes could see while the sweet scent of pollen and dew wafted up his nose. The gentle setting calmed his mind, and it eased his sore and weary body. Towering snow-capped mountains reached soaring heights far into the distance.

"8th Hell, my ass, ya stupid demon," he grumbled as he glanced to the far side of the meadow. The only sight his eyes could focus on was the woman sitting on a white blanket less than a hundred feet away from him.

"Ember?" he whispered. She smiled and waved as she slowly stood to greet him. He took a step forward and nearly tripped over his trembling knees. Tears fell from his eyes, and his throat swelled with joy at the sight of the woman he loved so dearly but had not seen in so long. He took another step forward as she rushed into his arms.

"Kael! You made it!" She cried into his neck and crushed him with her hug.

Holding her close, he struggled to find his voice. She felt and smelled exactly as he remembered. "How... what?"

Pulling back, she beamed. It still melted his heart every time he saw it. "This is Paradise, babe. The 3rd and highest tier of Heaven. You made it safely, and we never have to leave."

Her response sparked his suspicion. "But the Arkangel said you weren't here. This can't be real..."

"Kael," Ember said, gently touching his cheek. "The Arkangel has been gone from the Paradise heavens for years. Time passes differently here, babe. Max and I weren't here when she left the High Heavens, so she wouldn't know we were here. You can stop fighting, love. We have eternity together now. Max will be along later. I wanted some time alone with you first. I've missed you so much."

Kael grabbed her arms and forced her back a step. He could see the hurt in her expression, but the situation made no sense. "But the Arkangel said that..."

More agony danced in her eyes. "Babe, listen, please. We were minutes, less than an hour, behind you... Remember the Animus chamber? You died on the seal. I even know how you—" She choked on the last words and he involuntarily reached for his throat.

"You couldn't know that unless—"

"We were there. Yes, babe," she said, her eyes wet with tears. "Sythrnax was still there waiting for the seal to open. Devastated by what he had done to you, Max and I were no match for him and his men. We died the hour after you did. That's why Seraphi didn't know. The angel, Tydariel, told us Seraphi left to help you the very second you died and had not returned."

"I'm sorry." He gasped. "I... how does that work? I..."

She stepped closer, again, and gently cradled his face in her hands. "Shh, babe. Time passes much faster here than on

Talohna. While Seraphi helped you, the hour passed in Talohna. Since then, I've been here, waiting for you for days."

"Days?" Kael said, shaking his head in disbelief. "How much faster does time pass here?"

"Faster, but I'm not sure, and it doesn't matter anymore," Ember whispered calmly. "None of what happened in our lives before matters here. Seraphi will be along soon to explain, I think. Time is almost irrelevant here. You'll see. Now, kiss me, and tell me that's not real."

Ember melted into him as he laughed. All the pain, suffering, and loss of so many agonizing months fled his mind and body. He picked her up and twirled her around, happier than he had been in a long time. She giggled and held onto him tight as they crashed to the soft meadow. He opened his eyes to watch when her lips touched his. All his doubts faded in that moment. She did not disappear in a cloud of ash. She was truly there, in his arms, finally.

It was a moment so incredible that he never wanted it to end.

FLATWATER BAY, KAZZADOR MOUNTAIN RANGE
SUMMER'S DAWN 5025 PC

Dominique Havarrow stared across the still waters of Flatwater Bay. The dawning sun gradually peaked its way over the eastern horizon, and his hand rested on the hub of the ship's wheel even though his mind was far from well-rested. The events of the previous few days and the decisions he would have to make because of it weighed on him heavily.

He shook his head and pulled his thoughts back to the matter-at-hand. Eamon O'Leary had been right. The miserable and ornery dimensional traveler always seemed to be right. It had taken one month to cast, mix powder, test-fire, and then retrofit and rig two of Dominique's ships with the new armaments. Each vessel carried sixteen cannons per side and two chase cannons at the bow. All were tested several times while Eamon altered and reinforced the mounts for the ship so the cannons did not tear the decks apart the first time they fired. Still, he warned everyone that any cannon could just as easily explode as fire off at any time. It made everyone on board both ships twitchy and irritable.

Eamon's insistence on adding the chase cannons had already caused a serious blowout between his first mate, Shasta Trey, and the irritable Irishman. The grumpy transplant from the dimension called Earth was an invaluable addition to his crew, even if the old man and Dominique's half-sister did nothing but fight. The Northman shook his head as he chalked the dislike up to his sister's youth. Northmen pups were known for being brash and abrasive at times, and Eamon was the epitome of stubborn. If his chase cannons did not work as promised, all the demons of Perdition would not be able to keep Shasta from beating the crazy alchemist senseless. From what he had seen of Eamon, he was not sure it was a fight his sister would win.

The whip of a strong wind filled the dropped sails and bought Dominique back to the task at hand.

Captain Sandra Innac nodded as her ship, the Reaver's Curse, pulled even with his Twilight Reave. Dominique smiled wider at the sight of the floating weapon. It was an identical match to his own ship.

"Sythrnax's scouts said to the south," she shouted as the two ships moved close enough for them to communicate across still waters.

"Good," Havarrow yelled back. "Let's go show the bastard our new ships." Dropping his voice, he muttered, "Hunt me, you black-heart bastard. Never even thought of turning against you."

"Don't matter now," Eamon offered up from his right side. "Every fecking Suns' ship will be hunting us." Shasta smacked the short Irishman upside the head and received one in return. "God fecking dammit wenchling! Stop effing doing that. Next time, I swear to the Lord almighty, I will shove my boot right up your tight ass—" A second smack would have knocked him to the deck planks had he not ducked beneath it. Planting his boot on her backside as she passed, he gave her a light push.

She stumbled but easily recovered and whirled back around, her fists raised for a fight. "Stop complaining!" she barked. "It's all you've done for months, and you wanted Captain Havarrow to betray Bauro. Now that we're forced to fight him, you whine even louder. The only time you're happy is when you're blowing shit up."

"The Irish don't whine, womanling. We just state the fecking obvious that yer stupid pirates seem to overlook."

Shasta sighed and lowered her fists. "Go mount those useless chase cannons. Prove they work better than our ballistae draglines. That way, if they explode in your *fecking* face," she mocked, "then I will never have to look at it again."

"Yeah?" Eamon asked. He stared at Dominique, but slowly raised his right arm toward Shasta and lifted the middle finger attached to it.

"I know what that means now, you little fuck," she snarled and took another swing at him, but the Irishman was already up and over the railing.

"You made them," Havarrow shouted after him. "Go operate them, and slow that BlackSpawn bastard as if all the ghost ships below us were dragging him to the deep." Eamon spun from mid-ship and grinned. Dominique heard him mutter something about whiskey making for a perfect day and laughed his agreement.

"You know, that crazy bastard is gonna be the death of us both, right, brother?" Shasta said, looking back at Dominique.

"Probably. But no one lives forever, and I get a hell of a lot of enjoyment from the little bastard in the meantime." The words were barely out of his mouth when his crow's nest spotter hollered from above.

"Suns' ships off the bow and to the starboard side!"

"How many, Scag?" Shasta yelled and glanced up.

"Eight? No… ten…"

"Bloody bastard." Shasta cursed, glancing back at Havarrow.

"Sorry, first mate. The last two just cleared the point," Scag shouted. "Twelve ships total! All flying the Bastard's flag!"

"That means Bauro's there," Dominique said, frowning.

"But twelve ships? Against two?" Shasta asked. "We won't even get you close enough to offer a leadership challenge."

"Let's just worry about Bauro's swamp scout," he said. "Make sure Eamon's ready. I can't form a battle plan until I know exactly what these cannons will do to a wooden ship, and the scout will be the first one at us when they try to swamp this ship."

Shasta frowned. "If that drunk misses, the elementalist aboard the scout will carve through our hull like a red-hot blade through fancy leather armor."

"If that happens, make damn sure the flagmen signal Innac to unleash all she has, and then get to safety."

"This," Shasta began, but paused and stepped closer, "is a foolish risk, brother."

"I agree," he replied. "But something about Eamon's crazy stories… I can spot a liar, sys, and he is not."

"I agree, but these noisy bastard weapons better work. Cause I doubt these so-called flying machines and men who walk through the stars work as easily as he explained."

"We shall see," Dominique hissed. "Bauro's swamp scout is away."

Shasta growled and hopped the railing. Landing on her feet, she headed straight for Eamon. "Irishman!" she barked. "Now's your chance to show us what these weapons of yours will do. That small ship headed our way, destroy before it gets too close."

"It's moving too effing fast," he snapped back. "How the hell does a ship move like that on only wind power?"

"There's a magic user on board, you idiot," Shasta answered. "If he reaches us, he'll use that magic to tear out our hull. Sink him!"

Dominique frowned, and the Irishman grumbled and pulled the chase cannons up, locking them in the stow position.

"Never hit him with these," Eamon said and pointed to their starboard side. "Broadsides. Shot balls and don't pack them too tight."

"Fill the starboard monsters, boys. You heard the man! Pack them too tight and we dream the deep blue," Shasta yelled. "Firing order, Eamon?"

"I need a bloody rangin' shot from the forward most cannon. I will aim and fire it. Have your men ready to spark the rest when I shout."

The first mate nodded and passed Eamon's orders to her crew. The earlier hatred and their mocking banter vanished as the seriousness of battle set in.

The scout ship sped up, and Dominique frowned. The smaller vessel's sails bulged as the mage pushed his magic and the ship even harder.

"Eamon?" Dominique barked.

"Aye," the Irishman growled. "Give me a second, I have to take in the wind."

"Eamon," Shasta began, but the Irishman stood and touched the flame stick to the top of the cannon's barrel. The ship shook violently as the barrel belched flames. Dozens of gasps and a few shrieks rolled through the crew as the cannonball slammed into the water behind the approaching craft, tossing water ten feet in the air. Several of the youngest crew members ducked under the lifeboats and hid.

"You missed," Dominique stated calmly.

Shasta stared at Eamon and shook her head. "That was not impressive, at all, Irishman."

"Really? Water displaced the pressure of the shot, Einstein," Eamon quipped. "Coulda swore the Bastard's whole fleet was on its way to Davy Jone's locker."

"What?" Shasta barked. Her voice cracked as she continued. "Eamon! Five seconds, and *we* feed the deep blue."

"Eight seconds, actually," he replied, "but then you ain't an engi—fire!" His shout rolled out across the ship, and the crew responded. The remaining seven cannons on the top deck roared to life, and the whole ship careened under the stress of the detonations. Dominique glanced to his right just in time to see the scout sail into the hail of metal. The smaller shot balls pelted the ship from bow to stern. One struck the mage and jerked him overboard at the same time as a second metal ball hit the rudder man in the face. His head evaporated, and his body slumped forward as splinters, cloth, and chunks of wood splashed across the ocean.

An eerie quiet settled over Dominique's ship while everyone stared at the obliterated scout ship. Moments passed before Eamon laughed.

"Feck, yeah," he hollered, and the crew followed suit. Cheers and yelling bounced across the deck from all sides of the ship.

Dominique shrugged. "I'll take that over the deep blue. We'll sink the bastard, instead."

Shasta's laughter reached his ears as she howled and pointed across the water. "The Bastard's got his ships clustered in order to protect the flagship," she said and looked back at Dominique.

"Good thing we doubled the side cannons then," he said. "One broadside shot can drop his strength in half as long as the chase cannons take out their sails before we're surrounded."

Shasta gave him a quick bow and screamed at her men. "Let's go, boys! Swab the hot metal and get us into deep water!"

"Heavy shot this time!" Eamon yelled as he returned to the bow to prep the chase cannons.

"You heard him," Shasta continued. "Let's show Bauro BlackSpawn what these new babies can really do. Drop every ounce of cloth and load every cannon! I want all sixteen monsters on each side ready to fire on my or Eamon's order.

Castaine, be ready on that anchor, I want the Reaver spinning like a top if we need 'er to!"

Extra sails dropped on all three masts and caught the wind as they left the calm waters of the bay. Both the Twilight Reave and the Reaver's Curse lurched forward and went straight for the Suns of Blood armada.

In a matter of minutes, both of Havarrow's ships were within ballista range of the oncoming fleet, and Bauro BlackSpawn wasted no time. The air filled with dozens of flaming ballista bolts. Most of Bauro's ships only held two or three of the large ballistae, but they fired metal bolts inlaid with hollow obsidian, both to lighten them as well as to hold an extra gallon of pitch to splatter and ignite on impact. Dominique thanked the sea god the bolts could only be launched one at a time or else the torque would damage the enemy ships. Of course, if even one ship had a mage or wizard aboard, all the ballistae could be fired at once if magic reinforced the ship. He frowned. Bauro always had at least one magic user on his flagship.

"Now, Castaine!" Shasta yelled. Castaine McGraw immediately kicked the lock pin out of the windlass, and the massive anchor plunged into the shallow waters of the bay. A handful of other sailors pulled the sails, and the Twilight Reave groaned to a rough halt as the Reaver's Curse cut hard across their bow. The ballista bolts fell short while Havarrow spun the wheel to port and turned the Reave hard. As Castaine and his men worked the windlass to pull the anchor from the sea bed, the sails dropped and filled with wind once more. The Twilight Reave raced forward, hot on the stern of the Reaver's Curse.

"Fire!" Shasta screamed when Eamon gave her the sign. All sixteen cannons belched flames. Cannonballs soared across the distance and smashed into several of Bauro's ships. Captain Innac's ship roared as her cannons let loose a volley of heavy metal. Three ships on the outer edge of the fleet peeled away from the cluster and made for deeper water. The ships at their side caught the full force of Innac's cannons and broke apart under the hail of cannonballs. Bauro's flagship and three others continued straight for Dominique. The six damaged ships burst into flames when the destroyed pitch ovens set them on fire.

"Swab and reload!" Shasta ordered while she paced the row of cannons on the top deck. "Bottom deck, ready?"

"Aye, first mate!" a voice called up from below her feet.

Smoke billowed into the air around Bauro's burning ships, and Dominique lost sight of the last two enemy ships closest to the bay's point.

"First mate," he barked. "Where are the rear two ships?"

"Scag!" she roared. "Fleet position?"

"Three ahead, first mate!" he yelled back down. "Four coming at us from the starboard side and the last two will be on our stern in minutes."

Shasta waved him off and rushed up the stairs to Dominique's side. "We're nearly surrounded." She gasped. "The port side is the only way open to us for now."

"We're too heavy with the cannons. We can't out run him. Half sails," he ordered, and she nodded, relaying his orders to the crew. As his ship slowed, he watched the sails on Captain Innac's ship come together and drop to catch the full winds. With their sails full, her ship cut hard to the left, and he saw her port side cannon doors were closed. "Good plan," he muttered. "That's my girl." Her thoughts had to be the same as his. The moment her bow swung full around and her ship barreled toward him, he knew what her strategy was.

"Let them come!" he bellowed across the deck. "Let the Curse come to our starboard side!" Turning to Shasta, he added, "Tell our port side gunners to drop the doors until told. Hide the cannons."

"Of course," she replied. "If we switch sides with the Curse, Bauro won't realize there are cannons on both sides of the ships. If we can hold out that long, that is."

"Put up a token resistance, first mate, and then raise the white flag once the Curse is alongside," he commanded and spun the wheel to port so Captain Innac could pull alongside them. Both ships' port side cannons were hidden by closed doors, and there was no way Bauro would know they had cannons on both sides. He hoped the risk would pay off. He frowned when the first flaming ballista bolt slammed into the top deck railing and tossed burning pitch to the deck. Two crew members dumped sand over the fires and covered them with small sections of dampened canvas before returning to their assigned positions. Each took turns glancing back to make sure the fire stayed out.

Dominique smiled at his crew's efficiency. His pride was short-lived as Bauro's fleet slowed and surrounded them and the Curse. A single flaming bolt struck the side of his ship just below the water line. They were just out of range.

"You won't be able to challenge if you surrender," she reminded him.

"We are not surrendering, just buying time," he snarled.

"What else does a white flag mean besides to surrender?" Eamon asked, climbing the stairs to the helm deck.

"It's a ploy to draw him in closer, Eamon," Shasta replied curtly. "Surely, you'll be able to target more accurately if they are closer, and Sandra, too?"

"That's..." Eamon began but his voice faltered for several seconds. "That's like kicking a man in the swinging stones. Ain't there like rules against shyte like that?"

Shasta stared at him with her mouth open, but she remained wordless.

Dominique snorted. "By the sea gods wrinkled nutsack, Eamon," he said and burst out laughing. "We're fucking pirates. The only rule we have is to survive the day to plunder another." He deliberately slowed his words as he stared at the Irishman. "Let the Bastard get close, and then, fire your fucking cannons. Is that clear?"

Eamon shrugged. "Perfectly clear, boss, but that won't get them all," he said. Dominique frowned, and Eamon nodded. "We'll be ready." He turned and rushed to the port side row of cannons.

"We have two ships on each side of us," Shasta said as Captain Innac's ship arrived and slowed. His men pulled all sails up and the Curse did the same. Both ships came to a rest in the rolling waves only thirty feet from each other. Captain Innac nodded to Dominique, and he returned the gesture. "Bauro's ship is hidden behind the two at our starboard side. Innac won't get him."

"Always the bastard coward," he muttered.

"They are nearly in position to—" Shasta's words were cut short as several more flaming bolts landed in the middle of the main deck, and his crew rushed to contain the damage. "Pull all our sails and drop anchor," he yelled. "Raise it, first mate. Now!"

Shasta waved up at Scag. "Raise the white flag!" she screamed. The crow's nest spotter obeyed and tied a large flag to the main mast. The white cloth peeled open and snapped in the wind. The flaming ballista bolts came to an end, and Bauro's remaining fleet closed.

"Eamon?" Dominique shouted.

"Almost… a few more seconds," he replied

"Make sure Sandra knows to run if we get out of this alive."

"Already done," Shasta replied.

"Now!" Eamon hollered, and Shasta waved at Captain Innac. The port doors slid back on both ships.

"Fire everything!" Shasta screeched. Dominique closed his eyes and covered his ears as the sixteen cannons roared, and Sandra's ship followed a second later. The two vessels to Dominique's port side exploded, smashed to splinters by the onslaught of metal cannonballs. As he glanced to the right, he saw the two on Sandra's right had fared a bit better. Without Eamon to aim, the ships remained intact but listed heavily from the fires racing across their decks and up their masts. Bauro's ship was untouched.

"Pull the anchor and raise all sails," Dominique barked. "Straight ahead. Eamon, target the two ahead of us."

The Irishman saluted and went to work while Dominique glanced back in time to see the Reaver's Curse race after the two ships at his stern. The targets raised sail and separated as they turned toward the deeper waters of the Sea of Storms. Havarrow spun the wheel and pursued.

"Don't let them get away, Eamon. The chase cannons!" Shasta yelled. Cackling like a madman, Eamon ran to the front cannons and kicked their lock pins free.

"Load them!" he barked to two sailors, and they poured black powder down the throats. He took a step back and spun two flame sticks like swords. The tips flared as the two crew members eased the cannons into place. Eamon lit them both, and they discharged, vomiting lengths of heavy chain attached to small cannonballs. The spinning chains hit hard, tearing the cloth sails and smashing the wooden masts on both of Bauro's fleeing ships. They were left adrift in the deep water. Eamon cheered and pumped his right fist in the air.

"Yes," Havarrow hissed.

"Bauro is running, Captain," Scag called down from the crow's nest. "He split the gap 'tween us and the Curse."

"Hard to port," he yelled and spun the wheel hard. The ship groaned as it leaned in response. The crew adjusted the sails, and they sped away, hot on Bauro's stern.

Bauro's ship jumped ahead and accelerated unexpectedly.

"Shit." Havarrow cursed. "The BlackSpawn Bastard has a wizard aboard. Shasta, we need to get him before he's out of range!"

"Eamon?" she snapped.

"Need to be closer," he growled back, but grinned suddenly as he carried on. "Wait! Use the angle to cut him off when he swings wide to clear the point on the bay's far side. That should get us close enough."

"Dammit, Eamon! I love you, you little shit," Shasta exclaimed.

As Dominique eased the wheel toward starboard, the main deck cannons aboard his other ship roared. In the blink of an eye, the second deck cannons spewed fire and smoke as well. Bauro's last two ships each fired a ballista shot off as Captain Innac's ship turned hard. The ship headed for him, but he realized she was not coming to his aid. With her sails and masts on fire, she managed to come full about as her speed slowed. Her sixteen cannons fired while she came to a halt less than a hundred feet from the last two enemy ships. The hail of cannon fire ripped through both ships. They shattered and broke apart, beginning an agonizing descent to the sea's floor.

Dominique returned his attention back to Bauro's fleeing ship. Its bow swung out as Bauro BlackSpawn tried to edge past the shallow waters of the bay's far point.

"Closer!" Eamon barked while glancing to Dominique.

"We won't get much closer," he shot back. "Bauro knows these waters as well as I do." He held his breath as he watched his old commander clear the shallows. "That's it. He's clear."

"Fire, Eamon. Now, dammit!" Shasta screamed. Eamon lit the cannons once more and turned his back as they erupted. Chains whistled through the air. Both ball and chain smashed into the side of Bauro's ship and did minimal damage but not before taking out the main and mizzen masts. With only the foremast remaining, Havarrow's ship quickly caught the BlackSpawn Bastard and, once alongside, his men tossed hooked lines over the rails of Bauro's ship to tether the Reaver secure.

Dominique grabbed his sword from its sheathe as his crew scurried onto Bauro's ship. Fighters jumped from the shrouds and dropped on the men battling along the deck. Considerably outnumbered, Bauro's crew fought to the last man. In the end, only Bauro, his sorceress, and a single crewman survived.

Havarrow tore free his new gift from Sythrnax from the last of Bauro's crew. The forged obsidian cutlass sliced through flesh and bone with surgical precision. Dominique took the stairs up to the helm deck two at a time and came face-to-face with his old captain. Shasta and Eamon were right on his heels, so he had only a moment to take in Bauro's female wizard. The gaunt woman held a hatred in her eyes Dominique knew all too well, but it was not aimed at him. The lone surviving crew member was frighteningly familiar, but he could not place the thin, scraggly-haired man out of the hundreds of pirates who sailed under the Suns' flag. A chill ran up his spine, but he shrugged it off and turned to Bauro.

The Suns' commander laughed and gripped his sword with white knuckles. "Now I see why the traitor ran," he snarled. "You found the crazy alchemist."

"Feck you, pirate," Eamon snapped, blatantly insulted. "My crazy alchemy just blew yer ass all over this bay."

Bauro growled as he continued, "Instead of bringing him to me, you kept him and these new weapons for yourself. Northman traitor!"

Shasta smashed Bauro in the mouth with the butt of her dagger. "The only traitor here is you, bastard. We weren't keeping the alchemist for ourselves. We were delivering people to these mountains, an unexpected, but urgent paid job. You came after us, not the other way around."

Snorting, Bauro shook his head. "Lying wench."

Havarrow stepped forward. Nose-to-nose with Bauro, he trembled with rage. "I have sailed at your side for over twenty years, every single second of it faithfully. I never once considered keeping the crazy fucker for myself until you started your hunt for me. You sank one of my ships along with our paid fare's protection ships in this very bay not two months ago while I unloaded my charges and their supplies. With no warning and no chance to parley. Had you not done that, we would have headed to you the second they were unloaded. But, instead, we outfitted my ships with these weapons. You caused this with your cursed paranoia and greed."

"Matters not, Northman." Bauro grinned. "Question is, will you follow the Suns' creed and fight me for control of the Suns' so I can kill you?"

"If that is what it takes."

"You know you cannot beat me one-on-one," Bauro sneered. The bastard was right, and Dominique frowned while Bauro continued, "Or, perhaps, you will just kill me like the coward traitor you are, huh, Dom?"

"Fine I challenge—"

"No, you don't," the pirate standing behind Bauro growled, interrupting him. With no warning, the last crewman bent over and yanked a dagger from his boot. A snarl of hatred marred his face. It was a face Dominique had seen in battle many times.

"Cassel," he let out as the man viciously stabbed Bauro in the back. Ripping the blade from Bauro's flesh, he kicked the back of his knee and stabbed him once more as he dropped.

"This is for my fucking wife, you black-heart bastard," the pirate barked. He eased the blade into the side of Bauro's neck and spat on the twitching corpse as it fell to the deck. Bauro's sorceress shrieked with rage and magic leapt from her hands. Shasta stepped in front of Dominique with her daggers crossed in defense, but instead, the magic gripped Bauro's corpse. Pivoting, the sorceress lifted Bauro's corpse into the air with magic before flinging it overboard.

"Good riddance, you gods-cursed pig!" she snapped, earning a curt nod from Shasta.

Dominique stared at the man who had killed Bauro. It was a face he recognized through the grime and a hundred pounds of weight loss. It was also a face he was certain he was never going to see again. The man was paler than he remembered, and his eyes hollowed from sickness, but the familiar face he knew was underneath it all. "You've lost weight, but I know you, pirate. I thought you were dead," he said.

"You fucking better well know me."

Dominique shook his head, repeating himself. "We thought you were dead, Cass."

"Close as I could get, I promise you, brother."

"Wait," Shasta whispered, "Cassel Moranax? Your old partner?"

"Aye," Dominique said, smiling. "Where you been, my brother?"

"Witches," Cassel replied. "Ella the White. I think she brought me back from the dead after that Broken Blade killed me. Woke up and found out it's been almost eleven years. My Suns' mark and sailing experience got me aboard the Bled Trader. Heard rumors Havarrow had gone rogue."

"Damn lies," Dominique snapped. "Bauro was paranoid. Yes, we had the alchemist, but we weren't running, just finishing a job. How'd you end up on Bauro's ship?"

"I woke up under the care of one of Ella's witches but managed to escape. I overheard the Twin Cities' port guards talking about Captain Orion shipping out. I remembered Hack Orion. He was an anchor winch-man on a low-level ship a decade ago. He never recognized me, but he was short on men. It's hard to fake Bauro's magical Suns of Blood tattoo—bloody Broken Blades were good for something at least. Once Orion sailed out, I explained who I was. Bauro sent Orion back to Rejtett a week ago, so I jumped aboard the BlackSpawn Bastard in the hopes he'd actually catch up with you." Cassel shook his head as he laughed.

"Wait," Shasta interjected. "You can't be serious. You were with Ella this whole time?"

"Pretty sure that's what happened, young one. Yes," Cass said.

"Good enough for now." Dominique snorted, dragging Cassel in for a hug. "Ha! Welcome back, my brother! Gods-damned good to see you. Now, let's find you a ship. It seems several of Bauro's need a new captain, and we still have an escort and protection run to make. I have to keep my word before I kill that bastard Sythrnax."

"Yeah?" Cassel asked, grinning. "Business as usual then, even with these new improvements."

"Far from it, old friend. It seems the Ancients have returned to Talohna, and they want us to take them home. Then, we're gonna kill one of their generals and start a war with the rest. A war so big Tyr will weep with envy."

"No shit? Why?"

"Their general killed a brother of ours, one who held my kreeda, an offer for saving my daughter's life."

"Guess that's what I get for sleeping for a decade. You have my sword and sail always, you know that. Any chance you know where Yrlissa and my little girl are? Hack told me Bauro tried to kill her, that my death fell at her feet. Why, Dom?"

"I know not what happened to your young one, but you know how it works. From our side, you were cut down during Blade internal business. Merethyl Bellas paid the gold-weight, but Bauro wanted a point made. Yrlissa is still alive, though. I saw her myself months ago. The Broken Blades believe she is dead. Bauro ordered all Suns to keep the knowledge she's alive as a secret. I agreed. But you're not dead, brother. So, we get this job out of the way, and you can take a couple ships to find her. I will sail at your side until we do. You have my word. Besides, starting a war takes time." He laughed.

Cassel nodded. "We're taking these Ancients home before we start a Kreeda-war with them, then? You know what that means?"

"I do," Dominique answered, his voice dropping. "Before we call in our oaths, we're going back through the Jaws of Ice and Rock, and this time we have to make it to land."

"We barely made it out alive last time, Dom. We lost four ships and over thirty men. Three were wizards!"

"I know, but this time we'll have cannons to help with the wildlife, and we'll have *Ancient* wizards commanding the decks."

Dominique chuckled a second time as he stared at his previous first mate and closest friend.

"Well," Cassel stated, "we didn't choose this life to live forever or to grow fat from merchant gold, did we?"

Dominique shook his head and lifted his arm, pointing at his flag man. "We did not, we do it—"

"Because we can." Dominique, Cass, and Shasta said in unison as they laughed.

"Wrap the other ships up, Shasta," Dominique ordered. "Let's head back to Arkum Zul. We have special arrangements to make."

Chapter Four

'In one and the same fire, clay grows hard and wax melts.'
Francis Bacon

"An English philosopher from the sixteenth century by the name of Francis Bacon once said that. I remember reading about him in school, and this quote can be applied to almost any situation involving the changes of life and death. With what has happened to us, to Kael, and to our group, I think this quote applies more now than ever before. The fire that is our life can either melt us or harden us depending on our own resolve and strength of will. Kael refused to melt under the torrential firestorm that was his last year of life and he will always be an inspiration to me. Very few people could have experienced what he did and still pushed forward every single day, but he did. Even after all that he suffered and all that was taken from him, Kael forced himself to keep moving forward, to keep helping those whom he did not know, and to keep living. The only way to do this was to harden himself. I know this, so how can we not do the same? We have to follow his example and rise from the fires of loss harder and stronger. We will do the same and we will live on."

Ember Symes, Kael's Eulogy.
Field of the Fallen, Dyrannai Forest

DYRANNAI FOREST
THE ANCIENT KINGDOM

Kael had been laid to rest, and the preservation spells cast by Yrlissa completed. The moment she finished, a lone Luhnee warrior walked out from the forest carrying a clear sarcophagus lid to place on Kael's tomb. It was meant to protect his body further. The young man, a Druid, entered the crypt and placed the cover himself before nodding to Yrlissa and bowing to Ember.

"My people have guarded his kind for a score of millennia. The other half of your heart will always be safe here. By my word, and that of the goddess, you will always be welcome in this holy place. As your kind have always been." With a final nod to Yrlissa, he left and vanished into the forest.

Ember returned to the fire and sat down to share the evening meal with the others, but she was not in the mood to eat. Instead she glared at Yrlissa for several seconds, nervously spinning the broken vial through her fingers.

"Enough of this shit," she said, staring at Yrlissa. "You have some explaining to do. You know a lot more about what's happening here. I heard what you told Max and the others. You will elaborate further now. No more secrets, and no more lies. Those are the actions of a *Vohkra*," Ember snapped, purposely using the Dyrannai Elvehn term for traitor. "Those aren't the actions of a friend."

"Call me what you will, *mai nahlla*."

Ember held up her hand, interrupting Yrlissa. "Never call me that again. Ever," she said. The low growl in her voice made the implication of violence clear. "You demean yourself and insult me at the same time. Now, tell me the goddamn truth."

"The truth?" Yrlissa asked. She turned to the fire and stared into the flames as if in a trance. "All right. But the truth will only make things worse."

"Kael is dead, so I doubt that. But I'll decide for myself. You owe me," Ember told her, shaking with anger.

"I owe you more than you will ever know, *mai*... Ember. What do you want to know?" Yrlissa sighed.

Ember did not know where to begin, and the silence opened the door for DormaSai's king. Nekrosa sat quietly with Sephi cuddled into his arms. He said nothing while Ember pushed Yrlissa for answers about the horrific events of the last couple of days. A frown curled his brow as he straightened, and Sephi slid over to give him room to stretch his bad leg.

"The Ri'Tek," he interjected. "Start with them. The Arcane Library in DormaSai has nothing on them."

Yrlissa nodded. "The Ri'Tek? I guess it's as good a place as any. What came before that matters little anyway. The Ri'Tek are the second of Talohna's original two races. They truly are the Ancients. They had incredible magic at one time. It was powerful, amazing, and unrivaled even among the other races. All you have to do is look at all the wonders across Talohna to know what they were capable of."

"Were?" Sephi repeated.

"Yes," Yrlissa said, carrying on. "The Ri'Tek are not like us. Their emotions and morals are far different than ours. Although, I don't believe evil is a word that qualifies to describe them. They don't act out of malice or to purposely be sadistic. They just do the things they do to achieve their objectives. Their natural magic was stripped from them long ago by gods aeons older than ours are now. Even though they could do some amazing things with magic, the Ri'Tek soon grew tired of building wondrous cities and artifacts. They thrived on challenges and perfection. So, instead of continuing to create wonders for this world, they shifted their focus: to emulate their gods. By using magic, the Ri'Tek attempted to create new life. They worshiped the Old Gods and wanted to be like them in every way."

"That's frightening," Sephi commented. "The arrogance..."

"Exactly," Yrlissa said. "They quickly discovered creating life was not so easy because they were not gods with infinite power drawn from another dimension. Instead, they mutated and perverted life that was already present instead. Using the Lesser races as a start, they created an assortment of sentient creatures and some not so sentient."

Absorbed in the story, but confused, Ember asked, "The Lesser races?"

"Yes. Humans, the Elvehn, and the Dwarven people before any of us had access to magic or technology in the case of the Dwarves. Later, the magical races joined us in the eyes of the Ri'Tek. The Dragons, the Fae, and the DemonKind all became known as the Lesser races. They were young races. All of them just trying to live, to survive. They were easy targets for the Ri'Tek. The Lesser races were twisted and mutated into creatures so vile that Perdition's strongest demon lords cowered in their fiery hells, too afraid to face the walking nightmares even to save their own children, the DemonKind."

"The DemonKind?" Ember let out. A jagged edge of the broken glass snagged the flesh between her fingers, but she barely felt it. "God in Heaven," she croaked, nearly choking. Her mouth dried out, feeling full of cotton, and her heart hammered in her chest as Yrlissa continued with the horrific story.

"The Gods of that time stopped the Ri'Tek by stripping their magic and sealing it away. But in doing so, the Old Gods destroyed themselves. However, it was far too late as the Vascuul had already been born."

"These Old Gods really didn't screw around, did they?" Max demanded as he dropped an armload of wood by the fire and eased down on his sleeping mat with a wince.

"This happened several millennia before I was born, but yes, my Ker'Myhnera— my mother's mother," she explained upon seeing the confusion caused by the Elvehn term. "She read me the entries from the Dyrannai Avalath—"

"Avalath?" Ember interrupted.

Getting blank stares as she glanced around the campfire, yet again, Yrlissa sighed with frustration, and Aravae took the chance to explain.

"It is a book kept by the Elvehn," she told them. "A record of history as it affected our people."

"That wasn't the end?" Nekrosa asked. "I can't imagine any race surviving once their magic was taken from them."

"It was only the beginning," Yrlissa said, shaking her head. "Soon after, in a matter of a few hundred years, the original Lesser races discovered their own magic — the earth's power we use today, but back then magic was much more powerful than now. Low class citizens had the power of gods. Accidents happened daily, and those who had been abused and oppressed became power-mad or were driven by revenge. Others snapped under the euphoric effects of newly bonded magic and gave birth to the Braiga."

"Insane wizards," Ember mumbled.

"I can't imagine the suffering," Sephi added. Turning her nose up at her plate of food, she set it aside. "The deaths alone caused by the new magic must have been staggering."

"They were," Yrlissa replied. "And the Ri'Tek, having no defense against this new magic, tried their best to help the Lesser races use it responsibly. They really did try, and it worked for a while — for decades even. Accidents still happened, though the blatant attacks against the Ri'Tek lessened. Lessened, but didn't stop. Eventually, the Ri'Tek refused to tolerate it any longer. You can't begin to imagine the cunning intellect possessed by this race. They will out-think and out-maneuver you every time. It didn't take long before they figured out how to take this new magic granted to the Lesser races for themselves by using binding stones and a rare kind of wizard unique to the Ri'Tek — the Syddic priests. When the accidents and deaths continued, they attacked all the Lesser races, and the war started."

"Shouldn't the Lesser races have won? You'd think the Ri'Tek wouldn't have lasted long so outnumbered and using unfamiliar magic." Nekrosa wondered aloud.

"You forget." Yrlissa reminded them. "They're smart and devious, but more importantly, they didn't just have stolen magic. They had the Vascuul. Most of the Lesser races had no knowledge of these... creatures before facing them in battle."

The utter disgust layered in the assassin's voice was obvious, and a look of recognition ghosted across Nekrosa's features. "You've fought them, haven't you?" he asked.

Yrlissa raised her head, locking eyes with the DormaSain King. "Yes. I was a child of ten years old when I saw my first Vascuul long before the war started. It wandered into the forest and killed a dozen Druid forest guardians before it found our village. It attacked the group of children I was with. My mother, my aunt, and two others sacrificed their lives to save us. My father led the twenty warriors and mages that killed the Vascuul. My sister and I watched as we hid in the trees. We never found out where it came from or why it attacked."

"One of these things did that?" Nekrosa asked. "Just one? By the Void, I'm sorry."

"It is the far past. it only matters so you understand exactly what these things are." She paused for a moment. Ember flipped the piece of glass in her fingers and watched as the ghosts of the past drifted across Yrlissa's memory. Her friend struggled to wrestle them back.

Feeling guilty about how she had been behaving, Ember forced her anger to calm. "It's okay. Take your time," she said. The painful glance Yrlissa gave her nearly broke her heart.

"I am all right," the assassin said quietly. "No one understood the point behind the creation of the Vascuul. Eventually, we learned they were created to emulate the Old Gods, to create new life, but they failed in their attempt. Later, the Ri'Tek discovered how well they killed, and how they thrived on senseless violence. They began breeding and creating Vascuul specifically designed for war in case the day came when they needed them. The creatures grew bored easily and had a battlefield blood-lust unlike anything we had ever faced. They attacked and attacked relentlessly. I once had a Vascuul gorgon track me for days on end even though it was mortally wounded. It just kept coming and coming until... until it fell dead from its wounds. Another hour and..."

She paused and took and breath but continued before the horror of the story left the others. "The Vascuul refused to stop until they were down and dead. To try and counter them, the Broken Blades were formed. Magically enhanced killing weapons that never tire, are immune to most poisons, can ignore pain, and feel no fear. They are killers who will not stop until they have their corpse. And they... we... didn't stop until the Vascuul were dead or gone."

"Broken Blade assassins still live by that creed today," Nekrosa said.

"True," Yrlissa replied. "But the guild has been corrupted and bastardized into a money and power-hungry organization ruled by a select few. I had hoped to be in control of the ruling council when all this came to pass. I even had an ally—the son of a Guardian—on the ruling council who would have helped, but I underestimated Merethyl Bellas' desire for greed and power."

Ember frowned and her anger flared back to life. The stories were nothing, but tangent stories designed to avoid the real questions. She pointed two fingers with the piece of broken glass between them at Yrlissa.

"I..." Ember began.

Yrlissa cut off her off. "Where did you get that?" she asked and snatched the chunk of vial from Ember's fingers.

"Why?" she asked as the assassin examined it closely.

"Where did you find it?" Yrlissa repeated.

"It was beside Kael when we arrived."

"Oh," Yrlissa whispered. "All right."

"What is it?" Nekrosa asked.

Yrlissa looked up into Ember's eyes. "A reminder of a hopeless age."

"It looks like a piece of a potion bottle from long ago. It's square, not like the round ones more common now," Sephi offered. "I used one once to help Kael when we were in Dasal."

Yrlissa nodded. "I was," she said. "A potion first attempted by the Fae. Many wizards have tried to perfect it, to no avail. It means Broken Blade Purge and it has never worked, as you can see." She offered Ember the broken glass.

"Someone tried to help him, you think?" Ember let out as she took the broken vial back.

"Or it was broken during fighting or perhaps it has been lying in this field for an aeon—the likely explanation," Yrlissa answered. "It matters not."

Ember frowned. "No it doesn't," she said, perturbed by the distraction. "Any more than some stupid guild, Yrlissa. Tell me about Kael, about his kind. The DeathWizard. Where do they come from? Why? How the war ended. How come every story about the DeathWizard I hear is layered with corruption, evil, and insanity. Yet everywhere we went, Kael always helped people. Even the so-called priestess of Mylla lied to cover up why they had him tied up inside a tent. Tell me everything!"

Yrlissa closed her eyes. "All right, Ember. Your first question. Where?"

"Yes."

"The year was 549 ARI—549 years after the Ri'Tek invasion. Vascuul scouts had forced my people to abandon the Dyrannai Forest. Our home. Our elders had been trying for years to get the most powerful magic users from all the Lesser races in one place. The new gods had agreed to help build a magical weapon to fight the Ri'Tek. The DeathWizard. Though, that's not what we called them. That name and the Ri'Tek words *Kai'Sar* came much later, in our modern times."

"Gods." Sephi sighed in awe. "You created a living weapon from complete scratch with magic? As in, you created an entirely new entity—not just magically enhanced an already existing one?"

"Yes. Although, it was not by intention. We were desperate and stupid. We were naive, but worse, we had learned nothing from the Ri'Tek's mistake in creating the Vascuul. We were facing extinction, so every race willing offered the essence of their own magic and the gods offered theirs—a magic we had no understanding of. This essence was taken by ritual sacrifice to make the creature stronger. We needed magic stronger than all the gods combined. Dathac and Mylla, the gods of life and death, placed this mix of magic inside the sun and marked the unborn babes of six mothers to be. The magic was boosted by the sun, and the black rays triggered the marked babes. The weapons were spawned. The families who had offered a sacrifice, including the chosen mothers, were granted Elderblood powers as a payment for the lives of their own."

"Gods," Sephi whispered, but it did not slow Yrlissa's story.

"Eight months later the first six were born. There was just enough magic left to trigger the black sun a second time — or so the gods thought. Eight months after, another six weapons were born. Only three survived from each set of births. But we never could have predicted the black suns would continue or that the children would be born with an innate connection to all the sources of the magic used to create them: life, death, the Void, Fae, Dragon, Demon, and even the gods' own magic. With these connections a part of them, a DeathWizard's magic is not a foreign force like ours. It is a part of who and what they are. It is them. Like an arm or a leg, it's just there."

Yrlissa paused as she lifted her head. Ember could see the weight of history in the assassin's eyes, so she said nothing and let her continue. "Once a DeathWizard figures that out? There is almost no way of stopping them. The first three born are buried here in the Field of the Fallen. I laid each to rest here with my own hands, but not before they claimed over a hundred innocent lives. We quickly realized the danger of what we had created — the wizards were easily corrupted. By what exactly, we never figured out. By death, too much power, or perhaps it was just the effects of the new magic we created... it mattered not. Watchers were nominated to monitor these new wizards, to keep them in check. My twin sister and I were the first of many Guardians. For our service, we were granted immortality by the gods, but we are not invincible. Our numbers have died off even though we can pass our immortality on to our children in a ritual." Yrlissa took a deep breath and rubbed the small flower-like tattoo at her right temple. "This flower marks a Guardian and ties us to these wizards. The flower thrives or dies depending on whether a wizard is alive."

"You knew," Ember whispered, her tone accusatory. "You goddamn knew. You knew Kael was dead the moment Sephi and Nekrosa woke us in Kazzador. Your mark was smaller then. Aravae noticed it."

The Elvehn sorceress nodded. "I did, yes."

"I suspected, but I wasn't sure," Yrlissa replied. "The last wizard of Kael's kind I Guarded was different than Kael. She fought the corruption better than any other I had watched over. Still, she did horrible things to accomplish her goals right up until she nearly destroyed our world with the Cataclysm. After that, the gods stopped caring, and we Guardians became a dying breed."

"Why did the gods turn from Talohna?" Aravae asked.

"Once the threat from the Ri'Tek had been dealt with, the gods tasked the Guardians with killing every DeathWizard still alive and those born from then on — they decided they were too dangerous. Even the gods can't unmake magical creatures, and that's exactly what a DeathWizard is. Like the Fae or the Dragon Behemoths, the DeathWizard was born of magic. A decree from the gods fractured the Guardian Pact and those of us who were also Broken Blades. We had friends and family, all very young DeathWizards, who fought the corruption every single day. They desired nothing more than to grow up and do good, to help people. They didn't deserve to die. The gods believed those who tried to protect their charges betrayed the pantheon. After the Cataclysm, they blamed us and said it was proof of how dangerous they were. Apparently, we betrayed Talohna because we didn't stop it. They turned their backs on us and on everyone else."

"Then why was Kael so different?" Ember interrupted. "Kael never hurt anyone who was innocent. You told me that Sister of Mylla was lying, that your spell showed him tied up."

"It did, and I don't know why." Yrlissa sighed. "Perhaps because Giddeon sent him to your world? Kael developed his morals and beliefs without the magic's corrupting force or without any influence of magic at all. It matters little, Ember. I have watched countless DeathWizard's lose the struggle for their Humanity or their Elvehnhood, and in some frightening circumstances, their Fae essence. The corruption was still there with Kael. We saw the aftermath. He still pulled demons into our world when he was threatened. During the Ri'Tek war, doing so was considered a horrendous crime punishable by death. We heard the stories from when Kael first arrived in Talohna compared to those leading to when we caught up with him. It was becoming easier and easier for him to kill. He was losing the fight against the corruption."

"That's everything? Everything important?"

"Yes, Ember."

"No. It's not." Nekrosa interrupted her. "You are forgetting the most important part going forward." Yrlissa frowned but said nothing.

"How the war ended?" Sephi prompted. "And could the Ri'Tek possibly return?"

Yrlissa sighed as if weary of reliving a past so old it might as well have been a campfire story.

"We knew we couldn't beat the Ri'Tek with the resources we had," Yrlissa began, again, "the six DeathWizards alive and under our control came close to balancing our power against theirs, but we were still losing. To make a very long story short, the oldest of them, Asa Nahai, discovered a DeathWizard can crack dimensional barriers if they're strong enough and focused, if they're disciplined enough."

"Like the Fae," Sephi stated.

"Yes. The Still dimension was the first one he found. But where the Fae used finesse and inherent magic to open a dimensional doorway, the DeathWizard clawed his way through. It left a scar. One easily reopened. Asa worked closely with the god of death to design a lock to ensure that once the Ri'Tek had been forced into a stasis type of dimension, the scar would be sealed. We hoped that would be enough until there were enough DeathWizards alive to force a peace or win the war."

"They created the Animus Seals?" Ember asked.

"Asa and Dathac, yes. Asa then taught the others of his kind how to open a door to the Still dimension. We were engaged in battle with the Ri'Tek as they pushed at us from all sides. Asa believed if we lured the Ri'Tek into six different battles, his people could open a doorway at each location. The Dragons and Fae used blood from Ri'Tek prisoners of war and designed a spell using the Still dimension's energy to pull the Ri'Tek in. It worked, but the price paid was horrendous. Each DeathWizard was killed using their own life force to activate the Animus Seals."

"Jesus Christ." Ember cursed quietly.

"You have to remember, we were fighting a war against an enemy who wanted to eradicate our very existence. No price was too large and studying the new magic from when we created them wasn't an option. Even Asa had no idea how to keep himself alive, and he was the strongest of his kind. Like Kael, his vines had nearly spread across his entire body. Every race of Talohna fought against the Ri'Tek and stopping the Ri'Tek was the only priority we all had. The probability of another chance was scarce."

Ember could not believe her ears. "All races fought against the Ri'Tek and still you nearly..."

"All but the Lost," Yrlissa said, nodding.

"The Lost?" Nekrosa prompted. "That's new."

"The Lost are Talohna's other original race—all of our ancestors who were blessed with magic by the old gods, and those Ri'Tek who had no interest in creating the Vascuul. Some of the Lost you know as the gods we worship. Mylla, Dathac, and Inara were the first three Lost to use magic to ascend to godhood. Several others followed and the pantheon as we know it was created."

"The gods of Talohna were once mortal?" Aravae asked, disbelief riding every word from her lips.

"Yes, but they have none of their mortal essence, or Elvehnhood or humanity left. Like the Ri'Tek, the Lost worshiped the Old Gods and wanted to be like them, but they studied ascension magic instead. It took countless centuries, but eventually... well, some succeeded and ascended to godhood. Remember, the old gods were gone. They were destroyed sealing away the Ri'Tek's magic. The pantheon was empty, and there was no structured afterlife, just a pocket dimension created when the old gods sealed away the Ri'Tek's magic."

"How does that work?" Nekrosa asked.

Yrlissa smiled. "From what I know, the old gods were merely caretakers of the world they created. With no afterlife, upon death, souls — life energy — were absorbed by magical artifacts and gifted to family to use as they needed. Mylla, Dathac, and Inara created the afterlife we have now from the pocket dimension and the Tree of Life they found there. Only they know why or how beyond that."

"Incredible," Sephi said. "To have seen and to know so much."

"None of that matters," Ember snapped, again. "None of it! You should have told me, Yrlissa. I would never have stayed with Giddeon had I known what I know now. Max and I would have purposely stayed ahead of them... or... you... *you* could have told me how to jump to him, like you did to get us here."

"Told you," Max quipped, but Ember never even slowed.

"Kael would still be alive if not for you," she growled. "I swear to every god in existence, old or new, in your world and mine... I will never forgive you for that any more than I will forgive Giddeon Zirakus for his role in Kael's death!"

"I know, Ember," Yrlissa said quietly. "I understand. Giddeon will be paying for his mistakes, I promise you."

Ember stood. "And when do you pay for yours?" Shaking her head, she turned and walked away into the dark.

"Ember, wait!" Yrlissa yelled after her and got up to chase after her.

"Stop," Max said and groaned as he struggled to stand. "I'll go. You'll just make it worse."

"It wasn't my intention, Max. You have to know that."

"But I don't," he said and went after her the best he could. Ember was moving away too fast for him to catch her. "Ember!" he called. "Stop, please."

She turned and waited for him to catch up. "What?"

"Easy," he replied and held up his hands. "Not the enemy here."

"I... I know," she said and frowned. "I'm sorry."

"You all right?" he asked and took her into his arms.

She tried to resist, but quickly gave in. "I can't do this, Max. She betrayed everything we stand for. We could have caught up to him with one jump. One goddamn jump." Tears rolled down her cheeks, and it was impossible to stop them.

"I know, girl," he said. His arms squeezed her and for a single second she felt a bit better.

"I don't trust her, Max. She knows more than she's telling us."

"I doubt we know Sephi and Nekrosa's full agenda either."

"They haven't lied to us, yet," Ember offered.

"Yet," he repeated. "It seems like this world thrives on the idea of betrayal."

"Then, we have to watch our own backs from now on," she said.

"Always, but—"

"I mean it, Max," Ember snapped, speaking over him. "The next time some ones does this, I want them dead."

"Jesus, Ember. I know you're hurt."

"I mean it," she said. "I am tired of being pulled along in this world and following others. It stops right now. From now on we make our own decisions, you and I."

"I can live with that."

"Good," Ember said. "Then, we will leave this god forsaken forest when I am ready, not when any of them wish to."

"You are the only way out of here," Max added.

"Yes," Ember growled. "I am."

Chapter Five

'A sword must remain sharp, even when it lies harmless within a sheath. Even more so, the mind and soul must always be sharp when sitting idle within the body. A dull mind or soul will bring more devastation to oneself than a dull sword ever could.'

Northman Proverb, author and date unknown.

THE AFTERLIFE
YEAR UNKNOWN

Kael woke screaming from a nightmare. The images of demons tearing him apart slowly faded as he opened his eyes. Ember stared down at him and smiled.

"Bad dreams?" she asked as she caressed his cheek.

He nodded. "I guess even the afterlife can't wipe the mind clean of some horrors."

"It will, love. I promise. When we first arrived here, Tydariel said the mind heals slower and that it will just take time." Ember snuggled closer in the bed and pulled the blankets higher. Turning over, he kissed her forehead and wrapped his arms around her.

As Kael held her, he wondered if this paradise would last forever. Months, or maybe even years, or decades had passed since had first found Ember in the meadow of Heaven's third paradise realm. She was right. Time meant little when things were happy and safe. He hoped it would last eternity. The days passed easily as he and Ember settled into the strange existence of Talohna's afterlife. It did not take long for him to realize that all souls shared each realm's reality. Ember explained that the small village where her and Max had been staying was one of many and that the first city — for those who wanted to spend eternity in a city-paradise — was only a two hour walk down the trail. It was a walk where feet never got sore and there was no such thing as growing tired from miles of traveling. In the village where they lived, everything they could ever need was provided. Their home, food, water, and even clothing. The communal lifestyle was stress-free and relaxing. Farmers farmed, tailors made clothes, and there was no violence. It made him smile, and inside, he was bursting with happiness, with bliss.

It was Heaven after all.

"You'd better get moving, hun," Ember said as she ran her finger along his chest. "I need you to stop by the market before you meet Max, so I can make supper tonight. I need some spices. The list is on the kitchen table."

Kael sighed. "All right," he said. Leaning over, he kissed her forehead, again. "See you later."

As she rolled over and went back to sleep, he hopped out of bed and dressed in a pair of brown leather pants and set his Orotaq cloak on a chair. He had not worn his beat-up chainmail armor in months. There was no need. It hung in the closet with their other, more comfortable clothing. Pulling on a soft shirt made from a cotton-like material, he slipped on his boots and kissed Ember's head once again.

As he left their house with the list in his pocket, the sun was up high and he guessed it was close to noon. Turning toward the town's market, Kael inhaled the fresh mountain air and picked up his pace. The market was busy as always, so he spent time wandering to look at merchandise on the quieter side of the circular set up. Stopping at one of the jewelry stalls, he noticed a young woman watching him from the side of the clothing merchant's stall. She kept an eye on him from beneath a heavy wool hood. It was the fourth time he had noticed her watching him that week. Studying her without making it obvious, he struggled to make out her face through shadows of the hood. Her features were vaguely familiar, but he could not place where he had seen her before. Without access to his magic in the afterlife, the mundane tasks of normal life were inconvenient. Glancing back to the woman, he saw she had vanished among the crowd.

He made his way through the market to the far eastern side of the town and slipped between two houses. The simple route led to one of the town's most incredible views — a cliff's edge over a wide, imposing valley. Sitting on a rocky outcrop, he stared out over the miles of green valley floor. The awe-inspiring sight always made his day all the better than it already was. The greatest thing about Paradise was the lack of hurry to be anywhere, and Max always knew exactly where to find him no matter what part of Paradise he wandered to.

Kael smiled. A crunch on the grass let him know his friend had found him quicker than he expected.

"Ember's making supper tonight," he said. "Supposed to ask you if you want to eat with us."

"I don't think that would be a good idea," a female voice replied from behind him. Sliding off the rocks, Kael spun and immediately recognized the woman in the heavy hood.

"Have you been following me?" he demanded.

Shaking her head, the woman took several steps before answering. "Following, no. Watching... perhaps."

"Why?"

"Why not?" she answered flippantly.

"Because it's bloody creepy," Kael retorted. "Creepy things aren't supposed to happen in Heaven. I'm pretty sure of that."

"Heaven?" she repeated. He heard the incredible surprise in her voice. "Heaven?" she repeated, stepping back. "Can't say I've ever heard anyone call it that." Her hood caught the mountain breeze and lifted for a split second, giving him a better look at her face. A cold chill burst to life inside his stomach—the woman was beyond familiar.

He knew her. The dark hair, the pale skin, the startling beauty, and her Elvehn features... he had seen it before but had no idea when or where.

"Well, what do *you* call it then?" he asked.

A hint of a sly smile crept out from under the hood. "You are dead. You know that much, right?"

"Uh... yes..."

"Then, if you're dead and this isn't Heaven or Paradise, what's left?" She scoffed and shook her head as if she was dealing with an imbecile.

Kael laughed as he wondered if Max had put this woman up to pulling a practical joke on him. "If this is Hell, miss, then I'll burn here for all eternity. Happily, in fact. Compared to real life, this is Paradise for me." Shaking his head, he turned to leave but glanced back over his shoulder. "You'll have to tell Max to do better next time." Turning to leave, he had not made it two steps when her voice stopped him hard.

"Kael? Please, look at me." The cold spot in his stomach returned and he turned to look at her. "Why can you not sense what or who I am?"

"Uh... because there's no need for magic in the afterlife. Our magic doesn't work here because there is no need for it. Tydariel told me that when I first came to this town."

"Of course, she did," the woman said. Shaking her head, she massaged her temples in frustration. "Your magic will work just fine if you believe it will."

Having enough of her cryptic garbage, Kael took several steps to move closer to the woman. "Who are you? What do you want?"

"Use your magic, and you'll have your answer. I cannot use magic, they will know."

"Who will know?" he snapped, realizing for the first time since arriving in the afterlife that his anger was much closer to the surface.

"Demons, Kael! This isn't Heaven! You have bought into this illusion with everything you have."

"You're insane," Kael retorted.

"Stop. You know who I am, don't you? I know you do."

"You're familiar, nothing more," he said as the woman put her hand to her hood.

"You know me, Kael, you do. I heard you when you said a prayer for me and wished me an afterlife of peace."

"Impossible..." he stammered. As the hood fell back he recognized her. "Jasala Vyshaan..."

"Yes. And if I'm here after what I did in my mortal life, then where are we?"

Kael's thoughts came crashing together as the reality of who he was looking at settled in. "You're the most evil DeathWizard who ever lived. You're the boogeyman of Talohna!"

"Well, that is nice to know. And after all I sacrificed for mortal-kind." She scoffed, but Kael could see the hurt in her eyes. "If so, what does all that mean?"

He shook his head as his mind whirled at the complications. Footsteps behind him made him glance over his shoulder.

"Kael?" Max called from between the wooden cottages. "You all right? You look like you've seen a ghost." Kael turned back toward Jasala, but she was gone. It was as if she was never there.

"Yeah... maybe. Thinking about ghosts of the past, I guess."

"Not worth thinking about anymore, buddy," Max answered. "Come on. We have an afternoon of heavenly fishing ahead of us."

"Yeah, on my way," he said quietly as he stared at where he had last seen Jasala standing. No longer as naive as he used to be, he would never take anyone's word at face value. It would only be a mistake. Unsure of what else to do, he shook his head clear of the situation and followed after Max.

HELL
8th DIMENSION, YEAR 30

"You are sure you want to continue with this, mistress?" The large demon layered in scales paced nervously around the demon queen's putrid cave.

"What is your concern, Taymahk?"

"I fear you take too many chances, Mistress Reetha. This creature is not typical of his kind. Should he break free of the illusion, we will not be able to control him. This is not the living world. If he realizes what he is capable of here... we will lose Kroa lives and we are already outnumbered in the eternal fight. Kael can decimate us here, possibly even destroy our Hell."

The demon queen turned and snapped. Her vicious jaws missed tearing his face from his skull by a single inch. "Just worry about keeping the female away from him, and we'll have nothing to worry about. The illusions will hold. He has no reason to be suspicious. and his soul is at peace. He wants this reality to exist with all he has. It tightens the grip the illusion has on him. Just... keep... her... under... control."

The demon bowed. "The female is secure." The demon queen glared, and her eyes bored into the demon commander. "At least, as secure as we can make her. Her strength of will is surprising, much closer to his than others of their race." The demon queen hissed at him, her jaws dripping toxic venom. "Yes, Mistress. I will personally make sure she remains secure."

"Yes, you will. We have made a deal with the Ri'Tek. They will take as many black power stones as we can provide. In return, the souls of those they kill will come here to us. Except for the woman, all the souls of the black ones have been depleted. They will take many millennia to recharge. Draining this DeathWizard's soul is the only way to fill the energy stones the Ri'Tek use to power their magic."

The demon commander persisted. "But surely keeping both here is a mistake, no? Rajazeye would gladly take the woman, and he will still pass the odd stone she produces to you, my queen. The threat will lessen for the few Kroa that are left."

"Risking these two being here is a small price to pay to acquire more souls. The Ri'Tek conquest of Talohna will make the 8th Hell a true power once more. It will let us keep Garz'x at bay while we work to bring the Archdemon home."

Taymahk bowed as Reetha's form shifted. Her height vanished, and her several legs retreated into her body until a nude young woman stood in her place. Coils of red hair grew from her head, blazing in the cave's fire light as it stopped halfway down her back.

"I will make sure the female remains in her nightmare and is allowed nowhere near him," he said.

"Good," Reetha replied. Her voice, her body, and her face were an exact match to that of the woman Ember. "I will return to the Dreamscape and keep a close eye on Kael."

Still holding his bow, Taymahk backed away carefully before he turned and left the queen alone so she could ready herself for the transition back to the Dreamscape.

Kael struggled to stay awake while he leaned against a tree and watched the tip of his fishing rod. With his dreams still plagued by nightmares, sleep was not something he desired although he needed it. He sat up and yawned, attempting to banish the fugue of exhaustion assaulting him.

"You should have gotten up earlier." Max pointed out. "Too late for good fishing already."

Kael laughed at the asinine comment. They had never gone fishing early back home. "Maybe. I just figured the fishing would always be good in heaven."

Max quickly glanced his way with a frown, but it immediately turned into a laugh. "Guess not. Or perhaps you're just as much bad luck here as you were back home." Max cackled, and Kael couldn't help but join him.

"Perhaps," Kael said, shrugging. "Think you've been here too long, you're starting to speak native."

"That is completely possible. But you're still bad luck."

"Yeah, you're probably right." Kael chuckled.

Max got up, and he pulled his rod from its stand and brought his line in. "I'm gonna go for a run and then get ready for supper. You coming?"

"God, no," Kael said, frowning. "Why the hell would I want to go for a run? Had enough of that when I was alive. Never bloody running again."

"Yeah, of course. Sorry," Max replied. "All right, bro. See you at supper. You sure it's all right with Ember?"

"Her idea, so I'm pretty sure. Good thing I remembered her spices though."

Max laughed and headed back toward town, disappearing among the trees a minute later. Kael sat back against his tree and relaxed. It took only seconds before his eyes drooped, and he nearly fell asleep, again.

Jerking awake, he shook his head and yawned. "Holy cow, why am I so tired all of a sudden?"

"Because of the nightmares."

He recognized the voice to his right without even having to look. "You don't give up, do you?"

"No," Jasala said. "I don't."

"Well, you should. You're wasting both our time."

"I have nothing but time." She laughed. "And I would much rather be here than the alternative."

"What do you want from me?" Kael demanded.

"For you to wake up," Jasala answered.

"I am awake. Tired, but awake."

"Not awake as in sleeping, Kael. Awake as in this illusion around you. I understand you had a rough time before you died, and you want this," she said, turning her finger to indicate all around them. "I know you want it more than anything, but it's not real."

"Close enough," he replied

"The nightmares. You still have them?"

"Yeah."

"Demons tearing you apart? Pain? Agony?"

"Yeah."

"The demon who controls this hell drains our power by creating strong emotion, both good when you are awake and bad while you sleep."

"Oh... okay, then," Kael muttered, getting up to pack his fishing gear. He could see Jasala's frustration growing.

"You can't tell me you haven't noticed the subtle differences in your friend and your wife, Kael. Listen to me—"

"No. Stop bothering me. If this is hell, then they can have my power. I don't care. I don't want it. I'm happy here, and the nightmares are nothing compared to what I suffered in the real world. It's a small price to pay to be with those I love." He grabbed his fishing rod and tackle box and turned to leave.

"It won't stay like this forever, Kael. Once the demon drains enough of your power, this," she circled her hand to gesture around her, "will all end, and your real suffering will begin."

He shook his head but refused to look back as she screamed at him.

"Kael! It won't last."

Sighing with relief when no further words came from her mouth, he tried to clear his mind of the strange conversation while he walked home. He refused to believe it was not real. Ember was everything he remembered, and Max was mostly his same old self. They had been through a lot so a little change was not surprising. As he arrived home, he forced the thoughts from his mind and focused on the night ahead with his family.

Opening the door to their small home, Kael grinned when he saw Max was already there.

"Fell back to sleep by the river again, didn't you?" Max teased.

"Uh, yeah. Taking some time to catch up on sleep, I guess," he replied.

Ember rushed out of the kitchen with her hand out and a frantic frown on her face. He tossed her the spices he was responsible for and winked as she blew him a kiss.

"You two relax on the front porch, and I'll bring you some drinks," she ordered. Her tone was playful as she nodded toward the front door.

"Yes, Mom," Max replied, adding a mock bow. Kael smiled to himself at the familiar sign of affection the two had shared long before Talohna had taken over their lives. He frowned as he stepped onto the porch. The attempts to clear the crazy thoughts put into his head by Jasala seemed futile.

"You all right, brother?" Max asked, sitting on a wooden porch chair.

"Tired," Kael answered. He sat across from his friend and sighed.

"Still not sleeping well?"

"No. These frigging nightmares. Lingering effects of real life, I guess. You told me you had similar problems when you came back from Iraq. How'd you get past it?"

"What do you mean?" Max asked, frowning.

"Your PTSD? How did you get through it? The shit you witnessed on the march to Baghdad... Christ, man, it was far worse than what I saw."

Max shifted in his chair, and Kael recognized his friend was uneasy. It was a rare sight. "I don't know," he responded. "I guess you just deal as best you can as the horror fades."

"Don't have much choice," Kael said softly. "No shrinks here to help."

"Shrink?" Max snorted. "Nothing works to shrink the shit we've seen, brother."

Kael stared as he processed the second asinine thing Max had said in less than a few hours.

"The memories will shrink, Kael," Max offered. "Give it —"

"Time," he interrupted, having heard it before all too often. "Yeah." The hairs on the back of his neck stood on end. Something *was* off with his friend. They had shared memories since he had arrived in the afterlife so how could Max miss the slang meaning for a psychiatrist? He had no idea what was happening, but he needed to figure it out.

"You sure you're all right?"

"Sorry, Max," he said. "Just shit memories."

His friend nodded. "You've never spoken about what happened before you died."

"Not something worth reliving. What happened in Arkum Zul... the things I did..."

"You did what you had to." Max pointed out.

"Like you did in Iraq?" he asked. Max nodded but said nothing. Kael jumped on the opening. "Like in Nafar?"

"Yeah, among others."

"You always said Nafar was the worst." Max stared at him hard, as if looking into his very soul. Kael recalled the memory forward in his mind of what Max had told him about how his unit had cleared the small Iraqi town.

A frown etched itself into his features. "It was. They hit us at night after hailing us as heroes."

Kael's skin crawled. It was exactly the memory in his mind, but with the purposeful distortions he added. Max had told him that attack happened in Baghdad, long after the fighting in Nafar. There was no possible way Max would forget the details to his time in Iraq. Kael swallowed his panic as he slowly watched his paradise begin to crumble.

"Who would've thought a night out at Tinker's would have led to this?" he prompted.

"No doubt," Max said and nodded to the front door of the house. "Did you get the chance to give her your ring?" Max's clarity of the night's events convinced Kael something was *very* off. It was as if the thing in front of him had the memories he and Max shared, but only had access to what Kael saw in his own mind.

"You're good. Both of you," Kael said, laughing. "I should have known."

"Kael?" Max asked. "You all right?"

"*Perhaps,*" he said, putting a heavy emphasis on the Talohna vernacular.

The front door opened, and he spun to see Ember step onto the porch with a tray of drinks.

"Kael?" she asked. "What's wrong?"

His heart ached as the full weight of his predicament settled onto his shoulders. With no magic and no weapons, there was no way to fight whatever was happening to him.

"You're both very good. Especially you," he said, looking to Ember. He shook his head. "Had it been only you here, I never would've suspected anything. You even smell like her."

Ember put her hand on his shoulder, gently and in a way only Ember could. Any strength and defiance he had left vanished. "Smells are easy, love," she said. "Memories are the tricky part. We can only see the events that you've experienced yourself."

"More lies and illusions. The real Ember and Max?"

Ember leaned closer. "I do not know, my dear, and I certainly do not care."

"Of course not. Who are you?" he asked. "What do you want? Christ, why can you all just not leave me alone, or let me die?"

Ember crouched in front of him, and he stared into green eyes that quickly melted into the black of her pupils. "You probably know me as Reetha."

Kael sighed. "The demon queen of suffering."

"Yes," she answered as her other features slowly changed. Though Ember's red hair remained, her face grew thinner and her cheek bones rose. The demon's mouth widened, her full lips shrunk, and Kael caught sight of a hint of sharp teeth behind her thinning lips. The sweater and jeans she wore quickly faded from sight, replaced by a tattered black dress that reeked of damp and rot. Though terrifyingly dangerous, the female demon also held a surreal beauty.

Kael gagged as he studied her closer. A putrid black aura swarmed the demon's body and soul. "What do you want from me?" he repeated.

"Power," she said, smiling. "What we all want."

Pushing at his eyes with the heels of his hand, Kael grunted. "Then take it and send me to one of the heaven realms. I never wanted this power that everyone's been fighting for, both when I was alive or now that I'm dead."

"It doesn't work that way," Max offered. Kael shot him a dirty look, and the demon quickly took on his own natural appearance. There was no doubt in Kael's mind — if the female Kroa demon was made for seduction, the male was bred for violence. Though he was the same size as Max, the demon was easily twice his weight with corded muscle making up every inch of its body. Horns, tusks, and fighting spurs covered his arms and legs.

"My commander is right," Reetha said. "Your emotions give us what we need. The stronger the better. This paradise doesn't have to end, Kael. You can carry on with this 'heaven' if you want. I can even erase your memories of this day, and you can go on being happy with Ember." Her tail slid from underneath her dress and slithered over her leg until it was between them. A small but sharp stinger topped the tail. "The poison in this barb will remove today from existence, and you can enjoy your death in paradise... just here in hell, instead."

She grinned as a drop of black toxin fell from the stinger.

Kael struggled to see a way out. He was exhausted from the dreams, lack of sleep, and the scheming and lies. A scream from across the lake to his right caught his attention, but his captors did not seem to hear it. He ignored it and faced the demon queen.

"It won't be real," he said.

"You are dead, Kael," Reetha purred. "This is the only reality you have left. Is it not better to accept your best possible option? You were happy for many years before today."

"How long have I been here?"

"Forty-two years have passed since your arrival in the meadow."

He shook his head and tears rolled down his cheeks. he had nothing left to fight with. No magic, no weapon, and no desire. "All right," he whispered, surrendering.

Reetha's tail quivered, ready to strike, but another scream erupted and ripped through Kael's head.

"No, Kael!" He whirled and saw Jasala at the foot of the patio's steps just as Reetha's stinger plunged into his chest. The poison quickly spread through his body, and his hold on reality slipped. Colours and sounds swirled together as the lake, the town, and his home vanished. He found himself secured to a wall in a hot cave. Tentacles, webbing, and putrid red veins of filth coursed through and around his flesh. Reetha held him even tighter as her stinger pulsed, driving toxin into his body. The poison raced through his blood, and he struggled to stay conscious.

"Fight her, Kael." Jasala's voice rolled through his head like a freight train. Out of nowhere energy surged through his body, and his eyes snapped open to see her chained to the wall across from him. She was unconscious. Reetha's commander stood guard as he held a jagged wrist spur to her throat.

You have the power here. Someone has killed for you in the real world and sent you the soul. The energy… use it. Jasala's voice echoed inside his head again, but quickly faded. *Never give up.*

Kael used the unfamiliar power coursing through him to battle the cloud of exhaustion covering his mind. Panic flared in his chest, and the immediate danger sparked a renewed desire to fight.

Remembering what Jasala had told him days earlier he grasped at his magic out of instinctive desperation, but there was nothing there. His renewed energy peaked as he struggled to tear his right arm free. The pulsating webs finally snapped. He grasped Reetha's tail and ripped the stinger from his chest. A quick head-butt to the demon queen's face allowed him the time he needed to claw his way free. The last of the webbing and veins tore and he fell forward, stumbling. Shoving the demon queen out of his way, he collapsed to his knees. He was exhausted and spent, but he could not stop.

Knowing he needed a weapon, he glanced around the cave but only saw broken bones and chewed scraps of dried flesh. A violent scream hit his ears for a full second before he recognized his own voice.

"If I had a weapon, I'd kill you both," he roared, scouring the cave floor for something to help.

Reetha laughed as she lifted herself off the floor. "But you don't," she said, kneeling in front of him. "I don't make mistakes like that. You can look all you want, but there are no weapons here. Demons don't *need* weapons, fool."

There has to be something to use as a weapon here! Kael screamed inside his head desperately.

There is. A voice answered back. *They are always with you. As am I.*

Kael stared at his hands as his reaper blades materialized from thin air. The blades were black, not silver as he was accustomed to. He was not quite sure they were even real. Reetha's surprise gave him the answer he needed, and he swung while her tail whipped around and went for his chest. His blade sliced through her tail and opened her shoulder wide. Kael forced himself to stand and swung again, aiming for Reetha's head. Black spurs appeared in front of him and hooked both his blades as the demon queen scrambled away. He broke off the attack and stepped back to catch his breath.

Thank you. he thought.

About time, Wizard. The voice shot back. Mischief danced in the tone of the voice, but he quickly refocused on the trouble at hand instead of dwelling on it. Energy coursed through him as if his weapons had revitalized his body and soul.

The demon commander planted himself between Kael and the demon queen. Kael squared his shoulders, ready to fight them both, when it dawned on him that he needed her charm.

The Arkangel's words washed over him: *Every underworld dimension has an overlord, nine demons, and three angels, all of whom must surrender control of his or her dimension to you… You must have all twelve tokens before the Tree of Life will open a doorway back to Talohna so you can return to the mortal world.*

Kael laughed. "An awful elaborate scheme to keep me from getting your realm token, Reetha." He pointed a reaper blade at her, but it was her commander who attacked. The spurs whistled passed his head while he ducked and slashed both of the demon's knees with his blade.

"Stop!" Reetha shrieked. She threw herself in front of the massive demon protecting him as he crumbled to the dirt. "You can have the token." Already swinging his blade, Kael pulled it short and came within an inch of the demon queen's neck. "You can have it," she repeated, her tone desperate. "Just take it and leave. I only have two alpha commanders left."

Kael touched his blade to the big demon's throat. "Why should I spare him?" he yelled. "After what you two did to me."

"We didn't hurt you, Kael!" Reetha pleaded. Pointing to where Jasala hung from the wall, she added, "I could have hung you on the wall and made you suffer! It would've given us just as much or more power, but I didn't. I gave you your heaven."

Kael growled and pressed his blade against the demon's throat until dark blood trickled across the dark blade.

"Please!" Reetha wailed.

Easing the weapon back, Kael snarled, "Demon, toss me your token."

Reetha reached inside her mouth and yanked out a long fang. "It is toxic to the dead," she told him and tossed the fang at his feet. She spat blood and venom to the cave floor to clear her mouth before continuing. "Now, leave. You are out of the DreamScape. Garz'x will know you are here, and he will come with his armies. You must leave."

"Gladly," he snapped. "And she's coming with me," he added, pointing to Jasala.

"That is not part of our deal, you shit," she hissed.

"Tough."

"You cannot take her," Reetha shrieked. "You idiot. Her soul was marked by the gods for the 8th Hell—my hell. You take her, and she will cease to exist the moment you leave my realm."

"Goddammit." He cursed.

"Perhaps a deal?" the demon queen offered.

"Demons and your goddamned deals. What do you want?"

Reetha smiled and slowly climbed to her feet. "You have a deal with Rajazeye. I can sense two of his tokens on you, not one. My offer is the same. You have my token for defeating me that you need to leave the afterlife. I will trade you the ownership of Jasala's soul in return for you delivering this… a second token," she pulled yet another tooth from her mouth as she spoke, "to Salo Redmaw should you ever return to the living. Deal?"

"Deal," he growled while the demon queen threw the second tooth at his feet.

"This deal is different than your others, Kael. Pay attention. If you do get out of here and do not give my token to Salo within a reasonable amount of time—say, one year after returning to life—Jasala's soul will return to me. Soul deals are very tricky, you little wizard. Should you die a second time, your soul will become mine, too. Do we have a deal?"

"Yes," Kael barked, and magic leapt from the demon queen's fingers and struck the front of his neck. Pain seared into his throat as soon as he answered her. He touched his neck and pulled back fingers covered in black ash and scorched flesh. "What the hell was that?"

Reetha shrugged and slowly put her hands in the air before turning to her commander. "The mark of the Kroa. It means your soul is destined to come here should you die, again. Jasala had one, given to her by the gods upon her death. It now belongs to you, and she is allowed to roam the afterlife freely, beholden to no Brethren Lord. Break our deal, and the mark will return her to me and she will find herself here."

"You miserable bitch," he muttered.

"Thank you, my dear, but compliments really are not necessary. Oh yes, you may also find the mark gives you some, uh… unique abilities, if you actually manage to return to the living." She smiled and clapped her hands. Kael watched her closely as she removed a rope from around her commander's neck. She opened the small leather sack tied to the rope and emptied the contents before tossing him the sack.

"Do not touch my teeth with your bare hands, and only carry them in that pouch. It is the tanned flesh of a KiPara demon. It will protect you from the toxin."

Kael nodded and gathered the teeth without touching them. He placed the pouch inside the pocket of his Orotaq cloak for safe keeping. Keeping the demon queen and her commander in his line of sight, he circled his way around the cave to Jasala. Taking a quick look, his stomach dropped. The strong woman in the DreamScape was not the woman hanging on the wall. At one time perhaps, but all that remained was a haggard, drained woman. It was the price paid for five thousand years in Hell.

Fury lit up inside his chest. "I should kill you both," he barked.

"We have a deal, you foolish…" Reetha hissed, and Kael smiled as she struggled to control her anger. She snapped, "Break it and both your souls will belong to me forever."

"Fine," he muttered. He swung his blade and shattered Jasala's shackles. Her limp body fell, and he caught her in his arms. "We're leaving. How?" he asked, making it clear it wasn't actually a question.

Reetha glanced at her commander and he nodded. "To the left of the cave's exit," he said. "There's an open rift there. I know not where it will land you."

Kael frowned while the demon howled with laughter.

"Go," Reetha ordered.

He sheathed one blade, and he lifted Jasala onto his shoulder. With his eyes never leaving the pair of demons, he backed out of the cave. A purple ripple beside the cave hung in the air, waiting for him. Glancing back to make sure he was not being followed, Kael slid his second weapon into its sheath on his back when he knew it was safe.

Taking a deep breath, he held Jasala tight and stepped through the rift.

8th HELL

"Are you all right, Mistress?" Sovik asked as he offered Reetha a claw.

She nodded, and he pulled her to her feet. "Taymahk was right, it seems," he added.

"We knew he would break the DreamScape's hold eventually," she replied. "I had hoped it would hold him for several centuries, not a mere few decades. Especially with how hard he committed to the 'scape's effect."

"The wizard was betrayed several times in life. It made him unnaturally suspicious."

"True." Reetha agreed. "But I underestimated his strength of will and his ingenuity. You saw the weapon who came to his aid?"

"I did." Sovik nodded, and he held his right claw palm out. The hairs around the edge of his palm shone white in the fire's glow and his flesh bubbled with black necrosis. "When we crossed blows, the metal from his weapon brushed my palm."

The demon queen frowned. "Somehow, while still alive, he managed to find the Vai'Karth—a weapon of the old gods. Our brothers and sisters in the other realms are in for a surprise." She laughed. "Where will he land?"

"Rajazeye's rift will take them to the Vorali, deep inside the 7th Hell."

Reetha cackled louder. "Good. Hopefully, Kael will wipe out the feral mutts Garz'x uses for ground forces."

"With luck, but you know Kael will have to face Inys and the Fails eventually."

"Inys will never surrender control of his domain, which means Kael will have to kill him." Sovik grinned as Reetha carried on. "And every high demon or angel he kills with that weapon will strengthen the effects of my toxin coursing through his blood. Kael's reality is about to become very unstable, especially if he ever returns to the living world."

"It matters little," Sovik added.

"True. We had him long enough to fill three power stones for the Ri'Tek and also managed to collect the biggest prize—" A black rift tore open the air inside the cave, interrupting them. Rajazeye jumped out of the distortion with Taymahk at his side.

"It worked then?" the small demon asked as the rift closed behind him.

Reetha merely nodded and rubbed her slightly swollen belly while Sovik answered the demon gargoyle.

"It would seem so," the demon commander replied. "We no longer need Kael or Jasala's kind. Soon we will have our own Kai'Sar. One with the raging power of a born DemonKind."

Chapter Six

"Living a life of depravity or sadism can only lead you to a very long fall into Perdition. But to live a selfless life dedicated to helping those with less, or those hurting and suffering because of the depraved will lift you up and lead you to the heavens of Paradise upon your death."

Teachings of Mylla, the Goddess of Life

7th HELL, DIMENSION OF THE VORALI
YEAR 33

Kael gasped as his feet hit solid ground after only a short fall. Heavy drifts of snow came to his waist and ice covered every inch of the terrain surrounding him.

"What the hell?" he mumbled. "Cold day in Hell?" Shifting Jasala's weight, he stared out across the barren landscape. Towering cliffs curled over a shallow valley with caves like hollow eyes looking back at him. Readjusting Jasala's weight again, he headed for the only shelter he could see.

It took him over an hour to cross the snow-filled valley to find sanctuary. Thankfully, the first cave he came to was deep and unexpectedly warm. He carried Jasala inside and laid her down against the farthest wall. He sank to the ground beside her and let himself relax for the first time in longer than he could remember. Closing his eyes, he exhaled heavily.

Mere seconds passed before a scuffle at the cave's entrance caught his attention. He opened his eyes and saw Ember standing in the entryway just outside his reach.

"Kael?" she whispered while she looked around the cave. "Where are we?"

"I... I..." he stumbled over his words as he tried to determine if she was real or not. The demon queen must have followed them. He dragged himself to his feet and pulled a blade from his back.

He took several steps forward but stopped when she spoke again. "Kael?" Ember let out.

"Not this time," he growled.

"Kael?" Ember's mouth moved, but the voice came from behind him. He turned to see Jasala fighting her way back to consciousness. "Kael?" She repeated. He glanced back to the cave entrance and saw Ember was gone, an apparition of Jasala's power. She was attempting to communicate with him so he sheathed his weapon and knelt beside her.

"You're awake," he whispered, but could not understand her response. It was a language he had never heard before. "Do you speak the common tongue?" he asked.

She managed the slightest of nods. "You heard me?"

"Took me a while, but yeah," he said.

"I am sorry," she let out. "I know what you gave up."

"It wasn't real."

"No, and it would have ended eventually. Even *your* power would not last forever in Reetha's presence."

"What power?" Kael snorted. "Besides my weapons, I don't have any."

"Then, let's fix that," she said. Her lips curled upward in the corners. "Come closer."

Kael settled down beside her and crossed his legs.

Careful! The voice screamed in his head a little too late.

With no warning, she snatched him by the throat. "If you can't use your magic, you are useless to me. I'll happily take it," she growled.

"Shit," he hissed through his teeth as his strength began to drain away. Waves of black energy fled his body and surged into hers. Jasala easily absorbed all of it. Pushing herself up on her knees, he watched helplessly as her physical strength returned at an impressive rate. The woman who had nearly destroyed Talohna once grinned down at him and drew more power from him. Waves of nausea swarmed his mind, blackness ebbed into his vision, and he knew his time was finally up. His consciousness wavered while the darkness dragged him closer to the edge.

Kael! The voice blasted through is head. *Stop her or she will use your magic to return to life.*

Everything he had ever heard about Jasala Vyshaan came rushing back on him suddenly. The Mistress of Death, the creator of the Cataclysm, and the destroyer of a hundred thousand innocent lives. He could not believe he could be so stupid. The vilest DeathWizard to ever live had him at her complete mercy.

"No." He gasped. He clawed at her threadbare shirt and reached for his magic as it passed between them, but it slipped through his fingers fluidly. He desperately wracked his mind for a spell to save him.

I cannot help you. I am sorry. The voice faded, swallowed by the intense pounding in his ears as the last of his oxygen disappeared.

"No," Kael let out a second time. He felt himself slipping away when two words entered his mind. "*Foss hrinda.*" The weak whisper sparked a concussive blast of black magic between them. It slammed Jasala's chest and drove her into the wall behind her. Busted stone and powdered rock exploded around her. Frantic, Kael sucked in ragged breaths, and panic sparked a primal urge to destroy the woman. Rolling to his knees, he grabbed Jasala in his left hand and dragged her to him as a long blade of purple and black ice formed in his right.

She smiled at him.

"Finally," she said. "Now, we can get you out of here."

"You tried to kill me," he screamed, his voice hoarse.

"Yes. I did," she snapped. "You need your magic to survive here, let alone attempt escape."

"Lies," he snarled, and pushed the dagger of ice to her throat. The familiar power surged through him, and he forced himself to stop his blade before it punctured her throat.

"I willingly return what I took," she said. "All of it." As the energy created by his own magic flowed back into his body, Kael let the ice shard slowly dissipate. Jasala grew weaker with each passing second until she no longer had the strength to hold herself up. He caught her and eased her back against the wall. "I am sorry," she said. "It was the only way to wake up your mind."

"How did you do that?"

"You did not have a Guardian, did you?" she asked, though it seemed rhetorical.

"A what?"

"Gods, what has happened in the real world since my death?"

"I don't really know," Kael replied. "I'm not from Talohna. I was brought here from my world, Earth."

Jasala gasped. "What else has happened?"

"Probably better if you don't know," he said. He was certain she would not react well to how Talohna felt and spoke about her.

"I need to know if we are going to get you out of here. I had a Guardian, Kael. I know exactly how to get you back to the living world. It has always been the goal of our kind. To walk from death and to gain the power of both life and death — immortality."

Kael stared openly. "How?" he asked. "How do I get out?"

"Tell me what has happened first. A Guardian never showed up for you. My god, your power must be completely uncontrollable."

"Unpredictable is a better word," he answered. "It works off and on more than a light switch back home."

"Light switch?" she repeated, but he just shook his head. "Oh, Kael. That is the easiest fix."

"How?"

"We are magical creatures. You spit out the words to a spell to stop me when you were desperate and on the verge of blacking out, yet you formed that blade of ice without a spoken spell. Why?"

"No idea," he admitted. "I was in Talohna for about a year. I was hunted like a rabid dog the entire time and then killed. Most of that year, my magic refused to work. And when it did…"

"People died," Jasala said, finishing his sentence when he paused.

His anger vanished. "Yeah."

"I know. I can show you how to use your magic properly once I've recovered. Understanding how it works will make a big difference, I imagine. You must know my story?"

"Some form of it, yes," he replied. "You're the demon of nightmares in Talohna. From what I was told, you caused a lot of death and destruction."

"Well…" She paused as if choosing her words carefully. "I killed a lot of innocent people, but I didn't destroy anything."

"Your death caused a major Cataclysm, Jasala. Hundreds of thousands died, and Talohna's landmass broke apart. Oceans rushed inland, mountains rose on flat plains, and the Black Kasym was created, separating the entire north lands from Talohna's mainland. Your tower is in a magical wasteland, and it is against the law to even enter the area. Some of your creations are still alive and wander the entire zone, which has been quarantined by magic for thousands of years."

"Oh, no." She moaned. "The Sepulchre spell."

"What is that?" he asked. "You mentioned it in the letter you hid in your bedroom."

"You have been to the Black Arc?"

"Yes," he replied.

"You really are something, aren't you? Do you know why I fought all of Talohna, except for the Fae and DragonKin?" He shook his head but said nothing. "Where do I start? Do you know about the Animus Seals?"

He nodded. "Intimately. I died on one."

"Oh, no," she said, wincing. "So, it has already started. All right then. In my time the seals that held the Animus gateways shut had grown weak. They were mere years from failing. My Guardian and I created a new spell that allowed my magical energy to reinforce the seals upon my death. My only goal was to live long enough and grow strong enough to enhance the seals with a magical sepulchre, and if not, for the sepulchre to activate upon my death in the hopes Talohna had a few more centuries without the Ri'Tek."

"It did work," Kael offered. "For five thousand years."

He could see the pure surprise in every feature of her face. "I never dreamed for so long..." She stopped and studied him closely. "But not for much longer," she added with no hint of it being a question. Kael shook his head as she continued. "We weren't ready, yet. I needed an artifact—a weapon—one carried or created by a god so I could control and direct the raw power of my life force."

Me. The voice said, returning.

"Without the weapon, it was only a temporary solution." She stared at the reaper blades poking out over his shoulder.

"These," Kael stated, pulling the second one from his back.

"You found them." Jasala stated. Still, there was shock in her expression.

"More like they found me," he corrected.

"Of course, they did. Do you know what they are?"

"Just a story a Dead Sister told me."

Jasala scoffed. "I know that one. It's not true. The Vai'Karth are a weapon of the gods. That is all we ever knew about them. But they are supposed to amplify our magic, are they not?"

"They do, to some extent," he replied.

Some? You would be in the Dreamscape if not for me. The voice snorted in his head, but Kael ignored it.

"May I take a closer look at them?" she asked.

Kael frowned, but the voice in his head was adamant. *No!*

"I know I cannot physically touch them," she quickly added. Kael stuck both blades in the dirt at her feet. "Amazing." She gasped. Pointing, she added, "You can see the carving in the handles. I don't recognize the glyphs..."

The language of the Kahge... it causes the attraction to me that your kind have.

On cue, Jasala grabbed her own hand as if having to forcibly stop herself from touching them. "Why do use them in that form?"

"What?"

"The offset double reaper's type blade? Why not something more practical?"

"Uh..." Kael shook his head, completely lost.

"You know you can change their shape, right? From what Yrlissa told me, anything from a sword to full length reaper blade, even daggers or an axe."

Not without my help you can't. The voice mocked.

Care to explain? Kael said to himself, not expecting answer.

No. You are not ready.

"So, you do speak," Kael said aloud.

"Of course, I speak," Jasala replied, staring at him funny.

"Not you," Kael barked. Realizing he snapped, he shook his head. "Sorry."

Jasala's eyes opened wide. "They talk to you?" she whispered. "Yrlissa guessed they might."

"Not they," Kael answered. "Him, and I wouldn't call it talking. It's more like I sense these thoughts."

Now, you're just being an ass. The voice said.

"Do you have a goddamned name?" Kael barked again out loud.

"Akai," Jasala said.

Akai. The voice told him at the same time. *Ooh. She is good. Hang on to her and maybe we can make you a real weapon.* The spirit laughed, and Kael felt his presence slid away.

"He says you're right."

"So, he does talk to you?" she asked.

"It seems so. He's said more in the last ten minutes than in all the time I've had the weapons. Didn't even realize he was real until today. I thought it was just more of Reetha's games," he said rubbing his chest.

"May I?" she asked

Kael nodded and shrugged out of his Orotaq cloak. Jasala lifted his shirt and ran her hands over his scarred shoulder and down across the dark wound in his chest the demon left him with.

She continued down over the scar caused by the Zakair's greatsword in her tower. "Your death wound?"

"No. I survived that one." He bent forward and moved his hair to the side and revealed the scar at the back of his neck. Jasala gasped and did the same. As he sat back up, it was impossible to miss the identical scar on her neck as it bisected a heavy brand.

"Broken Blade assassin," she stated. "Someone wanted you dead. Badly."

"You have a brand," he replied. "It's similar to the Orotaq brands."

"Yes," she said. "My Guardian used it to keep me safe from the death spells used to kill our kind. It is a long story. If you'd like, I can..."

Not entirely interested in hearing it, yet, he shook his head and tapped the dark scar from Reetha's stinger.

"Yes. Sorry. Reetha's Ichor," she said softly. Pulling down her threadbare shirt, she revealed a similar mark between her breasts. "It is designed to weaken your hold on reality and even your sanity. Had she hit you when you were in the

DreamScape, you would never have escaped, and no one could have helped you."

"Why did she wait then?"

Jasala scoffed. "The Ichor — the toxin — it weakens you, your strongest emotions especially. She wanted your emotions peaked, not dulled. She leeches more power from you that way. I am sorry, Kael, but you are in for some serious problems. No wonder you thought Akai wasn't real. That is a problem you will have to deal with. It'll take a millennia's worth of years to wear off here in the afterlife. Less in the living world, but the effects will be far worse there."

"Then, let's get out of here," he said. "What do you need to recover?"

"You happen to have a thousand years you can give me?" she said, but he could tell she was not serious. "It will take my magic that long to regenerate."

"But I have plenty of power. Take some of mine back."

"I cannot do that, Kael. It is against our beliefs. We do not syphon off our kind. I only did it to help you."

"Whose beliefs?" he barked. "Those of a dead society? A dead order of wizards? Take enough to be able to get back on your feet and fight. Take enough to teach me how to use mine properly."

Sighing, she held out her hand. "If you are sure, then I suppose we must."

"Yes," he answered.

"Fair enough," she said, and he took her hand.

The pull of magic from his body was much slower and much easier to handle. An initial wave of weakness washed over him, but it dissipated as Akai's voice returned.

If you're going to give it away, then give her enough to make her the weapon she is. Your chances will be better.

Kael gasped, and Jasala groaned. The power between them intensified as black energy rocketed from his body and into hers. She screamed and arched her back in pain, forcing him to quickly sever the contact. Pulling his hand back, he gasped as she tumbled onto her back.

"You all right?" he asked.

She laughed. "What happened? I haven't felt like this since before I died."

"Akai helped I think," he replied.

"Thank you," she said, sitting up. "We should go. This dimension of hell is run by Inys and the Fails. We have to find them to get your tokens."

Too late.

"We're out of time," Kael stated.

"Akai?" Jasala asked. He nodded as the sound of growling hounds echoed through the cave's entrance.

"Goddammit. I hate dogs," Kael muttered.

Getting to her feet, Jasala smiled. "You met my pets at the Arc?"

"They call them darga now," he replied, pulling his blades from the dirt.

"Elvehn for Demon dogs," she said, translating for him. "Appropriate."

He turned toward the opening as a pack of white dogs raced through the entrance. Over half his height and made of solid muscle, Kael frowned and quit counting the number coming for them when he hit ten.

"Too many," he growled.

Jasala laughed and he glared at her sideways as she winked.

Lifting her hands above her head, Jasala spread the fingers on both her hands and raised them palms up. As the last dog entered the cave, she pulled her hands together in front of her. Kael held his breath. Hundreds of stone spikes exploded from the ground, ceiling and walls. The light vanished from the cave as the overlapping spikes blocked the cave's pathway.

Kael a deep breath and held it in the dark as he listened for any sound of the dogs. Some whines and some scuffling reached his ears but nothing else. His hands ached from holding his blades so tightly and sweat trailed into his eyes as Jasala summoned a globe of light.

"Jesus Christ," he whispered. The dogs he could see were beyond dead, either crushed or impaled. as the devastating spell destroyed every mutt in its path.

"How?" he managed to get out.

Jasala laughed and glanced his way. "Let's find a new hiding spot, and hopefully you can figure it out," she said. He nodded, still dumbfounded by her display of power. "With some help, you'll be able to do far more than I, Kael. It's time you learned exactly what it is our Kind can do."

7th HELL
LOWLAND CAVES

Kael sat against a cave wall with Jasala by his side as he wiped the sweat from his forehead. It felt like months had passed as they fought and hid in and around the valley where they had first arrived in the 7th Hell. The further down the valley they went the more sweltering the caves became. Now, they had nowhere left to go. Hordes of Hell's minions roamed the lowland valley floor, waiting for them.

Not before long, Kael realized something in the caves and out in the valley had changed. He cautiously crept to the entrance with Jasala on his tail.

"What's wrong?" she whispered.

"I don't know..." He trailed off. He peered over the top of a piled stone wall. Outside, the valley swarmed with denizens from the 7th Hell along with those from another dimension.

He grunted softly and frowned. "Those are KiPara demons," he said.

"They are." Jasala agreed. "And look over there," she added, pointing to her left. "There are also Ferro and Tanz'I demons marshaling the Verali dogs."

Kael shook his head in disgust. "It won't take them long to find us."

"The Ferro demons will find us the moment they get to this side of the valley," Jasala told him. "They can smell the scent of magic from half a mile away."

"They're searching the southern cave system. We should have a couple of days. Let's get some rest and practice before they get here."

She nodded and followed him along the wall back to their meager possessions. He sat back against the wall and closed his eyes as Jasala sat facing him.

"If we can't get you to better understand how your magic works, Kael, this escape is over. We haven't really had time to practice much, but Garz'x has to be nearby if the KiPara are here."

"I figured as much. Don't suppose I'll have any power over him here, will I?"

"No." She stared at him funny, and he could not meet her eyes. He felt her fingers on his cheek, and she slowly turned his chin back to her. "Why?"

He groaned. "I might've pulled him into Talohna while fighting Sythrnax."

"Holy shit," she exclaimed. "He is gonna tear you limb-from-limb, then get the Tanz'I to put you back together just so he can do it all over again. Demons hate being collared by a wizard, but demon lords? Ah, Kael. What possessed you to do that?"

"I don't know," he replied with a shrug. "His voice was always the loudest one offering to help."

"That's insane. Normally, only the weakest demons of the lowest hells offer the call. There is something very different about you."

"Doesn't matter now," he said.

"It might someday. You might just have what it takes to get us out of here. You are far more powerful than I was. I can feel it in your magic. You even recover faster too."

"I doubt that."

"Your power is there, Kael. If not, I couldn't have taken it from you, and you certainly wouldn't have been able to share it with me like you did. You gave me all I had in life and more, and it barely affected you. When you were alive, what did you feel when using magic?"

"It took a while," he started, but stopped to think about it before continuing, "speaking the words to a spell began a power build up inside me. When I finished the spell, the magic unleashed and gave me a rush like I have never felt before."

She winced. "That's how normal wizards cast magic. You shouldn't even be able to.." He stared at her as she went quiet, clearly thinking. "Turn and look at me," she said. He shifted and did as she asked. "Our magic isn't bonded magic."

"From what I was told," he interjected. "We are bonded to both life and death. We have two crua."

"That is what we always thought, too," she answered. "But I do not believe so. If that was the case, we couldn't cast what is considered *normal* magic here in the afterlife."

"How so?" he asked.

"A wizard's cruus collapses when he dies. Only his current reserve stays within the body. It is what produces the deathflower when a wizard's body decays. That means we should have no power here, but we do."

Kael sighed. "You do. Ugh. This makes my head hurt."

"Listen to me," Jasala said. "Our magic is unique compared to every other source in Talohna. We were born with this power, Kael. It's part of us. We don't draw our power from a source. We are our own source. Does that make sense?"

"It does actually," he replied. "Explains why we don't have to cast spells in a traditional sense. Though, I used to be able to."

"I never tried traditional spells. I had a Guardian. I knew it wasn't the right way for our kind to use magic. But it is also a lot more than just that. We can manipulate more than just the energy within us. We can affect our surroundings, nature, the dead, and even the living. Watch." Jasala pointed to the cave wall and gently wiggled her finger. Smokey-black magic swirled off as her fingertips brushed the surface of the wall. The stone responded and slowly grew outwards in a sharp point as if being coaxed out by her finger.

"Like you did with the dogs," he offered. "Bigger scale though?"

"Yes," she replied. "Our willpower and our magic can physically and mentally alter certain — most aspects of our dimension."

"What about a dimension that has never had magic?" he asked, thinking about Earth. Her lowered eyebrows prompted him to continue. "There's no magic where I came from. On Earth. It's common knowledge that there never was."

"I believe ours would work, Kael. We are our own source of magic, remember? It is always with us."

"Damn," he whispered. He wondered if the ancient gods of Earth had been like them, but quickly dismissed it. The theory created more questions than it answered. As he sat in silence, his mind buzzed with questions, but he did not know what to ask first. A black millipede crawled up over his boot.

Jasala pointed and gasped with quiet excitement while she held out her hand and curled her fingers. The bug immediately changed its direction, crawling off his boot and onto her hand. It circled her hand, finally coming to a stop when all eighteen inches sat comfortably curled in her palm. She pointed to a twig laying on the ground at his side. He picked it up and offered it.

"Hold it by the tip and place it here," she said, gesturing in front of her hand. He did, and with a slight twist of her hand, she activated her magic. The millipede lashed out.

Its massive jaws crushed the tip of the stick.

"Bloody hell," he snapped.

Jasala tossed the stick and millipede into the corner. "Yrlissa taught me as I grew up that our kind are limited by only two factors. Our imagination and how quickly we can recover, our health and our magic. I can recover incredibly fast for our kind. I could cast magic for hours and need only a single hour to recover. It is what helped me keep Talohna at bay outside the Black Arc for eight months. Had I not been fooled and betrayed, I could have held my post longer. Perhaps long enough for Yrlissa to return with those," she said, pointing to his Vai'Karth.

"How did you lose?" he asked. "I saw the battlefield outside your tower. Even now, it's littered with demon bones. Human skeletons are rare, but there were still a few there." He could see the shadow of memory roll over her facial features.

"You have to understand that at that time, the Guardians had split into two groups. One side wanted our kind eliminated from existence while the other defended us, trained us, loved us..." She trailed off, lost in her own thought. Moments later, she shook her head as if to banish the horrible memories. She carried on, but her voice trembled with emotion. "When Talohna moved against me, the enemy Guardians sided with the rest of Talohna. Yrlissa Blackmist was my Guardian. Her twin sister was also a Guardian who had defended our kind for many, many millennia. For some reason, she turned her back on us and pretended to be Yrlissa returning with the Vai'Karth. She brought two enemy Guardians with her. They fooled my guards long enough to get close to me and my personal guards while I was summoning demons. That's all that matters."

"I'm sorry," he said.

"It's all right," she replied. "I knew it wasn't Yrlissa, though, she blames herself for leaving. Deep down, she believes I think it's her who did it."

"How could you possibly know that?"

"The same way I heard you when you were in the Black Arc. We can hear the prayers of our kind and even sometimes our loved ones. I just didn't realize you were in the Black Arc at the time."

"That's crazy," he answered.

"The power of prayer," she said, laughing. "Want to try it?"

"No one in Talohna is praying for me, I promise you, Jasala."

"You are so very wrong. Close your eyes and concentrate. Listen for a connection to the living."

Kael closed his eyes instead of rolling them as he wanted to at the ridiculous notion. Deciding to try anyway, he took a deep breath and focused.

Seconds passed and nothing happened. Almost ready to give up, his breath caught in his throat.

Kael — miss — thank — I will — fine —

Words trickled through the silence, but the voice was unmistakably Cassie's. Focusing harder, he tilted his head and the words came together.

There are people here Kael. I think they will take care of me —

It crushed his soul to hear Cassie's voice while it slid through the Void and reached his ears.

She was safe, and she was alive. He smiled knowing that even though escaping the afterlife was ultimately futile, he had at least managed to save her while he was still alive.

FOREST OF THE FALLEN
DYRANNAI FOREST

Ember had been trying to rest for hours, but after the horrors recounted by Yrlissa and the fact she could not reign in her own anger, sleep was impossible. She quit trying and sat up, looking around the campfire. Surprisingly, everyone else was asleep. Welcome to the Field of the Fallen, where there was no threat and no watch was needed so everyone was comfortable enough to catch up on lost sleep. She sighed with frustration. Ember slipped from the campsite and walked to the crypt where Kael had been interred. After so many months of travel and countless hours in forests and mountainous terrain, she had become quite skilled in making little noise. She entered the mausoleum and descended the marble stairs without making a sound, but she knew immediately she was not alone.

Stepping off the last stair, she looked around the room. The center sarcophagus belonged to Kael. Beside his coffin, a young girl with long blonde hair knelt and sobbed.

Ember could not see her face but could tell by her blonde hair and familiar aura that she was the one who hitched a ride on her transport spell. Her foolish behavior had nearly killed the whole group When she realized the girl was speaking, Ember stayed inside the shadow of the stairs to watch and listened.

"… miss you, Kael. Thank you for being there for me… There are people here, Kael. I think they will take care of me."

The young girl turned and stared at Ember. The stairs had done nothing to hide her presence. Outed, she settled on the floor beside the girl and wrapped an arm gently around her quaking shoulders.

"You knew him, didn't you, sweetheart?" Ember asked.

"Yes," the girl whispered.

"Did you see what happened before we arrived?"

"I did. We'd been together for weeks. He saved me from the Orotaq. When they attacked our village, my aunt and uncle and my little cousins were killed. I was about to die when he saved me."

"You're from Cairnwood?" The girl nodded but did not answer. "Where are your parents, sweetheart?"

"They died when I was a year or two. It's funny, I can feel way inside me that they loved me. I think I was happy once."

"You weren't happy in Cairnwood?"

"I... I lived. My aunt and uncle didn't want me. My father and my aunt were very close when they were young. But something happened. I think it was my mother. They hated her. I helped around the house, and they fed me, but I was a reminder of something they wanted to forget."

"God in Heaven, those are some serious thoughts for a young girl. How old are you?"

"Almost thirteen, I had to grow up fast the last little while. Kael helped make sure I will get the chance to grow all the way up," she said, as she rubbed the side of the glass coffin lid in front of her.

"Yeah, he had a way of doing things like that, didn't he?" Again, the girl nodded but said nothing. Ember suddenly realized the girl must have been with Kael during the attack on the vested sisters of Mylla.

"Sweetheart?" she asked. The little girl looked up for the first time. Her eyes were red and swollen, yet frighteningly recognizable. "What happened the night you two stopped at the Sisters of Mylla camp?"

"We didn't stop. They took Kael by force the day before. They were witches. Dead Sisters." Ember's heart leapt at the revelation—Kael had only been defending himself when everyone thought he had murdered twenty innocent woman and girls.

"You are sure?"

"Yes, mistress—"

"—call me Ember, sweetie."

"Yes, Ember. The woman traveling with Kael was a Dead Sister. I watched her and another witch trick Kael and put one of those horrible collars on him, again. I followed them until they camped at the mountain's edge. When Kael fought to escape, I helped him run away until we found mistress Aravae. She healed him, and then... then..." The little girl grabbed her and started crying. She was unable to finish because she had witnessed Kael's murder.

"Shh. It's all right, sweetheart. I have you," she said. Ember held her tight. "You didn't have to run when we arrived. No one here would've hurt you. I promise."

"I am sorry," the girl said, turning her head to look at Ember with startling amber eyes. Again, Ember was struck by their familiarity. "I knew Aravae from when she helped us, but everyone Kael ever trusted betrayed him. I was scared because maybe you wanted to hurt him too. But I watched you after we got here. For two days you never left him until you put him here. You loved him. So does Aravae."

"You're right, sweetie, more than you could ever know..." Choking back her own tears, Ember stopped herself from saying more. It would only make her feel worse than she already did.

"He told me about you, Ember. He loved you too, with everything he had, and he missed you, but he thought you died." The girl's words crushed the last of Ember's resolve. She blinked the tears from her eyes and she swallowed the lump in her throat.

"I know, hun," she said. "There are a lot of people in this world who tried to keep us apart." The girl nodded for a third time without words. "You must be starving. How about you tell me your name and we go get you something to eat." The girl turned and stared, her swollen, yellow eyes wept with grief and the need for comfort.

"My name is Cassandra. Everyone calls me Cassie. I'd like to stay here for a bit, please? I don't know what will happen to me now that Kael's gone. He... he took care of me."

"Cassie? Your name is Cassie?"

"Yes."

As Ember stared into the young girl's familiar eyes and studied Cassie's aura even closer. It finally sunk in even though the odds were astronomical. She gently grabbed the little girl's face and checked her ears and the right side of her temple. Sure enough, though not Elvehn, the girl's ears tapered slightly, and her right temple had a small, black birth mark Ember bet would eventually grow to be that of a deathflower.

Ember spun and yelled at the top of her voice. The name echoed through the crypts and out onto the Field of the Fallen, all the way to the group's campsite.

"Yrlissa!"

In only minutes, Max stormed into the crypt, both swords drawn, with Yrlissa at his side. Sephi followed while Nekrosa stood watch at the top. The necromancer was unable to enter the crypt with the magical wards designed to keep necromancers of his advanced skill out of the mausoleum.

As Max and Yrlissa barreled around the corner at the end of the stairs, Ember spun around with her arm out and shielded the little girl with her body.

Sephi was the first to speak.

"That's the brat who almost killed us all."

"Not now, Sephi," Ember barked. With one arm holding Cassie close behind her, Ember reached out and used her magic to trigger Yrlissa's aura.

"*Aurorus sala.*"

"What in the Nine Hells are you doing Ember? I told you to never—"

"Shut up, Yrlissa, and be goddamn grateful I'm even doing this much after what you hid from me," Ember snapped. The spell completed, and the assassin's most guarded secret bloomed to life. The Elvehn killer's spirit nearly overwhelmed Ember's sight with the vibrancy of her true age and the staggering power of long forgotten magic. It was much stronger and brighter, but it was identical to Cassie's.

"Jesus in Heaven, what's happening here?" Ember gasped, as the young girl clutched at her legs. "You said she was dead. You said she was dead! What the hell, Yrlissa?"

"What Ember? Who's dead?"

"Your daughter." Ember watched Yrlissa's stoic front start to crumble as she tried to get a look at the young girl hiding behind her back.

"She… she is dead. Her and Cassel. I buried what was left myself. You saw their graves, Ember. I buried them both in the Yusatan hills." Her voice trembled as it rose in volume and then dropped off, again. "I buried them... both..." Ember knew better as she coaxed Cassie out from behind her.

"This is the girl who jumped with us. Check her aura, Yrlissa. It's identical to yours."

"No!" Yrlissa barked. "No, dammit! It can't be..." Yrlissa stumbled forward for a better look at the girl. Ember watched as the defiance melted away.

"She's half Elvehn, and she has the black mark for an eventual deathflower on her right temple. Her name is Cassandra. Dammit, Yrlissa, check her aura for yourself."

"It can't... I... I... can't..." But Yrlissa stopped and spoke the words to the ancient Fae spell. "*Aurorus sala,*" she whispered.

Tears streamed down her face long before the spell activated. It blossomed the energy surrounding the little girl. Yrlissa laughed with relief for a lone second before it turned into a sob, and she dropped to her knees in anguish, no longer able to hold back the tears.

"*Mai nohva?*" she cried. Cassie looked up at the words Ember knew she must have heard countless times as a child, like some lost echo deep within her soul. She began to tremble as she looked from Ember to Yrlissa and back. Ember nodded to her, and Cassie took a single step forward.

"M... Mai..." Cassie stuttered and frowned before she tried again. "*Mynerha?*" The words crumbled the last of Yrlissa's shield as Ember watched her friend's heart shatter and reform in an instant.

"Yes, baby! You remember." Yrlissa burst into tears as Cassie rushed into her arms, sobbing.

Ember watched on, her heart filled with joy for both mother and daughter.

Chapter Seven

"Help often comes from the strangest of sources. The key is in knowing when the offer to help is real."

Garren Sallus, Talohna Peace Summit. 5020 PC

7th HELL
YEAR 65

"Dammit." Kael cussed as again his magic fired up and quickly failed.

"Easy," Jasala whispered. "Don't try so hard. You are trying to force it. Magic doesn't require physical strength, Kael, just strength of the mind. Will it to happen."

They had been trying for what felt like years to get his magic to work, and his frustration had grown steadily the whole time.

"Try simple fire," she suggested. "Nothing fancy. Create it and hold it — without using words from the VosHain language."

Kael frowned and tried again, closing his eyes. He held out his right hand and inhaled deeply. Flexing his fingers, the whoosh of magic hit his ears, and he opened his eyes to see a rolling ball of black fire in his hands. With a deep breath, he steadied his racing heart, and the fire hissed and spit in his hand, but remained steady.

"Easy… relax… gently," Jasala offered quietly. "Got it?" He nodded but kept his concentration on the burning fire. "Try to add more," she prompted.

Kael focused harder, and the fireball jumped, doubling in size. "Breathe," she added. "Stay calm. Now, try with your left hand."

His left hand filled with dark flames with an ease that surprised him. It was if the less he tried, the easier it became. He smiled, holding the magic strong.

"Bring the two together, Kael."

Bouncing both fireballs in his palm, Kael rolled his hands together, and the two magics became one, doubling in size just as a commotion broke out at their cave's entrance. The noise broke his concentration and his magic took off without him meaning to, growing exponentially in size while he struggled to maintain control.

"They're here. Shit," Jasala hissed.

Kael spun instinctively on his feet and released the fireball, hurling it toward the gathering demons. Black fire exploded out of the cave like a blast from a cannon. He pulled his weapons from the dirt and followed Jasala into the fray.

As he stepped from the cave, his heart sank. Even though his fireball had melted the ice and snow away for hundreds of feet, thousands of demons still pressed in on the valley. "We are seriously outnumbered, Jasala," he growled and swung his reaper blade, cutting a feral demon dog in half. Everywhere he looked, he saw only row upon row of demons.

Clearly having the time of her life, Jasala winked and leapt into a group of KiPara demons. Darkened roots exploded from beneath the four-armed monsters and with a flick of her wrist, four more were tossed through the air. Watching her for a single second cost him his ground as a massive wolf standing on its back legs stepped between them and cut him off.

"Dammit." Kael cursed. The wolf lunged and drove him back, further separating him from Jasala. The creature swung, and long claws whistled through the air past his face. A second swipe followed immediately, and he crossed his blades, blocking the strike. The wolf's claws locked onto his weapons. Kael grasped his magic and demanded more room. Reacting to his thoughts, a hazy blast of dark air detonated outwards from his blades. The pulverized wolf toppled through the dirt, dead. "Finally." He breathed out, smiling as he began to truly understand how his magic worked.

Turning to Jasala, he saw her surrounded by rows of demons. A way to help flit through his mind, and he sheathed his left blade. His hand shot out with four bolts of crackling electricity erupting from his fingers and raced toward the demons. Black energy popped and sizzled its way through a dozen demons at Jasala's back, ensnaring flesh and hair as it went. Kael yanked the magic back and dragged a dozen demons through the dirt viciously. A twist of his wrist tightened the magic, crushing each demon. All were dead long before they came to a stop on the ground.

He took his chance and claimed the open space at her back.

"I'm here," he yelled.

"Good. Watch—" Her words stopped short as a large demon dropped from the sky. It swung its massive hammer slowly, and the lesser demons bowed and skittered backwards, making way.

"One of Inys' Fails," Jasala muttered under her breath. "She's a high demon, Kael. A general. Not like these fodder," she said, gesturing to the bloody demon corpses surrounding them.

"Together then?" he suggested. Jasala nodded, and he touched off a blast of ice spikes, stitching the ground around the demon as she vanished in a cloud of black smoke. He grinned at the familiar tactic and stuck his blade in the ground at his feet. Summoning more spikes, he tossed them as fast as he could move his arms. The Fail slammed the handle of her demon warhammer into the ground and used it as a pivot, deflecting the ice.

Jasala stepped from the smoke behind the demon and swung an ugly blade of black magic. The Fail spun, and Jasala's blade struck the demon's hammer. The Fail roared and backhanded her, tossing her body to the dead grass and damp dirt in front of their cave. The distraction gave Kael the opening he needed.

He used his magic to erupt a spear of ice from the dirt under the demon, piercing its foot. Kael twisted his hand as the ice grew, spiraling up through the demon's thigh and out its hip. Never hesitating, he snatched his blade from the ground and vanished like Jasala had. He emerged from the murky magic and swung his blade, severing the demon's throat.

It crashed to the ground as Akai called to him.

Sai Kull'Vai

"What?"

Say it. Now.

"*Sai Kull'Vai,*" he repeated. The spell ripped from his mouth, leaving him weak. He stared in awe as black and purple smoke rose along his reaper-blade, drawing some type of energy from the dying demon. The black metal on his blade rippled like water in a pond and slowly changed to silver as it absorbed the demon's energy.

"Bloody hell." Kael gasped as his own energy returned and the weariness of battle vanished.

"Kael? What just happened? Your blades are silver."

"I don't know."

These weapons are useless. Akai snarled. *Use the power from the demon to change them. Quickly, before it fades.*

"How?" Kael demanded as he glanced across the battlefield. The horde of demons hung back as if afraid to attack.

"How what?" Jasala asked. He nodded and pointed to his own head. "Akai?" she whispered. He nodded once more.

Weapon of choice?

"I don't know," Kael asked, growing frustrated. "I've been using what I can get my hands on."

Akai snorted in his head. *Put both weapons handle-to-handle.*

Kael put his reaper blades butt-to-butt. "What now?"

Crack the bone handles with your magic.

Again, Kael did as instructed, using his magic to increase his strength to split the polished white handles. A graying mist rolled out, and Akai's voice stormed through his head once more.

Push the blades into the ground.

Kael eased the blades down until they stood on their own, stuck in the dirt. More pale smoke flowed out, and formed a spirit vaguely resembling a human. The phantom bowed to Kael and Jasala before turning and coiling around the weapons, transforming them into a single weapon. The handle grew in considerable length as three blades retreated, allowing the fourth to grow in size. The phantom evaporated into the handle and the cracks came together but remained visible on the shaft.

Kael lifted the scythe with ease, shocked that it took such little effort.

Better?

"I guess," he replied to Akai. "I've always used two weapons."

Of course. Akai chuckled lightly in his head. *You saw Jasala's weapon a few moments ago?*

"She created a dark blade from her magic."

Your kind are never defenseless, Kael. Use your magic to pull a second blade from the first, but don't fight it. An ideal match to your skills will answer.

Kael focused his magic on the weapon and inhaled sharply as the scythe answered, shedding a smaller weapon identical to a mountain climber's pick, but with a longer blade and handle.

"Much better," he said and grinned. As he slowly swung the magical blade back and forth, long strings of misty energy trailed behind the pick. It took no effort to keep both weapons active.

Jasala laughed. "I knew it," she said. "Ready to kill some demons?"

"We're still outnumbered. They do want us alive, right?" he asked.

"With the Tanz'I here, it doesn't matter, Kael. They can put what is left of us back together as many times as needed."

Kael turned and faced the demons gathering across the open valley plain. "Still not giving up," he stated. "You know that, right?"

She shrugged and offered a sideways smile. "Never doubted it."

With no other options, he once again followed her into the fray.

LOWLAND MOUNTAIN PASS, HALF HOUR EARLIER
7th HELL

Garz'x and Inys stared into the Lowland Valley as flaming magic exploded out the cave across the valley them. Both watched while their armies engaged Kael and Jasala.

"The witch has her magic back," Inys stated and spat to the side in disgust.

"The boy gave it to her. He is rather unique, even for their kind."

Garz'x grinned as the two wizards cut a swathe through the lower demons, but the gesture quickly turned to a growl as Jasala killed one of his own troops and Kael pounded a DemonKind werewolf to a pulp.

"Send in a Fail and bring those two to heel. Now!" he roared.

Inys nodded to one of his female Fails, and she leapt into the air, dropping over the edge of the cliff and diving into the battlefield.

Both demon lords watched intently as the other demons made way for the Fail. The fight was violent but short. Inys howled when the Fail fell dead.

"Impossible..." Garz'x let out, trailing off as Kael pulled the life energy from the high demon's dying body.

"They killed my Fail," Inys growled. Raking the ground with his back foot, he snapped open his wings. "They will not kill any more of my Fails or my soldiers, Garz'x. I'll deal with these wizards myself! We need our army for Hell's conflict."

"No!" Garz'x barked as Jasala and Kael engaged the army below once again. "I have seen enough. We cannot risk more lives if that boy can absorb our life energy so easily. Follow me and bring your remaining Fails." The massive demon lord jumped from the cliff with a snap of leather wings and plummeted toward the fighting, several more Fails flew after him.

Surrounded once again, Kael stumbled as a small hound backed away and his long scythe met no resistance with his powerful swing. He watched as the other demons backed off the more he tried to fight them. Even the KiPara soldiers had retreated by at least twenty feet. His heightened senses warned him a mere second before two massive demons plummeted from the sky. He reacted on instinct, grabbing Jasala and pulling her into his jump spell. They stepped from the murky smoke with enough distance between them and the demons that he hoped they would have room to fight. He stared up at Garz'x as the monstrous demon lord slowly approached.

"You are not the same boy from the Animus room so long ago," the demon said.

"Apparently not," Kael answered, readying his weapons.

"You have no control here, boy. You know that?"

Kael knew the question was rhetorical. "Yeah. I know. I'm not overly interested in talking to you, Garz'x. Get on with it."

The demon scoffed. "I have seen enough of your life, boy, to know I will have to kill and revive you a thousand times over before you will give up. If my Dead Sisters could not break you, I doubt I can, either."

"Probably." Kael agreed.

"I could," Inys barked.

Garz'x ignored him. "Unlike the other demon lords," Garz'x began, pointing to Inys. "The two of us do not covet your power. Though, Inys would like nothing more than to kill you. He will not. That leaves room for negotiation," he said and laughed.

Kael shook his head in disbelief. "You've been hunting me since I got here."

"Do not mistake me, boy. If I was willing to pay the price for it, I would take your power for myself right now and we all know you could not stop me. However." he said, motioning to the monstrous winged wolf beside him. "We are preparing for a coming war that will tear the heavens asunder, and for this alliance, there are important matters to consider, and you are not one of them."

"Make your offer then, demon," Kael snapped, not believing for a moment that the demon lord's good intentions were real.

Garz'x shrugged and the massive chains ringed through his horns clattered together. "Simple. The extra tokens you carry... do *not* turn them over to Salo RedMaw should you find your way out of the afterlife."

"You're serious?" he stated with disbelief. Every part of the demon's body language pointed to him telling the truth.

"I am very serious, boy." Garz'x growled as he nodded and held out an assortment of tokens. "And I will do one better. The tokens you need from me, a link of bone chain and from Inys." Garz'x nodded and the massive wolf grabbed the werewolf Kael killed earlier. Tearing off its tail, he tossed it to the defacto leader of hell. "The tail of a DemonKind. As well as a battle spur from the Ferro, a Tanz'I bone needle, and an eye from the Baallo demon clans. You'll have to claim the Chire and Moloch tokens yourself. They are not part of our alliance — though you had better grow some wings should you wish to do so. But it is a start. Do we have a deal?"

"I can't..." he began, but Jasala coughed, and he glanced her way. Her eyes told him not to mention the demon queen's deal.

I agree... if we are voting. Akai chimed in as he echoed her sentiment.

"Why?" Garz'x barked.

"Ah, goddammit." Kael cursed, furious at his situation. Lying to the demon lord would bite him in the ass and he knew it. "Because making a deal with you goes against my better judgment. Period."

"Good. We fight then," Inys said, finally speaking.

"Kael, you know I'm with you," Jasala began, letting the rest of her sentiment fall unspoken between them.

"Fine." Kael bit his lip, unable to believe he was about to agree. At the very least, it was a quick and easy way to get his hands on several tokens at once. "Goddammit. You win, Garz'x."

"Deal." The demon lord offered up the five tokens, so Kael grabbed them and placed the tokens in his pocket with the others.

Garz'x nodded, and again, his chains rattled as Kael watched him. "You have a token from every realm in my alliance. You will not be harmed while in the 9th, 7th, 5th, 4th, and 2nd Hells," he said as a sarcastic edge slid into his voice. "But do not linger. Every hell has feral creatures we cannot control. It would be a shame to see you fall now that we have come to an agreement." The demon chuckled as he took flight. Inys pulled his thumb across his throat in a warning and snorted before swooping away after Garz'x. The demon army took the initiative to retreat from the valley.

"Damn," Kael whispered. "I can't believe that just happened."

"We have to go. Now," Jasala ordered. There was panic in her voice.

"Why?" Kael asked.

"If he finds out you have a soul deal with Reetha, he will chase after us with that army of his, and they won't be testing us this time, Kael. This was Garz'x plan the whole time — to see if your power was worth losing a large part of his army. If not, he planned to cut a deal. If we jump out of here now, he won't know where we land, and it'll be more difficult for him to track us."

"Shit. Jesus Christ, Jasala. Does every goddamned aspect of Talohna have scheming and backstabbing?"

"In my day it did. Everyone has their own agenda," she told him.

"Then what's your agenda? How about telling me the truth?"

"I have no intention of hiding it from you, Kael. You ask, and I will answer. I have been here longer than either of us can imagine, and you might just well have the strength and cunning to get out of here. If you can and I observe you do it, then perhaps I can do it as well one day."

He laughed. "That kind of agenda I can deal with. Now, how do we get our asses out of here?"

"Oh, you will like this part," Jasala said. "It'll take you a while to learn how it works in the real world, but it is worth the effort. Here, it's like any other magic. Use your willpower to open a doorway, short or long distance." With a flick her wrist, a rift opened in the air in front of them. "To the Paradise realms?"

Kael nodded and followed her through the shimmering doorway.

ARKUM ZUL
HIDDEN DOCKS

Princess Corleya Bale heard Damien Krass walking toward her cell long before he arrived. The pirate's heavy boots clomped on the wooden floor as he approached the small holding cells.

"Ladies and vampyr!" he shouted. Like he did every time he brought them their meager rations, he taunted them. Laughing, he banged on the wooden doors and rattled the window bars as he passed. "Time for slop and spit, prisoners. I added a little something extra for you all this morning."

"You are so very generous," Lycori hissed from her cell.

"Took very little effort," he said, smiling through the barred slot. "You can thank me later."

Lycori snorted. "Step inside my cell. I would be happy to thank you now."

Damien laughed. "Nah. Got no problem waiting, demon-spawn. You can thank me when the time is right. For now, I suggest you eat and drink up. You *will* need your energy." The pirate slid a water pouch under the vampyr's door — Corleya knew it likely contained Keske blood. The small goat was prized for its nutritious meat, but its blood barely kept Lycori alive. Two bowls of gruel slid under the door of the cell Corleya shared with Alia, her lady-in-waiting.

"You are most welcome ladies," Damien barked as he walked away. "Enjoy."

Alia slid across the cell floor and grabbed her bowl, but it fell through her fingers. Corleya frowned at how weak the former Salzaran mercenary had become and was surprised by the confused look on her face.

"The bowl is heavier."

Corleya investigated her own bowl and realized Alia was right. The food bowl was much heavier than normal even though it held the same amount of food. Picking it up for a closer look, she saw the bowl was lined with leather.

"Odd," she whispered. "Look." Turning to Alia, she peeled the leather to the side and revealed the hidden pieces of roasted Keske underneath. "Safe, you think?"

Alia grabbed a piece and sniffed. "Seems to be," she replied, popping the meat into her mouth. "If I die, perhaps do not eat it."

"Lycori?" Corleya whispered towards the second cell. "Your food all right?"

"Better," the vampyr growled. "Human."

Corleya knew the starvation was making Lycori more volatile. She was also aging rapidly, approaching the appearance of a seventy-year-old woman.

"What's going on here?" Corleya asked aloud, more to herself than anyone else. Seeing as Alia showed no signs of poisoning, she dug into the meat and moaned at the savory sensation of real food. Reaching into the bowl for another chunk, her finger touched something metal. She frowned and pulled a key from under the meat. Alia stared at her in disbelief and checked her bowl, finding a second key from among her food.

"Lycori?" Corleya whispered. "Anything strange about your water skin?"

"You could say that," the vampyr answered. "You?"

"Two keys and roasted Keske meat under the gruel."

"Interesting," Lycori muttered. "There's a crude map drawn on the side of my water skin that leads to some tunnels further into the cave system behind us. Seeing as the skin was full of Human blood, I imagine the single word etched into the bottom here is telling us when to escape."

"Which is?" Corleya prompted.

"Dark."

Corleya laughed. "Good thing I can just make out the hidden entrance to these docks. If the vines hanging over the cliffs were any thicker they would block all the light from the outside. I bet one of these keys opens the cell doors and the other your silver shackles."

"Let's try that theory," Lycori suggested.

Stuffing another hunk of meat into her mouth, Corleya slid across the floor and handed both keys under the gap in their cells. She waited impatiently for any sort of discovery that it was true. Before long, a single key was returned to her fingers.

"Seems to be real. All my cuffs are open," Lycori said, though Corleya could hear the doubt in her voice. "No one is near. Try your key in the door."

Sliding back across the cell, Corleya stood and reached her arm through the barred window with the key in hand. "Good thing this little window isn't any higher up," she muttered as she fumbled to find the lock. Praying to every god in the pantheon, she rotated it and felt the lock flip back. Opening the door just wide enough for her head, she peered up and down the hallway to see if they had company. "It's clear. Should I go check further in and see if I can find the caves?"

"No," Alia answered. "If someone is trying to help us, we should wait."

Lycori coughed, clearing her throat. "I agree. Leaving now would be disastrous."

"Fair enough," Corleya said. She closed the door and flipped the locked back into place before pocketing the key in the rags of her pants. "But what if this is a trap?"

Lycori's doubtful grunt reached her ears while she watched Alia shake her head. "We are being held." The ex-mercenary pointed out the obvious. "A fake, yet elaborate escape plot would benefit our captors nothing. Always play the odds in your favor," her voice dropped as she continued, "Princess, odds say the escape offer is real."

Corleya nodded. Alia rarely spoke, so when she did say more than a word or two, she had learned long ago to listen.

"Tonight, then," she said, getting a nod from Alia and a whispered agreement from Lycori.

Chapter Eight

"The more we are betrayed, the more we are able to see betrayals and double-crosses on the horizon. Trust is a rare commodity in Talohna and within the walls of this guild it is rewarded handsomely. But when that trust is broken it is punished severely. Only a fool allows such a thing to happen twice."

Merethyl Bellas. Date,
location, and occupation unknown

HIGH HEAVENS
YEAR 155

Kael crouched on a narrow ledge half way up the 3rd Heavens tallest cathedral spire. His stolen cloak of white kept him hidden against the pale steeples and from the angels who guarded the underground prison. He had lost track of the passage of time so many years ago it hurt his head to try and figure out how long he had been in the afterlife. Jasala's rift to Paradise had been the worst mistake they could have made. Unlike Talohna's Hell, there were part of the Heavens united behind a Heretic angel named Arreal, and Jasala's jump took them right to him and his warriors.

Tired of slowly losing the eternal battle between good and evil as they lost souls to Hell, the angels had united and waited for Kael and Jasala to make their way to Paradise. Kael frowned as the memory of his escape crawled to the front of his mind. Jasala had not been so lucky. After trying to free her from the prison for over a year, he was forced to abandon her and jump into the nearest Hell to continue collecting tokens. It took him decades to track down the demon lord who ruled the 6th Hell and took what felt like centuries in the 3rd. Neither demons gave up their token without a fight, but in the end, it didn't matter. Their tokens joined the others in his pocket, and the only thing keeping him from going home were the three tokens that he needed which were held by the angels of Heaven.

Kael studied the movements of the angels below him. He could not leave Jasala to rot, drained of the power he gave her as years turned to a millennia. However, the angels took their duties seriously, and he could see no way into the cathedral's subterranean tunnels from the outside. Still, he smiled. Over a century of fighting in Hell had taught him a lot, and the angel's warding would not keep him out like it had before he left. His smile vanished along with the rest of him, leaving behind a puff of dark smoke.

Reappearing inside the prison, he remained crouched as he took in his surroundings. The cells in around him were empty and he cursed. It was the location where they had been keeping Jasala the last time he had tried to free her. His esoteric senses told him that she was not in the cathedral prison any more.

"She's at the coliseum," a low voice said behind him. He turned to see an old man huddled under a blanket in Jasala's old cell. Without moving, Kael reached out with his magic and ripped the door from its frame.

"You were left here to tell me that," he stated and walked into the cell.

The old man nodded. "Yes. I am to tell you that Arreal will be waiting in the arena below us."

"Coward angels," Kael spat.

The old man flinched at the heresy. "She said you'd come," he offered.

"Did she?" he asked.

"She never doubted it," the old man added.

"Of course, she didn't," Kael snapped. His long reaper blade appeared out of nowhere and he spun as he swung the scythe. The blade cut through the old man with ease. Kael slowly slipped into a crouch and watched as the years melted off the man's aged face. Wings unfurled on his back. "But she would never tell another soul that."

What a waste. Akai moaned. *If you know it's an angel, take its damn power!*

"We have more than we need," Kael snapped back. "Every soul we take, the harder it is to fight the effects of Reetha's Ichor."

Angels are different! Swallow your old religious beliefs and take the power as it's available. Killing demons is not enough. We will need every bit of power we can gather to get out of here.

"Yeah," Kael answered and mentally pushed the spirit away. The being inside his weapon had been growing more aggressive the more he used Akai to absorb demon energy. Akai thrived on souls, and both of their power grew exponentially with each one they took. It was frightening at first, but Kael guessed he was approaching two hundred years or more in the afterlife, and it was almost more frightening that he cared less and less with each soul they took as each year passed.

Knowing Arreal would be ready for him, he triggered his magic, jumping to the outer edge of the angels' coliseum with both his reaper scythes ready. The massive arena was nothing more than a cavern with sparse seating cut into the stone walls. Lighting from torches circled the arena floor and cast a surreal yellow glow.

Arreal stood in the center, a giant battle axe resting in his hands. "You do not look surprised," the angel said.

"You honestly thought I wouldn't know the old man was an angel?" Kael asked.

Arreal shrugged. "I had hoped. But you are here. That is what matters."

"Good point," Kael muttered. "What now, angel?"

"We fight. You win, you get a token. You lose, and Heaven can begin fighting for the souls that are rightfully ours instead of losing them to Hell. Your power under our control will insure it."

Kael scoffed. "More likely, I'll just kill you, and then Paradise will be weaker than it is now. I doubt Seraphi would agree to this."

"Seraphina has been gone for centuries. Every day we grow weaker as the demons steal more and more souls marked by the gods for Heaven while she is off doing who knows what."

"Don't say I didn't warn you when you're dead."

Arreal laughed. "The good thing about being in Paradise, Kael, is that our rules are the only ones that matter." He laughed harder as two additional angels dropped from the shadows above and landed beside the angel lord.

Though had never met either, Kael sensed that the new arrivals, Sarakel and Ramiel, were like Arreal—angel lords. High angels who each controlled a tier of Paradise. He could feel Akai salivate at the prospect.

They will get us home. Even one high angel will give us more power than we will need to crack the barrier between life and death.

"Taking the soul of an angel is gonna make karma drop a boulder on my head when I do get back," he muttered.

You and your stupid Earth superstitions. You were born in Talohna, Kael. Earth's karma does not apply to you.

"Talking to yourself already?" Arreal asked. "I heard the demon queen had you. A soul in the afterlife suffers hard once infected by her poison. You might as well give up. Even you cannot fight all three of us."

"I disagree," Kael said, snorting. "I have no qualms killing all three of you, but unless you're buddy, buddy with the Tanz'I, you won't come back." He paused to let the words sink in. Arreal growled, and Sarakel hissed at the mere mention of the demon clan. "You can't kill me because my power you need so badly will die with me," Kael added. "Sure you wouldn't rather strike a deal?"

Sarakel hissed a second time as she pulled a gold and white lance from her back. "Deals are for demons, soul."

Kael chuckled. "Soul? Not even worthy of my name, am I?" He pointed his smaller scythe at her as the smile disappeared. "You'll die last, and your *soul* will power my path back to the living."

"Blasphemy," Ramiel barked. He pulled two hooked swords from his waist and set his feet for battle.

"Where's Jasala?" Kael barked.

"In the arena's living quarters behind me. For now, her magic powers our soldiers at the Void's gateway as they fight the hordes Garz'x has sent to steal souls," Arreal told him. "If you manage to beat all three of us, you can have her. It will no longer matter."

"Fair enough," Kael said softly and attacked. Black lightning shot from his small scythe as he faded from view. The distraction failed. He materialized in front of Sarakel and swung, crossing his weapons. The angel's lance slammed into the ground at her feet, and Kael's blades clanged while they bounced off the metal handle. Not hesitating, he vanished in a puff of black as Arreal's axe passed through his immaterial body. Knowing the angels were much stronger than any demon he had ever fought, Kael held his magic constantly and materialized for only a second at a time. He re-entered the physical world long enough to feel his blade bite deep into Ramiel's thigh before he vanished again. Popping back in front of the angel, Kael sliced the other thigh. The angel fell to the arena floor swinging his sword wildly, but Kael was already gone.

He appeared twenty feet away and cast a dozen spiral spears of ice. The shards hammered Arreal and Sarakel as each shard connected, catching the female angel from foot to chest and pinning her to the ground as Arreal dropped to a knee in agony. Again, Kael vanished. Switching targets, he stepped from the shadows out in front of Ramiel. An explosion of dark air blasted from his weapons and pummeled the angel, tossing him over thirty feet into the arena wall. Kael was on the angel before he hit the ground. He walked from a swirl of black. His long blade vanished, and his hand filled with black and purple magic.

"*Sai Kull Vai,*" he growled. Pulling his hand up triggered the magic as black and purple swirls of smoke lifted the angel from the ground. The angel's life energy blazed in his face. The light was bright enough to make him wince as it poured into the short scythe. The angel screamed, racked with agony, and Kael closed his fist. The magic crushed the angel. Gold blood splattered the arena wall as the scythe absorbed the last of the angel's essence, and he let it fall dead to the arena floor as he turned, his long scythe re-materializing. He leapt to the middle of the arena and drove both blades toward Sarakel's head.

"Enough!" Arreal yelled as Kael stopped his blades an inch short of her throat. The urge to kill the angel nearly overwhelmed him, especially as Akai's voice roared through his head.

Kill it! Now!

He pushed the spirit away and his anger cooled the slightest bit. "The three tokens, Arreal. Now." Kael hooked the long scythe around the back of the angel's neck and pressed the short blade to the tender skin of her throat. A split second was all he needed to decapitate the angel if Arreal still wanted to fight.

"You are more powerful than last time. Here," Arreal said, and held out two rings and a bracelet. "Let her live. You have what you want."

Kael reached out with his magic and snatched the tokens. Pulling them back to his hand, he used one finger to grab them, refusing to let up on Sarakel.

"Get Jasala," he barked. "And I'll let your angel go."

The angel struggled with the order, and Kael pushed the blade of his pick until it drew blood. "All right," Arreal finally answered, and launched into the air, crossing the arena with one beat of his wings. He returned moments later with Jasala but stopped short.

"Let her go," the angel demanded.

"You first," Kael barked, losing his patience. "Unlike you cursed angels, I keep my word. Let Jasala go, and I'll let Sarakel live."

"You had better." Arreal growled and pushed Jasala his way. She stumbled, and he could sense how weak she was, but she made it to his side safely before collapsing.

"Kael," she whispered. "I can't jump us out of here. Why did you come back?"

"It'll be all right," he answered, but his eyes never left Arreal. The angel held his axe in a death-grip, and Kael knew his time was nearly up.

"Let her go!" the angel yelled.

"Very well." Kael released his hold on his short scythe and grabbed Jasala, pulling her close as he stabbed Sarakel and vanished in a cloud of black.

Arreal growled as he leapt for Kael, but his axe caught nothing but air. He turned his attention to Sarakel as she lay curled up holding her side.

"Let me see it, Sara," he said, his voice softening. She rolled over and bit her lip to suppress a scream as he gently moved her arm away.

"It's clean through your side. Shallow." He sighed. "Not fatal. Why would he do that?"

"He said to slow us down." Sarakel gasped.

"Why?" he asked as a snap echoed behind him.

"Because he's going for the Tree of Life," Seraphi said, stepping from the bright light.

"Arkangel?" Arreal whispered as he lowered himself to one knee. She gestured for him to stand. "He doesn't have all the tokens."

Seraphi scoffed. "What do think he was doing for the hundred or more years before he returned for Jasala? He hunted down and killed Toloc and Eligos. I told you not to fight him!"

Arreal stood and lifted his axe. "We are losing the eternal battle," he told her. Anger brushed each word. "If we don't do something, the barriers will fall, and Garz'x will rule all of the afterlife. He will become as powerful as our lord, Dathac."

The Arkangel stared at him for several seconds. "It is not your responsibility to alter that. The whole of the afterlife under Hell's command will be better than what the Archdemon had planned for all of existence. I gave you clear instructions to treat them as if they were honored guests until I returned. Now, because you didn't, Kael is on his way out of the afterlife with everything the Archdemon needs to return to Hell."

"Why would he do such a thing?" Sarakel asked softly as she sat up. Her side had already begun to mend.

"Because, the only way out of Reetha's domain with Jasala was to make a soul deal. If he doesn't do as the demon queen has asked of him, Jasala's soul will go back to her immediately and Kael's will go to her the next time he dies. I have been chasing him since the demon queen let him go. That is why I was gone. Garz'x is now aware that Kael will not honor their deal, so he has launched an attack against the barrier on his side of the Forest."

"My apologies, mistress," Arreal offered, dropping to a knee, again. Wincing in pain, Sarakel followed suit. "What can I do?" he asked, looking to her.

"I will weaken our barrier. It should let you enter the forest before Garz'x. Gather the Heretic army and engage Garz'x the moment he breaches his side. I will send Tydariel and our army to help you. You have to keep him busy long enough for me to talk to Kael."

"Yes, mistress," he said. He spun, and his wings uncurled from his back as he leapt into the air, disappearing into the dark of the coliseum's ceiling.

"Hopefully, it will be enough," Seraphi murmured and followed.

THE AFTERLIFE. YEAR 207
UNKNOWN REALM

Seconds before Kael stepped out of his jump to the Forest of Lost Souls, an unseen force ripped him and Jasala out of his magic. He crashed to a plush green meadow, and Jasala landed on top him with a grunt.

"What the hell now?" he snapped.

Jasala groaned and rolled off him as he got to one knee. "Someone tore us from your rift."

"Yeah," he replied as he stared cross-eyed at the golden lance touching his nose and the angel holding it. "I can see that."

"I am Tydariel," the female angel stated.

Kael snorted. "I know who you are. We met when I first arrived."

"We did not," the angel replied, scoffing as if he should know better. "You met who the demon queen wanted you to. You have one chance to listen to me."

Kael snorted. "I'd rather just kill you and be on my way."

The pressure of the lance increased, and the sharp blade cut the skin at the side of his nose. "If you do," she said, "you will die shortly after."

"Kael," Jasala whispered. Her voice held an edge of warning, but he laughed her off.

"Your three strongest generals couldn't stop me, so what chance do you have?"

The angel knelt in front of him, and he studied her emotionless eyes, searching for any hint of malice.

"You defeated three of heaven's generals, yes. But do not fool yourself for a minute that they were the best the heavens have to offer, Kael. They were merely the Heretics strongest fighters, lords of their tier and what not. Heaven's true army is led by Seraphi and me."

"I don't have to fight you anymore. I have what I need. If you or any others try to stop me from getting to the tree of life, Paradise will weep gold blood."

The lance fell away, and she stood. "I am not here to stop you. Only to help. One of your tokens is false. If you use it, your soul will be destroyed, and you will cease to exist."

Kael rubbed his head and immediately knew who double-crossed him. "Arreal," he said.

"Yes," Tydariel said, nodding. "He has much to gain. The Heretics would rather see you dead than risk any chance that you will someday fall into the hands of Perdition."

"I beat him," Kael snapped. "Do you know how bloody pathetic it is when you can trust a demon's word over that of an angel? It's goddamn ridiculous. How the hell am I supposed to finish what I started without that token?"

Tydariel shook her head and held out a lock of golden hair wrapped in glowing gold wire. "Arreal cannot give you the real token because it was not his to give. As the lord of Heaven's third tier, it is my right. Take it."

"How can I ever trust you?" he asked, taking the offered lock of hair. "I sensed the power of a realm lord on Arreal."

"Heaven's third tier lord died in battle many centuries ago. Arreal took her place, but he has become a heretic. The Arkangel stripped him of his post, but the power you sensed remains and cannot be reversed," she answered.

"Omitting the truth, does not stop a lie from being a lie," Kael muttered. "Your kind are worse than demons."

"Perhaps, at times," Tydariel said. "But you must decide whose word is the truth. I want nothing more from you, so perhaps therein lies your answer. Choose wrong and you will die. Now go, you must hurry. Garz'x has discovered the details of your soul deal with the demon queen. You cannot keep her deal and his. He will attack this forest to get to you, and I cannot enter the neutral zone to help you without my Arkangel's consent," she said, standing aside.

Kael stared at the angel. His mind whirled with uncertainty about the tokens and worry ate his stomach.

"Kael," Jasala prompted. "We should go."

He nodded and slipped the token into his pocket. Lifting his arms, he touched his magic and opened a rift once more. Hopefully, this time they would step out in the forest where the tree of life was waiting to get him home.

TAZMMOR MOUNTAINS
ARKUM ZUL

Corleya woke with a start. The only light came from the flickering torches, casting an unsteady glow from outside the cells.

"It's dark," Alia whispered.

Lycori's voice drifted into their cell. "All the guards have been pulled way back. Even the docks and forges are clear."

"Feeling better, I see," Corleya said, smiling. She stood up and reached her arm out of the barred window, opening the cell door using the smuggled key.

"Much," Lycori answered as Corleya unlocked her cell and swung the door open.

The Princess smiled wider. Human blood had done wonders for the vampyr. "You look more like yourself," she said, glad to see the vampyr had regained her youth and strength.

"Let's go," Lycori muttered and led the way into the cave system. It took less than thirty minutes to find the hidden tunnels marked on the map.

"I guess this mean us?" Corleya pointed to a message written on the wall above a torch sconce in the tunnel as they entered.

Snuff message and torches as u go.

"It's recent," Lycori whispered. She examined the marks and rubbed the charcoal residue between her fingers.

Multiple torches lit the way in the tunnel. Pulling the torch from the sconce, Corleya smothered it in the dirt before smearing the wall to make the message disappear.

"Let's go," she whispered and led the way into the tunnels.

They walked steadily for over an hour before coming to a branch in the tunnels.

"These tunnels... are they man-made or magic?" Corleya asked, glancing over her shoulder. Alia merely shrugged.

"Nature would be my guess," Lycori stated while running her fingers over the passage walls. "The walls are too smooth to be made by hand or magic."

"Where do they go, you think?" Corleya asked.

Lycori shook her head. "If they were part of an underground stream at one time, I expect we'll come out at a river or even a lake perhaps."

"Shh," Alia snapped suddenly. Seconds passed, but Corleya heard nothing. "You hear that?" Alia asked, staring hard at Lycori.

"I did, dammit." Lycori cursed. "They must use these tunnels too. We need to hurry. If they catch my scent, we'll be swarmed."

"Swarmed? By what?"

"Mahala, Corleya. Move," Alia snapped.

"Go," Lycori said. "I'll watch your backs, but hurry."

Corleya and Alia moved through the tunnels as fast as they dared. It took only a minutes before they could both hear the hunters.

Nook, nook, nook.

The sound grew louder as they grew closer. Talohna's cruel Deep Earth killers actively pursued them, and Corleya realized the childhood stories told to her by her nannies about the Mahala were true.

"Faster, Princess," Alia whispered more urgently.

Corleya stole a quick look back over her shoulder as all hell broke loose behind them. "Lycori." She gasped.

Alia grabbed her by the arm and shoved her. "Faster," she repeated.

"We can't leave her—"

"She is coming." Alia cut her off.

Glancing back again, Corleya saw Lycori's glowing eyes moments before she materialized out of the dark tunnel, moving faster than seemed possible.

"Faster, Corleya!" she screamed and tossed a headless Mahala to the dirt as two more dropped onto her from overhead. All three tumbled to the passage floor.

"Mother Santia," Alia yelled. "There are tunnels above us. Be careful, Princess."

Corleya nodded. The death cries of what she hoped were the Mahala reached her ears as she burst out of the tunnel, tripped on a root, and crashed into the sandbanks of a shallow stream. Scrambling to her feet, she turned in time to see Alia join her. A bruised and bleeding Lycori arrived seconds later. Corleya shook her head and rubbed her eyes, almost positive a set of wings had disappeared into Lycori's back. Her eyes had to be playing tricks on her.

"We should be safe for now. They were just ranging scouts," Lycori said, barely out of breath.

"We are not the first to be chased here by Mahala," Alia replied, walking toward the remains of several Mahala skeletons.

"Months old — close to a year even. There are a lot more tunnels on... that side..." Lycori gestured into the distance from where they came from as she approached. "Well done, Kael," she whispered.

"They were wizards," Alia added. "At least two... no, three. One was incredibly tall or fast, perhaps. You knew them?"

Lycori nodded. "They are long gone now."

"Yes," Alia said. "Many months gone."

"Here," Corleya called to them. "The stream heads out of the cavern this way." The stream emptied out into a sand-filled ocean bay surrounded by mountain rock. A man dressed in a black peacoat stared down at them from a high outcrop of rock.

"That's the Sea of Storms," Lycori said, pointing out to the ocean. "I always wondered how you did it, brother."

"Very good guess. Both guesses actually," Damien Krass replied, bowing as he jumped off of the piled rocks. "You can thank me now, if you like."

"Bastard," Lycori growled, but did not attack. They were surrounded by a dozen pirates and all held silver blades at the ready. "Those won't kill me, Damien."

"But they will slow and weaken you enough, so I can cut that demon-cursed head from your body." He chuckled. "That will kill you. But I don't want to kill you, Lycori. Trying to help ya. You are making it rather difficult, though."

"Help?" Corleya snapped. "Starving us and keeping us locked up for months? You bastard."

"Stop," Damien whined. "Gods, grant me some patience. Look. You want to go?" He sheathed his silver blade and ordered his crew to do the same. "You are free to go. The Suns of Blood grants you amnesty. Go."

"Just like that?" Corleya demanded.

Damien nodded and flung his hands to the side as he bowed, but Alia cut him off before he could speak.

"Not just," she guessed. "Suns, yes. Ancients, no?"

"That is the just of it," he shouted over her. Ending the bow, he pointed at her with both hands. "You *are* free to go. The inlet is that way, but currently about twelve Ancient controlled ships are anchored there, and you will never make it over land—not as weak as you all are."

"Let me guess," Lycori said, approaching the pirate. Damien's crew drew their weapons, again. She held up her hands as if to say she was approaching in peace while she continued, "The Suns have a way out."

"But, of course, demon. Though not the Suns per say. You will have to follow me if you want to remain free of that cell."

Alia nodded slightly, and Corleya glanced her way.

The vampyr shook her head. There was really no other option for them. "Lead the way, pirate."

Damien smiled and led them from the bay into a grass valley before heading back up the mountain. They walked for hours, circling the valley and slipping past Flatwater Bay without being seen. Just when Corleya was certain her feet were going to give out, Damien led them off the trail and through to a small clearing.

Corleya gasped. Dominique Havarrow and his first mate waited for them.

"My apologies for the cloak and dagger as well as the treatment, ladies," the pirate commander said. "I had no interest in any of you."

"You have a strange way of showing it," Corleya snapped.

Dominique frowned and shook his finger. "Be careful, Princess Corleya."

"You know?" Lycori asked.

"Yes. From the moment Sythrnax took her from the Sartaq."

"And you said nothing. Why?" Corleya questioned.

"Knowledge is always worth something, Princess. There was no profit in telling Sythrnax and the Ancients who you were. You were their prisoners, not mine."

"But there is profit in letting us go?" Lycori asked. Disbelief rode every word.

Dominique laughed. "Perhaps in the long run."

Lycori snorted. "How?"

"If I told you, Lycori Alatar, you would never believe me."

"Try me, Northman, you might be surprised."

"Fair enough. It took me a while to get the details, but it seems you and I had a mutual friend. One who meant a very great deal to us both."

"Bullshit," she spat.

"You are not the only one to escape this mountain of hell. In fact, there are still Dead Sisters in Arkum Zul," Damien told her. "Where do you think he ended up? The man you consider a brother?"

"Kael?" Lycori whispered.

"Yes," Dominique said, nodding. "After his escape from here, he eventually passed through Dasal, and he saved my daughter's life. He rescued her from slavers."

Lycori shook her head. "But you're a Northman... shit!" She gasped. "You offered him a kreeda? Even though Kael's not Northman?"

Dominique nodded. "I did. As was my right to do so. He accepted, as was his."

"Your clan owes him a life then."

"And he will get more than just a single life. By Tyr's bloody blades, he will."

"What does that mean?" Corleya asked, confused.

Dominique stood and moved closer. "Kael died a few months ago, Lycori. He was killed in Kazzador City by an assassin working for Sythrnax. I only found out a few days ago. One of his captains told me about what Sythrnax and the Dead Sisters did to you and Kael before your death, and then Kael's escape from the opposite set of tunnels you just used."

"No, no..." Lycori let out, slowly sitting on a fallen log.

Corleya's heart broke at the depth of devastation etching its way onto Lycori's face. She went to her friend to comfort her.

"I am sorry," Dominique offered up. "This world needed someone like him."

Lycori ran her palms over her eyes and took a deep breath. "You are going to attack the Ancients."

"No. At least, not right now. Unfortunately, Northman honor and the Kreeda Oath each work both ways. To satisfy the deal I have with Sythrnax, we will return his people to their homeland. After we do, I will recall all Suns and MyrkrVatn ships that are not tied to the civil war on Kastalborg Island, and we will devote our time to making the Ancients' lives pure hell."

"And what of us?" Corleya asked.

"Below us is small vessel. The three of you will be able to handle it. You cannot sail south, so you must go north through Dark Cliffs Pass along the Kasym's southern edge. If you follow the Black Hollow shoreline, you will come out on the north side of the WhiteWyrm Ocean. You need to go home, Princess Corleya. Your own country is also on the verge of civil war."

"I guessed as much," she answered. "With no heir in court, some of the nobles will question whether or not my father should remain on the throne."

"It has already begun," Havarrow's first mate informed her. "Several powerful nobles have called in their marks and are assembling troops. In a matter of weeks, the fighting will be at your father's door, and from what we are hearing, even the Pillars of Rule will be hard pressed to hold back the forces assembling against him. We should leave. Now."

Dominique nodded. "This is my sister and my first mate, Shasta Trey. She will lead you to your ship."

"I can't," Lycori said, shaking her head. "I must return to the RedMaw clan. I have been gone for over a year. I wish you all the best, Princess, but I must return home also."

Shasta frowned. "They will never be able to sail the Black River and the Dark Cliffs with only two and be able to operate the cannons Eamon installed."

"No, they won't." Havarrow agreed. "The two of them will never hold the vessel. The current will drag them into the Jaws."

Damien stood and stretched while he coughed and finally yawned. "Well then, I guess I will have to go with them." He laughed as Corleya and Alia frowned at the idea. "Seeing as how we Suns are being bloody gods-cursed heroes now."

"Great," Corleya muttered.

"Do not worry, Princess," he said. Laughing, he threw his arms wide. "Heroes are gentlemen, don't ya know." He bellowed as he turned. "I will even prepare the ship for our royal departure."

Alia glared after him. "He will die if he — "

"He will behave," Shasta interrupted, raising her voice so Damien could hear. "Or I will castrate him myself. Now, come. Weapons, clothing, and food are already aboard as well as a new weapon that your ship will most definitely need if you go astray or are forced into the Jaws."

Corleya turned to Lycori and hugged her tight. "Thank you for everything. I'm sorry about your friend."

Lycori nodded. "Thank you, Princess. You two take good care of each other. Travel safe."

"Time to go." Shasta prompted their departure gently before walking into the trees. "My brother and I must get back to Arkum Zul before Sythrnax or the Vikress become suspicious of our absence."

Corleya and Alia followed.

Dominique hung around, eventually sitting beside Lycori on the fallen log. "I am sorry about Kael. I would have never seen my daughter, again, if not for him."

"You knew what he was?"

"Aye. He was traveling with a Dead Sister, and he was brave, or stupid enough to walk right onto my flagship unannounced. Neither of them were anything like the legends have led us to believe Though, he was equal parts brave and crazy."

"He was not always like that," Lycori said, smiling. "Someday you will have to tell me that story."

Dominique nodded. "Agreed. On a day when we are once again on the same side."

Laughing, she nodded. "Talohna has a way of changing things like that. We may be enemies next time we meet."

"True, on both accounts. But Bauro BlackSpawn is dead and the Suns' armada belongs to me, so for today, you and I are allies. I will bet, that on any tomorrow, we will remain so. Our friendship with Kael assures it. Be well, Mistress Vampire."

Lycori raised her eyebrow at the pronunciation.

Dominique laughed while tossing her a small travel pack with several water skins of Human blood. Unbuckling a scabbard and short sword from his waist, he offered the rune-engraved Northman blade to her and bowed. "You may fool most, Demon, but you cannot fool everyone. You are not the only DemonKind I have met, rare as you are. That blade holds the angel of ice rune. It was forged by my father. I gathered it would be more fitting than a blade forged with a fire rune? Be careful." As Lycori nodded her thanks, he turned on his heel and nearly disappeared into the forest. For a brief moment, he paused at the tree line and called over his shoulder, "I know not whether it'll help, but I have heard rumors that the DormaSain king and queen knew Kael very well. I have also heard that the two wizards who escaped with Kael returned to Cethos. Perhaps they would be worth a visit before returning to Salo RedMaw?"

He vanished among the trees without another word, and Lycori grinned at the news of Kalmar and Galen being alive as she vanished in the opposite direction.

Chapter Nine

"*To my beloved Kael,*

It has been ten months your death. It's been a very long and difficult year. You would be sad to see what is happening to our surrogate home. Talohna has become a true and living nightmare for some countries and for many people. The Blood Kingdoms can only sit back and watch as Cethos tears itself apart with civil war, and a little over a month ago, there was a Black Sun. It was terrifying and surreal, but incredibly beautiful all at the same time. The eerie darkness lasted for three hours. As far as we know here in DormaSai, none of the children born during the three hours were found, and we pray that there was only one or two because there is no one left to find however many were born. The ArchWizard, Saleece, Kasik... all are still missing.

Max, Yrlissa, Aravae, and I have taken refuge in DormaSai under the protection of its king and queen. Protection that was short-lived, for now we are threatened by war as well. Ellorya's emperor blusters and threatens while having the audacity to demand my hand in marriage. King and Queen Kohl refuse to bend under his pressure, and war can be the only outcome if he does not back down. Elloryan people worship the Fae like gods, more so than the rest of Talohna worship the real gods. To most Elloryans, I am a living god. Because of this, they refuse to see reason or understand that an Elloryan-DormaSai war would be the stepping stone to a world-wide war.

I'm scared, Kael, and I wish you were here. I miss you more with each passing day. We should have reached you in time, but I failed you when you needed me the most. I will see you again someday, love, even if it is in the Halls of Paradise after my own death."

Excerpt from Ember Syme's personal diary,
5026 PC

DORMASAI, SOUTHERN KINGDOM
SUMMER'S DAWN, 5026 PC

Darkness settled over DormaSai's Capitol city of Drae'Kahn. Torches positioned throughout the city cast differing levels of light into the darkest alleys of the blackest neighborhoods as music and chatter from the taverns drifted out onto the evening's cool air. Even though threatened with war—or perhaps in spite of it—the city and those living in it continued unabated with their lives.

Ember Symes, the last Fae in Talohna, watched the flickering lights as the evening breeze peaked, and she listened to the sounds of happiness while standing on the balcony of her room high up in BlackVoid Castle, the home of DormaSai's king and queen.

The previous king had been the vilest of tyrants and had eventually led his country into civil war. A war that Nekrosa and Sephi had won. Ten years had passed and DormaSai prospered under their rule, but Ember knew their lenient laws on magic would always make them a target. Even though Nekrosa and Sephi had risen to power on a wave of blood and undead magic, Ember felt safer than she had in a long time while in their presence.

Nekrosa and Sephi granted Max, Ember, and Aravae, along with Yrlissa and her daughter, Cassie, official sanctuary after returning from the Dyrannai Forest where they had interred Ember's husband.

Ember could not help but think of the chaos that followed during their months in the forest. Rumors that the

DragonKin had captured the ArchWizard, Saleece, and Kasik, along with a priestess of Mylla, Sister Nikki, just moments before Ember, Max and their new allies arrived at the Animus Seal ran with intense abandon throughout the cities and towns of Talohna.

Wildly exaggerated tales that the Ancients had returned to Talohna were also spreading like an uncontrolled wildfire. Many of Talohna's citizens believed it was only a matter of days or weeks before it became public knowledge. After countless millennia of heralding the Ancients as the founders of modern magic and civilization, the people of Talohna had real hope for the future should they return.

Ember shook her head. She was beginning to doubt all she had heard over the last year. Though she remained loyal to Nekrosa and Sephi for their help, Yrlissa's warnings were starting to fall on deaf ears. The woman whose words she once trusted over all others now seemed tainted with lies and personal agendas. Betrayal had that affect.

A light knock rapped on her door. Ember's magic told her it was the Queen.

"Come in," Ember called out. She glanced over her shoulder as Sephi entered. Dressed in a flowing, white silk gown, Sephi seemed to glide across the room's polished marble flooring without stepping on it. Ember smiled as the Queen bumped against her playfully. Sephi was a warrior few could rival and an even more ferocious friend.

"Are you ready, my dear?" she asked. "The Conclave is about to begin."

"As I'll ever be, I guess," Ember replied. Not making eye-contact, she continued to stare out into the city. Sephi put her left arm around Ember's shoulders and held her tight.

"I know the past ten months have been hard, hun. Kael's death was a senseless loss caused by ignorant fools. I am so sorry this meeting has to take place."

Using the back of her hands, Ember dried the moisture from her eyes and took a deep breath. "I miss him, Sephi. Death took him from me, but time hasn't taken my love. We lost so much under that mountain."

The Queen laid her hand on Ember's shoulder with the softest of touches. "We did. The biggest were Kael and Luthian, but we need to start making up for it, especially tonight. If Emperor Mero sees that you are not here against your will, then he should stand down, and we can focus on the things Yrlissa has told us. Things of which you need to speak to her about. It has been eight months since we've returned to Drae'Kahn from the forest."

"I can't, Sephi. If she had told us earlier what she knew... what she was, God... we could have done things differently. Had Max and I known, we would have left Giddeon behind and traveled faster or jumped. If we had, Kael would still be alive. I'm not sure I even believe her anymore. It's like she wanted him to die. And now… the Ancients are worshiped by everyone in Talohna. They created so much beauty. If they have truly returned, how can they be evil like she claims?"

"I agree with you, you know I do. She should have trusted in you and Max enough to be honest, especially after she found out you were Fae. But she didn't, and it is the past. The secrets she kept from you... it was for the right reasons. Time and experience will show you that sometimes you must do things that will hurt your loved ones, especially if it keeps them safe. Had Giddeon overheard or suspected, or had you been captured… The Dead Sisters were a lot closer than we thought—ahead of us and behind us. It was a no-win situation for her. There was no right call. I believe deep down you know that."

"I disagree," Ember said, shaking her head. "You don't tell a trusted friend one thing, and then keep your own agenda hidden. We had chances to leave Giddeon behind. We could have traveled faster or used her knowledge to realm jump to Kael. The choices were endless. It's like she didn't want us to catch up to him. Kael might still be alive, Sephi. I will *never* forgive her for that."

Sephi sighed. "You are hurt because she kept it from you. That is normal, but we must work together in order to push on. She has knowledge and skills we need. You know her secrets now, and you know what is coming."

"If what she says is true."

"Because of the library below us, we know that enough of what she said *is* true. And we must prepare for if the Sepulchre falls."

"Fair enough, my Queen." Ember frowned as she bowed.

"Don't you dare," Sephi said, grabbing Ember's arm to interrupt the bow. "The Fae do not bow to kings and queens and what I just said to you is as a friend not a queen. Ultimately, Ember, you must decide whether you will forgive Yrlissa or not, but we still must work together toward our common goals."

Ember nodded. With her heart lifted slightly, she gave Sephi a hug. The two women walked from the room and headed to the peace conclave between DormaSai and Ellorya with the hopes of averting what could become the start of a Talohna-wide world war.

She was ill at ease with the pending situation. The power-hungry emperor had been threatening a forced marriage. It was the last thing she needed to deal with, and she prayed her magic would be her strength. Ember quickly banished her worries aside when she noticed the palace's guard-captain waiting for them at the bottom of the wide central staircase.

"Your Highness," he said before bowing as Ember and the Queen stepped off the last stair.

Sephi motioned for him to straighten himself. "How may I help you, Captain?"

"I know you are on the way to the Conclave, but the guards at the castle gate apprehended a young woman trying to sneak into the castle. She is asking to see you."

"We don't have time for this tonight, Captain. Send her on her way, please."

Ember could see the guard flinch as if unsure whether to push. True to her title, Sephi also caught it.

"Yes, Captain?" the Queen prompted.

"I am sorry, Your Highness. She says she knows Mistress Ember, that she has information you both will want... about Mistress Ember's husband."

Ember nodded slowly and tried to swallow the lump forming at the back of her throat. If she was shocked, Sephi hid it well. "Very well, Captain. The Conclave can wait for a few minutes. Take us to her."

"Yes, Your Highness."

"And Captain?" she added. "Next time, lead with that information, please."

"Yes, of course. I am sorry, Your Highness."

Bowing a second time, he led them from the castle to the inner bailey. As they grew closer to a group of guards surrounding a young woman in a heavy robe. she stood and lowered her hood. Ember's heart plummeted into her stomach the moment she recognized her. Sephi was quick on her feet as she attacked the woman, forcing Ember to jump between them as both the Queen's blue daggers flashed. The woman put her hands up when Sephi's dagger came to a stop against her throat.

"You dare show your face here, you traitorous—" Ember placed a hand on Sephi's shoulder to stop her.

"Easy, Seph," she whispered, but her eyes locked on the woman. "Why are you here, Sister Nikki?"

"I am sorry," Kyah said. "I had nowhere else to go."

Ember shook her head. "You betrayed us and got Kael killed. Why would we help you?"

"And you can drop the Sister Nikki routine," Sephi added. "The monastery in Corynth has never heard of you, which backs up what Yrlissa told Ember and Max about you and what happened with Kael in that mountain glade. If you want sanctuary here, then you had better start telling the truth and right now."

"Fair enough." Kyah nodded. "My name is N'Ikyah—Kyah. I was with Kael when he escaped from Arkum Zul. I was the Dead Healer charged with keeping him alive during his imprisonment there."

"Bastard Dead Sister," Sephi spat.

"No, I am not. I was a Dead Healer. It is why I escaped with him. But the real Sisters caught us again, just north of Cairnwood. I was just trying to stay alive."

"That's a lie," Ember interjected. She realized the words coming out of Kyah's mouth showed no signs of revealing the truth behind Kael's death. "Cassie saw you take down an Orotaq Shaman and then help the Dead Sisters that night in the glade."

"I did," Kyah answered. "To save my own life, I did help them."

"You know what?" Ember scoffed. "I don't even care. What happened when Kael died? Where did you all disappear to?" she demanded. Her voice rose along with her anger as she took a step closer to Kyah. "Who killed Kael?! Was the assassin working for Giddeon?"

Kyah shook her head. "No. Giddeon didn't kill Kael. When the assassin struck, he was just as surprised as the rest of us, and when Kasik caught the assassin, Giddeon severed the man's cruus as punishment. He died horribly."

Ember was too shocked to say anything.

"Then what?" Sephi asked.

"The DragonKin Queen and a Fae Matriarch appeared out of nowhere and took us prisoner. They knew I had nothing to do with Kael's death, so I was released almost immediately. Over the last year, I tried to go on with my life away from all this... and... I met someone. We had a child two weeks ago," she said. Kyah carefully opened her cloak to reveal a baby completely covered, swaddled in a blanket, and secured around her waist. "But word got out that I had traveled with a DeathWizard, that I helped him. My child's father died fighting them, so my child and I had time to escape from bounty hunters. I have nowhere to go. Please..."

"No," Ember said.

Sephi stared at her as if unable to find the right words. "Ember," she finally let out.

Ember stared at Kyah for several seconds. "I am sorry for what you've suffered," she replied and turned to the Queen. "She can't be trusted. She needs to go her own way, Sephi, and may the gods grant her exactly what she deserves." Taking a deep breath, she looked to Kyah. "A darkness washes off you unlike anything I have ever seen. You will never be welcome anywhere I live. Be grateful you have a child and we have a war to stop or you would not walk away so easily. I highly recommend you turn her away, Your Highness. Far away."

Sephi nodded and pointed to the guards watching Kyah. "Escort her to the city limits and have two DeathDog scouts escort her to Fathoms' Deep in Ellorya. Pay for her passage to anywhere she wants to go but be gods-damn sure she gets on a boat heading far away from the Southern Kingdoms."

"Ember?" Kyah asked, stepping forward. One of the guards placed his hand firmly on her chest, stopping her from getting closer. "I truly am sorry about Kael. He was a good man."

"He was," Ember said. "He helped people every day on Earth, and every single day that he was here in Talohna. He helped you. When he needed help, there was no one there for him. You were there and could have helped him, but you chose not to. I wasn't there, so I couldn't. We both have to live with that."

"I do," Kyah began.

Ember sighed. "I don't believe you. Leave my sight before I ask the Queen to arrest you." She walked away without another word.

"Are you all right?" the Queen asked, following her

"I'm fine."

"You just asked me to exile a mother with a very newborn child from a country known for helping those no one else will. My country."

Ember snorted. "I know, but trust me, Sephi. That woman makes me feel physically ill, as if my soul aches. More frightening is the fact that I can't read her at all. The farther from us she is, the better off we will all be. I've made enough mistakes, allowing myself to be carried along with the events occurring here in this world like a mesmerized animal because the situation was so ridiculous I didn't know what else to do. Never again. It may take me a while at times, but I do learn from my mistakes."

"I understand and I trust your council, Ember. She is a confessed Dead Healer, and the Dead Sisters are not welcome in DormaSai, but your Fae empathy is going to eat you alive for this decision."

"It already is." Ember agreed. "But I'll carry it if it means that vile woman is far away from us all."

"If you are sure, and if you promise me you did not do that because of what Seifer told us in Dasal."

Ember laughed, but there was no humor to the sound. "I hold no ill will toward her over the fact she might have been with Kael intimately. I may be a bitch for not helping a young mother, Sephi, but I'm not a monster." Sephi nodded and walked in silence.

"At least not yet I'm not," Ember muttered to herself, thinking back to the day Kael died. Ember could only shake her head in grief as she swallowed her anger. The ArchWizard had betrayed them all, rendering the group unconscious so his smaller group could do what? Ember had always believed Giddeon and those loyal to him had taken Kael's life. But it was beginning to look like Yrlissa's agenda might be the true path forward—that Giddeon did not do it, but instead, Kael was killed to pave the return for the Ancients—a race Yrlissa called the Ri'Tek. She shook her head and shoved the thoughts aside.

She had more important things on her mind, like avoiding a war between two powerhouse countries and avoiding the offer of her hand in marriage to solve the problem.

NORTHERN BLACK CLIFFS
BLACK KASYM, NORTHERN TALOHNA

"That's unbelievable," Princess Corleya breathed out as she stared out over the falls. "Beautiful and frightening." Water cascaded into the Black Kasym and reacted to its volatile magic. Energy exploded far below them as purple and black lightning bolts danced and sparked through the mist.

"And more dangerous than all the Nine Hells combined for anyone with a heartbeat," Damien Krass muttered as he worked his way through the treacherous current. Corleya frowned while the experienced pirate struggled with the helm in his attempt to keep their small ship clear of the currents' ever-increasing pull toward the falls. One mistake would leave them at the mercy of the Kasym's wicked magics or else strand them on the Orotaq-controlled Black Hollow peninsula.

Grunting as he fought the ship's wheel, Damien continued complaining. "Be a miracle if we don't run into an Orotaq slave trawler."

"You had to say that, pirate?" Alia barked, looking over her shoulder from the bow. She pointed out to the open waters. A looming ship was anchored in the deep waters inside the Jaws of Ice and Rock less than a mile ahead of them.

As the last of the Black Kasym slid away behind their wake and they entered the bay between the WhiteWyrm Ocean and the Jaws, the massive ship dropped sail and the squeal of the anchor winch reached their ears.

"That is not a slave trawler."

"Is that not a good thing?" Corleya asked. She grabbed two sail lines and planted her feet as she watched the massive ship with horror. It turned and barreled down on them. The front bow was decorated in the giant bones of a long dead creature and a monstrous set of shark jaws big enough to swallow their whole ship rode the prow.

"No!" Damien roared. "That is a hunting and war ship and here they come! Alia! They have no idea what those cannons will do! Let them get close before you touch it off! They won't ram us and risk losing three slaves, but they will get close enough for us to see the wood grain on their side panels. Try and hit them at the water line and they might take on enough water for us to get away!"

"The bow of that ship is armored with bone!" Corleya yelled back to Damien. "You sure they won't ram us?"

"Not at first," he answered. "They will get close enough to toss drag lines across if they can." Pointing to Alia, he added, "Make sure that cannon fires before they do!" The mercenary nodded and turned back to the cannon. Stoking the small burning coal cylinder, she blew hard and lit the flare stick.

The Orotaq ship surged through the waters toward them, and Corleya could hear the bow scrap against the submerged ice and rock, but the bone armor held. The ship closed quickly with chunks of broken ice rolling out from around its sides.

"Fire!" Damien bellowed.

Alia never hesitated. Spinning the flare stick, she touched it to the left cannon and then the right. Both belched flame and the cannonballs hammered the Orotaq ship right at the water line. Corleya tied off the sail lines and rushed to help Alia reload while Damien spun the wheel, heading deeper into the bay of the Jaws of Ice and Rock. As Corleya arrived at the bow, Alia tossed her a dry swab stick and pulled the wet one from the second cannon. The second Corleya jerked the swab from the first cannon, the mercenary was already pouring black powder down its throat. In a matter of minutes, both cannons were loaded, and Corleya returned to the sail lines.

"Slow them?" Alia yelled across the small vessel to Damien.

He nodded. "But they are still after us."

"Are we faster?" Corleya asked.

"Matters not now, we're inside the fangs. The deep blue sea will decide our fate long before the Orotaq get here. Be ready and pray the cannons scare off whatever creatures the sea sends our way."

Chapter Ten

"... and the DemonKind betrayed the ArchDemon, helping the powers of hell to banish Salotan from the Nine Halls of Perdition. Not born nor diseased, but the true DemonKind created by Salotan with magic stolen from the gods. With one last act of defiance, the ArchDemon cursed those who betrayed him so that he could one day return, find, and punish the betrayers with his own hand with the powers of Perdition once more at his command."

Partial document found in the
Arcane Library Catacombs.
Fact or fiction status unknown, 5026 PC.
Drae'Kahn, DormaSai

**BLACKVOID CASTLE
DRAI'KAHN. DORMASAI**

Sephi and Ember were the last to arrive to the meeting in the castle's banquet hall. With soaring forty-foot ceilings, the expansive hall with its black marble pillars and excessive space was the perfect place to hold meetings of magnitude. Six bone statues lined the outer walls from one side to the other. They were a tribute to the long history of necromantic powers held by both the kings and queens of DormaSai. King Nekrosa had told Ember he loved the intimidating presence the statues produced, as if hell's most powerful guardians where watching over him and his castle. Similar demonic effigies were scattered throughout the castle, some even perched like gargoyles on the castle's keep.

Upon the Queen and Ember's entrance to the hall, Emperor Mero stood as did his two masked advisers. While they were believed to be women, their identities were kept a protected secret so no one could reach the paranoid ruler through them. Others believed they were slaves whose sole purpose was to lay down their lives to save the emperor from assassins. With Mero's reputation, the later was likely closest to the truth. From everything she saw, Ember was sure the man was a coward at heart.

"Your Highness," Emperor Mero said, bowing to Sephi. When he saw Ember, he walked around the tables, approaching her slowly. An expression of awe was etched in his fat face. "May I approach, reverent one?" Before Ember could answer, he dropped to one knee in a generous bow, nearly prostrating before her.

"Emperor Mero. Please, stand. Let us speak face-to-face," Ember said and extended her hand to help him rise. He recoiled from her touch as if he was unworthy to touch Talohna's only Fae.

"As you wish, Madam Eminence. I thank you for meeting with us. The Elloryan people are elated the Fae have returned to Talohna. Our citizens have worshiped your kind for thousands of years. Your architecture and temples still stand in our cities to this very day." The emperor babbled, clearly elated to meet a living idol.

"Thank you, Emperor Mero, for your kind words. Please, sit, so that we may begin."

"Yes, Madam Eminence." As the Emperor returned to his side of the elongated blood-mahogany table, Ember took the seat opposite him, in between Nekrosa and Sephi. Ignoring

Yrlissa where she stood behind them, Ember was the first to speak.

"We are gathered here today with the hopes of averting a war between your two countries. With the civil war situation to the north, it is my hope the same does not happen here in the south," Ember began. She looked over all members present at the table to enforce her sincerity before she continued. "My people, traditionally, were always the voice of peace and reason. I hope to live up to their reputation here today. Emperor Mero, you have made it abundantly clear you believe I am being held here against my will. Do you still believe this is so?"

"I am not sure, Madam. Why would you willingly choose to stay among these vile practitioners of the dead? Return with us to Ellorya where you can take your rightful seat as the living goddess of my people. You belong with the only country in Talohna to worship you. Your people, the Fae, would never have lent their support to a country so obsessed in the dark workings of black magic."

"You know my people personally, do you, Emperor?" Ember replied testily.

"Of course not, Your Eminence, that would be impossible—"

"My people believed in peace and healing. My genetic memory tells me that, but they have also fought in many wars. Do not assume to know anything about me or the Fae. I mean you no harm, Emperor, and neither do the King and Queen of DormaSai, you have my word on that." Ember interrupted him before he could finish.

Emperor Mero shook his head, clearly not convinced. "How do I know those are your words, Madam? It is no secret that men and woman who practice necromancy can master the ability to control the minds of others, both living and dead. We have worshiped the Fae since the time they walked among us, and I know they would never stay in a country like this willingly. I'm sorry, Madam, but I have no choice but to believe they are influencing your mind."

Ember could not help but chuckle. "I promise you, Emperor, my mind is very much my own. Both Nekrosa and Sephi have become good friends to me and my companions. Their help in the depths of Kazzador Mountain saved our lives, even if not that of my husband."

Emperor Mero continued to shake his head. "That is another concern of my country's, Madam. You openly confess to be married to a DeathWizard. His death was a blessing for all of Talohna. Yet by your apparel, it is clear you still mourn for him. You should be open to the prospect of remarrying. Perhaps, if you were to consider my proposal — "

"Emperor Mero, we will not discuss your offer of marriage, again. I will mourn my husband as long as I see fit. I may never marry again, let alone when being pressured to do so to avoid the war you so clearly seem to want."

"That is a problem, then, your Eminence. Your actions and your words are sounding less like a true Fae and more like a Darkling the more you speak. Talohna is changing, Madam, you may be the last Fae, but you are not the last of the old races. The Ancients have returned as well, and their words will carry the final say when it comes to which countries your kind will ultimately support. Even the Fae once bowed to the Ancients."

Furious, Ember snapped, "I can guarantee you, Emperor, that no one, regardless of who they are, will have any say in whom I support. I will lend my help to whichever country I see fit and that will always be those on the side of peace. The more you continue to insinuate threats and try to blackmail me into marriage, Emperor Mero, the less likely it is my support will lie with Ellorya. Even a living, breathing Ancient will not change that!"

"I make no idle threats, Mistress of the Fae. The Ancients have returned."

Hearing enough, King Nekrosa finally spoke. "We are not here to argue which country the Fae will support. With Ember being the only Fae alive we know of, it's irrelevant anyway. As for the rumors about the return of the Ancients, they are nothing more than that, Emperor Mero. You know it.

There have been no sightings, no diplomatic requests, and more importantly, no demands for their former territories to be returned. Corynth was built by the Ancients. It was their shining masterpiece. If no declaration for its return has been made, then they have not returned."

"My husband is right, Emperor," Sephi added. "Lies, rumors, and conjecture, nothing more and irrelevant to the matter at hand."

"I beg to differ, your highness. The Ancients have returned. I have been one of the few blessed with a visitation from them, in fact."

Nekrosa frowned in disbelief. "You've gone mad, Mero. What you claim is impossible."

"Not so, Nekrosa," the Emperor said, obviously dropping the king's title on purpose as he flashed an enigmatic smile. He inhaled deeply, puffed out his chest and stared confidently across the table. "They have returned, necromancer. In fact, my closest adviser is a living, breathing Ancient. Would you like to meet her, king of the dead? She certainly has some words for you," he growled. He stood with his arm extended toward the same door he had entered earlier.

A smug expression rose on his chubby face. Ember, Nekrosa, and Sephi watched in awe as an elegant and graceful figure walked into the meeting room. Wrapped in a white hooded robe to cover her entire body, in with her presence rolled an unnerving silence. Strange black marks sparkled with silver flecks of energy were etched into the white leather of her entire robe. Strange purple eyes struck them speechless as they peeked from above the velvet mask hiding the remainder of her face. An aura of power radiated from the confident being. Emperor Mero grinned ear-to-ear as the woman sat beside him.

"Nekrosa and Sephi Kohl," he started before turning to Ember, "Your Eminence, I present to you the Vikress Illara. The Matriarch of the Ancients."

Though Yrlissa had been quiet up until that point, Ember let out a sharp breath as she felt the assassin instinctively reach for her magic and fail. The implication of who they were facing became undeniably clear. Bending down, Yrlissa whispered into her ear, but she already knew what was coming.

"We need to leave, *mai nahlla*, now. Something is very wrong."

"Not now," Ember snapped harshly.

"Ember! Your magic. Is it gone?" Yrlissa asked, pushing again. Ember frowned and reaching for her magic if for no other reason than to prove Yrlissa wrong. She gasped as she realized her magic was gone.

"It's gone. What's going on?" she whispered over her shoulder.

Yrlissa winced. "It's Mero's adviser. She is a real Ancient, Ember. It's a set-up. This entire Conclave is a facade to get the Ri'Tek into DormaSai so they can locate the Human Animus Seal. We need to go. Now!"

"Is there a problem, Madam Eminence?" Mero asked over their heated discussion.

"No, Emperor Mero," Ember said, smiling sweetly. "My adviser was just filling me on the identity of *your* new adviser. You honestly didn't think you could fool us. Did you?"

"What is it, Ember?" Nekrosa asked.

Emperor Mero grinned. "Fool you? No, not at all. Get away with it? Why yes, young Fae. In fact, we already have. We are here in DormaSai, and the Dead King has something the Ancients want very badly."

"Something that doesn't belong to them," Yrlissa barked in response.

"The Animus Seal, husband," Sephi murmured.

King Nekrosa laughed. "You won't get it. I suggest you make your apologies, Emperor Mero, and then leave my castle before I have you removed like the sniveling shit—" The Vikress stood as Yrlissa dragged Ember from her chair, interrupting the DormaSain king.

"We can't win this fight, Nekrosa," the assassin snapped.

"Oh, yes, we can. I have never lost a fight in my own home, even before it was my home. This castle feeds my power and mine alone," he stated. Pushing his chair back, Nekrosa stood, and Ember felt him tap the Void's power. She winced as the energy entered the mortal world and filled his being with the kind of dark power that made her stomach hurt. Unlike everyone's failing magic, Nekrosa's magic manifested into dark wisps and black phantoms that circled his body.

He grinned at the Vikress, but Ember saw no fear in the woman's violet eyes. "This is my castle and my country," Nekrosa barked. "My word is the only law here. You can nullify the power of the Fae and the Elvehn, but you cannot stop mine."

The Vikress returned his smile, her mask tugging gently to the side. "Foolish *dosa* child. Necromancers have always believed they were the spawn of Gods when, in reality, the offspring of primordial ooze is closer to the truth, King Nekrosa," she hissed, spitting the insult his way. "There is no power on Talohna the Ancients cannot stop."

"You've been gone for too long, Vikress. Times have changed. My power doesn't come from Talohna like other wizards. I am not bonded to the Void, but born of it, ripped from my mother's womb by the cold, rotting hands of the DeathGod himself. My power *is* the Void. The infinite darkness between life and death, and a place where you have no power."

The dark ghosts and trailing comets of black power around him intensified, multiplying until a phantom form was seen through the swirling haze. The Vikress stared, and Ember caught sight of the shock and disbelief in her ancient eyes. Still she refused to back down.

"Very well, King of the Dead," she barked. "You can join the bones of your grotesque statues, and my brother can reap your soul in the same way he gave birth to it. Emperor Mero, kill them all, except for the young Fae. Bring her to me alive," she ordered calmly.

With a nod, the emperor's troops moved to attack, and runners fled the meeting hall to pass the word to units all over the city of Drae'Kahn. Nekrosa's personal guard leapt to meet the threat, and Ember watched on in horror as a noisy rattle erupted from under Vikress Illara's hood. The realization of the century slammed into her, taking her breath away.

The war they had been trying so hard to avoid for so many years had finally begun.

Emperor Mero grinned and ducked into the hall, but not before Ember pulled his thoughts from his head as he went. The emperor had been ordering his very best soldiers to hide through DormaSai in the weeks prior to their peace meeting. Dozens of units were positioned strategically throughout DormaSai's Capitol city of Drae'Kahn waiting for the command to attack, and it had been issued.

With only the magic to sense thoughts and feelings and no active magic to defend against Nekrosa's Void energy, weakness nearly overcame her while she fought to stay conscious. Ember gagged as the necromancer sneered and raised his spear into the air, calling forth every ounce of raw energy he could handle. The endless power of the Void poured into his soul and thundered through his veins. She collapsed on the floor, unable to help herself up.

"My grotesque statues are insulted, Vikress," Nekrosa growled from inside the shifting murk of shadows. With her magic, Ember could feel the way he ground his teeth, to suppress the agony of controlling such an abundant amount of Void-magic. Her body shook with tremors, mirroring his own struggles. Still, he carried on, "They would like to discuss it with you... Bones of the Brethren, hear me... return to life and protect what is yours." He gasped, his labored lungs barely able to draw in a breath. As the last word ripped free from his lips, Nekrosa drove his arms down and slammed his spear into the floor. A wave of magic exploded outward, billowing through the room with a sonic blast. The black mist and shadows came together and created six long tentacles. They multiplied a dozen times over as they raced toward the decrepit bone statues of the Lower Brethren lining the room. Hundreds more rocketed into the hallways and disappeared into the castle.

The aged and rotting bones of all six demon statues stirred with life for the first time in countless millennia as

Nekrosa crumpled to the mosaic tile; The activation spell for the demon skeletons completed.

Ember winced as the bone monuments came to life with a violent pop and the grind of dust-dry bone. The long forgotten KiPara remains—Perdition's most sadistic demon clan and rulers of the 9th Hell—rose with a roar of thunderous rage.

Not waiting to see the results of the battle, Yrlissa dragged Ember to her feet while Sephi grabbed Nekrosa's unconscious body. Together, they fled through the door and into the main castle as the sounds of ancient magic followed them in a monstrous battle.

Exploding granite and the ear-splitting screams of the dying assaulted Ember's ears as she gasped for breath. "Mero has troops all over the city! I saw it! In his mind!"

"So do we, dear, and Max is below us somewhere with the DeathDogs," Sephi told them, flashing a confident smile. "Only a fool trusts an Elloryan Emperor. You better?"

Ember nodded. "Close."

"Help me with Nekrosa?" she asked. "Yrlissa can scout back and watch our asses. It should be clear ahead."

Yrlissa let Sephi and Ember take Nekrosa while she brought up the rear, guarding their backs diligently. Her newly acquired Broken Blade daggers were ready in each hand, but Ember sensed she was still unable to use her magic. A tear ran down her cheek as she thought about how much they needed Kael—now more than ever. She heard Yrlissa say a quick prayer to Acathryl that Max would find his way to them from the barracks. He had spent every day for eight months building and training DormaSai's elite military unit, the DeathDogs, who they desperately needed.

TRAINING GROUNDS
BLACKVOID CASTLE

Max sat alone in the officer's quarters located off the eastern side of the training grounds in the royal castle in Drae'Kahn. He wanted no part of the peace Conclave. He was not born yesterday. Not for a single second did he believe Emperor Mero was sincere about peace between their countries. An influx of foreign mercenaries into the city over the preceding weeks had led him to believe Ellorya was up to something sinister. It was far too close to be a coincidence. He dearly hoped Nekrosa's men were up for anything that might happen. The number of mercenaries had even prompted him to advise the King to covertly post his best DeathDog squads throughout the city. They remained hidden in warehouses and rundown homes until—or if–Ellorya made a move against DormaSai while Max stayed with the newest DeathDog recruits.

As the shouts and grunts of the trainees' vigorous workouts buzzed in the background, Max's mind was far away. His was lost in his memories of finding the body of Kael over a year ago. The events of that day had tortured Max nearly every waking moment for an entire year. Though Kael's death was not his fault, he still felt responsible for letting Kael down in the moment he had been needed most.

A lone tear crept its way down Max's cheek to his jawline as he forced himself to remember their arrival in DormaSai as a distraction. Their arrival put them under the protection of its king and queen. The jump itself had been devastating. Like the others, Max felt like he had been hit by a truck several times. Yrlissa made sure they passed by the Kasym's volatile magic instead of going through it, but Ember had still lost most of her control on the spell. They arrived unconscious in the outer bailey of BlackVoid Castle. It had taken two full days to recover, but once he had, Nekrosa had sought him out.

He sighed, perfectly recalling the conversation that had followed.

"*Max?*" *Nekrosa asked, knocking on the big man's chamber door.*

"*Your Highness,*" *Max replied, slowly opening the black mirewood door. He started to bow, but Nekrosa stopped him by placing a hand on his shoulder.*

"*Max, please, we've been through enough. You don't have to bow and call me Nekrosa. I never held to titles well. I was born a commoner like everyone else.*"

"*Fair enough, Nekrosa. What can I do for you?*"

"*I would like to talk to you, but there's also something I need to show you. Can we talk while we walk?*" *the King asked.*

"*Lead the way,*" *Max replied as he stepped into the hall and closed his chamber door behind him.*

Max walked side-by-side at an easy pace with DormaSai's popular king. The King's limp from an old battle wound slowed their progress considerably. They went in comfortable silence as they passed the additional guest chambers and approached the main staircase.

"*I hear you've been down working out with the new recruits since you woke. How do they look?*"

Always the pragmatist, Max spoke his mind. "*Green, Nekrosa, but they're miles ahead of most kids their age. How does a sixteen-year-old have the technical skills of a man three times older, yet have no practical experience, no battle readiness?*"

"*That's a bit of a story, I assure you.*" *As they stepped from the bottom of the stairs, Max stopped and looked at Nekrosa.*

"*I have nothing but time, I assure you.*"

"*Fair point. This world can be a brutal place. We took this country by force from a man who made many orphans. A man who destroyed nearly everything this country is, and in the process, made the rest of the world suspicious of us. We try to do everything we can to keep people safe, but sometimes children are still left orphaned.*"

"*I get it, Nekrosa. People die. Accidents happen. Every world is like that, Earth was no different.*" *The King nodded while they resumed walking. Max noticed they were heading toward the barracks and the military training grounds.*

"*Since I have become king, orphaned children anywhere in DormaSai become wards of the crown. If they are younger than six, they are taken care of by young maidens here in the castle — most are teenage girls from noble families or other women interested in it as an occupation. They are paid very well to give the children a happy childhood — noble or not."*

"Are you serious?" Max asked.

"Very. If the children are over six years of age, they are cared for the same, but they take classes for education and train for the military. Once they reach age twelve their options for adulthood are explained to them, and they make their education choices accordingly, though it is never set in stone. At eighteen years of age, they are offered a choice of what they will do with the remainder of their lives. Those who wish to do so can continue their training and devote their lives to the DormaSain army — whichever branch they choose. If they decide they would like to do something different — say be a farmer or a blacksmith — they are placed in a way that will give them everything they need for an independent, successful life."

"For such a hated man outside your own country, you rule with more compassion and fairness than most," Max stated.

Nekrosa frowned. "People outside of DormaSai don't live here. We survived under the rule of two necromancers whose only concern was power gained through the death of others. We fought to free ourselves from the horrors that necromancers — the kind of horrors that my kind can inflict. I won't be the one to lead us back there."

"I understand. It is a noble goal, but I can't imagine the cost."

"It is expensive, and we do have a high tax rate, but it is eighteen percent lower than the tax rate in Ellorya. And everyone pays fairly. We get surprisingly few complaints because we have no magical taboos or restrictions here." As they approached the first wing of the soldiers' barracks, their progress slowed further as recruits raced back and forth in a clear attempt not to be late for their next class or workout. "Surprisingly, about seventy to eighty percent of those training from youth stay on and become lifetime military. When they do, their classes change to strategy and command and a lot more training. Families with too many mouths to feed are also welcome to bring their children here. They are welcome to visit at any time and the crown will cover the cost of their stay. It has worked well for the ten years I have been king, and I don't have children starving, begging, or whoring on the streets."

The two men passed through the remainder of the barracks quietly. When Nekrosa turned right just before the entrance to the training grounds, Max knew they were headed to the armory. Upon entering the weapon room, they had to wait as a squad of DeathDogs — men from Nekrosa's personal guard and DormaSai's most experienced warriors — finished gearing up for their daily practice routine. When the large room was empty, Nekrosa led Max to the secured back vault. It was the room where all unused magical weapons and the King's personal collection were kept.

As he began to unravel the complex spell placed on the door, Nekrosa smiled. "There's something in here I'd like you to have. The gods know that no one else here will ever use it." With the magic dispelled, the three heavy lock bars slid back into their recessed sleeves with the quiet rasp of metal on wood. The inset door swung outwards, for added protection, and the two men entered.

Max followed Nekrosa to the back wall of the vault where a weapon hung suspended on two wool-covered hooks. His eyes shot wide and his heart raced with a familiar excitement at the sight of the massive black warhammer.

"It is yours if you want it," Nekrosa offered. "We know the handle has been rune-forged, yet it predates the arrival of the Northmen by several millennia at least. We have no idea what it's enchanted with or how it was done. None of my men can lift it, let alone swing it. Four of my strongest DeathDogs struggled to lift it high enough to hang it there." Max was not sure what to say as he reached out and gently touched the engraved handle of the big hammer. His fingers glided across the carved bone, feeling the crisp edges of the archaic writing that looked to be melted into the bone and metal. Not a square inch of the hammer was without the strange markings.

"It's different," Max said. "Any ideas how it got here?"

"No. The hammer's head is made from a material we've never seen before, and it's inlaid with forged obsidian. All the writing and symbols are coated — perhaps stamped — with kinrai, the God's metal. We believe the handle is carved from the bone of a Dragon tail."

Max sighed, too tired to lie any longer. "It's not Dragon..." Max stared at the hammer as a need to possess it called from deep within his own soul. It had been so long since he had felt such a *feeling that it ached. He wrapped both hands around the handle and lowered it from the wall with ease.*

"... it's made from a demon's attack spur, from a KiPara demon..."

"I knew it." Nekrosa breathed out in awe.

"Knew what?" Max asked absent-mindedly, his attention still fixated on the war hammer.

"That hammer was found among the demon bones cataloged in the catacombs below the Ageless Library of the Arcane. The script with the hammer was written in the cypher of the gods. It cost me a fortune to get translated. One of which means: forged by the hands of the ArchDemon for the hands of a true Demon. Your strength and speed, the fact you can lift that hammer; it all adds up, Max. You're a demon, or you have demon blood in you, at the very least."

The weapon hummed in Max's palms. It reminded him of home. His real home. Memories he had not thought of for many millennia flashed in his mind... watching Vaighar... the mighty white Behemoth fall beneath the frenzied claws of the Vascuul... the oath of the Guardian Pact... and of his promise to the Gods of Talohna.

The most powerful of the memories were the twelve thousand years spent on Earth, waiting for two newborn Talohna children to be delivered to the small city of Rockton, South Dakota. For twenty years, he watched Kael and Ember grow to love each other, and he hoped his own world would not be destroyed by it. The charade was over. There was no longer any reason to hide the truth.

"DemonKind, Nekrosa. True DemonKind, and the second to sign the Guardian Pact."

Nekrosa was stunned by the revelation. "Ah... how is that even possible? Is history really that wrong?"

Max scoffed so suddenly, it turned into a snort of laughter. "You're a smart guy, Nekrosa. There are six Animus Seals, why?"

"From what Yrlissa said, I assumed there was one for each Lesser race?"

"All right, six seals means six races. What are they?" Max prompted.

"Well," Nekrosa began, "from what we know, the one here in DormaSai is the Human seal. the Dwarven seal is somewhere far to the north, close to the Black Kasym, likely on our side of it from what

we know about the land shift from the Cataclysm. I assume the Dragon's Seal is on Ver Karmot." Max nodded as Nekrosa continued. *"That leaves the Elvehn and Fae Seals, but we don't know where they are."*

"I think you're one short, Nekrosa."

"Didn't I have six?" he said, puzzled and began counting his outstretched fingers. *"Human, Dwarven, Dragon, Elvehn and Fae... shit, that's only five. Who are we missing?"*

"The DemonKind," Max answered. *"The one Kael died on. The first one to open."*

"Then, history is wrong. There was no war between the Ancients and the DemonKind."

"Technically, yes there was, but it was the same war everyone else fought in. We fought alongside the other races against the Ri'Tek. We gave our blood in battle to seal them away just like the others. The Ri'Tek are who most of Talohna call the Ancients. But the DemonKind were small in number. Those like myself were created by the ArchDemon Salotan when he mixed the soul of a demon with that of a mortal soul suffering in his realm. Demonic magic was used to bring the joined souls back to life. It was magic he stole from Dathac. We acted as his generals, but other DemonKind were born in the living world from the pairing of demon and a member of the Lesser races. Vampyrs and were-creatures are these Kind's weakened ancestors, yes, but neither of them ever are true DemonKind Not by a long shot. I was one of only a few purebred Kind created by Salotan left alive before the Six sealed the Ri'Tek away. The Ancients started secretly wiping out my entire race long before the war started. Our strength, our immunity to magic, and some who could command our creator's magic... all of that made us a target. On the battlefield one of us could easily destroy a fifty-man troop of Ri'Tek warriors in minutes."

"What happened?" Nekrosa asked.

"The few remaining true DemonKind died in the same chamber as Kael while defending Asa N'ahai — the DeathWizard who sacrificed himself for our seal. I commanded the army at that seal's location, but I was fighting above ground while my people and a Guardian protected the DeathWizard."

"That's incredible. What then?"

"I wasn't a Guardian like Yrlissa. For that you needed to wield magic and very few DemonKind did. Instead, it was my job to command the armies, but I was severely wounded fighting a white Vascuul dragon. A young Fae jumped me to Vaenaria where the Fae Matriarch saved my life and tried to get me back in the fight, but the plan worked and the Ri'Tek were sealed away. With no battle to return to, Eva and another Fae woman healed me slowly over the next few days, but before I was fully recovered, prophets began seeing the Ri'Tek's eventual escape from the seals — Kael and Ember's prophecy. I was asked to wait on Earth for them to arrive, should such a thing ever happen. The Fae matriarch, Eva Thornwing took me through a Fae-rift to Earth when Humans there were still far from evolved. The Last Light prophecy was old even then, but it never made sense until the Ri'Tek were locked away. Every prophet since has seen it. Ten thousand years' worth of planning, more even."

"Oh, damn. If you were the second to sign the Pact, why doesn't Yrlissa recognize you?" Max spun towards Nekrosa, and the necromancer stumbled back, only his cane kept him from falling.

"Never will you tell her what I've told you, do you understand? As far as she knows I fell on the battlefield aeons ago."

"Max, I won't if that's your wish, but gods, don't you think she'd want to know? She's the only one left from back then, and she has been alone for five thousand years. Give her some peace of mind."

"I can't, Nekrosa. I'm not the same as I was then. A DemonKind couldn't go to Earth. There was magic... it mutated my body, changed me into what I am now. I am not what I used to be or who she knew, and I no longer want to know her. She evolved into the persona of an assassin, driven by her own agenda and she is not... the woman I knew would have had Ember jumping us to Kael the moment she figured out Ember was Fae, not let him die when she could have helped. That is not the woman I knew."

Max did his best to hide the deeper more intimate story behind his argument, but he could tell Nekrosa did not buy it.

Even so, the King still let it go. *"Fair enough, you have my word, but she will figure it out sooner or later."*

"Yeah, she will," Max muttered aloud. As his thoughts returned to the officer's barracks, he grinned at how well Nekrosa had kept his secret, but the King had been right about Yrlissa. Her attraction to Max was almost unnatural, and only he knew why. Over twelve thousand years ago, no two souls had been closer than theirs.

Now, it scared him. It was just one more reason why he missed Kael. He had never judged, and he had always listened. Max hoped beyond hope that Kael's soul had made it to Paradise, that the real magic of the DeathWizard was indeed broken. If not, he feared for what torture his friend's soul would be going through.

Shaking his head, Max grabbed his warhammer and stared at one of Nekrosa's grotesque demon skeletons as it sat motionless in the corner of the barrack's recreation room. Though demons and the DemonKind seldom agreed on anything, the bones of the massive Lower Brethren still incited a sense of longing inside him for his true home.

With a need to distract his thoughts, Max forced himself to go join the DeathDog trainees in the yard. He nearly made it but stopped short as a ten-foot long shadow of magic snaked its way into the room. The shadow coiled tightly around the demon bones. The giant construct shivered to life as its eyes lit up, glowing a menacing blue. Max knew the origin of the demon bones well—the Kroa from Perdition's 8th Hell. Bones cracked, and dried sinew stretched as the eight-foot-tall demon bones unfolded to its full height. Clicking its razor-sharp claws, the demon snapped its tail stinger. The bones quivered, distorting the image to Max's eyes. Even in death, he realized the Kroa's deadliest ability still worked as the bones disappeared only to be replaced by the most beautiful woman he had seen since his own days walking the 8th Hell.

Smiling at him, she lunged without warning. As Max easily sidestepped the attack, he whirled to see the Kroa demon land in front of two Elloryan knights. Approaching both knights slowly, the demon smiled playfully over her shoulder at Max while her claws punched through each knight's metal chest-plate. Hypnotized by her beauty, the knights never stood a chance. She ripped her hand from their chests, clutching their hearts in her fists. She bowed to Max and dropped both hearts on the floor at his feet. The demon rushed from the room too fast for him to follow.

"Over twelve thousand years and those sisters are still a nasty piece of work," he muttered. He did not have time to focus on her as he heard the cries of dying men coming from the training arena. Grabbing his warhammer in one hand and sliding his bow and quiver over his shoulder with the other, Max raced out to the training arena.

Chapter Eleven

ELLORYA

"... and finally that brings me to. Emperor Mero. What is there to say about this Southern Kingdom ruler who controls one of Talohna's largest standing armies? He runs a tight country and, on the surface, it looks like he is an amazing man politician and leader. That being said, I have met the man in person and found him to be, well, unimpressive. As explained above, Ellorya is often a country where money and power have more say than the law and I believe that a ruler's behaviors and ideals filter through to affect a country's personality. Emperor Mero has built an impressive military machine, but his country will forever suffer from the lack morals that he himself possesses."

Garren Sallus, A Traveler's Codex Volume 1

BLACKVOID CASTLE
DRAE'KAHN, DORMASAI

"Yrlissa!" Ember cried as she stepped in front of Sephi and Nekrosa. The Elloryan wizard ten feet away unleashed a hell-storm of sizzling red fire on them. She pulled the DormaSai's King and Queen into her arms. The wicked spell scorched Ember's back, eating through her formal gown and into her flesh. The roar of the flames died, and she glanced over her shoulder in time to see the wizard fall. Yrlissa stood above him, a broken dagger in her right hand.

"You all right?" the assassin demanded.

Ember grunted to hold back the pain. "Fine. Already healing," she lied. Even though she had her advanced Fae healing, it would still take some time for the heavy burns to heal. It was time they did not have. Looking at Sephi as she supported Nekrosa, Ember added, "We are too outnumbered to keep doing this. We need a way out of this castle, so we can regroup and find some support."

"If Nekrosa were conscious, we could fight our way deeper into the castle," Yrlissa suggested. She turned to look around the corner while she slid her broken dagger handle first into its sheath. "Can either of you help him?"

"I can wake him using Void-magic. Thank Dathac, they can't counter it," Sephi offered.

"Yet," Yrlissa mumbled. "It won't take them long to figure out a way. Believe me."

"He won't be able to use magic for several days if I do wake him. The risk—"

"Wake him," Ember interrupted her. "We're fighting with weapons anyway. My magic is still gone. Only my innate magics like accelerated healing and senses are working. Yrlissa?"

"Nothing," the assassin said, shaking her head as Sephi and Ember propped Nekrosa against the wall. "Every one of Ellorya's unit commanders will have one of those Ancient amulets. Only Void-magic and that—like what Kael had—will work in its presence."

Sephi gently slapped Nekrosa's cheek. "Come on, luv. Wake up. We need your help. Come back to me, husband. Follow my voice. The Void can hold you another day. *Na gravasay dal toc.*"

Nekrosa jerked awake, grasping at Sephi's gown. "Did they walk?"

"Yes, luv, you did it. The demon bones rose, but we're still outnumbered. We're losing. We must flee through the Library catacombs — if we can even make it that far."

"Fair enough." He agreed, climbing to his feet with Sephi's help. She handed him his walking cane, and he immediately twisted the handle. The long and smooth javelin blade slid out. "We're on the east side of the grand staircase. The barracks are on the west. They would have hit it hard and fast at the start of the attack, so getting there for soldiers and weapons is out of the question."

"Max was there," Ember whispered as she chewed her bottom lip.

"I know. He will fight his way to us sooner or later," he told her, and Ember nodded.

Yrlissa shook her head. Pulling two metal daggers from within her boots, she sighed. "Whether he finds us or not, it won't matter if we're dead or captured. We need to get out of this castle," she said. "Is that door behind the shelving of your personal library still working? The one that leads to the backside of the inner courtyard? It's close enough that we should be able to avoid the heavy fighting, and we can use the hidden entrance to the Arcane Library by the outer wall of the castle."

Nekrosa frowned at Sephi. "Don't look at me, luv. I never told her."

"No one told me," Yrlissa barked. "I walked the halls of this castle long before your ancestral line was born."

"That is..." Nekrosa's voice trailed off. "Yes, it's still there. Let's go." Using his spear for support, Nekrosa limped around the corner with Yrlissa at his side. They moved as quickly as they cold down the narrow hallway without being seen. However, as they rounded another corner, two Elloryan wizards stood between them and the library door.

"Back, now! Shit," Yrlissa hissed.

"I can take the one on the right with my spear," Nekrosa whispered, peering around the corner.

Ember slid two throwing knives from the sheathes along her waist and offered them up to Yrlissa. "Quietly?" she asked.

Yrlissa took the knives and nodded at Nekrosa. "Can you distract them?"

He frowned. "No. Not without blacking out."

"I got it," Sephi interjected and took Nekrosa's place. "*Na gravasay, shadus mal.*" The shadows behind the two wizards came to life in wisps of black as she moved behind Nekrosa. A light hiss rose from the doorway, catching their attention. When they turned, the shadows vanished, teasing the guards. Yrlissa took the opportunity and rolled into the hallway. The throwing knives and Nekrosa's spear whistled down the hall in unison. The spear hammered the wizard on the right, pinning him to the library door as the second wizard fell with two knives in his neck. His shield sputtered, spazzed, and winked out.

Yrlissa climbed to her feet as the others walked toward the dead wizards. "It's a good thing that crazy druid blessed those knives of yours, Ember. Gods, what kind of a wizard keeps a shield active all the time?"

"A paranoid one?" Sephi answered. "He is in Mero's employ after all."

"Good point." The assassin agreed.

"Let's go" Ember said. She pulled her blades from the wizard's neck and throat. Standing slowly, she stared at the way the second wizard was pinned to the library door. Even though she had seen it happen, it was a bizarre and surreal sight. "Like some bizarre Hollywood movie."

"Ember?"

"Never mind, Yrlissa. Help me get him off the door so we can get out of here."

Nekrosa stepped up and wiggled the spear loose. The wizard's body crumpled to the floor as he eased his weapon from the heavy door. Ember helped Yrlissa drag the body aside before heading into the library with the others. Quietly closing the door behind her, Ember turned to discover an Elloryan knight's steel sword touching her nose. Another knight and two Elloryan military swordsmen held the others captive. Yrlissa and Sephi reached for their weapons, and Ember could feel Nekrosa preparing to tap into his magic.

"I would not advise doing that." Emperor Mero told them as he emerged from the shadows. A dozen more soldiers appeared with him.

"Don't, Yrlissa," Ember said, shaking her head.

"I suggest you listen, assassin. Captain, remove their weapons and secure them, please. Make double sure the Dead King and his insane wife cannot utter a single word. The Ancients' pendants don't seem to work when it comes to suppressing their vile magic."

"Yes, Emperor." The captain and one of his men stuffed rags into Nekrosa and Sephi's mouths and secured their placement with a tie around their faces.

Ember frowned at the sight. No speech meant no magic. She stood still as the Elloryan knights searched everyone, stripped their weapons, and tied their hands behind their backs. With a blade to their throats, there was no good way to resist.

She winced as the Captain's hand lingered a little too long around her waist and her thighs while he felt for hidden weapons. Hoping to distract the man from his search, she rotated her hips into his hands when they slid along her ass. Looking her up and down, the Captain licked his lips. Ember smiled coyly in response and winked. She pressed into him harder, letting her body rub against his slow enough to make the Captain blush. He tugged at the bindings around her wrists as he clearly tried to compose himself, and Ember smirked, proud of herself. He missed the throwing knives sheathed inside her sleeves thanks to her flirtations.

The Captain and his knights placed the wide assortment of weapons on one of the library tables and made way for Emperor Mero as he approached.

Stopping in front of Ember, he grinned. "My future bride-to-be... I'm starting to think that you do not want to marry an emperor. In Ellorya, the Fae are worshiped like gods. Why would you not want that? Everything you could ever want would be yours." Reaching out, he gently caressed her cheek and guided her closer to him. "And everything I ever wanted would be mine. A perfect arrangement, do you not think, my beautiful Fae?"

Ember struggled to control her rolling stomach. "I have tried to be polite for months. I have tried too many times to make you see that I am not interested in marrying you or anyone else. My only concern since my husband died is to make sure Talohna doesn't fall into the chaos of war. The Blood Kingdoms have watched helplessly as Cethos is torn apart by civil war, the ArchWizard is still missing, and the Northmen are also on the verge of civil war while fighting back an Orotaq invasion all while you threaten to do the same here! Why can you not see what war here in the south will do to this world?"

"Because it does not matter, my dear," he said. Stepping closer, his hand grazed her body as it trailed from her cheek to her waist. "Wars are for making people like us rich and for those below us to wage. Besides, the Ancients will put an end to the all the troubles both here and there, and you and I can enjoy the pleasures this life has to offer like those of real power should." His hand fell further. Grabbing her ass, he pulled her against him. Ember slipped a knife from her sleeve just as Yrlissa dodged the sword at her throat and leapt to Ember's side.

"Leave her alone, Mero," she snapped. Before the assassin could do anything, Mero grabbed her by the throat.

Turning her sideways, he growled in her ear, "Because you are a friend to my bride-to-be, I will not have you killed right now, but you will not get another warning, elf." Yrlissa stiffened at the rarely-used racist insult. Ember brushed her fingers against her friend's hand, quickly pushing the blade into Yrlissa's hand. The assassin took it discreetly.

"Fair enough, Emperor Mero," Yrlissa spat, her voice full of disgust.

"Good," he said. "Captain, please, make sure this interruption does not happen again. I have a beautiful young Fae to woo." He laughed lightly as the Captain led Yrlissa back to the others. "Now, Miss Ember, where were we?"

"You were wasting your breath about marriage proposals, again."

"Right. I guess if I'm wasting my time, there is little to do here then. Are you sure that's your decision? Be warned, though, the alternative is not nearly as enjoyable for you even if it is much more so for me."

"I will never marry you, Mero. I'd rather die slowly," Ember hissed.

"Fair enough, my dear, but you won't die. No. I was thinking perhaps you'll become a new addition to my harem. Our enjoyment will make for interesting offspring. Do Fae and Human offspring still retain their Fae magic? We would have a pantheon of god-children. Do you not think?"

"Never."

"Yes," he yelled back, his anger flaring. "And, perhaps, we start right now." He grabbed her by the hair and shoved her to the library table, pressing her face painfully to the hard wood.

"Emperor Mero, sir!" the Captain interrupted. Ember hoped the man was among those who worshiped the Fae. "Stop. This isn't right —"

The Emperor glared over his shoulder but did not stop. "Captain, take your men and secure the far hall."

"But, Sir..."

Ember forced a smile for the Captain to see. It was her attempt to thank him, but she also nodded for him to go before he ended up dead. The least she could do was ensure his safety.

"Now, Captain! My knights will be enough protection. After all, we are in control of the Dead King's castle. With his mouth stuffed with cotton rags, he and his crazy wife are no threat to anyone." The Captain hesitated, his conscience clearly bothered him. "If I must give you the order twice, Captain, I will strip you of your rank. Am I clear?"

"Yes, Emperor. Let's go."

Ember struggled as she stared after the Captain. He led his men from the library with an emotionless mask pasted on his face, never looking back at her.

"Now... where were we, my dear?" Mero asked, lifting Ember's face from the table.

"You were about to prove how much of a pervert you are."

"You are right. I was," he said and slid his hand up under her evening dress. He slammed her head down on the table, leaving her dazed. The feeling only lasted a moment thanks to her accelerated Fae healing, giving her the chance to continue struggling.

The rough touch of Mero's hand slipping around her hip to between her thighs set her off. Panic made her heart race. She dropped all her weight on the table's edge and pushed with everything she had, catching his hand between her hip and the wooden table. The bones in his wrist flexed and it strengthened her resolve. Grinding her hip harder, she could sense his ulnar bone crack. It did not snap, but she knew he was hurting. He smashed her head into the table repeatedly until she finally released him. Swearing under his breath, he moved away to inspect his hand.

"Fuck!" he nearly shouted as one of his knights offered him a strip of soft leather from one of his bracers to help.

Waves of nausea overtook her stomach and her head spun uncontrollably. Ember collapsed on the floor and stared at Mero, trying to keep him in her sights. He swam through her dazed vision, though, and she blinked rapidly to clear her head. "What's the matter, love?" she mocked, her voice cracking as she put on a strong front. "Can't handle what you found down there?"

With everyone watching Emperor Mero for his response, she eased her last throwing knife from her sleeve and balanced the blade on the floor.

"Hold her down across that table," Mero ordered, as he wrapped his hand.

As they turned on her, she scrambled backward with little hope of getting away. They yanked her from the floor, cutting her bindings as they went. She fought for her life, kicking and screaming. The tactic doubled as a distraction, letting her slide the knife along the floor to Sephi. It was short lived as they tossed her to the table on her stomach, and Ember was unaware if the DormaSain Queen caught her blade but hoped it made its mark. they pushed her face down on the table once more. Each knight held her down by the arms, stretching her while one immobilized her by a fistful of hair.

The position forced her to stare at Sephi. The Queen gave her a quick nod, letting her know she had the blade. Still, Ember caught sight of the Queen's lips trembling with a knowing fear.

Ember shook her head as best she could with hopes Sephi would know not to risk an attack just to save her. As much as she wanted it to end, she would not risk her friend's life for her dignity. "Your tin cans have done this before," she muttered. The Emperor stepped behind her and forced her legs apart.

"They have, my dear. Not all my harem girls take to their duties right away," he told her. He bent over to nuzzle her ear and the smell of him washed over her, making her stomach turn. She tried to shift away to no avail. "Neither did young noblewoman when I was younger. Most women need to be properly trained, and it seems you do as well. It is so much easier now that I have *tin cans* to do the hard work for me." He confessed in her ear.

Ember fought harder but knew she was no match for the two knights. The longer she struggled, the more exhausted and hopeless she grew. "You touch me, you disgusting pig and I'll break something a lot more important to you than your hand!" she threatened.

"I highly doubt that, little Miss Fae," Mero said as he pushed her dress up over her hips and draped it over her exposed flesh. "The only thing that *will* be broken, is you." The Emperor opened his robe, and the rustle it made as it hit the floor sent her heart racing wildly. His good hand rubbed her hip almost fondly and she shivered.

Out of the corner of her eye, she caught a flash of movement. Fear and worry surged through her but were quickly replaced with relief as she understood what she was seeing. A smile overtook her lips with the emotion. Mero's erection pushed against the back of her leg and his fat belly settled on the small of her back as he nuzzled her neck, again. "See?" he said, licking her ear and drawing the affection out. "I knew you'd change your mind. You're already smiling."

Shifting to stare over her shoulder, she said, "Of course, I'm smiling, Mero. You're about to die, and you don't even know it."

Distracted by her, he never saw the other three captives move. Her hands came free as Sephi and Yrlissa each stabbed a knight in the neck, sliding Ember's throwing blades past the gaps in their armor. Nekrosa yanked Emperor Mero back and snaked his arm around the naked man's throat in a rough choke hold.

Ember turned and, after several attempts, managed to pull her dress back down over her legs as she shook uncontrollably. Acting on impulse, she snatched up one of Sephi's blue-bladed ice daggers from the table and rushed the Emperor, swinging it madly. It severed Mero's manhood and half of its companions. The blade's magic flashed blue and froze the wound shut while Mero's missing body parts fell to the floor with a resounding smack.

"By the Gods," Nekrosa exclaimed almost painfully and stepped back, releasing the Emperor. Mero stood on the tips of his toes and trembled. The frosted blade tumbled from Ember's numb fingers as she tried to back away. She lost her footing, falling over herself as her body was out of her control. Tremors and quakes raced up and down her body as the full weight of the situation crashed down on her. Scrambling backward, she put as much distance between her and Mero until her back hit a wall. Her chest heaved with quick sobs, and she pulled her knees to her chest, but kept her eyes glued to Mero.

Emperor Mero shrieked, but she barely registered the sound.

Sephi stepped forward, untying the leather strap around her mouth and spitting out the cloth gag. In a hurry to help Ember, her and Nekrosa had foregone helping themselves. Now that she could, Sephi took the opportunity to ram the ball into Mero's mouth to muffle his screams.

"Sit here, you fat bastard," Yrlissa snarled as she shoved the emperor into a chair. She knelt beside Ember and gently rested a hand on her shoulder.

"Don't touch me!" Ember shrieked, slapping Yrlissa's hand away. "Leave me alone!"

Sephi glanced at Yrlissa. "Give her a few minutes, will you? Go keep an eye on the hallway."

"A few minutes is all we have," Yrlissa persisted. "She needs to get up."

"And I said give her a damn minute," Sephi ordered, putting her body between Yrlissa and Ember. "She needs it."

"I can hear you, both. I'm fine," Ember whispered and lifted her head as if to prove her point. Rearranging her dress, she pulled it down to her ankles where it belonged and took a deep breath. "Help me up, Sephi, please."

Ember stood but barely. Her legs trembled, and she still struggled to keep her feet under her. "Find those Ancient amulets and destroy them. I want my magic back, please," she whispered. Turning toward Emperor Mero, she stared at the man but said nothing more.

"Ember?" Yrlissa asked. "Look at me? Please?"

"What?" she answered. Her voice held a cold edge of defiance, but her eyes never moved from the emperor.

"Hey..." Yrlissa touched Ember's chin, and she flinched. pulling away before finally shifting her glare to the assassin.

"You're all right, it's over," Yrlissa added. "He'll bleed out once the magic from Sephi's dagger melts. We have to leave, Ember."

"No," she said softly. "He has to pay for what he did. It is what's right."

"Stop, Ember, please," Yrlissa whispered and moved closer. "I know what you're thinking, but you cannot. Fight the desire to make him suffer. If you give in to what you are feeling, it is a long road back—if you ever manage to find it. Your mind is twisting your Fae sense of justice into revenge, but the Fae cannot act on those feelings."

"I... don't... care. I am tired of listening to you. You betrayed me in the worst possible way. Your words mean nothing to me. What happened here today does not change that. Help the others locate those amulets and get the hell out of my face," she said, the icy edge to voice never wavered. She pushed her former friend away.

"Ember, stop." Yrlissa tried one more time. "If you do this it will send you down a dark path. The Fae cannot act on feelings of revenge until they're much older—if ever. It is how Darklings are formed."

"She is right about that, hun," Sephi added in as she returned from checking Mero's clothes and a knight's body. Two Ancient amulets hung from her hand by their leather ties. "You know me well enough to know I won't stop what you're planning to do but calm yourself first."

"No," Ember countered. "I am going to tear his brain apart, piece-by-piece, until nothing remains but a slobbering, dickless fool, and then I am going to heal the wound between the fat fuck's legs, so he can live out his life as a drooling idiot."

Nekrosa bent over to check the last knight for an amulet, clearly uncomfortable with the conversation. "Thank the Void's black ass, this guy's clean. No amulet. As long as the Elloryan captain took his men to the far hall as ordered, we should be good if you smash those."

"Smash them?" Sephi asked, getting an adamant nod from Ember.

"Please, don't do this, Ember," Yrlissa begged. "It will change you."

"Maybe that's a good thing. Maybe if Kael had changed — been what everyone in Talohna wanted him to be so badly — he'd still fucking be here," she snapped. Ember turned her attention back to Emperor Mero as he whimpered in the chair.

Sephi grabbed her other dagger from the table. "Oh, babies, I missed you," she whispered and wiped Mero's blood off the first before kissing both daggers on the handles. Hammering the butts against the amulets shattered them, and the powerful magic-silencing effect vanished.

"Hold him still," Ember ordered with no emotion. Nekrosa and Sephi held the Emperor down in the chair.

"Ember. Please," Yrlissa began.

Anger rolled through her unlike any she had ever experienced, and she whirled on her heels to face Yrlissa. "No!" she yelled. "*Naolass tongh.*" Her arm shot out and magic blasted Yrlissa in the chest. The assassin's eyes rolled back in her head, and she collapsed to the floor unconscious.

"Shit," Nekrosa let out, and Ember glared at him. He put his hands up in immediate defense. "No complaints from me! Just… she is gonna be pissed when she wakes up."

"Tough," she grumbled and focused on Mero. "Hold him still."

Nekrosa pressed down on Mero's shoulders as he and Sephi held the Emperor tight.

Ember rested her hands on the arms of his chair. She snapped her fingers in Mero's face but got no response. "*Tongh aidora,*" she whispered. Wisps of blue and green mist drifted from her fingers, and she pushed the magic down into the Emperor's wound. The variation of the spell she had used on Yrlissa to deaden her mind would also take Mero's pain, making him coherent once, again.

It worked surprisingly fast and the Emperor sighed as the pain faded. "You healed me," he said. "I knew you would come around —"

"You are a fool, Mero," Ember cut him off, her tone harder than steel. "I did not heal you. I numbed the nerves around your wound, so you can understand and comprehend what I am about to do to you."

"Ember," Sephi whispered. "We cannot handle you if you go Darkling here."

She looked at her friend. "The more you listen to Yrlissa, the worse off we will be, do you understand that?" Sephi nodded. "You like to rape and abuse women, don't you, Mero,"

He laughed. "Just until they learn their role."

"You are not a coward, Mero," Nekrosa said. "I'll give you that." The Emperor blew him a kiss over his shoulder.

Ember grabbed his chin and forced him to face her. "Their role?" she demanded.

"But of course, their role," he answered, "is to serve me." He laughed again, louder.

Ember snorted. "That just makes this easier," she said. "Emperor Mero, as the only Fae present in Talohna at this time, I find you guilty of crimes against your own people and against the Fae."

"You cannot judge me, young Fae," he growled. "My army will grind this country to dust for your disgraceful behavior—"

"Silence!" Ember hissed. "I am done talking with you, Mero." She clutched his head between her palms and whispered. "*Naolass tongh.*" As his brain shut down, Ember closed her eyes and thrust her consciousness into his. Only one thought went with her and she used it to rifle through the Emperor's memories until she found his very first act of depravity—sixteen-year-old Mero had forced himself on a young noblewoman a year older than he was. She followed the consequences of his actions as the woman's family brought official charges to Mero's father. money and favors had kept the family quiet.

Before she could dreamwalk to the next memory, Ember sensed a trace of pleasure that bordered on giddiness. Tracking the emotion took her to the throne room in Ellorya where young Mero had learned the young woman had taken her own life in shame. The pleasure the young Mero felt was depraved and sickening.

Again, and again, she bounced from memory to memory as Mero took advantage of women from all walks of life in both his own countries and others. The destruction in his wake was staggering to her senses and left her with a cold knot in her stomach. Each time, the bastard had no sense of the shame he caused. He had no understanding that his violation of such an intimate act left them hopeless victims. Several were unable to cope, and their lives were cut short by the cruel actions of the man in front of her.

Ember opened her eyes and had to blink several times to clear her tears. "*Amaeh Noalass*," she whispered, and Mero slowly blinked his own way back to the real world.

"What did you do?" he barked. "You were in my head! My memories. You have no right to be there—to do that!"

"I have every right," she snarled. "Crimes against innocent civilians were investigated by the Fae and punishment handed out as recommended or needed. No justice will ever reach you in Ellorya because money and corrupt favors is the only justice your country understands. But not in DormaSai."

"How dare you?" he growled. "I am the Emperor of Talohna's most powerful kingdom. You wouldn't dare—"

"Yes, I would," she said over him. "For the sake of women everywhere, and unlike the Fae used to do, I will tell you exactly what you will experience for the last moments of your remaining life. For whatever time you have left, you will experience every single second of terror you have inflicted on all the woman you have done this too. You will feel what they felt as if you were them. A small part of who you are will remain—just enough for you to understand. The spell will only end when you die."

"No… wait… please," he begged, his eyes widening. "I…

"*Naolass relamus kreevic reptasante*," Ember whispered and grabbed Mero's forehead. His flesh sizzled as a myriad of colours lit up underneath her palm and burned their way into his mind.

"Damn," Nekrosa whispered.

Ember stepped back and watched Mero's consciousness convulse its way to somewhere deep within his own memories.

"Are you all right, Ember?" Sephi asked, releasing Mero's shoulders.

"No," she replied as tears fell from her cheeks.

"I know," the Queen said and wrapped her arms around her friend. "But you will be some day."

Nekrosa ran his fingers through his hair. "If it helps any, Emperor Molester will be dead within an hour. Once Seph's dagger magic wears off."

Yrlissa moaned on the library floor as she came around. She sat up just in time to see the last of Mero's convulsions. "Oh, Ember," she whispered. "What did you do."

"Justice, I would say," Nekrosa replied. "And we have no Darkling to deal with."

Yrlissa stumbled to her feet and stepped past him for a closer look. "That's a punishment brand," she said quietly. "For mass crimes against innocent civilians. Ember, no Fae had cast that spell for hundreds of years before the first war with the Ri'Tek even began. It was ruled inhumane."

"Good," she replied. "Then all that is left to do is heal him so that he can live with it for the rest of his long and natural life. *Amaeh shalanes.*" Pink and blue magic misted from her hands and swirled together as it entered Emperor Mero's body. The magic from Sephi's dagger melted, revealing the raw, bloody wound between the man's legs. Ember concentrated harder, not wanting to the touch the vile man to make the healing process easier. "*Amaeh shalaness!*"

The blue and pink magic doubled in intensity. As the wound closed and began to heal, her magic winked out, nearly causing her to fall over. "No! Goddammit!" she cried. "No!"

Yrlissa sighed, not even bothering to hide her relief. "More Elloryan soldiers must be in range We have to leave, now."

Sephi and Nekrosa grabbed the rest of their belongings from the table. Ember stared at Mero, trembling. She gave herself the well-needed space before finally grabbing numerous throwing blades from the table and rushed to join the others.

"Over here," Nekrosa muttered. He reached behind one of the library's massive book cases and lowered a lever. Situated against the outside wall, the bookcase slid over to reveal a door in the castle's outer wall. "Gotta love the secret door that Talohna's best assassin knows about."

"Be grateful I'm the only Broken Blade who does know, King Kohl. Merethyl would've already had you assassinated years ago if she were aware of it."

"I'm walling this door up the minute we take this castle back. Can't have an assassin with a back door into my home. No offense." Yrlissa nodded his way but didn't say anything. He opened the door. The squeals of rusted hinges screeched through the library and out into the castle's rear courtyard. Ember led the way out as the others followed.

Stopping short as she stepped into the courtyard, Ember made room for the others. "Apparently, Yrlissa's not the only one who knows about this secret door." They were surrounded by over two dozen Elloryan knights, soldiers, and two Ancient wizards. One of which she knew all too well.

"Right you are, my dearest Ember," Sythrnax said. "But we did build this castle, you know. It is so nice to see you, again."

She sensed Nekrosa and Sephi reach for their magic, but Sythrnax raised his hand. "Do I really have to stuff your mouths with a bloody cloth?" he asked. "I will make it simple. I can sense the moment you even think about touching your magic, King Kohl. Should you do so, a simple gesture from myself and every knight and soldier here will attack. Ember and your assassin will die before your magic can manifest. Am I clear?"

Ember frowned as the King and Queen both released their power, standing down.

"Much better," Sythrnax replied. His strange purple eyes twinkled with joy.

TRAINING GROUNDS
BLACKVOID CASTLE

The young men training to become DeathDogs in the DormaSain army were the best young up and coming warriors the country had to offer. Even so, they had still been taken by surprise when six battle-hardened Elloryan soldiers entered their training grounds and attacked. The Elloryan swordsmen cut down every DeathDog trainee but one.

Dalen Toth stood alone and faced the four remaining soldiers. Dalen's entire squad of twenty young men had been mercilessly butchered by the older, more seasoned fighters with an almost laughable ease. Though he had managed to kill two of the attackers, it was of little consequence. He was surrounded and cornered in a doorway. His long-winged pike was the only thing separating him from certain death on an Elloryan steel blade. It was a separation that would soon disappear.

The Elloryan unit commander took a step forward and stared down the young pike man who had killed two of his men. His crooked smile beamed as he taunted Dalen.

"Look men, the last of the dead man's little pups. What do ya say, pup? Put the pike down and walk away. Let us into the barracks, and we will spare your life. You have my word."

"Elloryan words are more worthless than the shit that spews from your diseased asshole, you limp-dick cowards. You attacked under the white banner of a peace Conclave. Your actions and those of your spineless emperor are that of a useless chicken-shit."

The Elloryan commander's face flushed with anger, but he chuckled. "You make me laugh, pup. We are here to euthanize all you animals that follow the Dead King. Cowardice has nothing to do with it."

Dalen's face went pale as the commander's words cut short in mid-sentence. His head evaporated in a spray of red mist and crumpled bone while his body collapsed in a heap of mangled armor. A massive blue and black war-hammer swarming with orange markings settled atop the twisted remains.

"Max!" Dalen shouted, the relief in his voice more than clear. Wasting no time, Dalen lunged with his pike and pierced the throat of the nearest Elloryan soldier. A quick twist of the smooth wooden handle opened the doomed man's throat from ear-to-ear. Their commander's death had proven to be a well-timed distraction.

The two remaining invaders froze with indecision and were crushed under the sideways swing of Max's massive hammer. The broken bodies spun through the air like twisted marionettes before what was left splattered against the arena wall. The mangled armor and broken bodies dropped to the dirt surrounded by the stillness of death.

"Dalen?" Max spat with disbelief. "Fuck me, boy! Twenty of you lazy bastards, and you're the one who survives? You have gotta be the bastard son of the goddess of luck and her boy toy."

Dalen saluted. "Yes, Max, sir! If you think so, Sir!"

"We've already lost too many men. Follow me. BlackVoid Castle is full of Elloryan soldiers and so is the city and maybe even the rest of the country. Don't hesitate, dumbass, I won't wait for you."

"Yes, Sir. I won't let you down, Sir."

"Shut up and follow me. And stop kissing my ass. Worry about your own fucking backside," Max barked as he left the training arena. He went straight for the castle to look for Ember and DormaSai's king and queen.

Fury boiled Max's blood at the sheer cowardice of the sneak attack. Racing out the door to the castle's main staircase, Max and Dalen stopped short at the carnage that lay before them.

"Gods, Max. What's wrong with these Elloryans?" Dalen asked, as both men stared openly. The bodies of slaughtered servants had toppled side-by-side with those of nobles from DormaSai's ruling families.

"Mero's taking no chances," Max replied. "The orders must be to kill anyone in the way."

"Why? You don't invade a country and kill civilians."

"Unless you're not planning to stay," Max stated. "Fuck. He's after something. Come on, Dalen. We need to get to the upper tier of the castle. There's too many to fight. The ramparts by the barbican above the inner courtyard will give us cover to even the odds by bow."

Chapter Twelve

"A brave man and a foolish man never fear the consequences of their actions because the fool acts with only himself in mind and the brave acts because of those on his mind. Only during the final act of a man's life will he learn whether a brave soul or the soul of a fool resides within..."

Duchess Kathryn Akyyr's interrupted graduation speech, 5026.
Corynth Chapel of Cortina

BLACKVOID CASTLE
DRAE'KAHN, DORMASAI

The Elloryan attack commander prodded Ember in the back with his steel sword. The steel blade punctured her flesh, but the wound closed even as the blade slid from her skin. Alongside Yrlissa, Nekrosa, and Sephi, Ember was forced to march back to the castle's elegant courtyard.

As they walked beneath the final barbican into the castle's spacious inner bailey, Ember searched around for Max, but he was nowhere to be seen. However, the Vikress and her three hooded companions waited for them. They were accompanied by a handful of Elloryan knights.

Even though they were likely headed for their own execution, Ember leaned toward the Elvehn assassin chained by her side.

"Ellorya's Emperor seems to be missing," she said loud enough for everyone to hear.

"So it seems. I wonder what could ever have happened to him?" Yrlissa replied, her voice light and airy with a laudable sense of mockery.

"Maybe he fell," Sephi added, mocking concern as a pout crept onto her lips. "Oh, and worse? Maybe he can't get his fat ass up now."

"Actually," Yrlissa replied. "I bet the fat fuck stroked out. Probably long before he bled out." Yrlissa retorted. It was clear none of them cared if they were overheard.

With a smile that tugged at the corners of her mask, the Vikress stared at the captives. "I like your suggestion better, Mistress Ember. If he is missing we will find him," she crooned.

"I'm sure you do." Yrlissa snorted. "But my version is closer to the truth."

"It is what it is," the Vikress said. She turned her attention back to Ember. "I'm so glad to see you were rescued before these heathens absconded with you, Mistress Ember. You need not worry about them anymore. We will execute them all here and now, so you can return to Ellorya. We do have your wedding to plan after all." She held her hand out and nodded to the Elloryan Captain from the library. "Please, proceed with the execution, Captain."

"No," Ember barked at the Captain, hoping his reaction in the library would be repeated. He sighed and it was a heavy sound. Ember knew instantly the man struggled to see her being mistreated. "You know full well they didn't take me against my will, Captain." She turned to the Vikress. "Even if you did have Mero for a groom, Illara, you'll be hard pressed to have a wedding when the marriage can't be consummated."

"Worry not my dear. We will find out where Emperor Mero is, and we shall all return to Ellorya together."

Yrlissa laughed. "Good luck with that plan. Emperor Molester will never return to reality if he didn't already bleed out."

"A minor setback, Yrlissa. I will resurrect him from the dead if I need to. Or Ember will marry his replacement. Either option will suffice. You really should know that by now." Turning to Ember she added, "Even a dead man can consummate a marriage with the help of my magic."

"Not the one you have in mind," Ember scoffed, shivering at the prospect.

"Why, Ember, my dear," Yrlissa said, smiling. "I do believe the Vikress thinks we're joking."

Ember shrugged her shoulders and stared at the Vikress, but it was Sephi who answered.

"She'll get it when they find the cockless wonder —"

" —enough!" Vikress Illara hollered, her patience clearly tested. "Captain? I asked you to proceed with the execution. I will not ask again." As if struggling to obey, the Elloryan Captain wiped his sweaty forehead as Ember continued to argue.

"If you execute them, our people will be in a permanent state of war," she growled, pulling against her guard.

The Vikress shook her head at the idle threat. "So, now you do speak for your people, do you, young one? You are a people and race of one, my dear, Ember. I have been to war against your race. The Fae were formidable when they numbered in the hundreds of thousands, but you alone? A newborn? My dear, you are not a threat. You are nothing but a political tool and a figurehead who will return with me to Ellorya and remain at my side so the Elloryan people can worship you as Emperor Mero had hoped they would. Until a new emperor is chosen and your marriage can proceed. If—and when—the rest of your people do show up in Talohna, they will also swear their allegiance to the Ancients, or they will die, all of them this time."

With a violent twist, Ember tried to free herself from the hooded Ancient holding her neck. "No. They won't, and you won't find me so easy to control either," she hissed, as her breath rushed through her clenched teeth.

The Vikress scoffed. Ember could hear the genuine mirth in her voice. "Just because you believe something, d*osa*, does not make it a universal truth. The Ancients have already accomplished what we came to DormaSai to do, especially if Emperor Mero is dead. We can put a true ruler on his throne. Once the necromancer king and his queen are executed; our plan is complete. They die now," she said calmly, her strange purple eyes never left Ember's as she spoke.

"Commander," the Vikress continued, raising her voice. "Seeing as how our Elloryan Captain cannot follow orders, begin the execution yourself. Now!"

"At once," Sythrnax replied as he bowed.

Knowing Sythrnax owed her no loyalty like the captain, Ember wasted no time. Snapping her head back fast, she struck her guard in the mouth. The velvet mask offered no protection, his nose crumpled and lips split against her skull. The inside of his mouth filled with blood as broken teeth sliced his cheeks and gums, choking him long enough for her to break free.

Yrlissa also lashed out. Reaching back, she snatched her captor's hood and wrenched the handful of cloth forward as she dropped to her knees. The warrior spilled over her back and landed in a crumpled pile at the Vikress' feet. With no access to their magic, the attempt was a futile protest and nothing more. The two masked women beside the Ancient Vikress raised their hands and the crystal stones sown into their gloves pulsed with vibrant blue light. Ember and Yrlissa moaned as foreign magic assaulted both their body and senses. Collapsing to the dirt, they were forced into submission.

The Vikress approached, kneeling before them as they heaved in the dirt and grass. "I admire your determination, but your magic and martial skills are that of inbred insects. The people of Talohna call us the Ancients out of adoration, but the truth is that our existence, our magic, and our knowledge is just that ancient. We walked this world when your kind wallowed in caves, too stupid to be more than a pest… a d*osa*. You are the Lesser races for a reason," she explained, her voice calm. Standing, the Vikress turned to Sythrnax. "Commander! I gave you an order of execution for the king and queen! Why am I repeating myself so often this day? Carry it out. Now."

Obeying his Vikress without hesitation, Sythrnax ordered four of his Ancient warriors to drag Nekrosa and Sephi forward. Forced to their knees, DormaSai's King and Queen looked at each other and smiled as a moment passed between them. The Vikress, lacking the understanding shared by the royal couple, backhanded Sephi hard on the chin.

"Care to share, Your Highness?" she asked. Noticing Sephi's blood on her knuckles, the Vikress held out her hand and one of the hooded women by her side wiped it clean. "Perhaps your friends would like to know what it is that you find so amusing about your own death." Sephi snorted and Nekrosa's smile doubled in size.

"You can't hear it can you, Vikress Illara?" he said. "Listen closely. The winds of death are blowing, but they're not here for us."

Glancing around the courtyard and seeing nothing, the Vikress scoffed. "I think your mind has finally cracked under the strain of your putrid magic. I am in control of your castle, your city. and very soon, your country," she told them, bending over in front of the royal couple. "But don't worry, your death will be quick, which is more than you both deserve."

Vikress Illara stood and nodded to Sythrnax. His eyes danced with delight as he lifted a large battle axe from the top of a supply crate. Wiping the curved blade, he stood before Sephi and the two Knights pulled her arms behind her back, pushing her into a sitting position. They applied enough pressure to force her head forward.

"Any last words, Queen Kohl?" Sythrnax demanded.

As she answered, a hollow screech echoed off the castle walls. "The winds of death will carry my last words." Even with her neck craning forward, she still managed to laugh as a second, high pitched wail traveled through the castle, reverberating off the walls.

Nekrosa smirked. "Last chance, Vikress, the winds are almost here. It's your death it wants. Let us go and walk away, otherwise you will forfeit your life." The last words had just left Nekrosa's lips when a third shrill cry, much closer this time, ripped through the air with god-like power. The sound made the earth shake and the castle walls vibrate. A heavy cloud cover prevented anyone from pinpointing the direction.

"Enough of these games, necromancer. Your tricks of illusion fool no one. Commander, proceed with the execution. Now!" the Vikress ordered angrily. Doing as he was ordered, Sythrnax raised the battle axe above his head. At the apex of his swing, the monstrous shriek returned from above their heads this time, and much closer. Unlike any sound from the mortal world, the cry blasted through the cloud cover and was followed by an enormous figure as it slammed into the ground. The impact shook the earth inside the castle courtyard and dust billowed out, swirling through the air as everyone except Yrlissa and the Vikress were knocked to the dirt.

Slowly getting to her feet, Ember gaped at the surreal scene before her. The Ancient knights holding Sephi and Nekrosa for the execution were dead. Each flattened by a clawed paw. Their bodies had been pushed a full foot into the ground, yet the DormaSain King and Queen remained unharmed. The impact from the creature's landing was staggering in its strength.

Ember tried, but could not stop her gaze from drifting up, following the spines that lined the dragon's legs until reaching the growing spikes at its shoulders. Taut muscles flexed and trembled as the massive wings folded in against its body. The dragon's long neck swayed slowly back and forth while the creature took them in, assessing the threat they posed to it.

Its mouth was lined with smooth, white, teeth, ranging from twelve to sixteen inches in length. Horns protruded from the flesh on both sides of the tense jaw to match the spines covering the rest of its head. The vertical, slit pupils of its feminine eyes gave away the dragon's sex.

It was a gorgeous creature called a Behemoth by most of Talohna. However, she stared in awe at the supposedly long-extinct being. Beautiful white scales ranging in size from her hand to some as large a tower shield covered every inch of the dragon's flesh, making it impenetrable.

"Nekrosa?" she whispered.

"It's all right, Ember. She's here to help us." She nodded as if that was the natural assumption to make, unable to stop her staring. A dangerous violence boiled just below the creature's surface. Its prominent aura was alight with hatred and a wild, savage urge to kill. The vibrant colours, some of which she could not find the words to describe made her head ache and throb with pressure.

The Dragon race had returned to Talohna, and it was obvious there was a vibrant hatred for the Ancient Vikress.

Six DragonKin descended from the back of the dragon, a clear force to be reckoned with. With them was Saleece, Ember's former travel companion. Gone was the beautiful young woman she had come to know. Instead, she had been replaced by a scarred Zephyr with feline eyes covered in battle scars on her arms and throat.

As Saleece touched the ground, the other DragonKin warriors followed. Ember recognized Commander Zatassa from their time on Ver Karmot. He nodded her way before approaching the Vikress. Saleece moved to Ember's side and faced the Vikress while drawing a thin green sword from the sheathe on her back. It was obvious her job was to protect her, and Ember let out a sigh of relief.

Quick to act, one of the hooded Ancients by Illara's side pulled the staff from her back. The magic inside the deadly weapon crackled as the Ancient Sect priestess prepared to attack the dragon. Saleece's hand shot out and bright green magic leapt from her fingers, seizing the priestess and halting her attack. With a roar of annoyance, the dragon's tail slashed forward too fast for the common eye to follow. The Vikress' protector, focused on fighting through Saleece's magic, had no defense as a bladed tail-spur punched through her chest. With the second roar, Saleece released her magic, and the dragon snapped its tail. The priestess' body, along with her sputtering staff, cart-wheeled up and over the castle walls.

"I tried to warn you." Nekrosa spat as he and Sephi rejoined Yrlissa and Ember, seeking sanctuary beside the white dragon.

Commander Zatassa continued as if unaffected by the priestess' sudden and violent death. "Illara. Always a pleasure," he stated with a cold sarcasm, earning a scoff from the Ancient's matriarch.

"Commander Zatassa. All these years and you're still licking the claws of these overgrown vermin," Illara sneered. "I had truly hoped that when Vaighar WhiteScale fell, I'd never see another damned Dragon so long as I lived."

Zatassa grinned, flashing dozens of sharp, saw-edged teeth. It was the first emotion Ember had ever seen by any of the stoic DragonKin.

"The Dragon race isn't as easy to exterminate as your kind likes to believe. However, I am not here to discuss the extinction of our forefathers with you. I am here to give you fair warning—"

The Vikress laughed, interrupting. "Then let your Behemoth give me the warning. But I bet she can't, can she? Your mighty Behemoth looks a little young to be taking Kinform, Zatassa. Somehow managed to hide away an egg?" she mocked. Turning toward the majestic dragon, she added, "Dragons are mere children until they can change form at will. Yet you propose to threaten me, young lizard? Come back, baby White, when you at least have a full set of teeth."

A growl emanated from the Dragon, but quickly turned into a fierce challenge as the Dragon snorted, stepping toward Illara. The Vikress smirked, refusing to back down. "Careful child. My magic dragged your fellow White from the sky so many eons ago. Vaighar was seven thousand years old at the time. What chance do you have, little tadpole?"

Ember could tell the Vikress' words touched a nerve. Stomping its front feet, another dangerous growl rumbled deep within the throat of the Dragon. Sulfuric smoke curled from its nostrils as it gently nudged Commander Zatassa aside. It stood eye-to-eye with the Ancients' Vikress as the two ageless creatures seethed with a mutual hatred so intense Ember had to divert her gaze to avoid their swirling auras.

In some absurd mockery of emotion, the Dragon Behemoth smiled, and a vague female sound ushered from its throat, like the twist and pop of grinding quarry stones. "You assume too much, Mother of the Ancients."

Waves of magic shimmered around the Dragon. Wisps of power arced, racing around her limbs and over outstretched wings as she continued speaking. Her voice changed along with her body, both becoming softer and delicate. "I know exactly who killed Vaighar WhiteScale. It has been passed down and told to what few DragonKin have been born through the millennia." The dragon paused, grunting as bones began to pop and shift. Scales cracked before they shrunk, receding into pale flesh. Spikes and spines retreated, not quite disappearing. In a matter of seconds, the Dragon was gone, and a beautiful young woman stood in its place. Eyes identical to the Dragon's, and a row of small horns along her eyebrows all the way to her ears. were the only sign a Dragon was ever there. One of the DragonKin Zephyrs removed a white cloak from her travel pack and draped it over the woman's bare shoulders, covering her naked form. With everyone else too shocked to speak, the Dragoness frowned.

"A Dragon's memory is eternal. I remember well the day my father fell as if it were only yesterday. I will make sure to pass the story of his death and those responsible on to each new generation through our genetic memory. The skies above Talohna will be filled with beating wings again someday. You will pay the debt of my father's death with your life, Vikress Illara, but it won't be now. Today, you will take your remaining Sect priestess and leave DormaSai forever. It is now under my protection."

"Y... you" the Vikress stammered. "That is impossible! You're not... you weren't..." A white flash of magic erupted from the far side of the castle grounds, followed by a crack of energy.

"The greatest illusion magic, Mother Illara, is in using no magic at all to fool those weak of mind. My father believed that more than anything, and a young man reminded me of that just recently before he died." Another concussive blast of magic snapped from just inside the city, drawing away the Vikress' attention for a split second.

"Your father was the last Behemoth, Shelaryx WhiteScale. Our spies watched you from the day you were born. You were not a Dragon." Another ear-splitting detonation and flash of light echoed from deeper within the city limits of DormaSai.

"Your spies saw what Vaighar wanted them to see, and then, they died screaming for mercy, spilling every secret they had. Did you really think it would be that easy? Just because the first Animus Seal has been opened doesn't mean the rest will fall without a fight. We will keep the Sepulchre in place for as long as we can."

More bright magic lit up the darkening sky across the entire city. They continued to split the Vikress' attention for seconds at a time, clearly irritating her as the clicking under her hood increased.

"You know what those flashes are," the Dragon Queen continued. "All over Drae'Kahn, the Fae are jumping in my Talon warriors and Zephyr mages to finish off any Elloryan military and Ri'Tek warriors that may accompany them. And I promise you, these Fae will *not* swear allegiance to you. You should leave, Illara, before the Fae Matriarch gets here. Between her and I, we will make sure your stolen magic never drags another dragon from the sky or takes another Lesser race life. I was birthed from a royal egg at the dawn of our war. I am nearly twice as old as my father was at his death. This is your only chance to leave."

Fury radiated from the Vikress, but she refused to back down. "How did you know the seal was here? This world looks nothing like the one we left behind."

Queen WhiteScale glanced at King Kohl.

Nekrosa answered, stepping forward. "We managed to piece together what happened. We went to the Dragon Ilses immediately after I took the throne. If you want the Human Animus Seal, you're gonna have to convince Ellorya to go to war against us, and then, you'll have to find the real location of the Seal because it's not here in this city."

Vikress Illara burst out laughing. "You are a fool, Nekrosa Kohl!" she barked. "Ellorya will invade, and backed by our magic and warriors, we will have DormaSai under our rule in a month. The fact that Shelaryx WhiteScale is a real Dragon is irrelevant — even one, lone eon-aged Dragon cannot help you. Queen or not, Shelaryx, Dragons take several millennia to grow, and no more lizards will scamper from the Crystal Castle. Everything that happened here went better than we could have ever planned. Emperor Mero and his hand-picked Conclave delegation are all dead at the hands of the evil necromancer King and Queen. The only known Fae is under the mind-control influence of said powerful necromancers. The Fae jumping in DragonKin warriors now won't stay in Talohna. If I capture even one lone Fae with any real magic, unlike this one," the Vikress glanced Ember's way and scoffed, "I'll have the power I need to open the other seals. Mero's senate will vote for war within hours of my return, and the Blood Kingdoms will join us the moment we help them end the threat from the Wildland natives. I now know you won't stop me from leaving because your Dragon isn't strong enough to do so. We win, Nekr — "

The Vikress' words stopped short. Several long, shiny appendages jumped to life from under her hood, darting out like striking vipers. The first two knocked black arrows from midair, but the third was a split-second too slow, only deflecting the projectile. It pierced the Vikress' shoulder, pushing her robe two feet out from her body as it punched through. The blood-soaked obsidian arrowhead slowly cut its way through the cloth. The robe slid down the shaft and stuck to Illara's flesh as it soaked up blood from the wound. The Sect priestess moved to her aid, helping the Vikress stand.

"You know you can't win. Either of you," Illara snarled. "Before long, the Blood Kingdoms will be allied with the Ancients, and then, all the seals will be opened. The Sepulchre will fall one way or another. What was ours will be returned. There aren't six DeathWizards to stop us this time. Thanks to that fool, Giddeon, you don't even have the one that was here," she laughed.

With a flash of white, the Vikress and her priestess disappeared with a crack of power just before three additional arrows struck the dirt just past where they stood.

"You know, it really pisses me off that they can do that so easily," Ember admitted, referring to the stolen Fae realm jump magic.

She searched for the archer and was not surprised to see Max with his Orotaq bow on the far ramparts.

A second crack of power snapped from behind her, but she was so glad to see Max, she did not bother to turn around. The words that reached her ears sent shivers down her spine.

"A young Fae should not anger so easily. However, I can help you with making jump spells much easier, my daughter."

Ember turned and knew from the moment she laid eyes on the stunning woman that she was staring at her birth mother. "You're..." she started but couldn't finish.

"Yes."

Nekrosa cleared his throat. "Ember," he said, "let me introduce the Fae High Matriarch, Eva Thornwing. From what I understand, she is your mother."

JASALA'S FANGS
JAWS OF ICE AND ROCK OCEAN

Corleya tore her sword from one of the winged monsters that attacked the ship. She glanced up in time to see Damien shove the last one over the railing. "What the hell were they?" she shrieked.

"Welcome party," the pirate yelled back as he turned his head to the sky and howled. He was having the time of his life, and it drove her nuts. "Stay sharp, Princess. The blue bastards gave up, but we're still an hour from land, and the sea will try her best to stop us yet gain."

"More coming will suffice," Alia barked. Damien laughed, howling even louder while she shook her head.

Damien bowed low and offered a flourish with his right hand. "My apologies, my lady." Straightening, he grabbed the wheel and spun it to the left. "You thought this would be easy?" he asked. "Never occurred to either of you that no one has ever made it through here because... oh, I don't know? It's fucking impossible?!"

"Because of the creatures?" Corleya asked, getting a nod. "I just assumed it was the sea itself. Rocks, ice, storms."

Damien snorted. "These creatures are part of the sea, Princess."

Before she could process what happened, the ship lurched to the right suddenly, and long tentacles of spiky green exploded from the deck. She jumped back as another one shot up between her legs. The appendage pulsed, and hundreds of barbs snapped out before the tentacle pulled back. It was stuck in the deck planking, and the ship was righted by its attempt to leave before the creature slowly began to drag the ship under.

"Get down," Damien screamed, and Corleya dropped to the deck against the door of the captain's cabin.

Dozens of projectiles struck the deck and rails. Corleya stared dumbfounded as the source of the deadly weapons rolled up onto the railing of the ship's bow like a giant wheel. Thousands of spear-like quills stuck out of its shell. The tall creature stood, and the giant snail shell slid, compressing like an accordion. The humanoid snail removed a spear from its back with one of its dozen hands and lowered itself to the deck. Corleya shook with fear.

"What the hell is that?" she shrieked, and Damien swung past her on one of the sail lines. He smashed into the creature and shoved it back overboard.

Landing on his feet, he turned and waved. "Quickly! The rowboat!" he ordered.

Alia was at Corleya's side to help her to her feet. Both women ran to the side of the ship and hopped into the lifeboat.

"Get in, Damien." She gasped as she sat and grabbed a paddle.

"Sorry, Princess. Someone has to stay with the ship and keep them occupied or they'll just come after us," he growled back.

"No," Corleya yelled at him. "Get in here! The ship's lost, Damien." She stood and grabbed for his wrist but missed.

Damien stepped back and raised his sword. "The ship is, but you're not. Good luck, Princess," he said. He winked. Alia dragged Corleya back onto her seat as the ropes securing the lifeboat parted under a swing of the pirate's blade. Three more spear-wielding snails rolled onto the deck behind the pirate. A spear exploded from Damien's shoulder, and Corleya lost sight of him as the boat plummeted to the water's surface.

"Row," Alia screamed. "He has given us a chance."

"All right," Corleya let out as she struggled to hold back her tears. For all his faults, the pirate had done everything he could to get them to safety.

As both young women pulled at the oars, they shot away from the ship and headed toward the closest stretch of land. In their wake, they caught the full view of the ship. Dozens of tentacles rose from the water and wrapped themselves around the railing as the ship slipped further underwater.

"It will not hold long," Alia said, grunting as she rowed. As if her words were prophetic, the small vessel cracked in the middle as several human-shaped warriors burst from the water and landed aboard. Corleya watched as blades flashed across the deck of the sinking ship. Damien fought for his life, and there was nothing they could do to help.

"Worry about us, Princess," Alia snapped. "He made his choice knowing the outcome. Now, row before—" Her words stopped short as the rowboat scraped against something below the surface of the water.

"Land?" Corleya gasped. Glancing back over her shoulder she saw there was still quite a bit of distance between them and land. "Or not..."

"Do not stop rowing," Alia growled, but kept her voice low.

Corleya dipped her oar in the water and another scrape rolled across the boat's bottom. Both women stopped and stared into the water as the scrape continued up the bow until a pair of clawed hands appeared over the bow's rail. A beautiful face followed, and Corleya jumped as Alia's whip snapped out, curling around the creature's throat. A quick tug pulled the creature onto the boat and the metal wire opened her throat. A slimy tail covered in thick scales thumped against the gunwales.

"Gods," Corleya let out. "What in the Nine Hells of Perdition is that thing?"

"A siren, perhaps" Alia replied. Confusion marked her features. "But too far north."

Something slammed into the boat, and it lurched to the side, nearly tossing them overboard with it.

Alia moved to the bow and shoved the siren's body over the side as a dozen more hands grabbed the railing. "Fight," she yelled, pointing behind Corleya.

The Princess turned and unraveled her whips. Lashing out, each snapped across the faces of sirens and cut deep. She flung her whip to her left as yet another tried to board the small boat. "There's too many!" she cried out. Frustration and panic took over as her whips slashed out over and over.

"Princess!" Alia barked. Corleya spun as Alia plowed into her and knocked her to the bottom of the boat. Countless spears from a snail stitched the side of the boat above their bodies, and both women looked up in time to see a massive green tentacle explode from the water. It hovered over their boat for a split second before it dropped. Alia's body took the incredible force of the attack, and she grabbed at Corleya before the boat cracked under the Princess' back. A second impact left her dizzy and surrounded by water.

She never felt the powerful impact of two more attacks before darkness swallowed her mind.

Chapter Thirteen

"The darkness of the Deep Earth holds an eerie calm just before battle. You cannot explain it to others, and you can never get used to it. Our people know this calm very well – personally, I would say. Its disturbing silence is like death's embrace. We welcome it and will spend our last hours with it should the gods of stone deem it so. This day, the gods have spoken clearly. My people – the very last of the Dwarven race – will welcome the final calm before what could be our last battle. My people have been vigilant. We never once neglected our duty or wavered in our responsibility. Our numbers have dwindled over the years, but still we remain loyal to the task that was handed to us. We are the First Sentinels of the Guardian Pact. We are the strength of the Host and the last of the Dwarven race."

Draven BloodPounder, Priest of Izotan: Channeler for the God of Living Stone.

DEEP EARTH

Sythrnax stood perched on one of the Deep Earth's yawning chasms, several days' worth of traveling below the surface of Talohna. Almost a mile in the distance across the yawning underground valley stood the formidable metal gates of the last Dwarven stronghold. Dal Dagore was the pride of all the once great Dwarven strongholds. The slithering of scales scraped along the granite surface behind him.

"Well?" he asked without turning around.

A soft female voice drifted to his ears, surreal and dreamy. "They are ready, Master. The Dwarves want to play," she purred softly, reminding him of the giant snowcats of his homeland. Her words calmed the slow beat of his heart to a dangerously slow pace. "We want to play. My brothers and sisters need something to do. We are bored." He never heard her move, but her velvet finger caressed his cheek. Struggling to keep his eyes open, the insistent rattle of his tresa from under his hood brought his senses storming back. Realizing almost too late the trouble he was in, he moved.

"Bitch," he snapped. Whirling on the creature with a speed that far outmatched hers, he snatched her throat. Lifting her off her toes, he slammed her into a crumbling wall of stone. "Save your tricks for the enemy, Gahainna. You pull that shit on me again and your sisters will fight for a new leader. You are Vascuul. Use your skills on the enemy."

"I am. You will be our enemy until the day we die. We are Vascuul! We are not slaves!"

Sythrnax squeezed harder until cartilage crackled in her throat. "You are what we made you, and you will serve us until your dying day." Pressing down on her tail, Gahainna clawed at him with her feet, trying to tear his bowels from his stomach. Once again, he was reminded of the big white cats of home. Her talons raked off his kinrai mail but did no damage. The black stone set inside the palm of his glove sizzled with dark power as he flexed the muscles in his wrist. Its magic pulsated against her throat as a flash of bright lit up the veins under her skin, super-heating her cold blood and causing instant pain.

"You will answer to me or my commanders, am I clear?" Gahainna hissed, her beautiful Elvehn face distorted with raw hatred and intense pain. A forked tongue lashed out, sliding over hollow fangs just enough to pick up traces of potent venom. Licking his face, she sneered. His cheek twitched as the venom sizzled and burned through his mask. Slamming her into the wall a second time, he growled. "Last chance. Tell me what you saw and return to your own kind until the attack or die here."

The creature thumped her long, scaled tail against the ground in frustration. "Fine," she hissed. Venom-less saliva sprayed across the remains of his mask. He could see the lines of holes at the side of her tongue quivering with the desire to open. If they did, he knew it would not be a simple kiss this time. Should she decide to spit for real, he would be in serious danger. "The Dwarves are holed up. The fortress is impenetrable. We couldn't get through. No cracks in the foundation, no grates, no sewer access."

He nodded and released her, watching as she slithered away, her legs tucked in beside her tail for added speed. Her clawed fists shook with fury as she glared over her shoulder at him. Sythrnax wished once more that the Ghul had found a way to calm the Vascuul temper before he had died during the war. Perhaps, when the Human seal opened, the Syddic priests would succeeded in creating more and some of those would be without the trouble they frequently caused.

"I see all that slithers is not well." Sythrnax turned, recognizing the voice immediately.

"Kurse. That gorgon blood runs hot in those freaks. Your reconnaissance from the sky go any better?" he asked. He watched for signs of aggression as a pair of glowing eyes emerged from the shadows. The Vascuul did not take well to being called freaks, but he was beyond caring. Emotionless, Kurse blinked and the glow in his eyes dimmed, giving way to the slit orbs common among the DragonKin.

"They are Dwarves. They do not have weaknesses to exploit."

"Of course not. Damned bearded *dosa*. Ideas?" Sythrnax turned back toward the cliff, staring out over the valley toward the Dwarven fortress once, again.

"I could send one of the Blacks to see how strong those walls really are. I don't believe we can pull those gates apart.

Though, they might buckle under a Black's barrage." Tilting his head to stretch his neck, Sythrnax frowned as the bones along his spine cracked and popped. His tresa lightly rattled under his hood while he weighed his options.

"Fair enough. Let's show these cursed Dwarves that you Vascuul are still very much alive."

"As you wish," Kurse said, stepping clear of Sythrnax. Long black wings unfurled like the snap of leather. He whirled toward the precipice with a speed that rivaled his master's. His waist-length green and purple ponytail trailed behind him as he leapt clear of the ledge and soared to the right, disappearing into the underground cavern's heavy mist. Sythrnax crouched, settling in for a comfortable view of the commotion to follow.

DAL DAGORE
TWO MILES SOUTH OF BLACK KASYM
DEEP EARTH

"What's the word, priest?" Dravik BloodPounder hollered to his brother, Draven, the moment he saw him approach. Draven easily sidestepped yet another massive Dwarven catapult as it rolled past.

"The last scouts never made it back." He slowed to a walk as he met his brother at the base of the city's forged metal gate. "They've been declared lost by scout command. They're close, Dravik. It'll happen soon," the priest of Izotan predicted.

"Has your god got any advice? Or perhaps information on whether or not the Vascuul survived the exile?" Dravik asked. As commander of the Host, it was his responsibility to be prepared for whatever was coming. They had prepared for this battle for too long to lose.

"No. If they did, a safe wager on numbers would be one or two for every Ri'Tek freed by the first seal's rupture. Asa's journal entries prior to the battle claimed at least a thousand Vascuul would have taken the field at the battle to open the

DemonKind seal. Though they have yet to show themselves in force, Izotan believes the first seal held the Ri'Tek's highest ranks. This includes their Vikress and their strongest military warriors, including Sythrnax," Draven explained.

With a smile only a dwarf heading into a battle outnumbered could give, Dravik growled his orders. "Gather the Host, brother. I been waitin' ten millennia to kill that cursed son of a godshyte." Clapping his brother on the shoulder, he laughed. "Smile, priest. We finally go to war."

Dravik nodded and turned to leave. The priest was the strongest of the few god-blessed channelers the Host had. He knew Draven would gather the commanders and then his own priests. The time had come for the Dwarven Host to defend the seal they had been tasked with protecting so many thousands of years ago. The first of the six seals had fallen ten months prior. The DemonKind had put up no fight for reasons they knew nothing about. Dravik smiled, thinking about the fight the Host would put up. The Ri'Tek would scatter like a Mahala with its tail between its legs or the Dwarven race would finally join the mighty Dragon Behemoths in the obscurity of extinction.

A massive explosion outside the monstrous gate pulled his attention back to the matter-at-hand, and he cursed himself for being distracted.

"Throw the side-bolts on that cursed gate, before the blood-thirsty bastards come through!" Dravik BloodPounder bellowed. With a grimace of pain, he tore a foot-long sliver of granite from his forearm. As blood spurted from a partially torn artery, the stubborn Dwarven General wrapped a leather tourniquet around his arm above the elbow and twisted it with his blade until the flow of blood became a trickle. He pulled himself back to his feet and was immediately tossed back to the ground like a rag doll by a second concussive explosion.

Dravik glanced skyward seconds before he hit the dirt. Among the falling rock and granite of the destroyed ballistae tower, he saw what appeared to be the outline of a massive black Dragon with long back spikes and tattered wings. Once he saw the wall was still intact, he prayed to the gods he was wrong about what he saw. "Lock bars. Now, goddammit!"

"Aye, General!" The shout came from three veteran warriors as they muscled the heavy mechanical levers into place with a solid clunk. The rest of the Dwarven Host cheered as the massive lock bars slammed into place, securing the underground fortress' front gate even further.

"Quit your yappin!" Dravik barked. "There's an army kicking down our gate! Shape up, Host! Keep your heads right, or it'll be over. I want reports from all commanders in ten minutes! Move it! You all know where you need to be!"

Draven stepped up to the General from behind. "Brother?"

As always, his soundless appearance made Dravik jump.

"Brethren's bloody balls, Draven! Make some cursed noise! You're a Dwarf, not some prancin' Fae. Gods, even Elvehn scouts make more noise than you do."

"Sorry, brother, but you wanted reports from all the commanders."

Draven always seemed at least one step ahead of everyone, and he was the first to report on any given matter. "Fair enough. What's new from your... from Izotan's priests?" Dravik asked. With a quickening pace, he turned toward the command tower.

"You're injured, brother. Let me heal it," Draven offered.

"This?" the Dwarven General said, lifting his arm as blood dripped from his elbow. "Just a ball-sucking love kiss from a bloody Vascuul dragon unless the trickster has me seeing grog visions. It can wait. Report?"

Draven followed beside his brother. "We've seen the bulk of the horde."

Dravik stopped dead in his tracks. "Horde? I knew that last attack was a bloody Dragon. You sure?" he asked.

Draven nodded grimly. "I'm afraid so. Except for the dragon they're trying to hide them, but the stone has shown us everything else. The army will follow in the wake of a full Vascuul attack."

"Gods of stone and earth… We don't have the numbers left to turn back a Vascuul attack. I had hoped we would never have to face those god-cursed abominations, again. They should have died on the far side of the Animus Seals. How is it possible, Draven?" The fact that Dravik had used his brother's birth given name spoke volumes to the dire circumstances they faced.

"I do not know. The magic in their dimension was unknown to the gods, let alone us. It is why they and the Lesser wizards trapped the Ri'Tek there to begin with. The stasis atmosphere must have kept the Vascuul alive as well. We had hoped that, without an active connection to the magic of this dimension, the Vascuul would die. We were wrong, and so were the gods."

Silence followed on the heels of the two brothers' conversation, but it did not last long. "You haven't used my real name since Izotan chose me as a vessel, brother."

"I am aware. So many of our people hated magic. I never did, you know that. How could I with it woven so deep into our family? But it seemed more respectful to use your title. He chose you for a reason. The power given to you and your priests by Izotan will be the only hope now that we have to stop the Vascuul. Our warriors cannot fight magical creatures and hope to win. My magic is not what it used to be, and my axes are the only enchanted weapons we have left after all these millennia of fighting the Mahala and the creepers."

"We will do all that we can. I promise many of the enemy will feel the teeth of stone before we fall. They have no idea what the Host is capable of now. The Ri'Tek have been gone a long time," he said, then bowed and took Dravik's arm.

Pulling the tourniquet, Draven scoffed as blood pumped from the wound, forcing him to grasp it tightly with his right hand. "A mere kiss, brother?" he requested.

Dravik grunted as the light of Izotan flared in Draven's eyes. Bright white magic pulsed through the veins and arteries in Draven's arm and down through his hand. The blood squirting out between his fingers sizzled as the Dwarven god's power seared and cauterized the wound. Draven held his brother's arm as smoke and the stench of burnt flesh rose from his fingers. Finally releasing Dravik's arm, both Dwarves could see the burnt hand print left behind had closed and sealed the wicked cut.

"Thank you," Dravik muttered as Draven nodded, turned, and left.

The Dwarven General wondered if Izotan and the other gods, in the coming of days, would call home the last of the Dwarven people to the halls of Paradise. They had been vigilant and would fight to the last standing man and woman, but they had faced the vicious creations called the Vascuul before on many occasions. Even with much larger numbers, they had lost every time. Dravik sighed, knowing the fight was merely a formality—a losing one now that they had confirmed the Vascuul had survived. A light blazed to his right, followed by the sharp crack of magic. He smiled. Though he had not seen it in an aeon, he still recognized Fae magic. However, it was not a Fae who spoke.

"Mother Inara! We made it!" Seifer Locke gasped with genuine surprise.

Dravik scoffed. "An Elderblood wizard and Mistress Thornwing all in one day. I must have shat in the gods' dinner last night to be blessed with such a visit," he grumbled, not bothering to turn his back. "Ah, gorgeous, I bet my commanders a barrel of grog you wouldn't have the stones to try getting this close to the dark Wizardess' breach."

The Fae Matriarch snorted and wiped blood from her nose. "You should have known better, you grumpy old bastard," she barked. "The real prophecy has started. I brought you what help I could—one last gift from the Dragons."

Dravik grunted. "Won't be enough," he said. Turning toward the beautiful woman, he smiled wider and took her into his arms.

"I know," she replied. "And you will fight to the last, you stubborn bastard."

"Of course, we will, gorgeous. We volunteered for this duty, remember?"

Eva shook her head and gently placed her hands on his chest. "Let them have this seal, Dravik. Work your way back to Jasala's tower and defend the Elvehn seal instead. At least you will be within range of help. Their seal is undefended, but Shel and the DragonKin will be close enough to help the Host."

"The DemonKind Seal was also undefended when it fell. What happened, gorgeous?"

"We made a mistake. I took the last of the true DemonKind from this world a very long time ago. We knew their Animus chamber was undefended, but it was sealed against the enemy. It was our mistake, Dravik. It appears one of the ancient warriors tunneled in through the mountain's far side. He must have escaped one of the seals during the Cataclysm, probably just before the Sepulchre went up."

"You are correct. I saw the DemonKind seal and the black one who died on it just hours before it opened," Dravik said, disappointed. "Your kind rely on magic too much, gorgeous. It will be your down fall someday."

"It matters no longer."

"No, it doesn't," Dravik growled. "The concern is here and now."

"It's why I came," Eva replied.

"And it's why you must leave now," Dravik told her. "Once the Vascuul begin their attack, there will be too much magic in the air for even a Locke wizard to protect your jump."

"I... I got us here... I'll get us out," Seifer huffed out, clearly tired and shaken. Blood dripped from his right ear and he kept shaking his head.

Dravik ignored him and instead turned back to the Fae Matriarch. "That jump should have killed you both. There's only one explanation. How in the Nine Hells did the Locke family manage to keep their bloodline pure? The gods forbade it. You should not have gotten here."

"What?" Seifer asked, mockingly wiggling his finger inside his ear as if he was having a hard time hearing.

Eva shook her head. "I don't know, but I'm glad they did. Now, please, Dravik, go to the Elvehn seal and let the Ri'Tek have this one. Don't let another of the great races— your race and our children's race—become extinct."

"The old and very young have already fled. The attack will come before we could evacuate my fighters and Draven's priests, Eva. It is too late to run even if I wanted to, and I don't. Sythrnax is out there. I can smell the bastard. The Host will stay and fight, and I will get one last chance to kill that backstabbin' traitor. Now, get yourself clear before—"

A giant explosion rocked the fortress' front gate. A second and third followed as the gates groaned under the stress and pressure of the detonations. Dravik stared in shock and awe as the gates that had kept them safe for over ten thousand years came crashing down.

"Defend the breach!" he yelled as a Vascuul dragon shoved its way through the opening. Dozens of Dwarven warriors and several priests obeyed immediately and the thump of two catapults rolled through the air while Dravik turned to Eva and kissed her briefly. "It was good to see you one last time, gorgeous, but you have to leave. Now. Or everything we sacrificed and the lives we will lose here today will be for nothing."

Eva nodded and turned toward Seifer, grabbing his arm. "Get ready, Master Locke. We are leaving."

"Eva?" Dravik asked.

"Yes, my love?"

"You tell her... tell her I'm sorry I never got to meet her."

"I will. She was devastated she could not come with. Her and Yrlissa jumped through the Kasym twice after Kael's death."

"And a third jump this close would kill her," Dravik said, finishing her sentence when she trailed off.

Eva nodded. "She will help save this world, I know it."

Dravik laughed and a proud smile spread across his mouth from ear-to-ear. "How could she not?" he said softly. "She is our daughter."

"I'm ready," Seifer replied.

Tears ran down Eva's cheeks as she smiled at Dravik. "You say hello to our boys for me when you get to Paradise, love," she said and nodded to Seifer. A white light sparked around Eva and the Elder Wizard. The crack of magic reached Dravik's ears just as he grabbed the two bags of DragonKin weapons and ran to assist his men. Dozens of Vascuul spilled through the gap as the dragon took to the sky.

Tossing the weapon bags to his men, Dravik pulled his axes from their sheaths and smiled.

"It is a good day to kill Ri'Tek. *Tahl Vah Kai,*" he muttered and banged his axes together. Black sparks jumped from the blades as the spell activated, and the first axe sunk into the flesh of a magically-mutated gorgon female while Dravik side-stepped its stream of spit venom. The creature screamed in agony as a dense fog flowed from the axe blade into her flesh. The DeathGod's poison spread through the gorgon's veins like wildfire, and she was dead before Dravik pulled the axe from her scaly hide.

"Even you monsters cannot stand against Death's magic and those who wield it," he hissed. Spitting on the corpse, he waded deeper into the battle. The black corruption of death dripped from his axes as if possessed by a dark, living entity, and dozens of Vascuul fell dead in Dravik's wake.

DAL DAGORE

The Dwarven brothers had retreated as far as they could as they fought. Dravik cursed as his last two shield sisters fell under the claws of a mutated creeper and the Gorgon Queen, Gahainna.

"Nasty viper," he barked, stepping in front of Draven. "Come! I'll add a match to that scar on your ugly mug I gave you an aeon ago!"

Gahainna hissed, but he easily sidestepped the spit poison. Draven shadowed him, also avoiding the sizzling acid as he chanted a prayer to Izotan for even more power. Dravik winced. Already the priests' hands and arms were burnt black—scorched from the insane amount of power he had already released onto the enemy.

Gahainna hissed a second time, but no poison followed. "Dwarves," she snarled, spitting air. "No fear to feed the frenzy of the scaled clans. Surrender, and face justice."

Dravik shook his head as his brother's chant continued. "I will not live on my knees, gorgon. You shouldn't have, either. You should have accepted our offer and united the Deep."

The creature shook her head. "For cold-blooded death is a mercy the Ri'Tek will never offer, even had we fought against them. Only the Black can free us."

"Then you die here, Gahainna. The Black are long gone," Dravik said, and a crooked smile crossed his lips. Draven's prayer was complete, and he ducked as the Dwarven god's power exploded from Draven's hands. The white light raced for Gahainna, but the gorgon snatched the creeper from the ground and held it in front her body. The overgrown millipede's shell cracked under the torrential magic as it detonated and threw her through the air.

Draven collapsed. "Brother." He gasped.

Dravik turned in time to see his brother's scorched fingers curl into his palms. "I'm here, Draven. Come on. Get up. Dying on our feet will have to suffice."

"No... no... no," the priest stuttered. "You must flee."

"Never," Dravik growled.

"The Lost, brother. Find them. The Black one is on his way back."

"Impossible."

"Izotan told me." Draven persisted. "He comes from across the Kasym. Set him on the path, and then, find our ancestors. They have to help."

"I cannot leave you. It is against all we stand for. Never abandon a brother in battle. The Host live and die as one."

"I know, brother," Draven said, sighing. "Forgive me when you next see me — *to the stone we come, and to the stone we rise. From the power of the one god, rise to defend our leader and to save our people.*"

The priest chanted, and Dravik whirled as he recognized the prayer, but he was too late. The stone golem burst from the ancient Dwarven wall and wrapped its arms around him. It turned and carried him through the hole, running across the flats behind the old Dwarven fortress. It ran until Dal Dagore was a smoking pile of rubble miles behind them while Dravik struggled against its grip.

"Damn you." Dravik cursed. The golem released him and stood guard as he stared back toward the home he had protected for over ten thousand years. "May Izotan take you to Paradise with his own hands, brother."

Chapter Fourteen

"For centuries my Sisters and I have trained, planned, and prepared for the re-emergence of a matured DeathWizard. Master Kael's return to Talohna was an event in our history that should have been celebrated as my fellow Dead Sisters, and he began our campaign to conquer Talohna. It wasn't to be. For some unknown reason, the corruption of morality and conscience had eaten into Kael's very soul. My Sisters tried valiantly to purge Kael of this filth that held his true soul captive, even giving their lives in the attempt, but to no avail. Kael died with the stench of this rot embedded in his soul. I hope all the demons of Hell tear him to pieces for every second of his miserable eternity.

But all is not lost. several children were born during the Black Sun two months ago. The Dead Sister's sole purpose for existing has been renewed, but we were betrayed by one of our own, and the only child whose location was known to us was stolen before we could retrieve it. I now hunt the thief and our child. I will not rest until the betrayer vomits her own insides from her mouth and our young messiah is brought home where she belongs."

Journal entry of Voranna Talavyr,
Dead Sister's Cardessa.
Found on a body in a side alley of
Soena's slum district. 5026 PC

SOENA, SOUTHERN CETHOS
PRESENT DAY

The young woman sat in the mud with her hand out, begging for the smallest amount of coin the poor of Soena's slums could offer. A filthy black shawl covered her head and a tattered blanket so dirty its colour was unknown wrapped around her body. As a passerby dropped a single copper coin into her open hand, she looked up. Her swollen gray eyes offering her thanks even though they held the agony of those completely lost. The generous soul disappeared into the crowd of people long before her thanks could be given.

Glancing down the way, the beggar quickly ducked her head and pulled her shawl further over her face as a group of three men approached, all stumbling drunk. Though she wanted to curl up and hide, the woman knew drunks were often loose with their coin, and the single copper would not go far enough to soothe the savage ache of hunger eating at her insides. Keeping her head down, she slowly raised her hand. The three men stopped, but no coin was offered.

"Filthy beggar," Kanin snapped, bending over to inspect the woman. "You a man, woman, or beast under there, ugly?" He lifted her shawl from her face. "Ah, my mistake, pretty little young thing."

"Pretty, you say?" the second man asked, almost tripping over his own feet.

Kanin smiled. "Very pretty, Jake. What say you, pretty? Care to earn more than a few coppers. My boys and I'll show you a right time. Give you a silver and warm you up, too?" The young beggar shook her head as she lowered it and moved the shawl back over her face.

"Don't think she likes you, Kanin," the third man said, laughing. "Think maybe she just wants me and Jake."

Again, the woman shook her head. "Please, leave me be. I am not a whore," she whispered.

"Hear that, boys?" Kanin laughed. "She's not a whore. Guess that means it's free!" he said. Grabbing a handful of her hair, he dragged her further into the alley. The young woman screamed. Her blanket fell away, revealing a baby in her lap. Exposed to the cold air, the child wailed miserably.

"What the fuck?" Jake yelled. The young beggar grabbed her baby, holding her close as she did her best to make sure the little one was not harmed.

"No, please! Don't hurt my baby —" The back of Kanin's hand slammed into her jaw, dazing her. Tearing the two-month-old baby from her arms, he handed it off to the third man.

"What the hell, Kanin?" he demand.

"Crush its head in, Shaig. Toss it in the mud." Kanin pulled the dazed woman to her feet and bent her over a stack of boxes as she mumbled incoherently, trying to reach for her child.

"Fine, if only for the sake of my ears," Shaig hissed as he laid the baby on top of one of the other crates. "But I get her first for killing this ugly thing."

"Fair enough." Kanin grinned as he pinned the struggling mother down. Glancing down the alley, he saw a tall woman walking toward them. Unlike the young beggar, she was dressed in an expensive robe of black velvet. The wide hood, lined with fur, surrounded her head even though it rested on the woman's shoulders. "Look boys, Miss Rich and Tasty has come to join us for some fun."

"I assure you, young man, I am here for no such reason," she said, disgust laced every word. "Release the child and the woman. Now."

Jake stepped across the alley, stopping in front of the well-dressed woman as he pulled a dagger from his waist.

"That is not going to happen, Miss Rich-Bitch," he said, sneering.

"Oh, Miss Rich-Bitch." She mocked him. "How original. You will let them go," she whispered. Leaning forward, the woman stroked the thug's cheek. Lost in his own heightened desire, the thug never saw the danger in front of him until the woman poked him between the eyes with her fingernail. A dark green and black corruption immediately spread out under his skin. "Just die. You are not worth the effort of the Ichor's dreams." The woman took a step back, and Jake's body shook with tremors. White foam traced with strings of red blood frothed from his mouth, and he died before he hit the ground. Shaig left the crying child lying on the crates and pulled his sword from its sheath. He attacked, but a putrid green energy tore through his abdomen and opened him wide before he could take two steps in the woman's direction.

Kanin shoved the beggar to the mud and took off up the alley. Sticky black webbing wrapped around his knees as the witch cast more magic. A second black web hex smacked his face as he looked back over his shoulders in panic. The corrosive webs ate into his flesh as he crumpled in the alley. The young beggar crawled to her child and picked the baby up off the crates. She cradled the wailing baby while she slid down the wall of the building behind them.

The witch approached and knelt close by her side, slowly caressing the beggar's cheek. "Kyah, my dear. So good to see you, again," Voranna Talavyr said. "We have missed you. All the Dead Sisters have. You shouldn't have stolen our child like that."

"My child," Kyah whispered. "She's my child."

Voranna snorted and shook her head. "You truly are delusional. The child of a DeathWizard belongs to the Dead Sisters. Now, say goodbye, Kyah, and I will send you to Hell to join your lover. The two of you can suffer forever in the Halls of Perdition."

Kyah pushed herself further away from the Dead Sister's most powerful witch, but the building pushed at her back like a living entity. "I won't let you take my baby, Voranna. She's all I have left."

Voranna smiled, her eyes heavy with mock pity. "You know you can't stop me, my dear. The child took your magic from you the moment you decided to steal it and spend every waking moment with it. You did well tracking down the woman who would give birth to this child. I arrived at the small farmhouse only three days after you left with the baby. You really didn't have to massacre the whole family like that."

"I didn't harm them, Voranna. If they are dead, then you did it."

"If you say so, my dear, but the Cethosian Wizard's Council is now hunting you. They don't take kindly to murder, especially when that murder takes place, so a young woman can steal a newly born DeathWizard. You are lucky the ArchWizard is still missing, or he would have already found you."

"I will stay ahead of that fool if it means keeping my baby."

"How?" Voranna scoffed. "Look at you. You barely have the energy left to stand. How long has it been since you've eaten? Sooner or later, you will not be able to find or buy milk for it, and the child will suffer as you do. Both of you will die. Is that what you want?" Voranna reached out and gently caressed her cheek, a smile of tenderness and love curling her pursed lips.

Kyah frowned at the cruel expression of false empathy. She wormed away from the deadly poisoned nail growing on Voranna's corrupt fingers. She had heard that the demon queen, Reetha, had awarded the new Cardessa well.

"No," Kyah whispered.

"Let me end the torment, love, and you can see him again—even if it is in the eternal suffering in Reetha's hell." The smile of pity vanished. "Or you can suffer now, for hours, or maybe days, while the child listens to your cries of agony until your heart finally gives out under the torrential stress of my magic. You've lost everything, Kyah. Your magic, your place with us, and even the man you so deeply loved. Once you are rotting in the ground, this child will become the most powerful DeathWizard ever to walk Talohna under our tutelage. You have no magic and nothing left to fight with Kyah, just give u—"

Voranna stopped short as she stared wide-eyed at Kyah. A puzzled expression crawled over her face. She gasped twice, but no words followed.

"I don't need magic," Kyah spat, twisting the blade in her hand as the hilt thudded against Voranna's chest and the blade slid into her heart. "Kael taught me that a steel blade kills a Dead Sister better than magic ever did." Kyah twisted the dagger back and forth, pushing the blade harder even though it had nowhere to go. "The DragonKin Queen gave me this blade. It will mark your soul and send it straight to Kael. He will absorb it as raw power, and you will cease to exist. It will help him escape from your queen and any others who try to use him in the afterlife. You are not the first he has received and I will make sure you are not the last."

Voranna slowly collapsed backward as the blade slid from her heart and blood trailed down the front of her robe. Kyah crawled forward and quickly searched through Voranna's belongings. She ached to take the fancy warm robe, but Dead Sisters worked in groups of three meaning Voranna's ternion wouldn't be far away. Taking the robe would make her a glowing beacon to the other Sisters.

Instead, she grasped the necklace and ruby charm from the dead woman's throat. Kyah pulled, snapping the leather choker. Tying it around her neck, she knew the obscurity charm would keep unfortunate incidents from happening if she kept her head down. Every Dead Sister wore one to keep prying eyes from looking their way when they could not use cover provided by the vested robes of the goddess Mylla. A small pouch of coins on Voranna's hip jingled, and Kyah quickly snatched it for herself. The prospect of eating real food nearly overwhelmed her. Struggling to stand, she held the baby close and checked to make sure she was all right.

"Oh, sweetie... that stupid witch bled all over you." Bending down, Kyah cut a piece of Voranna's inner robe. She wrapped her child in it, leaving the bloody rags in the mud. The cold sparked another outburst of crying as Kyah walked down the alley past Kanin. He was still alive, whimpering as the hex magic slowly ate away at his face and legs. Kyah used her toe to push him onto his back. Looking around, she knelt at the dying man's side.

"You tried to kill my little girl," she whispered. The man's eyes and nose had dissolved under the caustic effects of the hex. His lips were also gone leaving him with a gruesome dead man's grin. "Can you hear me through the haze of agony?" she asked and poked at the hole where his left eye used to be. He screamed and nodded. At least, she thought he did. The quaking tremors rippling through his body made it hard to tell.

"H... h... help... help me.... pl... please..."

"Help you? Why would I help you when you tried to murder my baby? My sweet Kaylla..." she said, gently rocking the cooing baby.

"No... no... no. Please..."

"Stop begging. It's distasteful, and it will do you no good. You want to know why?" Kyah glanced around the alley, making sure she was still alone. "I'm trying to decide whether to let my baby devour your soul or whether to let you suffer until you die. My love? Now, he would put you out of your misery, and he'd never let our baby devour your soul. But he's dead now, murdered by betrayers. Your friends were lucky. They died fast. Their souls are already in one of the Nine Hells."

"K... kill me. Pl... please."

"Very well, Kanin. Because it is what my love... what Kael would have done—shown mercy. I know it is what he would have done. Besides, there are plenty of souls for my baby to feed upon and many years for her to do it." Kyah drew the blade she used to kill Voranna from within her baby's new velvet wrap and eased it slowly into the thug's heart.

"Say hi to my Kael when he finds you, Kanin. If you manage to retain your self-awareness, and if not... eh, I really don't care," she admitted as she stood. Leaving the bodies in her wake, she meandered away, singing soft lullabies to her baby.

DAL DAGORE

Sythrnax grunted as the very last of the Dwarven Host fell. Every Dwarven man and woman had fought until their last breath—though, he had expected nothing less. Even with the Dwarves outnumbered five-to-one, over half his force had been slaughtered by the bearded bastards while securing the Animus Seal. Most were Vascuul so the Vikress would be satisfied once the Dwarven Seal opened and it released more of their kin from an exile far worse than death. From across the city square, he saw Gahainna heading his way. She was walking which meant the Vascuul frenzy had been minor. He smiled. The Dwarves feared nothing, and the Vascuul only frenzied on fear. His smile widened when he noticed the two creepers with her were dragging a prisoner through the dirt by his feet—a Dwarven priest.

He clapped his hands together and the sharp report echoed off the high stone walls. "Well done, Gahainna! A Dwarven prisoner! That's a first after over eight hundred years of war. I am impressed."

The gorgon hissed in disgust. "Do not be so easily impressed," she snapped. "The priest is burnt from channeling too much pretender magic." She clicked her teeth together, and the Creepers dropped the priest to the ground. He immediately struggled to stand and eventually regained his footing.

Sythrnax grinned. "Draven BloodPounder... my, my. Of all the priests to give up, I never for a minute would have believed it would be you. Dwarven royalty we have here, Gahainna."

"He is yours, Sythrnax. I care not who he is."

"Then, return to your sisters and enjoy the feast." The gorgon queen nodded and slid past Sythrnax, but he grabbed her arm. "The General. Is he dead?"

Gahainna shrugged. "Know not. This fool's explosion probably killed him and nearly me as well."

Sythrnax grasped the gorgon by the throat. "Is he dead?" Gahainna tried to shrug and lifted her hands. "Then, you will gather your sisters and search until you find him. He uses magic that can harm us. Do you understand?" Gahainna gurgled and he released her. "Search the entire Deep Earth if you have to but find that Dwarf and the axes he carries. Am I clear?"

The gorgon nodded and turned to leave. Tucking her feet back beside her legs, she slid away, cursing and spitting.

"So hard to control the more primal species, is it not, old friend?" Sythrnax said turning back to Draven.

"Friend? Long ago maybe, coward. Wouldn't know about controlling others. My people had no interest in the subjugation of other races."

Sythrnax nodded. "As long as they didn't have magic, true. Not so true if they did, though. Correct? I found your little device in Arkum Zul."

Draven laughed. The effort nearly dropped him to a knee. "We never even tried that until after you cowards attacked the Lesser races. Using the Arterius device was about survival, not control."

"Semantics, really," Sythrnax shot back. "It no longer matters. Even your... god cannot help you now. All your people are dead."

"Not all of them, coward," Draven snapped. "The young generation fled, and Dravik is on his way to get help."

Sythrnax shook his head. "My Vascuul will find your brother and kill him, but your young are already dead, along with the old, the infirm, and everyone else who fled hours ago."

"You lying bastard!"

"Come now, Draven. We both know better. Perhaps visual stimulation will help." He grabbed Draven by the neck and dragged him across the street and to a collapsed building. Tossing the Dwarf to the dirt, Sythrnax laughed as Draven took the scene in. Hundreds of bodies had been tossed into the depression created by a destroyed house. Young children and old women, along with the oldest warriors sent to protect them had all be killed and thrown into the pit like garbage. Deep claw marks and bite wounds scoured most of the bodies, but many others had been killed by bladed weapons.

Draven let out a slow breath of air as he stared at the last of his people. Warriors he had respected, young ones he had trained, old women who had stitched him up, and one who had saved his life when he was wounded fighting the Mahala.

"You bastard," he whispered. "You did not have to kill them all."

"No, I didn't. But your kind are worse than all the other Lesser races combined. You are stubborn, and you never quit. Even your youngest fought to the death. That is why the Dwarven race will join the Dragon Behemoths in extinction today, old friend," Sythrnax said. "Nothing else matters. There is no help coming."

"You are wrong Sythrnax. It will matter when others hear what you have done here," Draven barked with anger. He calmed quickly and smiled. "And my god is on his way to help."

"You're burnt," Sythrnax said, laughing. "You have nothing left to give to channel your phony god's power."

"Nothing, but my body and my life," Draven smiled.

"Even your pathetic god would never dare enter this world and face one of our kind let alone me! Your insolence has only grown over the aeons."

"Perhaps. And perhaps, the other gods will stand by and let you destroy Talohna. But mine won't. *Izotan, the one god. I am always your vessel, and I am your body for as long as my flesh can hold you,*" Draven shouted as light poured from his eyes, ears, and mouth. White flames erupted from his hands and arms while the fire quickly spread throughout his body.

"You dare!" Sythrnax roared, summoning his staff. "If you are so foolish, child, then today one of Talohna's new gods will die."

The threat was answered as the white flames exploded and Draven was gone. A fifteen-foot, flaming white avatar stood in his place.

"This world has changed, Sythrnax," the avatar told him.

"You are a fool, Izotan. You waste your power and your existence for nothing."

"Wrong." The raw power of the god's voice boomed against Sythrnax's mind and body as it echoed in the underground cavern. "We helped the Lesser races once. We will help them, again."

"At what cost?" Sythrnax yelled, his anger growing. "You are not a true god! None of you are. Your presence here and the life you just took is proof of that. Only our true gods could act in Talohna with impunity — those we both used to worship! Those who are long gone. Those you try to mimic with your blasphemy! Your actions here will be catastrophic for the Lesser races, yet you still make an appearance in this reality." Sythrnax smiled. He could feel the god weakening already. The vessel could not hold him for long.

"Any cost to this world will be better than the life they will live on their knees under your rule," Izotan roared. The white flames danced higher. "You will die today, Ri'Tek." The avatar's hand slammed into the earth.

Ready for the attack, Sythrnax stepped back into his jump vortex and vanished as the massive fist cracked the earth open wide.

Reappearing a short distance away, Sythrnax used the connection inside his staff to call forth the Vascuul dragon Behemoth. As the beast dropped from the sky accompanied by several of its DragonKin, he disappeared into a vortex, again. Izotan bellowed with rage when Sythrnax stepped out of his jump doorway further away. The dragon smashed into the god's avatar, and both rolled through the city as they knocked over buildings and destroyed walls. A trail of white fire followed in their wake.

Sythrnax stared in awe as Izotan called forth more magic from the gods' realm and his size doubled. Easily snatching the dragon by the neck, white flames and molten rock roared from the massive avatar's fists and poured through the dragon as it bit and snapped at Talohna's god of stone. The

DragonKin dropped from the sky, trying desperately to help, but the god smacked them from the air like the pests they were.

Kurse crashed to the dirt beside his master and slowly rose to his feet. "Ideas on how to bring down a god?" he muttered. The mutated Vascuul seemed more indifferent than hurt even with jagged pieces of broken bone pushing through both arms.

Sythrnax laughed. "Of course," he chuckled. "Kill a god with a god, not a fledgling god-child." Turning to Kurse, he handed the DragonKin commander his staff as the Vascuul dragon exploded among Izotan's roaring white flame. "Take this to commander Nyr at the seal and tell him to proceed. I will stall the phony god." Kurse folded his broken arms around the staff. He nodded and leapt into the air, his wings carried him away.

Sythrnax slowly headed for the towering god. The dragon fell dead, nothing but a pile of charred bones. The avatar turned to face him, so Sythrnax slid into another vortex as the ground exploded around him and stepped out of the modified Fae magic much closer to the Dwarven god.

He winced. The heat from the white-hot molten stone surrounding the charred dragon was intense, even behind his magical shield. "You probably should have left the dragon alive, Izotan."

"Still the dictator," the god rumbled. "You Ri'Tek will never change. That is why we fight, Sythrnax. Regardless of the cost."

"Even at the cost of your own life?"

"Yes," Izotan thundered.

It made Sythrnax's head and body ache, but he felt the sudden change in the atmospheric pressure around the ruins. He smiled up at the creature who long ago had been considered one of his own.

"Feel that, Izotan? The seal your precious Dwarves protected for so long has just been opened."

"It won't save your life," the god barked. Snatching Sythrnax in his giant hand, Izotan lifted him to eye level. It took all his concentration to keep his shield in place while the god's power raged against his magic. "I can feel the hatred this vessel and that of his brother had for you. The crimes you committed against their family, their race—"

"How dare you judge me?" Sythrnax snapped over him. "You may have ascended, but I was born centuries before you. You were still Ri'Tek at one point in your life."

The avatar growled. "I see the Vikress is still polluting our true past with lies and propaganda. You know well that I was one of those whom you call the Lost. I gave the Dwarven race my protection because I am one of their ancestors—not a scaly, treacherous Ri'Tek bastard."

Sythrnax laughed in the god's face as he saw the first inhabitant of the Dwarven seal rocket from the dimensional rift almost a half mile away. He had stalled long enough. "Perhaps, but you have retained one of our weaknesses—you talk too much. That dragon you killed so carelessly?" Sythrnax asked as he nodded over Izotan's shoulder. "It's very big brother just escaped the seal." The avatar dropped Sythrnax and whirled, but it was too late. As he fell into his vortex, Sythrnax watched the Behemoth Vascuul slam into the god's avatar and drive it into the ground. Stepping through another vortex well out of range of the monstrous battle, he saw the Vascuul dragon unleashed over twelve thousand years of frustration on the Dwarven god. Putrid black flaming acid tore into Izotan's avatar, snuffing the white flame. The attack went on relentlessly uninterrupted until the avatar shrieked and melted, leaving behind no trace it or Draven BloodPounder had ever existed.

Kurse dropped from the sky and landed gently at his side. "Primal god," he said. "Makes sense."

"They were in a sense, yes. More so now that they are Vascuul," Sythrnax replied. "Unfortunately, that is the only one left."

The mutated DragonKin commander shrugged, indifferent as ever. "Better than none. There is one of your kind from the seal who wants to speak to you."

"It can wait. There were none of important rank stationed at the fight when the seal opened," Sythrnax said.

Kurse frowned. "Perhaps tell him that, then." The DragonKin turned and held out his hand. Sythrnax stared bewildered, not quite sure if his eyes were showing him reality.

"Son?" Sythrnax let out. "Can't... be..." The naked man walking his way was undoubtedly his son, though he was certain his son had been dead for decades before the exile. "How?"

"Father? What happened?" The young man stumbled on his feet, but Sythrnax caught him. The connection was immediate and he knew the man was his son—one of the most powerful Syddic priests to ever live.

Sythrnax grinned and held his son. "Ghul..."

The Vikress would be extremely happy the High Syddic priest who had first created the Vascuul was alive and free.

FOREST OF ABANDONED SOULS, YEAR 210
THE AFTERLIFE

"Which one?" Kael asked as he hung the second last token from the ninth limb of the Tree of Life and dropped to the ground.

Jasala frowned. "I don't know, but it is not going to work if we choose wrong, and we are out of time. Perdition's barrier is already starting to waver. Garz'x and the others will be here and soon."

Kael rubbed his forehead in frustration. They had been trying for decades to reach the forest, but every time they tried, they had been pulled into a different hell by demon magic under the command of Garz'x. Now that they were finally here, he could not decide. "Yeah. Tydariel or Arreal?"

Jasala pushed her hair back over her Elvehn ears. "I cannot guess. If it were me, I would use Tydariel's."

Kael sighed. "She did seem more honest, and she didn't try to capture us—or kill us." Taking a deep breath, he closed his eyes and hung the lock of wired golden hair from the highest branch on the tree's Paradise side. Nothing happened.

"I'm alive," he proclaimed. "So, that's a start."

"Tydariel told the truth," Jasala said. A nervous laugh of relief slipped past her lips.

"Uh, yeah, but why isn't it working?" Jasala shook her head and stared at him. "Everything you were told by Yrlissa, and what we've learned over the past two hundred years all lead to the Tree of Life being the doorway out of here. Nine branches on the Perdition side and three on Paradise's side. We must be overlooking something... think, Jasala. You've been here for like a million years."

"I'm sorry, Kael. The tokens represent your control of all the realms of the afterlife. Joining that power with the Tree of Life is supposed to be your way back."

"Is it because Garz'x surrendered his realm and then changed his mind when he discovered the double cross? He's not exactly a normal demon lord like Rajazeye."

"No, he gave it willingly. From what I was told, that is all that matters. His token is good. They all are. He's only coming after you now because he knows you will turn over the extra tokens to Salo RedMaw."

The barrier on the forest's left side ruptured, exploding outward as Garz'x and his hordes poured onto the field. The demon lord's distance between them was uncomfortable.

"Jasala?" Kael asked as he prepared to fight.

The ancient DeathWizardess cursed under her breath and both her hands flared with magic. "I am sorry, Kael. I have told you all I know. Yrlissa Blackmist told me that joining my control of the afterlife with the Tree of Life would get me home. I have told you all of what she shared—knowledge from the mouth of a god. But like every other Kai'Sar who has died and arrived in the afterlife whole, I could never accomplish what you have. My vines were far from growing to maturity at the time of my death. I never had a chance. Even if they had, I do not have your affinity for magic, your intelligence, or your will." She paused for a second and quickly gave him a hug. "I will hold the demons back for as long as I can. You will have about five minutes to either figure out how to leave or else run so you can try again another day."

"Jasala, wait. I can't let you do this."

"You have to, Kael. I could not come with you anyway." Her voice caught in her throat, and regret danced in her eyes as she released him. "Thank you for the years of freedom you gave me and for all you shared during our years together. Now, I must go. They're coming."

"I should be thanking you," he said. "For everything. I couldn't have done this without you. I am going to miss you."

"Good luck, my friend," Jasala said as she turned away. Without looking back, she added, "If you do get back and you find her… tell Yrlissa I know it wasn't her fault."

"I promised you. I will," he said and nodded. Jasala vanished in a cloud of black smoke. A moment later, stepped out of the jump spell and met the first part of the demon army. As he stared, her words came back to him, but it was Akai's voice he heard in his head. Words that Jasala had repeated dozens of times during the nearly two centuries they had fought together.

Join your control with the Tree of Life.

"Dammit," Kael muttered. "I did that, Akai. What the hell am I missing?"

The tokens. Akai prompted. *If the tokens are the control, putting them on the Tree of Life should work. Why hasn't it? Think, Kael, think.*

A loud explosion rocked the glade, and the barrier to Paradise fell away, giving him a hint. The Heretic angels followed Arreal through the breach.

Arreal's fake tokens… like the others, they were just tokens — teeth, claws, and hair.

"Found you, little wizard," the angel roared.

Kael ignored the Heretic but stared hard as the dilemma rolled through his mind. "Control is having the power... the magic... of all the afterlife dimensions. Dimensional doorways are opened by using magic..." he whispered. His voice trailed off as the answer finally dawned to him, and Akai screamed in his head.

Magic! Hit the tokens with your magic!

Turning back to the Tree of Life, Kael raised both of his arms and grasped his magic. Watching his tokens closely for a reaction, black magic rolled off his fingertips like oily black smoke, and he focused on the first dimensional token he received so long ago. He forced his magic into Rajazeye's pendant, and it flared to life. Small vines grew from the bark of the tree and gently enveloped it while he moved on to the other eleven, activating each in proper order. The second his magic touched the last token, the snaking vines around the tree stirred from their slumber. Veins of purple throbbed within the tree and vines — like a heartbeat, a startling mockery of life.

The vines jumped and curled around his legs, quickly spreading up his body before they plunging into his chest through his deathflower. Overwhelming agony followed. only lasting seconds as a strange rush of energy entered his body. Identical to the rush that had helped him escape the demon queen, Kael opened his mind. The tree granted him knowledge he could not fathom. He smiled as a soul had been gifted to him by someone in the form of raw power, and it helped him push back the agony from the vines. At last, he knew how to get home.

The battle between Jasala and the demons echoed in his ears and he felt Arreal coming closer, but both meant little to him. He knew the Heretic angel would never reach him in time. A new arrival would ensure it. As the thought flit through his mind, Tydariel appeared on the field. She cut Arreal off, engaging him in battle.

The Tree of Life pulled Kael closer and his mind expanded further. Scenes of the past and future flashed through his mind faster than he could make sense of. A crack of magical power shook his body to the core. He saw the Arkangel, Seraphi, with her army standing at his guard. Her numerous soldiers split into two separate forces. Half followed after Tydariel and engaged Arreal's Heretics while the others took to the air and dropped down on the demon hordes. He knew what would happen and he knew what Seraphi would say to him before she spoke.

"Stop, Kael. Please. You don't know what you're doing."

"No," he snapped. "This time, I'm looking out for myself."

"The consequences," she said, trying again.

He was not interested in hearing it. "Damn the consequences. Goodbye, Seraphina."

"Kael!" Seraphi screamed. "Never hand those tokens over to Salo."

"I have to or Jasala—"

"—Kael, please, listen. Salo RedMaw is the Archdemon, Salotan. He was banished from hell for a very good reason. Please, trust me when I tell you handing those over to him will be the worst possible thing to happen to everyone, everywhere."

"How can I trust you?" he retorted. "You said I'd be welcome in heaven. Your angels were worse than any demon. They used Jasala as a living energy source."

"I am sorry," she told him. "I truly am. There are heretics among the angels. My absence allowed them to grow stronger. I am so sorry. This was not supposed to happen this way."

"But it did," he told her. "The demons of hell have been more honest and trustworthy than you and any of your goddamn angels, so why should I break any deal with them?"

"I didn't know, Kael. I have been tracking you through hell and to heaven and back this entire time." She stopped talking and closed her eyes for only a second. "I am so sorry."

Her emotions were legitimate as they rolled through his esoteric senses. "Then, I'm sorry too," he said. "I will not sacrifice Jasala's soul for you. She is the only one I can trust, and as long as her soul belongs to me, she can move freely through the afterlife and stay out of both your hands."

"Then the Queen." Seraphi gasped, trying one last time. "Only honor the Queen's deal. Please! For the sake of all existence. Just the Queen's. Please."

Kael sensed that the tree would wait no longer so he shrugged and turned.

As he did, the Tree of Life dragged him inside.

"Please, believe me, Kael," Seraphi whispered as a bright bolt of purple light rocketed from the tree up into the sky. It pierced the Void and disappeared. "Goodbye."

The Tree of Life groaned under the pressure, and the trunk split from the ground up to the first branch and all the way to the twelfth—from the first tier of Paradise to the ninth hall of Perdition.

"Gods, no. That's impossible!" Seraphi gasped and gently placed her hand on the tree. A liquid silver metal oozed from the cracks and wormed its way into the throbbing purple veins until both pulsed together, spreading throughout the entire tree. "That cannot be... what have you done, Kael? By the gods, what have *we* done?"

Seraphi stumbled away from the tree as the silver lashed out at her, continuing to spread. The Arkangel spread her wings and leapt into the air. Banking to the left, the Arkangel tucked in her wings and dove hard. Grasping Jasala by her hood, Seraphi jerked the DeathWizard into the air with her and flew away before signaling a general retreat of her forces.

A snap of angelic magic rocked the glade as both angel and DeathWizard disappeared back into Paradise with both the Heretic and heaven armies.

Chapter Fifteen

GODS

"Ever wonder where the gods came from? I am not a religious man. I do not pray and the closest I ever seem to get is when I take the name of numerous gods in vain, quite regularly. But have you ever really thought about where they came from? Or how they came to be? Why would they create this world and all the life within it? Like most other historians, philosophers, faithful, or minstrels, the thought has crossed my mind. Have the gods like Mylla and Dathac, or Lady Cortina always existed, or were they too created by yet another higher being? They created our world and yet they barely glance its way the past many thousands of years. There are dozens of myths and legends that talk of a time when gods walked by the sides of men and women. Perhaps they are just that — myths. I know not. Whether you are a devout faithful or not, the gods do not speak to us directly and personally I doubt they ever did."

Garren Sallus, Excerpt from:
Myths and Legends of Talohna. Volume 1

THE ETHER

Kael opened his eyes to blackness—a blackness far beyond total dark. It was unlike anything he had ever seen or felt before. He had no spatial awareness or recognition of sight. It was as if he were a small part of the infinite black void of nothing. Blinking did nothing, and he realized he had no eyes to blink with, nor a body to feel with.

His unbound chuckle tumbled through the void around him. He thought to himself, *What next?*

You feel no fear. The gravely female voice boomed in the darkness, but he could not make out whether anything had changed in the utter black.

Because it isn't real. he answered back.

Explain,

Danger is real, but fear is merely a product of the mind — a reaction to real danger. That makes fear a choice, and I've seen far too much to choose to be afraid of the dark. The worst dangers walk in the light of day.

Insightful — fear can be controlled with such beliefs. That surprises us. Mortals never see it that way.

You're not mortal, then? he asked.

We are... eternal.

Of course.

How did you come to be here?

Considering what I tried to do, I imagine I'm dead or god only knows what else...

God?

You don't know what a god is?

Explain.

Kael sighed at the unusual demand. *That's a difficult request to answer. The simplest reply — a god is an all-powerful being who watches over a world. Often, they are credited with the creation of that world and may or may not interfere with it at their whim. Most don't interfere from what I've seen. Benevolent or malevolent, a god or gods rarely seem to be interested in or concerned with their creations.*

Understood. How did you come to be here?

I have no idea, he answered honestly. *I have been somewhere similar before. No chatty megaphones there though.*

You have died before.

It was a statement and not a question. *Yeah, so they tell me.*

Then, why are you here?

Cryptic, aren't you? Remind me of these three wraiths... never mind. I imagine I'm here because I did something wrong trying to return to life.

No. You are here because you broke through the barrier separating death and life.

I wasn't trying to break it. I just wanted to pass through it.

The barrier is a universal governance that applies to all life regardless of power or dimension.

Okay, he replied. If he had a head to feel with, it would have been spinning with confusion.

Why return to the living? the entity asked.

Call it unfinished business. Or I had it back when all this started.

Explain

There were people I needed to help... things I still need to do in that life, meaningful things, Kael offered.

What gives a mortal life meaning?

Loved ones, children, passions.

Then, why return? You have none of those in Talohna.

Enough! Kael barked. Hearing what he already suspected fueled the rage riding so close to the surface. *I'm not answering your stupid questions. Send me where you will.*

Enough? The voice thundered with anger. *You violate the natural law and sanctity of life simply by being here.*

Who are you, or what? Show me who I'm talking to.

We are the beings that have always been. Some leave, some return, most live, and very few die. Your word... god... it seems appropriate.

On instinct, Kael covered his eyes as a bright light blazed out of the dark. As it faded, he realized he could lower his hand. He found himself staring at the strange female being in front of him. She was shrouded in a misty white light and an all too familiar armor and mask set adorned her body.

"That mask looks familiar," he said, unable to hold back the disgust in his voice.

An image from your mind. For your comfort. Strong emotion is tied to this appearance. I assumed the emotion was good.

"Not even close," Kael mumbled.

My true appearance then, seeing as fear does not rule your heart or soul.

The Ri'Tek mask melted away, replaced by a veil and hood of black and white lace. The being slowly pulled the dark veil down under her nose. Solid black eyes stared back at him. Black vines crawled over her cheeks and forehead and cracks across her face began where they stopped. More intricate and delicate than his own, her vines were missing the barbed thorns that marred his entire body. Instead, long and wicked thorns burst from the cracks around the vines, protruding inches from her flesh above her black eyebrows.

Any other similarities between them ended there. The woman's face oddly resembled that of a young child. Smooth and soft, her marred skin held a sprinkling of freckles across her cheeks. Everything about her was youthful, but an extremely dangerous aura of black and gray wafted from her and mixed with the white mist. The contrast to her pale skin was disturbing as was her ageless aura.

Better?

"Better than looking into the face of evil, yeah. Where am I? Who are you?" Kael demanded.

You are in the Ether. If your dimension's true... creators... gods... were not long dead, they would defend your transgression. However, because of your connection to the Ether, you may speak on your own behalf. Without it, you would have already ceased to exist.

"What connection?"

Your magic. The vines and thorns growing throughout you are products of the Ether and of our kind. It puzzles me how that is. You are not of Kin. The weapons you carry were forged here... for Niis. She was Kin. Her and Treach left long ago to create your world. They are dead now.

He decided to test what Jasala believed. "I was told the Vai'Karth were forged by the Dwarven race of Talohna by sacrificing an angel and a demon."

No. Both your power and weapons were born of the Ether. From here and from the energy around you. Can you feel it?

He had felt it the moment he regained consciousness. His awareness tingled with electricity and he felt amazing, yet comfortable and at peace. If it was a place to spend eternity, he would have been happy to do so. "I don't *feel* it," he answered, "it's like I am… it"

That is the Ether, and it is you now. That has to be why the Vai'Karth accepted you even though they were forged for my kind. This is… problematic. Both tie you to the Ether even though you are not one of us. Does the spirit speak to you? Did it help you to arrive here?

Akai slid into the furthest reaches of his mind, as if hiding in response. "He didn't help me get here, but he does speak. He's awfully quiet right now, though," Kael told her.

It knows its place among us and should not speak unless commanded to do so. That is even more problematic. In the hands of a mortal, the Vai'Karth could be cataclysmic weapons capable of destroying a world. The energy of each foe killed is absorbed by the weapons if the wielder so chooses. The weapon's spirit increases in strength exponentially each time and this strength can be passed to the wielder. Even its personality can change.

"Jesus," Kael breathed. "That explains his crap attitude lately. A literal soul-eater."

An intelligent and proper analogy.

"How did he come to be?" he asked.

Kin Akai was formed from traces of exhausted – leftover… souls as you call them. Energy is the term we use. The weapons are not supposed to accept a mortal master. One touch should have killed you. It did not, so this creates a unique dilemma. Therefore, when not in use, the Vai'Karth remains here in the Ether. They cannot fall into the hands of a mortal being ever, again. Should we deem it so, you will return to your old life as more than what you were before death, and the weapon will come to you when called. The cypher – the word to call them for this "Sai."

"Thank you," Kael replied.

I would not. If we deem it necessary, you will cease to exist here, and the Vai'Karth will remain in the Ether where they belong. Your answers and what rests in your energy will decide.

"What the hell do you want to know?" Kael barked, losing his temper, again. "Huh? That I want to go back so I can kill every goddamn Ri'Tek bastard I can get my hands on? That I have nothing else to fight for because my wife and friends died over two hundred years ago? Or do you want to hear that I want to go back to try and help all the people who will suffer under Ri'Tek rule? Which one? Because they're all true after every goddamned thing I've gone through and everything I've lost since being ripped from my own world. You won't stop me from returning!"

No. I will not. But the Ether itself may. It has shown you favor. You would not be standing here if it did not allow it, but that can change. Returning will make you immortal, but not invincible. It is rare for a god to walk from death. A mortal doing so is unfathomable. Do you understand the weight of what that means?

"Probably not," he answered honestly.

You surprise me, again. Mortal minds are rarely so honest.

"If I lied, I'm sure you'd know."

Your perspective is still refreshing.

"Thanks, I think."

You could live for thousands of years while others age or die and the world changes around you. Life is a part of death. Death is what gives mortal life meaning — knowing that your life will not last forever, that each moment is precious and should be cherished before there are no more moments. It is what makes being mortal so special. Can you live a long life with no meaning? Possibly forever?

"I'll find a meaning, a passion."

For a while, perhaps, but eventually you will understand. And once you do, you will never be happy, and it will be far too late.

"Being happy is not reality, anyway."

Again, we agree. You will return to Talohna, much, much more than what you were before death. Exactly how much more and what you do with it will depend on you. Listen for the call of the Ether. It is a part of you and within it you will find your real power.

"I never wanted any of this power." Kael sighed.

That is why it found you. True power should only make itself known to those with no interest in it, just like those before you — Niis and Treach — the true... gods... of Talohna. They died many aeons ago, so perhaps it is time Talohna had a protector once more. Someday... that may be you. Perhaps. But until then, I warn you, mortal. You must reconcile with the new energy that is part of you, before it forces you to. If that happens many may die.

Panic settled over Kael's heart as he realized what the being meant, and his tongue refused to cooperate to offer an answer.

The Ether is now a part of what you are.

Forever.

The last word rolled over and over inside his mind until it felt like the words where pushing him head over heels through the Ether.

He groaned as the blackness shut him down.

DYRANNAI FOREST
FIELD OF THE FALLEN

Kael opened his eyes and quickly came to understand he was on his back with a glass dome over top of him. The scent of dust and ancient death clung to the air around him like an oppressive fog. Pushing his hands against the glass, he tried to heave it aside. It refused to budge, his numb hands and arms were not helping. Taking a quick glance around, it took only seconds to realize he was likely in an underground crypt or mausoleum. Panicking, he beat on the glass and screamed as the overwhelming sensation of claustrophobia crawled into the recesses of his mind. Frowning, he grabbed at his magic. Black and purple mist swallowed his fists as he punched the glass above him repeatedly. The dome exploded into tiny shards of glass. Sitting up, he looked around, more confused than before. He could not recall how he had gotten there. The last memory he had was of walking through Kazzador City's sprawling ruins with Cassie.

Kael rolled off the marble slab to stand, but his legs gave out and he crashed to the stone floor.

"What the hell?" he muttered. He could not feel his legs.

"How long have I been laying there?" he whispered aloud as he massaged his legs, trying to bring back the feeling.

"A long time," a voice said drifting out of the darkness. "But far less than others."

Kael squinted and peered around the room a second time, taking in several other glass-covered slabs. Covered in layers of thick dust, he could not make out who or what had been interred inside. All but his own were recessed into the stone walls. With feeling slowly returning to his arms, he didn't really care. Walking and defending himself would not happen any time soon, so his recovery became his only concern.

"Where are you?" he asked. The voice in the dark had said nothing more, and the hollow echo of the chamber made it impossible to pinpoint where the words originated. His esoteric senses were also numb and no help.

"Here," the male voice said as a pair of eyes to Kael's right lit up the dark corner with a steady red glow. "Mean no harm," it added.

"Wouldn't matter if you did. I can't stand up let alone defend myself," Kael muttered.

"Foolish. Should keep such things to self. Dangerous. Give body time."

"Time, yeah." Leaning back against the cold marble, Kael sighed and tried to think of how he came to be in a dusty crypt with a very short creature in the corner nearby. His mind drifted back to the Animus chamber and to his final fight with Sythrnax. Remembering how the Ancient being had trapped him on the Animus Seal with its magic brought back a cascade of memories. His discussion with Giddeon flashed before his eyes. Kael gagged and reached for his neck as he felt the wooden dagger pierce the base of his skull and a second blade cut his throat. He remembered the pain—so much pain—and he remembered dying... and falling... and Hell.

He remembered every goddamned dimension of it.

More magic swarmed his mind as caustic images assaulted his senses and agony throbbed inside his skull. He grabbed his head and screamed.

"No!" the voice barked. Kael heard a stomp a split second before a new type of magic entered his mind. Strange and powerful, but mostly soothing. His racing heart calmed as the pain and nightmare visions fled from his mind as if something far more sinister was hot on their heels. He finally regained enough control to push the remainder of the caustic images aside.

"Dammit, why does that happen?" he moaned.

"Magic. I send away," the voice from the corner said. "But. You need Fae. They fix."

"Why would you help me? he asked. "What do you want?"

"Want nothing."

"You'll be the first then."

"Then, I be first." The creature agreed.

He snorted at the asinine suggestion. "Says it all really, doesn't it." he stated even though it sounded like a question.

The creature in the corner returned his grunt. "Move legs. Arms. Must leave, soon."

"Where are we?" Kael asked, again, as he massaged his legs with hands that were starting to spark with feeling. He moaned from the pins and needles buzzing in his nerves.

"Place not safe."

"Guess that means I'm back in the land of the living, then," Kael said hopefully.

"Yes."

"Who are you?" Kael asked.

"You people call me Raven."

"You're not Human or Elvehn then?"

"No."

"What do your people call you?"

The creature shifted, and its eyes glowed a second time, rising to three feet. "Once Vog. Now, nothing."

Kael grinned. "Nice to meet you, Vog. How about you come closer, so we can meet properly?"

"You run?"

"Why?"

"You always run."

Kael shook his head, finally understanding. "You mean people like me run when they see you?"

The red eyes bobbed up and down.

"Well, Vog, you probably can't hurt me, so I won't run."

A sinister laugh growled its way out the shadows. "You not stand. Even if so, Vog kill."

"No wonder people run, Vog. You need to work on your social skills a bit. Here, look," Kael said, offering his hand. "Come shake my hand, then there's no need to kill anyone, right?"

The eyes bobbed up and down, again, and Kael stared as the short humanoid slowly walked from the shadows. Wrapped in rags, the creature carried a black staff made from raw obsidian the same height as himself. It took everything Kael had not to pull his hand back in disgust and rage.

"No wonder everyone runs from you, Vog. You're a Mahala."

"No," Vog said and retreated back into the shadows. "Mahala sick."

"Yeah, that is one word for it. You going to come shake my hand?"

Again, the creature crept out slowly. "Yes."

Kael watched closely as Vog approached and gently took his hand, shaking it. "You're not like the others, are you?"

The short Mahala shook his head. "Not sick," he said and unwrapped his face scarves. The gaping mouth and long invasive tongue typical of the Mahala—both of which Kael knew too intimately—were missing from Vog. His mouth—only half as wide—had rows of sharp little teeth, but they were nothing like the long fangs and monstrous jaws that attacked him below Tazammor Mountain so long ago.

Moaning, Kael shifted his body as his legs and feet also began to spark with feeling. "The other Mahala are sick, you said?" he asked, and pulled his shirt to the side revealing a scar from a Mahala bite mark.

Vog nodded and traced a razor-sharp talon over the scars. Kael barely felt the grazing touch. Snorting, the little Mahala put his outstretched hands by the sides of his mouth and wiggled his fingers. "Sick."

"Good impression. Sorry," Kael offered.

"Long done," Vog said, shaking his head. "Walk? Danger."

"Yeah. I think so," he replied. For some reason, he felt he could trust the little Mahala. That was, at least until they got somewhere, and he could jump away. "Just gonna be slow going. You'd think whoever went through all the trouble keeping me whole would have put me someplace safe."

A strange squeaky noise crawled from Vog's mouth. Kael was pretty sure he was laughing. "You whole, you safe. Follow. Not safe long," the little Mahala added.

Kael struggled to stand and felt Vog's hand on his thigh. "Call weapon."

He blushed as he realized he had never even thought to pull his weapons from the Ether. The god-woman said the trigger for the spell was *Sai*.

"*Sai, Vai'Karth*," he whispered, not sure if what he dreamed was even real, but the long scythe appeared in his hands.

Vog nodded as a crooked grin crossed his lips. "Change? Staff help walk."

Kael chuckled at what was obviously a challenge, one he would have failed if Jasala and Akai had not taught him how to manipulate his weapons' shape by using the soul energy stored inside. Twisting the handle, Akai's voice echoed inside his head.

You were allowed to return?

"It seems so," he whispered.

I am… surprised… but pleased. A staff then? Like the little one says?

"Thanks, Akai," Kael said softly. The blade retreated into its handle, and the ornate bone shrunk down the five feet as an intricate webbed oval formed around a black stone at the top of the new staff. The weapon's signature twist at the halfway mark made for a perfect hand hold.

Vog raised his arm for Kael to follow and headed up the stairs. He limped after the creature, not sure what to expect. As they reached the top of the stairs and exited the mausoleum, Kael gasped. Dozens of crypts identical to the one behind him circled an open field of grass for a mile in every direction. Everywhere he looked people were fighting against monstrous creatures he had never seen, not even during his time in the 7th Hell.

"Come," Vog said. "Not much time."

"We have to help these people. They're outnumbered." Kael shook his head as archers in the trees released arrow after arrow in a forest he recognized from his time with the Tree of Life. He also knew the kind of men and women who fought. "Druids," he whispered.

"Yes," Vog said. "They die so you may live."

"We have to help them," he said, again.

"No," Vog snapped and grabbed his wrist. "They help you. They fight for you. All for you. Come, escape and live. Come."

"They'll die, Vog. We—" Kael did not see one of the nightmare creatures break off and come after him until it was almost too late. The female creature lashed out with her claws and forced him to duck. His numb, sparking feet failed him and he stumbled. The female hissed like an angry snake and green mist sprayed from her mouth. Kael raised his arms, knowing it was a futile gesture. Vog grunted and smacked his staff on the ground. A bubble of shimmering blue formed around the creature while Kael got his feet back underneath him. The green mist was trapped inside the blue less than an inch from his face.

As if the spirit inside his weapon could read Kael's mind, a blade snapped from the end of the staff, and he swung the scythe, cutting through the blue shield and the creature.

"What the hell was that thing?" He gasped.

Vog poked the dead creature in the eye with his staff. "Vascuul gorgon. Ri'Tek weapon. Must go. You cannot fight yet. Reflex gone, senses dull. Take—"

"Time," he said. "Yeah, I get it."

"Follow."

"Yeah, good idea." Kael agreed, shaking his head in disbelief. "And I thought Hell had some nasty shit."

Vog squeaked another laugh. "Demons cower, hide from weakest Vascuul. Come."

He followed after Vog once more as the Mahala headed down the stairs of another crypt. Unlike the one Kael had woken in, the mausoleum had been mostly destroyed. Signs of intense fighting and powerful magic scoured every surface. Cracks adorned the walls and gaping crevices split the floor in dozens of places. Vog stepped around them with ease, and Kael frowned at his own clumsiness. Finally, they reached the bottom, and Vog disappeared through a crack in the wall. Kael stumbled after him but immediately lost his footing and fell, sliding down a narrow chute of smooth stone. He hit the bottom hard and it left him dazed. The Vai'Karth vanished back to the Ether, and he slid across the stone and dirt. He stared at their surroundings.

He groaned. "Goddammit. We're in the Deep Earth."

"Upper shelf, yes. Home," Vog stated as he patted his chest.

"Hate this place."

Vog snorted and pointed above his head. "Better than Vascuul snack."

"Of course," Kael said. "Because becoming a Mahala snack is so much better."

"No sick here," Vog explained. "Must show you. Then, take to safe place."

"Actually, Vog, I'm good. Thank you for your help, but I'm going to jump out of here."

"No!" the Mahala barked.

"Why?"

Vog stamped his feet and ran to a pile of rocks. Using his staff, he pried up a large stone and a black millipede rushed out. The Mahalan scout snatched the creature and brought it back to him.

"Jump bug. Small, just bug. Jump ten feet, there to there," Vog ordered as he pointed.

Kael reached out and opened a jump vortex. Pain seared through his arm, but he held it open as Vog tossed the millipede in. Kael collapsed the door as he reached out with other hand to open the exit. Agony rolled up the other arm, too, but hit with more intensity as the vortex opened. The millipede flew from the jump door and slammed into a boulder, shattering both bug and rock.

"Okay," he said. With no other options, he would have to stay with the Mahala for a while longer. "Guess you're stuck with me, Vog."

"Good. Come, show why."

"Where are we?" Kael asked as he followed the scout.

The Mahala stared at him and crooked his head as if he did not understand.

Kael pointed his hand to the surface above them and made a circle with his finger. "Where in Talohna are we? Below Cethos? Under the Free Lands?"

Vog rubbed his head and pointed to the left. "Kasym." Pointing to the right, he continued. "Ri'Tek."

It dawned on him just how screwed he was. "Holy shit. We're on the far side of the Black Kasym," he whispered. "There is no way I can jump through that."

Nodding, Vog stared at him through a wide grin. "No, splat like bug. Not fit for dinner."

"Me, or the bug?" he asked.

Vog frowned at him. "Jump. Only if you die, anyway."

"Last resort only jumps," he muttered. "Got it. Hey, how did you get here?"

Vog tapped his staff and a familiar blue shield formed around him.

"You can't do that for me?" The grin grew wider as Vog tapped his staff, again. A blue shield formed around Kael, and he could not move a single muscle just like the female gorgon who attacked him. However, he also could not breathe, as if the spell immobilized every muscle in his body—including his lungs.

The shield fell away, and he gasped for air. "Uh... your magic only protects you. Yeah. How did those things get through the Kasym?" he asked, pointing up.

"Vascuul?" Vog asked. Kael nodded. "Like bugs, filth. Always find way. Ri'Tek magic," Vog paused long enough to spit on the ground, "help? Not know."

"Fair enough. Not a fan of the Ri'Tek, either," Kael said and began to relax. If Vog hated Sythrnax's kind, then he might be an ally—an ally of one. "I can get behind that," he added, talking more to himself than Vog. "What do you want to show me?"

Vog waved once more, turned, and walked away.

With no other options, Kael followed. No longer needing a staff to help him walk and with no visible threats in sight, he left the Vai'Karth in the Ether.

Several hours passed as they tread deeper into Talohna's dangerous underground terrain. Slowly, Vog worked his way south and up the mountainous side of the Black Kasym's northern edge. Kael guessed it had to border the Ri'Tek land behind them, what people called the Ancient Kingdom. Magic danced in the air like a living entity. Sparks of white and blue drifted in the underground current and where they met, charged bolts of orange energy snapped out, cracking and popping around them.

"No let touch," Vog said as an orange streak lashed out, melting stone. A second bolt, blue this time, danced over a pile a stones and small rift appeared. A scream of unearthly pain rushed out of the rift but was cut short as the narrow doorway closed.

"Jesus, Vog. What the hell was that?"

Vog motioned to him, and Kael walked with him up over the crest of rocks they had been climbing for an hour. As he reached the top, he took a breath and gasped at the incredible, but surreal sight the lay before him. The Black Kasym stretched as far as he could see, but the craziest sight appeared at the far reaches of his vision.

"Magic wound," Vog said and pointed a clawed finger across the expanse of dancing blue and orange lightning. "Time, dimension—magic, all hurt."

"No wonder," he sighed. The throbbing wound in the earth make his head throb. An inexplicable urge to heal the wound came over him but quickly passed as he realized the futility of the thought. Miles to the left and right, and for as far as he could see, the Kasym continued. Water poured through the cracks and seams of the earth above as if a huge ocean rested above the stone and rock ceiling.

Vog grunted as he slowly pointed at it. "Jaws of Ice and Rock. Ocean," the Mahalan scout offered.

"I can't believe it hasn't eroded and collapsed, flooding the Deep Earth," Kael said softly.

"Kasym own magic keep it, perhaps," Vog replied.

"Makes sense, I guess."

Vog bumped him gently and nodded back across the expanse of stone, magic, and water.

Kael gasped at the smoldering ruin. "That's ancient Dwarven architecture," he stated.

"You know?" Vog asked.

"Yeah," he whispered, refusing to acknowledge the memories that jumped to mind and threatened to swallow him. It was much easier than usual, and he knew Vog was the reason. "Spent a lot time in one and died in another. What happened to that one?"

"Attack. Ri'Tek, Vascuul," Vog said, matter-of-factly. "Dwarven Animus there."

Almost afraid to, Kael asked anyway. "That seal is open?"

Vog nodded.

"Was there no one there to protect it?" Kael wondered aloud as Vog whirled on his left foot. Boots scuffed the stone to his right, and Kael spun to face the newcomer.

"Sai, Vai'Karth," he whispered.

Think it! Don't say it. Akai screamed inside his head. *It's faster.*

Kael checked the knowledge away for later as the long scythe materialized in his right hand, and a short-bearded man stumbled and fell less than ten feet away.

"Aye, sonny," Dravik BloodPounder said. He struggled and tried to stand but failed. "There were, for... for what little it... mattered..." The man fell unconscious as his words trailed off.

The short man could only belong to the Dwarven race. At just less than five feet tall and slim like the Elvehn, there was no doubt to the identity of the long haired, bearded, and battle-scarred man. He had been through hell and back. A cauterized gash on his arm still wept blood plasma, and his neck and chest were covered in acid burns. Kael bent down to help as the sound of scales scraping on stone reached his ears.

"Nackt," Vog said, spitting the word out and rolling sideways as a gorgon exploded over the rocky outcrop. She landed in front of Kael.

Swinging his scythe to force the gorgon back, he stepped over the Dwarven man in order to protect him from the snake-like creature. As if unsure of who to attack, the gorgon hissed and glanced quickly between him and Vog.

"Back off," Kael snapped, filling his hands with frosted black and purple magic. He was willing to bet the cold would slow the gorgon enough, so he could kill it. To his surprise, the creature instantly settled back and lowered herself onto her feet in a far less aggressive stance.

She stared and pointed to the magic in his hand. "You?" she asked. "You are a creature born of black. How?"

Kael refused to drop his guard. "Long story. If you're not going to attack, perhaps you should leave."

The creature's head slowly moved side-to-side, like a snake mesmerizing its prey.

"Take care," Vog whispered from behind him.

"Don't worry That crap won't work on me," Kael snapped.

"Not trying to," the gorgon said. "I am Gahainna. I will not fight one born of black."

Kael scoffed. "Too bad your relatives don't feel the same way," he said, thinking about the creatures back in the field above where he woke. Gahainna smiled at him, and he noticed her beautiful face could only be Elvehn. As he studied her, it finally dawned on him what the Vascuul were—a mix of two or more races forced together by magic.

"My sisters will not oppose you, again," she said. Rising onto her tail, she bowed and retreated back over the edge to disappear.

"Not that I'm not grateful, but, fear? Or a trick?" Kael asked, turning to Vog.

"Nah." He snorted. "Vascuul crazy, not coward—no fear. Sensed respect for you."

"Keep an eye open for her, will you? Don't need her returning with the rest of her sisters from the crypts," Kael told him. He took Vog's offered water skin and bent over to help the Dwarven man.

Splashing water on the man's face slowly brought him around.

"The priest was right," he muttered as Kael stared, confused. "Thank Izotan's hairy nards."

"All right," he said. "You must be feeling better." He held out his hand to the man. "My name is Kael. This is Vog."

"I know who ya are, boy," he growled, and grabbed Kael's hand to pull himself up. "Me name's Dravik BloodPounder," the man said, weaving and unsteady on his feet. "That Vascuul wench gone?"

"Boy, scared." Kael rolled his eyes. Vog winked and laughed

"Ha!" Dravik barked. "So, the myths are true then, you old raven."

Vog smiled and nodded. "Seems. Creatures of dark bow to black."

"Bout goddamned time something went right," Dravik quipped as he slapped Kael on the shoulder and nearly fell over.

"Easy," Kael said, grabbing the man. "Would either of you two like to explain what the hell you're talking about?"

Dravik laughed. "Of course, boy. One prophecy — two meanings — both older than time and both talk about the return of darkness to Talohna."

Vog giggled. "Both true. One is... flawed, misunderstood."

Kael frowned, and Dravik laughed harder. "Mildly understated, old friend. Two powers rise at the end of the prophecy, the dark and the black. Guess which you be, boy?"

"Let me guess? Black," Kael muttered as he traced the black vines on his neck with a finger.

"Aye, and that *dark* power is goin' to rise if that bloody Sythrnax manages to open all six seals. You stop him."

Kael shook his head. "I tried. Twice. The second time cost me my life. This isn't my war. Even if it were, it can't be won. This isn't even my wor—"

Dravik moved too fast for Kael to see, but he felt the slap bounce off his head, and his ears rang like a church bell. Before he could recover, Dravik grabbed him by the scruff of his neck and pulled him down to eye level.

"My brother gave his life, so I could get here to you. The last of my race gave their lives to protect that goddamn seal! Look," Dravik barked. The man's strength was incredible, and he forced Kael to his knees, pushing him toward the far the side. "The last Dwarven city burns, fueled by the bodies of my people. For over ten thousand years, we defended that city and thousands of others have died — my sons died — so that one day you could help all of the races of Talohna defeat the Ri'Tek for good."

Kael jerked himself from Dravik's grip. It took a large amount of magic to break the dwarf's hold. "Then you wasted your long life, Dravik. I'm not going to waste mine again. We're north of the Kasym. I'm right where I want to be. Eventually, the Ri'Tek will return here, and when they do I will kill every last one I can get my hands on, but one at a time. Only an idiot would try to face them as a race head on."

"No," Dravik snapped. "You cannot kill them all by yourself."

"You've been hiding in your walled city for too long, Dravik. My kind are a pariah to those above the surface and the Ri'Tek are worshiped as gods in some countries. They are revered as the Ancients—the founders of magic and society. You want a war with the Ri'Tek? Then, you will have to face all of Talohna. Jasala Vyshaan tried that five thousand years ago to buy more time to reinforce the seal locks, and all she got for it was killed."

"Not all," Vog whispered. "She cast Sepulchre spell."

"Yeah," Kael yelled. "At the cost of her own life and an eternity of torture in hell for her soul. No thanks. I'll go after Sythrnax and his ilk my own way."

"Your mind is made up, boy?"

"Yes."

"I do not agree, but perhaps the Ladies of Fate will bring everything we need together some day, including you. Vog?" The Mahala glanced up but said nothing so Dravik carried on. "El'Noray might have survived the Cataclysm. Take him there." The little creature nodded a second time as the Dwarven General turned back to Kael. "Wish you the best, boy, I do. Many years of planning and fighting lie ahead. If you get to kill Sythrnax before I do, before he takes his last breath, tell him I survived Dal Dagore, will you?"

Kael nodded. "That I can agree too. Where are you going?" he asked. "You can travel with us, you know—" He was cut off by a stiff shake of the hand.

"If I cannot convince you to help," Dravik said, "then I will find those who will. If Talohna will support the Ri'Tek, then I must find those who will not. Perhaps, the Lost. Do not fool yourself. War unlike any you can imagine is coming." He smiled. "Take care, boy. The land above us is far more dangerous than south of the Kasym. You awoke in the very birthplace of magic."

"Be safe, Dravik," Kael said and nodded. The dwarf turned on his heel and disappeared over the rise, heading in the opposite direction the Vascuul gorgon had gone.

"Nacht," Vog grumbled.

"What?" Kael asked.

"Come." Vog waved and turned, heading down the slope the Vascuul had used. Kael glanced back the way Dravik went but shook his head and quickly followed the little Mahalan scout.

Chapter Sixteen

"What lies beyond the Black Kasym has been a topic of debate for many centuries. Scholars, philosophers, and historians have researched what they could, but the only person with any credibility has been Salabriel Aranasse. A firm believer that life exists in the long abandoned kingdom north of the Kasym, Salabriel has tried for years to launch an expedition north. However, no one has had enough confidence in her findings to finance such a dangerous expedition. Myths and legends tell us that great magic and resources could be found there. Personally, I believe if people and civilization north of the Kasym survived the Cataclysm, we would merely find more of what we ourselves experience every day."

Garren Sallus,
Myths and Legends of Talohna
Volume 1

**ANCIENT KINGDOM
TOWN OF EL' NORAY**

Princess Corleya marveled at the bustling activity as her and Alia entered the small town. The weathered wooden sign outside the village was marked *El' Noray*. Considering no one else in Talohna even knew it existed, the large town was a sight to behold .

"We thought no one was alive up here. The Ancient Kingdom has been cut off from Talohna for so long," Corleya said, turning to her lady-in-waiting. Ever the stoic, Alia shrugged as the Princess continued. "There's a tavern over there. Look, by the market stalls."

"We have no money, Princess, and nothing to trade," Alia replied, keeping her voice low.

"Perhaps we can work for the owner. I'd spend a day peeling root veggies if it meant I got to eat something. I'm starving. The last of that keske you trapped was gone almost two days ago."

Alia merely nodded.

Full dark had settled over the southern tip of the Ancient's long abandoned kingdom, and oil lanterns lit the sign above the tavern door. As the two women approached, Corleya read the sign aloud.

"Dagger's Roost. That's quite the name for a tavern."

"Best be careful, Princess — Corleya. Forgive my lack of formality," Alia said quietly.

"Probably best no one here knows where we are from or who we are," Corleya said, smiling. She grabbed the wooden door handle and pulled. The murmur of steady conversation drifted out as the two women entered the tavern. Corleya stared openly, unable to believe her eyes. Humans and the Elvehn occupied the tables in the two-tier main floor of the tavern. The upstairs, split by a central staircase, was lined with doors to what could only be rented rooms. Thankfully there was no sign of prostitution. She sighed, relieved. It was a legitimate inn.

"Shut the damn door, girlie!" the man behind the bar yelled. He was older with gray hair, but a warm voice held no malice. "You'll let the bloody banshees in. It's cold and dark out, ya know." Smiling, he waved them over.

Corleya quickly closed the door, and both young women approached the bar, nodding to the man.

"Can I help you young ladies tonight?" he asked as he chopped up pieces of meat before reaching and tossing them into a large pot. "Something to eat or drink? Stew will be ready before too long, or if you have a silver, I can cut you a haunch of keske."

Corleya's mouth watered, and her stomach growled at the sight of the large goat roasting on a spit inside the fireplace. "I don't suppose you would happen to need any work done? Rooms cleaned maybe? We are rather short of coin right now," she asked.

"Sorry, but no. My missus takes care of all that. What are you ladies doing here if you have no coin, if you don't mind my asking? El' Noray's a dangerous place for two young women with no means to support themselves. If you wait till morning there's plenty to eat in the forest if you know which plants and mushrooms are safe. You from around here? Your accent is different."

"We're from up north," Corleya offered quickly before the man asked more questions. Hoping to divert suspicion, she added, "It's been a rough trip."

"I can certainly understand that, my dear. The boys from the day shift at the mine should be here right away, and this place will be a lot busier. Perhaps one of them might know a way for you to make some coin—"

The tavern door opened and banged shut, cutting the barman's words short. Corleya glanced back over her shoulder and felt her stomach run cold. A man dressed all in black walked her way. Though his face was hidden by his heavy fur-lined hood, his mere presence made her tremble. His long, black coat just touched the hardwood planks as he walked. When he passed them, all she could make out was his heavily patched chainmail and leather armor, a black goatee trailing to his mid-chest, and a set of strange weapons strapped to his back. She shivered as he nodded to the barman and sat down in the corner table furthest from the tavern's entrance.

"Gods," she whispered, lowering her voice as she turned back to the barman. "Is he a miner?"

"By the Ancients, no. He's a hunter. Been here a couple weeks now. Scares the shit out of me every time he comes in, but he pays in silver or gold. Just be careful around him. He can be a very dangerous man. Leave him alone, though, and he seems to be quite nice. Two local boys learned that the hard way the first night he came to town."

"Dead?" Alia asked.

"The young men? Aye, buried up on dumbass hill. Stupid boys, both of them. May the God's rest their souls easy."

"What does he hunt?" Corleya asked, glancing back toward the man.

"Creatures and monsters, mostly. The nastier the better. Damn bastard for punishment if you ask me, but the miners night shift get to work and home safely now. He killed a banshee the first night he was here. In the last two weeks, he's also taken down two feral weres and a fanged snowcat. Rumor has it he's hunting a White witch for the next town over. He might actually lose that one."

"He's a mage?" Alia asked.

"Wizard. He is Human under that hooded coat and armor," the barman answered. "One of the most powerful wizards I have ever seen, and that is saying something." Corleya nodded and smiled as if she understood, but she began to panic. Too many more references they did not understand, and their story would fall apart. "Sonny and Grath could attest to that, were they still alive," the barman carried on. "Guess you'd have to have a strong magic to hunt the creatures he does."

"Why is he here?" Corleya questioned.

"Says he's waiting for someone to return," he said. "Not sure if they are friend or foe. His business, I guess. For now, most folk are happy he hunts the creatures we cannot. The miners do not take to him, but that is just miners' ego."

"Do you not have an ArchWizard for that up here who." Corleya stopped short, realizing her slip too late.

"Arch wizard? *Up* here? I thought you ladies were from up north? What is an arch wizard?" The front door to the tavern crashed open, and a strong breeze blew through the ground floor, saving Corleya from explaining herself. Miners caked in sparkling black dust entered the tavern, and the last one struggled to close the door.

"Damn winds kicking up, Don," he shouted to the barman as the latch fell, securing the door. They were loud and rough, joking and laughing after a hard day of work.

"My name is Donovan, ladies," the barman told them, handing them each a mug of ale. "Here, on me. Go grab a table, and I'll see if any of the quieter boys might know of where you can find some work."

"Thank you," Corleya said, leading Alia to a table near the hunter. It was the only one vacant and away from the rowdy miners. The two sat and watched as Donovan cut slabs of the roasted keske and filled pitchers of ale to take to the miners. He served the most boisterous men first, finally coming to a table with three younger men.

Lowering his voice, he asked, "You boys know anyone who might be willing to hire a couple of young women for a few days?"

The oldest of the three smiled as he glanced at Corleya and Alia. "The widow, Reece, would be their best bet, Donovan," the man whispered.

"Stay away from the widow," the hunter growled, but offered no more.

"What the spook say?" one of the big miners asked.

"Nothing, Raz," Donovan answered, clearly trying to avoid trouble. The hunter never looked up from his table. "Just wondering if anyone knew where the ladies might find some honest work."

"Ha!" Raz barked, grabbing himself. "There's lots of honest work right here for them. You got plenty of spare rooms right, Don?"

The tavern owner shook his head. "You know I don't allow whoring in my establishment, Raz. Just enjoy your food and ale. Things have been too quiet the last few weeks to start trouble now."

Raz stood. "Perhaps we should ask the ladies whether or not they'd like to earn some coin on their backs."

"That's enough Raz!" Don said. "I promised these ladies my protection while in my tavern." Raz passed Don and gently pushed him into an empty chair at the young men's table as he approached Corleya and Alia. The lady-in-waiting eased her leather whips from her belt. The metal burrs within the braids shone off the candlelight but did not deter the big man.

"What do you say, girls?" Raz questioned. "Interested in earning a lot of coin? My boys and I have plenty to spare. Obsidian mines pay excellent gold."

"Not interested, big man." Corleya said. She turned her back, knowing Alia had her covered if the thug was stupid enough to attack.

"Don't turn your back on me, woman!" He reached for Corleya but stopped short as the hunter rose from his table.

"Go home, Raz" the man barked. "Your pretty little wife is waiting for you."

"What did you say, spook?"

"You heard me. Go home and leave these girls alone. Neither is out of their mid-teens. Leave them be, go home, and fuck your wife if you need it that bad. You should never neglect a woman as pretty as her. You'd not want *her* to wander, would you?"

"You best watch yourself, spook! You ain't looking at two boys tonight."

"I'm not," the hunter replied, stepping clear of his table. "I'm looking at man with a beautiful wife, two kids, and a foreman whose men need him in one of the most dangerous mines in the Ancient Kingdoms. Go home, Raz. I'm tired of killing stupid locals." The insult brought the rest of Raz's crew to their feet, ready for a fight.

"Raz, please, don't do this," Donovan said, pleading. "You didn't see what happened the night Sonny and Grath died. Let it go."

The hunter took a few steps forward and held his hand out to Corleya. "Come stand behind me, please. He won't back down."

"Damn right I won't. Magic-cursed spook, I'm tired of your stench reeking up our tavern. El' Noray and the south have been free of you magic freaks for centuries. It's time it went back to being that way," he said, pulling an obsidian saber from his sheath. Corleya took the hunter's hand and let him guide her behind him to his table. Alia followed backward as she uncurled her whips and waited to see what would happen.

"Last chance, Raz," the hunter offered one last time. "Just go home. I have made entirely too many widows in the short time I have been in this world." The threat caused several of Raz's men to pull obsidian daggers from their waists. The black forged glass weapons were well-known across Talohna. Deadly and razor-sharp, they could puncture even plate armor. The hunter, however, never flinched.

"Do you have any idea what these weapons can do to pathetic chainmail armor, spook?" Raz asked. He smiled as he spun his saber, making it whistle.

"Actually, I do," the hunter replied and removed one of the strange weapons from his back. He held it up for the big man to see. "But they pale compared to what this blade will do to your soul." The long-bladed pick in his hand blazed with magical power. Pulling his hood down and dropping his heavy cloak over a chair, the hunter added, "I prefer killing monsters than making widows."

"You won't be making any widows tonight, wizard." Raz grinned, spinning his blade once more and forcing the hunter back a step. "And don't worry, we'll burn your body to get rid of the filth inside your kind."

Raz attacked, his saber whistling again as it cut the air left and right of where the hunter stood. The hunter dodged the first swipe and side-stepped the second. His hand shot out. Black sparks exploded from his fingers as a wall of compressed hazy-black air followed and slammed into Raz's chest. The big man crashed onto his table, and the hunter hopped to his right as a second miner's sword passed through the space where he stood. The crack of a whip exploded in the air, and the hunter turned to see Alia's whip wrap around the throat of a third miner, his dagger stopped short inches from the hunter's back. The young woman yanked the whip back, tearing open the backstabber's throat. Blood sprayed out as the hunter turned back to Raz. The big miner dragged himself from the broken table, but a fourth man stepped forward and stabbed the hunter in the side. The hunter's pick spun, hooking the knife-man in the stomach.

"*Vai'Karth, Sai Kull Vai*," the hunter hissed as he dropped to a knee, dragging the miner down with him. The blade pulsed. Powered by the spell, the blade slowly pulled the miner's soul from his body. The wound in the hunter's side began to close even as the miner screamed in agony and stabbed the hunter, again. Alia's whip cracked as it lashed out, driving back two more armed miners.

"Stop! By the Gods! Please, stop," Donovan yelled.

The hunter tore his weapon free, leaving the miner alive. Struggling to stand, the hunter yanked the black dagger from his side and let it drop to the floor. His left hand filled with black lightning. Purple sparks hissed as they fell to the floor. "Take your men and leave, Raz," he barked. "Get help for the wounded."

"Help? That bitch killed Sem, and you damn near did the same for Rollins! You gotta pay for that."

The magic sizzling in the hunter's hand grew brighter. "Make your fucking choice, Raz. Take them for help or die here with them."

"Do as he says, Raz," Donovan pleaded. "You can save Rollins if you take him to the widow, but you have to go now! Her cottage is a fifteen-minute run."

"Fine, dammit!" Several of the other miners lifted Rollins while the others carried Sem's body. Alia wrapped her whips up and tied them to her waist.

Raz stared at her and pointed his finger. "You brought this on yourself, foolish man," she said before he could say anything.

"Enough, Alia," Corleya whispered. Gently touching her arm, Corleya slowly shook her head.

Raz stared back and forth between the hunter to Alia. "Better run, freaks, all of you. You won't get far once the mine dogs are turned loose." He warned them, slowly walking backward to the inn door. "Your spell failed, wizard. You're still bleeding. Tracking you through the forest with those hounds will be easy. We will come for you."

The hunter scoffed. "Then you will die in the forest."

"Just go, Raz," Donovan pleaded a second time. "The widow's hut is too far away to be wasting time." The big miner pointed at the hunter and the girls, again, before whirling around and disappearing through the door.

Corleya stepped forward as the hunter's magic vanished into nothing. "I know what you are," she told him. "You're a DeathWizard."

"You don't know what you're talking about—"

"You are so very wrong, young woman," Donovan interrupted. "He's a child of the Lost."

"Neither do you, Don. Are my things ready?" the hunter said as he shook his head and eased himself into his Orotaq cloak.

"Yes, most of it. Some of the meat is still drying, but the snowcat pelt is done curing."

"Good. Give me what you have. We need to go." The barman nodded and left.

"We?" Corleya asked. "We're not going anywhere with you. Your kind are the worst scourge in all of Cethosian history." She pulled a small dagger from her waist as Donovan returned.

"Cethos?" he asked. "You... you are from south of the Breach! From south of the Black Kasym? How did you get here?"

"We were on one of the ships that brought the Ancients home," Corleya lied.

The hunter spat on the floor. "They haven't landed yet, and they're certainly not the Ancients."

"They are the Ri'Tek," Donovan said.

The hunter turned, stepping toward the barman. "You've heard of them?"

"Clearly you are from the south as well," Donovan said. "Do you not know of them south of the Breach?" the barman asked.

"No," Corleya said. "We know them as the Ancients. They built the wonders of Talohna. Modern magic is what it is because of them. South of the Kasym, they are worshiped as the founders of civilization and modern magic."

Donovan shook his head, his skin growing pale. "If your people worship the Ri'Tek in any way, then your people are already doomed, young lady."

"We have to go," the hunter said, turning to Donovan. "If I come to you later, will you tell me what you know of them?"

"I would, but if you return here, you will be killed. Besides, all our history is founded by stories told through our elders—passed down over the centuries, millennia even. Life here in the south is simple, and magic is very rare and very feared. The northern half of the land is another story. My mother's mother told us of the far past," he said, handing a pack of supplies to the hunter.

"We're still not going with you," Corleya told him. "I saw that black and purple corruption in your magic."

Donovan snorted. "Foolish girl. That was the magic of the Lost, not corruption."

"What are you talking about? I've heard of the Lost," the hunter barked, and grabbed the barman.

"Easy, young man," Donovan whispered. "Your magic... my grandmother called it the magic of the Lost Gods."

"What?" the hunter snapped. As if regaining some control over his temper, he released the barman and his voice calmed. "I thought the Lost were a people. I've never heard of such a thing."

"Us, either," Corleya added. "He is a DeathWizard. No one south of the Kasym can use magic like that unless they're a DeathWizard. A Kai'Sar—a wizard who walks with death."

The barman sighed, shaking his head. "Oh, you foolish young girl. Kai and Sar are Ri'Tek words, yes. The language is still used today, especially far up north. Kai means walk and Sar means death. Which comes first or second and what words go before and come after could make that phrase mean a dozen different things. That is all."

"What else do you know?" the hunter growled.

Donovan continued, "You don't have much time."

"Quickly, then."

"I was taught that far in the past the Ri'Tek were punished by the gods, stripped of their magic for using it in a vile manner. But in doing so, the gods destroyed themselves."

"What about the Lost?" the hunter prompted.

"Yes. Not all the Ri'Tek were punished. Some lived by the laws of the gods, so they were spared. Because they still had their magic, they went into hiding. With the gods gone, the 'Lost' people of the Ri'Tek used their magic to ascend into today's gods of Talohna."

"That can't be right," Corleya breathed out.

"What does any of that have to do with my magic?" the hunter demanded.

"You don't see?" the barman said, staring at the hunter. "The Ri'Tek... the Lost... their original magic was believed to be black and purple and very rarely, silver."

"No, that can't be..." the hunter shook his head adamantly.

"What is your name, young man?" Donovan asked.

"Kael," he said. "My name is Kael Symes."

"If our history is true, then you are a child born of the Lost Gods of Talohna, Kael." Turning to Corleya and Alia, the barman added, "You will be safe with him, ladies, but if you stay here, Raz and his boys will hang you both for killing that man. *Eventually*," he said, emphasizing the last word as he pointed to the smeared blood on the floor.

Corleya nodded. "We have no choice, then. Alia, help Kael. That stab wound cannot slow us down. We'll find a safe place to stop and bind it when we can. Give me the bag of supplies," she said. Taking the bag from Kael, she turned to the barman. "You'd better be right about that history, barkeep."

"I assure you, mistress," Donovan stated. "It is the history taught to all of those who live on this side of the Breach. It is true as I know it."

Corleya nodded once more and rushed out the inn door leading the way.

"Kael?" Donovan yelled after them.

Kael turned to look back with Alia's help. "What?"

"Many people on this side of the breach believe the Lost still exist. There have been stories over the centuries of strange people helping those in need, especially in the north. The encounters are rare, but I do believe the Lost exist."

"Thank you, Don," Kael said as Alia turned him around, and they left. "For everything."

DASATER MINING COMPLEX
NORTH OF EL' NORAY

"Are you sure about this, Raz?" Daff Cole said. The mine boss shook his head.

"Of course, I'm sure. Rollins and Sem are both dead. We need to find their killers and now."

"Raz, if I turn these mongrels lose with the blood on that dagger for a scent, you won't get justice... you'll just have three dead killers." He turned to the dog cages and grabbed his ring of keys. Crossbred using magic and the northern white cats, the three hundred-pound dogs had originally been created for war but were now trained to protect miners from the Mahala and the odd Orotaq raiding party.

"I do not care," Raz sneered. "Give them the scent and turn them loose."

The lock clicked open, and the hound boss turned back to Raz. "All right, but we're even after this. My debt to you is clear. All my mutts had better come back alive, too. How many do you want?"

"Six should be enough." Daff handed him six whistles. "You ran dog crew before your promotion. It's the only reason I'm doing this. You remember?"

"Of course," Raz snapped and handed out whistles to the men with him. "One whistle for each mutt."

"It is the only thing that will bring them to heal, Raz. Don't lose even one whistle, or innocent people could get hurt. Even you."

"Yeah, yeah. Stop worrying, Daff. The only people getting hurt are the magic freak and his new female friends."

Daff wet a rag and ran it over the dagger transferring the dried blood. Handing the dagger back to Raz, he walked down the row of cages and let each dog catch the blood's scent. Once the sixth dog had the scent, Daff reached up and pulled a metal handle so all six cages opened.

"Kill them!" Raz roared and blew the whistle twice.

The massive dogs bolted, disappearing into the forest as Raz and a dozen men followed, most with heavy crossbows already loaded.

TIR NEANNE FOREST
ANCIENT KINGDOM

Kael glanced back over his shoulder. The baying of hunting dogs had faded to nothing. "I can't hear the dogs," he said. "Let's stop." Alia led him into a small clearing with a fallen log and helped him to sit. The entire time she had been helping him, she never sheathed her dagger. He struggled with the straps on his armor as he watched her step into the dense cover of the forest.

"Let me help," Corleya offered. Alia returned, staying within easy striking distance as the Princess approached. Kael smiled. They may have been acting friendly, but he could see the fear of him in their eyes.

Corleya helped him shrug out of his long coat so they could get to the buckles. "We can't stop for long, and that wound will only slow us until we bind it."

"There's a clean cloth in the bag Don gave us." The buckles came free and Corleya shimmied the chainmail armor over his head.

"Shirt, too," she added, her fingers touching the hilt of her small blade. Kael eased off his shirt, earning a gasp. "Gods. Some of these scars are from fatal wounds."

"Yeah, they are," he said.

Shaking her head, she ran her finders over a large scar shaped like a bite mark. The strange v-shaped scar marked the middle of the bite still made his stomach run cold.

"What did this?" she asked.

"Mahala. Many years ago," he answered while she tore strips of clean cloth and began binding the stab wound on his right side. "They clamp their mouths to you and then this barbed tongue digs in."

He gasped as she pressed against the garish wound. "Please. I don't need to hear any more. This puncture is deep as well," she said. "It won't stop bleeding."

"It'll heal. See if Don managed to track down any turrin moss in those supplies." Taking a deep breath, he winced.

"There are no plants at all," she said, digging through the pack. "I'm more worried about the pain slowing you down."

"It won't. I've had worse."

"I can see that. I'm sorry. There," she whispered as she finished.

"Thank you. let's go." He put his armor back on and stretched lightly. The wound pulled at his side and ached, but he would be able to walk and maybe even run without help.

Alia stepped back toward the trees. "The hounds should be back in range by now."

Corleya frowned. "Why can't we hear them?"

Kael stared out into the trees, probing with his senses. They had been extremely unreliable since he woke in the crypt below the Dyrannai Forest, but he did not know why. Whether it was from the strange energy pulsing through the earth in the Ancient Kingdom or if it was one of the many prices he would pay for returning from the dead, it did not matter. It was irritating not being able to rely on his senses to figure out his surroundings.

"I don't know," he said, "but we need to keep—" Kael turned toward a rustle in the bushes as he put up his hood. A giant brown and white dog exploded from the underbrush. Its massive jaws clamped around his arm and pinned it to his throat. Locking its jaws tight around both his arm and neck, the weight of the beast drove Kael to the forest floor. The dog's back legs raked his stomach as if it were a jungle cat. His mail tore, but no pain followed. Quickly putting his knees together to protect his groin, the mutt clawed at his thighs, tearing furrows down each leg.

"Kael," Corleya shrieked as two other dogs followed their leader into the small clearing.

Kael struggled to hold back the dog. He was already weak from the stab wound and blood loss, leaving him to fight a losing battle. The dog's jaws crushed his arm into his throat, cutting off his breath while claws pounded into his stomach. Pain followed as the torn mail offered less protection. Digging the fingers of his free hand into the mutt's throat, he closed his eyes and concentrated.

Jasala's words echoed in his mind... *we are limited only by our imagination.*

His eyes snapped open, and the vine-like markings in his skin fired back to life. Though they had not moved since before his death, the pain was still like an old friend coming to visit. The vines tore their way down his arms and out his hands, burrowing into the big dog as Kael swallowed the agony of his torn flesh.

The hound released him and pulled, dragging Kael to his feet by the vines embedded in its flesh. Like some demented marionette, the dog fought and snarled, snapping and chewing on the vines. Kael yanked the vines back and thorns burst from each vine, shredding the mutt instantly. Turning to help the others, he saw both were holding the dogs off with their blades but barely.

Kael knelt and pushed his palms against the ground. The vines writhing from his hands raced away, exploding from the dirt under the two dogs. Curling around them, he watched in awe as endless vines wound its way around the helpless animals. The thorns snapped out and tore into the dogs until nothing, but pieces fell to the forest floor. The vines disappeared back into the ground, seeking him out. He stood as they slid back into his flesh and settled flat to his skin, appearing to be nothing more than tattoos once again.

"Mother Mylla," Corleya whispered. The fear in her voice quickly changed to concern as he collapsed. "Kael!"

"I really am sick of big dogs with big goddamned claws," he muttered through clenched teeth.

Corleya reached his side. "Alia! Help me!"

"Any spurting blood?" she asked.

"I don't think so."

"Then he'll live," she stated, bending down closer with her dagger in hand.

"Stomach first," Kael hissed, peeling back what was left of his chainmail.

Corleya gasped as if unable to find her voice.

"That bad?" he asked.

"You are intact," Alia offered and turned back to watch the forest.

"Flesh wound then," Kael replied, trying to smile.

Corleya pressed a clean cloth to his stomach. "We're almost out of clean cloth, Kael. Gods, your legs are ripped wide open."

He pointed to the bag of supplies. "Just cover the wounds and use the rope in there to wrap my legs. We have to get moving before more of those things find us."

Corleya nodded and followed his orders. "Never seen dogs like that," she whispered as she emptied the supply bag and grabbed the rope.

"I have. Similar at least," Kael spat. "Magic does more goddamn harm than it does good."

"How can you say that?" Corleya asked as she started wrapping the rope around his right leg. "It's created amazing beauty and wonders. It helped us become who we are."

"It has destroyed far more than it has ever created."

"I disagree," she began.

He put up his hand to stop her. "I have been fighting for so many years, I'm tired of it," he told her. "How about we start over? You already know it, but my name is Kael. And you are?"

"Princess Corleya of Cethos," she answered honestly.

"Princess," Alia snarled. "We have tried hard to keep that secret."

"Hush, Alia," she ordered. "What does it matter now?"

"Nice to meet you, Princess," Kael said and laughed lightly. "I've never met a princess. Been hunted by the King of Cethos, but never met a princess before."

"I am sorry for that," Corleya offered as a sheepish frown marred her face.

"Why would you?" he asked. "It was long before you were born."

"What do you mean?" she questioned back. "Your name is Kael. You are Giddeon Zirakus' son. My father is Joran Bale. He sent the ArchWizard after you."

"That's impossible. I know time passes faster there, but... how long was I gone?"

"I can't answer that, Kael," she replied. "I don't know where you've been. If it helps, my father sent Giddeon after you about a year ago, perhaps a little longer."

"Only a year?" he asked, but it was not directed at her. "You were the one they were looking for in the Wildlands."

"Yes," she answered and blushed a vivid red. "Not my proudest moment."

He shook his head as thoughts tumbled over and over through his mind. Only a year meant Giddeon was still alive. After all this time, he might have the chance to get his hands on Giddeon and make him pay for the misery he caused.

"You know who I am?"

Kael nodded. "I came across Giddeon and his daughter in the Wildlands, but he abandoned you to hunt me. Him and your father hunted me to the very end."

"Your kind nearly destroyed this world and the one south of here."

"But *I* didn't. Even still, both you and your protector have kept a blade in hand, even when I'm torn apart." Kael sighed. "Magic changes you, but lack of magic changes you more so. I wasn't meant to handle magic. Because *your* kind played with my life, magic has destroyed everything I have ever cared about."

"Not all magic is like that, Kael," Corleya said. Finished wrapping his left leg, she sat back on her heels and stared at him.

"It might as well be, Princess. As long as I'm alive, your kind will hunt me for nothing more than a distorted history and the magic I have. Who I am doesn't matter."

"You know little of our history, Kael."

"I know it better than you do, and you know nothing of me... but honestly? I don't care. Help me up. We have to get out of here." Alia turned and offered her hand. Giving him her shoulder as the Princess led the way, they raced into the forest.

In minutes, the baying of dogs returned. Looking over his shoulder, Kael tripped and dragged Alia to the ground with him. His senses picked up her fear and panic as her elbow crashed into his mouth. Freeing herself from his legs, she jumped back to her feet with her dagger pointed at his chest.

"Alia, stop!" Corleya snapped. "He just tripped."

Kael shook his head as he looked up at the mercenary. "They'll hang me right alongside you, girl," he told her. Corleya helped him stand as more hounds barked from the opposite direction.

"They got ahead of us," Alia said.

Corleya shook her head. "We'll never outrun them. We have to fight."

"I can... can barely stand." Kael struggled to get the words out.

"Then, you die first," the mercenary snapped.

"There's another way," Kael offered, "but you'll have to trust me."

"Never," Alia sneered.

"How?"

"No, Princess," Alia insisted.

"I might be able to jump us out of here," Kael said. His voice trembled, and he was not surprised when Alia caught it.

"You offer this now? Convenient." She frowned at him.

"Hardly," Kael scoffed. "I've never jumped as far as we'd need to for us to be safe, and we'll be jumping through the Black Kasym and its magic. But these hicks will chase us all the way to the Black Kasym if we don't do something. They know this forest better than us."

"Are you talking about a realm jump?" Corleya asked. "Like the Fae myths and stories?"

"Similar, yes," Kael answered. "Jasala told me how it works, but I've never actually tried it over such a distance or through such volatile magic as the Kasym."

"No," Alia barked a second time.

Kael growled. "Either we die here..."

"Or risk the jump," Corleya finished for him when his voice trailed off.

"And likely still die," Kael stated.

Corleya nodded. "We'll definitely die if we stay."

"Where? Where will be safe?" Alia hissed quietly.

"Trust me," Kael said, offering them both a hand.

"Princess?"

Corleya took Kael's hand. "What choice do we have, Alia? Die here or try getting to safety." The lady-in-waiting nodded and took Kael's other hand reluctantly. Her eyes narrowed as he pulled them closer.

"Both of you take a step with me," he instructed.

A crack of power rolled through the forest as the trio stepped forward and vanished. A cloud of black and purple smoke exploded around a bright white light.

The magic faded, leaving the forest empty.

Chapter Seventeen

"The last links of mail 'ave been scoured with enchantments and the leather properly treated. I have hammered steel and sewn supple leather for nae on four centuries and ne'r ave I been more proud of a set of armor than the one 'fore me. Kinrai chainmail links heat-tapped in Dragonfire 'til the tell tale orange and purple veins have retreated to within the metal have created a n'er unbreakable chain of linked mail. Dragon runes mark the leather and Fae magic been weaved through all threadings. Aye, I hope one day it shae been worn by a warrior worthy of 'er. I 'ave named 'er Unity as tribute to all who created 'er. She will be this smith's shiny glory."

Dagor Dragonforge, Arkum Zul's last dragon fire blacksmith. Journal entries found in the Arcane Library catacombs, year and date unknown.

THE BLACK ARC
THE FORSAKEN LANDS

Kael stumbled as he stepped out of the magical jump that carried him and the two young women through the outer edges of the Ether. Though he did not understand it, he knew such magic skirted the laws of god magic in Talohna. No price was demanded when he used such magic. As Don's words returned to him, he finally began to understand why his magic did the abnormal things it did. He understood why people feared him so much.

Corleya and Alia both collapsed on the ground, the stress of traveling so far by magic was more than they could handle. The rift closed behind him, and he released the shield he had used to protect them while passing through the Kasym. He, however, had gone without any shielding of his own and the price hit him hard. An explosion of pain coursed through his body, and he dropped to his knees clenching his teeth. The waves continued to throb from head-to-foot for several minutes as his stomach turned cold with panic. He began to wonder if the price he paid would be permanent.

"I am going to kill you, wizard," Alia said as she wretched.

His body shook from the stress, but he could not get his tongue to work.

"Why is the world spinning?" Corleya gasped out. Her fingers dug into the dirt as if she were trying to re-center herself to the earth.

Kael snorted as the pain started to subside. "We... we... we..." His brain sparked as if short circuiting, and he rubbed his forehead repeatedly. "Just traveled... traveled two continents... through the Black Kasym... I can't believe... we... we're alive. I am not doing that ever again."

"Wish dead, be better," Alia groaned and gagged.

"Try... try traveling from the afterlife to the living," Kael mumbled. Shaking his head as the last of the startling shock from the Kasym faded, he groaned and fell on his face.

"Where are we?" Alia growled.

"The first and only place I have felt welcome since I arrived here," he said. Forcing himself to his feet, he offered Alia a hand. She frowned and ignored it. Standing on her own, she quickly helped Corleya up.

"Holy shit!" Corleya whispered as she pointed up. "That's..."

"The Black Arc," Kael finished for her as he rubbed his aching head. "The magical tower Jasala Vyshaan built to help her keep the Ri'Tek locked away."

Corleya gasped. "My father has a painting in his personal study."

"Welcome back, Master." Kael recognized the raspy voice even though he had not heard it in over two hundred years.

Alia yanked her dagger from its sheath and placed her body between the voice and Corleya.

"What in the Nine Hells is that?" the Princess asked, her voice trembling nearly as much as she was.

"Easy," Kael barked, "they won't hurt you."

The three WraithLords bowed. "You are severely wounded, Master. Come."

"You have got be kidding me," Corleya said.

"Wraith butler," Alia quipped.

Kael stepped inside. "WraithLords," he corrected. "We'll be safe here until we recover." He entered the stairwell down to Jasala's bedroom.

"You don't understand, Kael," Corleya said as she followed. "I need to return home. My father needs to know I'm alive."

He nodded. "I do understand. Just give me a few days to heal, and I'll escort you home myself. Though, I doubt you can guarantee my safety?"

"No," Corleya said, and he could hear the sadness in her voice. "My father wouldn't listen to me about Alia, and he won't about you either, no matter what I say."

"Wise man, our king," Alia added.

Sighing as he struggled not to lose his temper, Kael shot the mercenary a frown. "Your... lady-in-waiting saved my life in El' Noray, but I'm tired of listening to her shit. I will take you home, and we'll be settled. Even your father's Third Pillar won't be able to stop me from jumping out of Corynth once I know you're safe."

"We need to leave now, Kael," Corleya persisted.

"Neither of you will get out of these lands without me. Jasala's creations still roam loose here. It's a three day walk to the border. Believe me, they make those dogs up north look like cuddly pets. Then, you'd have to get through the barrier fog and walk to Corynth. Another jump so soon will kill me and leave you both stranded, lost within the magic. A couple days rest, no more."

"There are other ways, Master," the lead WraithLord offered as they stepped off the stairs into Jasala's study.

"How?" Kael asked, staring at the wall-size fireplace and the hidden room he knew contained Jasala's body. At least he knew why her body was so perfectly preserved.

"You have acquired the strength needed to free us. In exchange, you may take my soul to heal yourself and my brothers can return to their rest."

"I can't," Kael said. "I promised to release you all from your torment, not just two of you."

"You can," the WraithLord replied. "I was Jasala's first creation. More of who I am passed into this body than should have. Returning my soul to the afterlife will be a punishment. We committed horrors here... the weight of it will crush my soul once it is complete."

"I understand that," Kael said. "Give me an hour to think on it, fair enough?"

The WraithLord bowed and all three turned to guard the foot of the stairwell.

Kael waved the women over. "Come on. Let's get some rest so I can decide whether ruining another soul is the right thing to do." He grasped the lever behind the big fireplace and pulled, revealing the hidden stairs to the lower bedroom. Heading down, he did not bother to wait for them.

Arriving at the bottom, he smiled and removed his Orotaq cloak and battered armor. Nothing in the bedroom had changed. The bed, nightstands, alchemy table... all were the same. As his gaze passed over the large armoire, his eyes widened. The magic-laden black chainmail and leather armor inside called to him.

Remembering what had happened last time, he approached the armoire. His fingers brushed over the ornate carvings, which resembled his own markings. It made him smile, again, even though it hurt to do so. Jasala's deathflower never grew past her chest, yet she had hand carved the wooden armoire with markings to match the different stages of a DeathWizard's growth. Some were exactly like the ones on his chest, even though they had changed after traveling through the Tree of Life back to the land of the living. The deathflower on his chest was gone, replaced by a detailed replica of the tree of life.

"What are you looking at?" Corleya asked, her words breaking through his thoughts.

"Remembering."

"Remembering Jasala?"

"Yes. She never stood a chance. This world believes she was a monster when she willingly offered her life to give this world another five thousand years without the Ri'Tek."

Alia snorted. "All it cost was millions of innocent lives."

Kael frowned. "Yet she saved tens of millions — or more — from enslavement and worse."

"She turned this world inside out, Kael," Corleya said. "She resorted to the darkest magic when cornered. That is all she will ever be remembered for."

"She knows that, and she has paid for it every day for those five thousand years. She still helped me get back here knowing she couldn't come with. That's who she really was or is."

Another scoff from Alia made him look her way. "DeathWizard lies."

Kael stared at her. "I am many things. A liar is not one of them. I will make you a deal, Princess Corleya. As soon as I am able, I will return you home. You agree to do everything you can so that I can leave without any problems."

"Even more lies!" Alia snapped. "You want time to recover. Do not make this deal, Princess. We should leave now, avoid DeathWizard's tricks." Alia hissed as she carried the last word for several seconds. It was the first real emotion he had seen from the young woman.

He turned to her and scoffed. "You are aware that if I meant you any harm, I would have done so already," he said. "My weapons embedded in your stomach would heal my own wounds in seconds."

Corleya nodded. "I saw you do that back at the inn. The man you stabbed… you tried *not* to kill him even though doing so would have healed you completely, wouldn't it have?"

With his eyes still locked on Alia, he nodded. "Yes. And, yet, your *lady* here, killed a man when she didn't really have to. Things are not always as they seem are they, mercenary?"

"No, they're not," Corleya said quietly. "That is why, I agree. Once you are able, take us home."

"Please, Princess," Alia hissed again.

"It's all right, Alia."

"Think about what your father would say," Alia insisted.

"My father said to kill Kael." Staring at Alia, she added, "He said the same to you, and I risked everything to save your life. That is why we are both here now. My father is not always right, even if his word is law. Maybe I can learn something from this nightmare we have been living, so it may help us some day. I have the feeling our world is about to change more than at any other time in its history. Even you can't deny that, Alia. The Ancients are back, and I'm starting to think they are not what people have been worshiping, praying, and wishing for all these millennia. How could we have been so wrong?" The bronze-skinned woman finally backed down and bowed to the princess.

"I agree," he said, and paused as he considered addressing her other question. "Because the years have a way of distorting some truths and burying others. History gets lost over time in any dimension. Now, get some sleep. You two can have the bed."

Kale could feel their immense exhaustion. Corleya stretched out on the bed and sighed as Alia eased herself into the bed. She wrapped her arms around Corleya. Their excitement and fear faded as the exhaustion settled in, and they drifted off to sleep.

Kael lay back against the side of the bed and stared at the armoire. Corleya's soft snores reminded him of Ember, and it tore at his heart and soul, but they were short-lived as she fell into a deeper sleep. Minutes passed as he tried to wrap his head around the drastic time shift difference between the afterlife and Talohna. A year and no news of Ember and Max. He knew what he saw in the vortex that began his nightmare, but at least now he could find the real answers. He would take the Princess home and then track Giddeon. It was the only course of action he could think of that might give him some answers, and if not, the ArchWizard would die. It was long past time. Exhaustion finally took over his mind as well. He yawned and closed his eyes.

Jerking awake, he yawned, unsure of how long he had slept as he leaned against the bed. Something brought him from sleep, and he recognized the all too familiar itch in his mind returning. He stared at the armoire. It was as if the closet called to him through its locked doors.

Perhaps it was the armor calling to him. The Vai'Karth had called out to him in a similar way to help him find them. However, with the armor, it was a strong feeling instead of actual words. It should have terrified him — if he touched the suit of armor, again, and he wasn't strong enough, the defensive reaction would kill him. It did not scare him — not in the slightest bit. A large part of him vibrated with excitement at what the armor was. Jasala had explained it, though she had never laid eyes on it. Her Guardian had chased after it and the Vai'Karth for five years. It was clear she had found the armor and then hidden it away after Jasala's death and the Cataclysm.

Only those who have walked the darkest of paths can wear it, Kael. Walking from death to life is a path darker than any other. The armor will be yours once you return to the living world.

Jasala had told him several stories about the armor on the night they hid at the bottom of a sweltering hot cave in the ice covered 7th Hell. The darkest path. Knowing he had heard those words before, he shrugged out of his Orotaq cloak and reached inside the deep pocket. He grasped the letter written by Jasala that he had found it when he first arrived at the Black Arc so long ago. His heart hammered as he touched the second letter—the one he had never been able to read. Taking a deep breath, he opened the first and read it, again:

> *To the next of my line…*
> *Faithfully, Jasala Vyshaan,*
>
> *The wisdom herein is reserved for the darkest of wizards only, those who have acquired the power to walk the blackest of paths. I cannot tell you what it says for I have never acquired such power for myself, though not for lack of trying. If you have found this letter, it means that I failed, and my purpose is now yours.*
> *This tower is known as the Black Arc. It, and all that it contains, are now yours as well. But beware: It holds many secrets. Some will be many years beyond your abilities regardless of your age and experience, it is my creation, and it still holds many mysteries even to me. The enchantment on this letter will let you know when you have attained the power required to master all, including the Arc. Always keep it close to the death-flower over your heart. Only then can it speak to you. Be careful. This world has grown to hate our kind. Do not let anything from this tower fall into the hands of our enemies, please. And remember, above all, even if it means giving your life, the locks must never be allowed to weaken again.*

Kael shook his head. The letter held so much more meaning now that he understood it.

"I'm sorry I didn't understand, Jasala," he muttered, knowing from experience that she could likely hear him. "Two of the locks are broken. The Ri'Tek are out. All I can do is hunt them and kill them one at a time." He cleared the memories before the uncontrollable magic pulled him in and glanced down as he held the second letter to his heart where his deathflower used to be. It did not matter how many times he remembered that the tattoo markings had transformed from a deathflower into the Tree of Life, it still surprised him when he saw it. Magic rushed through his mind as the powerful enchantment on the letter activated. Strange letters and symbols rolled through his consciousness but lasted only seconds before fading. Opening the letter, his eyes quickly adjusted to the transformed letters and marks. He could read it as if it had been written in English — as if he'd spoken the strange language his entire life.

"Incredible," he whispered. He started to read:

I know not where this missive will end up, but with some luck and guidance from the gods, perhaps these last words will someday reach one of my kind. Someone who has acquired the power needed to successfully complete the experiment we began.

We tried... all six of us tried to gain the power to walk from death with the magic of the old gods in our hands, but we failed time and again.

It seems the process begins when our magic and markings grow. We have concluded that only when the tattoo-like designs have stopped growing will we be ready for the transition. However, we will not proceed further at this time. Venturing further means dying and none of our markings are close enough. Though only my arms and face remain clear of the vines, our experiences have shown it could still be decades or more before the vines are complete.

Saving the Lesser Races from extermination is more important now and all our focus is there. There are six of us that have reached beyond our twentieth year of life without falling to the vile corruption that marks our souls. We six have created a way to imprison the Ri'Tek for what we hope will be several decades. By using the dimensional magic, I discovered some time ago, myself and my fellow wizards will use it to open six doorways to a place we have been calling the Still dimension. It is a place that has a stasis effect on all living material. The Fae and the Dragons have created a powerful attraction spell that will pull all the Ri'Tek armies into the Still dimension by force once the doorways are opened. The coalition armies will deal with the few remaining enemies that may be left afterward.

The Fae are extremely upset about opening six doorways to one dimension, especially considering three of us have each opened one already, but they can see there is no other way even though such practices are against their fundamental beliefs.

The Six, as we have become known, will use our life force and the energy from our souls to lock the doorways behind the enemy. Hopefully, it will give the Lesser races enough time to find a permanent solution or perhaps, even a way to make a lasting peace with the Ri'Tek. The locks will eventually weaken as our soul energy dissipates and we cease to exist. It is a small price to pay to save the races of Talohna from extinction, even if only for a time.

When the locks weaken, and they will, a Guardian may instruct one of our kind on how to strengthen them by using their own soul to create a Sepulchre locking system. It will buy a little more time, but it is not a solution. My people were not created as sacrifices to keep the Ri'Tek locked away. A permanent solution must be found.

The power of the old gods is the only answer we can come up with. Which leads us back to the study of our powers: to walk from the realm of death and somehow bring with you the magic of the old gods. If you can achieve this, only the Lost can teach you to use the magic you bring back. Find them and pray to the old gods and the new that the pacifist purists will help you. Because no one else can.

Asa N'ahai

Kael stared at the letter as emotions crashed through him. The one man who could have helped him find the Lost was already long gone. He shook his head at his own bad luck and hoped Dravik could find them. Quickly realizing the barman from north of the Black Kasym, Donovan, could be right, he shook his head, again. The magic of the old gods... it worried him.

The letter fell from Kael's shaking fingers. Looking to his hand, he called forth the strange magic he had brought back with him from the afterlife. A silver and purple ore formed in his hand, but as if sentient, it immediately lashed out at him. Just as it did the first time, it tried to attack the nearest target. Kael snuffed the magic and frowned. He would eventually have to go back north of the Kasym and find the Lost if he wanted answers… that worried him.

Rolling his shoulders, Kael got to his feet and winced from his wounds. Answers could wait until after he examined the armor hidden in the armoire. Tired of waiting, he touched the armoire's wooden door. This time, the intricate designs reacted to his magic. The vines moved with a life all their own. Coiling and slithering, the vines slid out of the way, and the lock clacked. The doors slowly opened on their own. The full armor set hung untouched on the back wall. The black chainmail and leather armor stared back at him as if daring him to touch it.

Nervous?

"No," he whispered. Akai had been uncharacteristically quiet for weeks since their return to Talohna.

I may not have been created by the Dwarven people, but this armor clearly was, and it was made for your kind. You needn't fear it.

"Needn't?" Kael snorted quietly. "You sound more like me every day."

Yeah. Magical side effect of the Ether's power in the living world as it bleeds through you into me.

"Great. Another conscience. Just what I needed."

Akai scoffed. *Don't flatter yourself. Your influence isn't that strong.* He felt the spirit's presence slip away and knew he would say no more.

Taking a deep breath, Kael entered the armoire, going to the armor. The spells engraved within the links of chainmail sparkled as the light hit them. Silver vines identical to his own shone lightly along the leather's surface. A compulsion pulled at his soul and created an intense desire to possess the armor. Without thinking, he reached out and touched the chainmail links. Unlike last time, however, nothing happened. He chuckled to himself and closed the armoire door behind him.

The sleeveless chainmail and leather cuirass slipped over his shoulders, fitting perfectly as he buckled the straps together to secure it. Kael took the armored pants from the hook and quickly learned they were made from two sets of heavy leather sown together with light chainmail woven inside. Additional chainmail reinforced any weak points around the inner and outer thighs, knees, and even the shins. Surprisingly, though, they weighed very little. After removing his own worn out leather pants, he pulled the armor on. Again, it fit perfectly as if tailored specifically for him. He slid his feet into the heavy boots and buckled them before he pushed a black leather bracer over his left wrist. He gasped and dropped to a knee as the last bracer settled into place. Pain exploded from the stab wound in his side and forced him flat to the floor.

"Akai?" he moaned. The spirit remained quiet even though Kael could feel him.

"Answer me, you bastard," Kael hissed through grinding teeth, but again he was answered by silence. With no help from the ancient entity, he rolled onto his back and forced his left hand through the gap in the buckles of the cuirass to feel the wound as the pain slowly faded. "What the hell?" he mumbled. The wound was nearly healed, and in the following minute, the pain vanished. All that remained was a raised welt of scar tissue.

"Ah, shit," he whispered. "That was a bit too familiar." Memories of Dasal came storming back to the front of his mind, and he fought to hold them back but failed as he thrashed on his back. The searing agony of a crushed skull flooded his body and mind, and a dark-haired woman's face appeared above him. "Sephi." He gasped. He barely managed to recall her name as she pushed his head back and poured a vile acid down his throat. He screamed as the pain tripled.

"Kael! Wake up. What's wrong with him?" Corleya asked without turning to Alia.

The mercenary shook her head. "Dying. With luck," she quipped.

Her words broke through Kael's flashback. He used it to ground himself to reality, and finally, he regained control over his own mind. "Not yet," he grumbled. "Jesus, I'd hoped these memories would be less intense after coming back."

"Coming back from where?" Alia asked.

"Doesn't matter," he answered when he saw Corleya's mouth open. Instead of revealing his return from death, the Princess offered him a hand up. He accepted, letting her pull him to his feet. "Thank you," he said, getting a nod in return. "How long was I out?"

"I am not sure," Corleya said, looking to Alia.

The woman shrugged and pointed to herself and the Princess. "Slept eight hours," she offered.

Kael nodded and slowly readjusted his new armor. "Okay."

"It fits?"

"Yes, Princess," Kael answered. "Perfectly in fact. Though, it seems to be enchanted with some kind of healing magic."

Advanced Fae accelerated healing to be exact.

Now you answer, you bastard, Kael said inside his head, not wanting to make Alia and Corleya any more suspicious.

I felt what you felt. Even if I had wanted to, I could not interrupt the magic as the armor bonded to you. As well as it being a Fae enchantment, healing your side was meant as a test of your will.

"Thanks for the warning, asshole."

You think the Dwarven armor-smiths and Fae enchantresses and whomever else helped make this set would just let anyone wear it? Jesus, Kael. You should know better by now.

Kael shook his head and his mind swarmed with disbelief. "You can drop the act. You already told me my influence isn't that strong. No one likes to argue with themselves."

Then don't, Einstein.

"Now you're just being an ass."

Different from an asshole, is it? Moving up in the world. Akai laughed and went silent as Kael felt his presence retreat.

"Gotta have the last word, huh? Worse than being bloody married," he said, knowing the spirit could still hear him.

"Kael?" Corleya prompted, bringing him back.

"Careful, Princess," Alia said. The mercenary pulled her to the side and drew a small dagger.

"Yeah, I'm here."

"You were not a minute ago," Corleya suggested. He could see the worry in her eyes.

"Sorry, Princess. Just adjusting to the healing magic in the armor."

Alia spat on the floor.

"Healing," Corleya let out. "Did the armor heal your side?"

"Yes."

"Then, we can go home," Corleya said, smiling with excitement. "You can jump us back, right into my father's throne room. We can go now."

Kael shook his head and was shocked when Alia nodded her agreement to his response.

"No," the mercenary said. "We cannot."

Corleya whirled and frowned at her lady-in-waiting. "Why not? Cethos is probably in the middle of a civil war by now, and I can put a stop to it."

Kael sighed. "We need to get some information first," he said. "Find out who's actually in control of Corynth."

"I agree," Alia said. "Walking into the throne room may get us killed."

"But," Corleya protested, "the guards will still be loyal to me even if something has happened."

Kael scoffed, and it earned him a dirty stare from Alia, but he continued anyway. "You cannot know that, Princess. The fact that a rebellion began means that someone coveted your father's throne and enough people supported it. In open rebellion, murdering the Princess and rightful heir would not be beyond the realm of possibility."

"He is right, Princess," Alia stated. "We need to determine what has happened before we move. I suggest we jump to Sora's. The Hideaway Tavern is just inside the walls of GutterTown. We can gather information there for cheap."

"Good idea. If you can give me a detailed enough image so I know where we have to jump to," Kael said. "It will be easier than entering through the gates, and I'm not comfortable making two jumps so close to Corynth. Your father's wizard or the Council could detect the one jump we will have to make. I have a few silver coins, but my gold is from north of the Kasym and will only draw the guards down on us, so a slum area will be best."

"Agreed," Alia said.

"But first, you two need better weapons," Kael stated. "There's an armory in this tower. What kind of weapons do you prefer?"

"Show us," Alia demanded.

"No," Kael said. "To get there I must pass through a room. I won't betray a friend by allowing you in there."

"I have my whips," Alia said. "I need nothing more."

"Corleya?" he asked.

"I lost my whips when our ship went down," the Princess began.

"I doubt there are braided whips in the armory here."

The Princess looked to Alia. "The weaver who lives outside of the walls. Perhaps she can make a set, if not I can pick up a sword."

Kael nodded. "I'll bring two from the armory and carry them. Pack the few things you have, and we'll jump as soon as I get back. Don't forget. I'll need a description of that inn — somewhere nearby where we'll not be seen arriving."

"I know a place behind the tavern."

"Good," Kael said, nodding as he turned to leave. "Be ready and make sure neither of you will be recognizable to the public or guards. We'll be done before we start if you are."

Chapter Eighteen

"For thousands of years citizens across Talohna have prayed, dreamed, and hoped that one day the Ancients would return. As an historian, I understand better than most people how time can twist and distort the true events of the past into something far different than the reality of what took place. I believe proof is required before we blindly believe what history has laid before us. Having lost so much of that history during the Cataclysm, to meekly follow what has become known as our true past may be the biggest mistake the people of Talohna can ever make. Only cattle and sheep willingly follow their own kind to the slaughter while the wolves herd them from behind."

Salabriel Aranasse,
Stillwater dig journal entry, 5026

SORA'S HIDEAWAY TAVERN
GUTTERTOWN, CORYNTH

The little girl crashed into the clay chamber pots in the alley behind Sora's Hideaway Tavern and landed in a heap. Struggling to lift herself from the razor-sharp pieces, twelve-year-old Kenna gasped as yet another blow slammed into the underside of her petite body. The force of the vicious kick lifted her from the broken pots and sent her spinning into the oak barrels of lining the alley's far side. Unlike the chamber pots, the whiskey barrels did not shatter, and Kenna's body crunched against the wood. Her fingers scrambled in the dust and red sparks ground out in the dirt and faded. She did not move.

"Please, Sonny! Stop! Here!" A small boy, no older than ten, jumped to Kenna's defense. Holding up a small bag of jingling coins, he offered them to the older boy. "Here, Sonny. It's everything she got from the marketplace. Every copper and the silver. I promise. It's all there. Please, stop hurting her."

Sonny Talo, the great-grandson of Talohna's most powerful criminal mastermind, stared down at Tanner. "That's all of it? You're not lying, are you, ya little shit?"

"That's all of it, Sonny. I swear. Please, she can't pay your dues if she's dead." The sneaky backhand caught Tanner up the flat side of his head and the smack rang his ears ring like a temple bell.

"I am not going to tell you two to stay out of the marketplace, again. You can panhandle in TinkerTown or GutterTown or steal from the barracks if you're good enough not to get caught." Sonny's voice climbed with anger. It was an anger every street kid knew first hand. "But you will stay out of MarketTown completely. I catch you begging or picking pockets in the marketplace, again, you will both lose your right hands. Is that clear, Shitter?" Tanner winced at the nickname but nodded in agreement.

Knowing what came next, his hands shook uncontrollably. His stomach did a cold flip, and Tanner had to clench his scrawny butt cheeks together to avoid a recurrence of the affliction that had led to his nickname.

"You or her, Shitter?" Sonny asked, his belt already halfway off.

Well-aware of how much worse it would be for Kenna, Tanner never hesitated. A lot more than Sonny's belt would come off if Kenna were to pay the price for disobedience, and he would never let that happen to her, again. Broken bones and bruises healed, but a defiled body and broken soul would never mend.

"Me. Do me," Tanner said, as Sonny's belt slid free from his waist. Tanner dropped to his knees. Quaking with fear, he lifted his left hand. The yellow and green mottled bruising disappeared under the stiff leather as Sonny wrapped his belt around the hand once before slipping it through the buckle. With a sadistic grin, he yanked the belt tight around Tanner's hand, braced it, and pulled the belt strap with every ounce of power in his over-sized, sixteen-year-old body. The delicate bones in Tanner's hand snapped like kindling. Malnutrition-weakened bones popped and ground together as Sonny tugged again and again. When he was done with him, Sonny tore his belt free and kicked Tanner to the dirt.

"Dues are up in three days, Shitter. See you then." Sonny smirked as he turned and entered the back door to Sora's. Tanner knew the money he had just given Sonny would go straight to Sora's prostitutes and perhaps the lone silver to the dice table.

Even at sixteen, Sonny Talo and his twisted tastes were well-known on GutterTown's seedy streets.

Using his knees to stand, Tanner cradled his hand. Already, his right hand was bandaged up and due to be taken off within a week. Now, Miss Siona would have to set the bones in his left and wrap it, too. Again. One of GutterTown's most notorious alchemists and famous for her less than helpful concoctions, Siona Vakal was the only one who would help the street kids when they were injured.

Tanner hobbled over to Kenna and ignored his throbbing hand as best he could. As he knelt, a wave of relief washed over him when he saw her chest rise and fall. Unable to carry her, he did his best to wiggle her still body against him. Cradling his older sister in his lap, he waited for her to regain consciousness, so they could walk to GutterTown's only healer together.

SORA'S HIDEAWAY TAVERN
CORYNTH, CETHOS

Kael emerged from the realm jump magic with Corleya and Alia at the back of a tavern. Aged barrels, full and empty, had been stacked under the sloped roof hanging off the tavern's rear wall. He immediately sensed blood around them and searched for a reason. Looking around, he saw a pile of broken chamber pots.

"Someone was hurt here," he told them, kneeling to examine the dirt. "Badly."

Alia moaned as she held her head. "Kill you some day, wizard," she said, barely above a whisper.

"We cannot—" Corleya said but stopped short as a coughing fit overtook her. Kael was reminded of how hard realm jumps affected them. "We cannot spare time to find and help them."

"Not interested in helping them," Kael answered. "Just offering a warning about our surroundings. This is a dangerous place."

"We agree, again," Alia stated, still breathing heavy.

"I'll try not to let it happen again."

"Stop, you two," Corleya ordered. "There's no time for you two to argue about agreeing with each other, for the sake of Paradise."

Kael smiled. The jump had somehow restored the Princess' confidence and royal mannerisms. Or perhaps it was just the familiarity of home.

Both women pulled up their heavy hoods and Kael motioned for Alia to enter the tavern first with Corleya in the middle, so he could watch their backs.

As the door closed behind him, Kael's eyes adjusted to the gloom instantly. The stench of poorly fermented alcohol and the noise from the upstairs bedrooms nearly overwhelmed his senses.

"The far-right corner has an empty table," he whispered as he mentally worked to dial back his esoteric senses to ease the onslaught from the stench and noises. Alia led them around a boisterous young man sixteen or a bit older. Kael frowned as the large braggart boasted about pummeling someone for their weekly dues. He resisted the urge to snap the bully's neck just for the sake of doing so.

They sat at the table and scoured the tavern for someone who might be able to inform about the city's royal and political situation.

A waitress made her way to their table with three mugs of ale on her tray. "Traveled far?" she asked and placed the mugs on the table. Kael dropped a silver coin on her tray, and her eyes widened.

"A fair ways," Kael answered.

"Stew is ready any time if you are hungry."

Kael handed her another silver coin, and she stared at it in awe. "I cannot change a second silver coin, Sir."

"You don't have to. If you know of anyone in here who can give us some information about the troubles here in the city we heard about out on the trail."

"Dice would be your best bet," she said quietly and indicated with her chin toward an older man sitting alone at a table as he tossed a set of bone dice. "Buy him a drink or two."

"Thank you," Kael said. "Alia, go see that weaver about a pair of whips. Corleya and I will go talk to the dice man."

The mercenary shook her head. "I will not leave her alone with you."

"It's all right, Alia," Corleya said. "Kael won't let anything happen to me." She turned and offered him an embarrassed smiled.

"You are sure?"

"Yes, Alia, it's all right," Corleya repeated.

The Salzaran woman nodded and left the tavern, but not before giving Kael a warning glare.

"Come on," he whispered and worked his way around the tavern to the dice table. He nodded to their waitress on his way, and by the time they got to the old man's table, she was already placing two mugs of ale in front of the older man.

"Dice, I'm told," Kael stated, sitting across from the man as Corleya sat beside him. The dark shadow under her heavy hood hid her profile from the man.

"Aye, young man. Not many Salzarans enjoy a game of Bones, but all are welcome at my table."

"Salzaran?" Kael asked.

"Your tattoos, boy. Every man leads his own path, I know, but very few people outside Salzara mark their faces as thoroughly as you have."

"Right," Kael said, nodding slowly. "Haven't been gone from home for long. I forget how strange it must be to others sometimes."

"Understandable," Dice said. "Tough road getting here?"

"Deadly, yes."

"Well, boy. What's your bet? I don't toss bones for free."

"Actually," Kael began, "I was hoping you could just bring us up-to-date on the trouble we heard of on our way first. It's calm here. We heard otherwise. The civil war over?"

"Civil war?" Dice snorted. "A coup more like it. Especially at the end, anyway. Rumor has it that the first, second, and third Pillars of Rule are dead."

"I don't understand," Kael replied, puzzled. "We heard both sides had called in their markers — that war was imminent."

"They did. It was," Dice said, shaking his head. "Duchess Vakaran had at least twice the army King Bale had. She brought her forces right to Corynth's front gate with very little difficult fighting. I'm sure you saw them on your way in."

"Yes, of course," Kael answered, hoping not to raise the man's suspicions.

"The King's forces had been depleted by the units guarding the border to the Wildlands. The tribes are threatening war for trespassing. His gods-damned daughter caused that." Kael noticed Corleya slink further into her hood as the old man continued. "All both of those did was weaken the royal army and distract the King from the real threat and now it doesn't matter. Not enough nobles have stood against the change in our monarchy so whoever is in control will probably hold it. Us common folk will be the last to hear any real information."

Kael shook his head, but it was Corleya who spoke. "What happened to... to the old king and queen?"

"From what I heard, they are either dead or imprisoned in the Citadel's deepest dungeon cell," Dice offered with a shrugged. "It matters very little to us here in GutterTown."

"Nothing ever changes at the bottom," Kael agreed.

Dice lifted his ale. "Spoken by a man who knows." Kael nodded at the toast and clinked his mug against the old man's raised cup.

"Well," the old man said. "I gotta use the crapper. Be back shortly, and we'll throw some bones, yeah?"

"We'll be here," Kael replied as the old man walked away.

Corleya turned to him immediately. "We have to get to my father. Freeing him will be the only way to restore the throne."

Kael sighed. "There is no way we can get into that dungeon. The Wizard's Council will already be looking for us just from the jump into GutterTown. Especially if a new third pillar has been inducted already. A second jump will tell them exactly where we are. Unless you know of a back door into the very bottom of the dungeon?"

"There isn't one." Corleya shook her head. "As far as I know. My father would have told me if there was. The bottom level of the dungeon hasn't even been used in my father's time or even my grandfather's." He could hear the frustration in her raised voice and glanced around to see if anyone was watching. A woman in dark green leather armor and a hood watched them from a few tables over.

"We're starting to attract attention," he told her as Alia returned through the tavern's front door.

She shook her head and sat at the table. "The weaver cannot help. The heavy metal filament for the whips will take too long to acquire."

"It's all right," Kael whispered. "We need to leave now. People are starting to notice us."

"Back door?" the mercenary asked as Dice returned and sat down.

"We tossing Bones, young man?"

"Sorry, Dice," Kael answered and slid a silver coin over to him as he stood. "My thanks for the information, but we will be going."

"That is a true shame, my new friend," Dice replied slowly as he picked up the coin. "I will be here should you change your mind."

Kael nodded. "Thank you for the offer. Take it easy." Alia and Corleya followed him to the back door. He stepped outside and crossed the barrel storage yard before turning to talk to them. Instead of Alia and Corleya, he found himself face-to-face with the young braggart. Kael frowned. Though his senses had been notoriously unreliable as of late, he still should have felt the young man's presence.

"Everyone in GutterTown pays dues to the Talo family, newcomer."

"Is that right?" Kael replied as he swallowed the urge to strangle the bully, again.

"It is. My name is Sonny Talo, and these are my associates," he said, waving to the two older men at his side. Each had a hand on Corleya and Alia. Kael suspected each had a blade pressed into their side or back. "Your women do not have much, but by the looks of that armor, you do. A silver piece should cover you for the week."

Kael snorted and shook his head. "Little gangster, huh? How about you leave before you and your boys end up dead?"

Sonny glanced to his men and laughed. "Why are newcomers always so fuckin' stupid?" Both shrugged in response.

"Sonny Talo," a new arrival said. Kael only sensed her the second before she appeared. "Take your boys and leave, please."

"Like hell I will."

The woman moved quicker than Kael could follow and almost too fast for his faltering esoteric senses. Shocked by her speed, he stared openly as the woman knocked Sonny to the ground and attacked his two men by knocking them out cold.

"Take your leave, Sonny, or I will let this wizard tear you apart. I would rather not have to explain to your grandfather how your own stupidity got you killed. Am I clear?"

Sonny nodded as he looked up. "Yes, Pillar," he said. "My apologies."

The woman in the dark green armor turned to Kael. "Can you bring them around?" she asked, pointing to the two on the ground.

Kael nodded and knelt between them. Placing a hand on each, he released a trace of electricity into each, and both woke slowly before Sonny helped them back into the tavern.

"My apologies," the woman said and glanced around before she removed her hood and dropped to a knee. "My Princess."

"Mistress Spy?" Corleya gasped and gestured for her to rise. "We were told most of the Pillars were dead."

"We are. Myself and the Hunter are both here in Corynth, and the Corsair is docked in Soena with the royal fleet, all still loyal to your father. We believe the rest died during the coup."

"But you don't know?" Kael prompted.

"No," she said. "We were not here."

"Wait," Corleya said, smiling. "That means Father is still alive. Your magic..."

"He is, Princess, but I doubt he will be for long. Already our connection is weakening. We need to find him and quickly."

"How?" Kael asked.

"Perhaps I can help with that, young man," another voice said.

"Brother Donis!" Corleya cried out and ran to the monk.

He grabbed her in hug and laughed. "Princess. I have never been so happy to see you," he said as tears slipped from his eyes. "I feared you were dead."

"Too close, too many times," she replied.

"Come," the fourth Pillar said. "We need to leave GutterTown. Crossing the Talo Family is not wise, even for a Pillar of Rule."

"Of course, Pillar," Donis agreed. "Follow me and keep your hoods up as we pass through the gates to Nobility Row. Zaddyk has been trying to find a way into the dungeons for days now. We believe your father is being held there."

Kael nodded and followed the stern-faced monk. "How did you know where to find us?" he asked.

"Zaddyk," the monk said as if that explained it all. Kael offered him a frown as they walked, and the monk explained. "Right. You would not know of him. Zaddyk is a young prophet, but he has already fallen to the prophet's madness. He told us... 'the rightful heir will step from the shadows among the bones of the poorest drunkards'. It was the only words of prophecy from his mouth we have been able to understand in months. Luckily, Dice is well-known throughout Corynth for his Bone games. However, there is another tavern located near the old cemetery so me and the Pillar split up to cover more ground. When I did not find any sign of you, I returned here immediately."

"Where are we going, Brother Donis?" Corleya asked.

"To the temple," he answered. "I am hoping our new friend here can help interpret what Zaddyk has seen—a way into the dungeons so we can rescue your father."

"You know what I am?" Kael asked.

Brother Donis sighed. "I certainly hope you are not," the monk paused as if collecting his thoughts before continuing, "Zaddyk has become obsessed with a future that prominently involves you, and he has seen where the *'blackness'* or the '*darkness*' will decide the future of Talohna. He believes *the black will return the rightful heir from among the shadows.* We hope that is you."

Kael's stomach sank at the monk's words. They were frighteningly familiar to what Vog and Dravik BloodPounder had said when he first arrived back.

"You have your suspicions, then?" Kael asked as the last of the rundown buildings and shanty homes passed them by and they emerged in a large marketplace three times the size of the one in Dasal.

"I know what and who you are, Kael. I helped plan your exile, and Giddeon Zirakus was one of my closest friends."

"Was?" Kael prompted as they moved along the bank of a wide river flowing through the marketplace.

"The ArchWizard has been missing for some time, but that is a conversation for later—should the time arrive. But, you... I do not know whether history is true or if perhaps the accounts I have read concerning your kind are mostly fact or the ramblings of the terrified." Again, he paused, and Kael got the feeling that Brother Donis only spoke after he weighed his words carefully. It made him an intelligent and dangerous man. "Until your actions prove otherwise, your secret is safe with me and those you've already trusted. Though, I would enjoy a very serious conversation with you some day."

Kael laughed and shook his head. "Your King might not be so keen."

Brother Donis stopped walking as they approached a large bridge over the river. The carved marble footpath led to a massive fountain. The bridge had been shaped around the fountain and was clearly a late addition. The polished Fae statue inside the fountain pulsed with magic unlike any he had seen in Talohna before. Brilliant colours danced in the water and even throughout the mist in the air. The monk touched Kael's hand and caught his attention as the others continued walking ahead.

"The Pillar's powers are waning," he whispered, "which means King Bale is dying. If we cannot get to him in time, but still manage to restore the Bale monarchy, I believe you will have a friend on the Cethosian throne for as long as she lives. Do you not?"

"Maybe," Kael said. "Power and political pressure can change even the best of people."

"This is very true. You are wise beyond your years, son. It will serve you well in the coming years," Brother Donis stated. As they continued walking, Kael took one last look at the incredible fountain and smiled. Talohna had some amazing sights, there was no doubt.

"What happened while we were gone?" the Princess asked as Kael and Brother Donis caught up.

"We do not know for sure," he answered as they approached the gate to Nobility Row. "The nobles are still swearing fealty or protesting from what we've heard."

"Who was the instigator?" Kael asked.

"Originally, it was the Duchess Vakaran," he said and turned to Corleya. "But she had a legitimate claim. You know there are two interpretations of the law." The Princess nodded but gave the monk a frown. "Sorry, off subject. Her army was outside the gates when the attack on the castle began. Whether she led a quick but stealthy and decisive strike or whether it was someone else, we do not know yet."

"Vakaran scum," Alia growled and spat in the dirt.

"I am well aware of your history with the family, Madam," Brother Donis said. "But not all children are the same as their siblings." Again, the mercenary spat to the side as she turned her back on the monk.

They reached the gate to Nobility Row, and Brother Donis got them through without any trouble. Kael let his senses linger at the gate as they walked into Corynth's wealthiest district, but the guards went about their normal business without any suspicion.

It took minutes to walk to Mylla's temple, and Kael stared in awe at the castle across the road.

"Impressive sight, is it not?" Donis asked.

"Very," he said. A waterfall poured over the mountain cliffs on either side of the castle. Both powerful waterfalls fueled the castle's moat. The separate waterways circled the castle and came together to form the river that ran out into the city. "Never see anything like that back home."

"I imagine not. Now, come," the monk said as they turned and entered the temple. "I'll take you to Zaddyk. Pillar? Can you take the Princess and her lady to the kitchen? Their rumbling stomachs are making even me hungry — it has only been an hour since my last meal." He laughed, and his instant change in personality was astonishing. As if more relaxed to be back in the temple, a harmless but mischievous aura rose from the monk. "Shall we?" he added, leading the way.

Kael nodded and trailed Brother Donis around the prayer room and to the dorms at the temple's far side. The monk stopped at a room guarded by two other monks. Unlike Brother Donis' excessively wide frame, both were extremely fit and corded with muscle.

Brother Donis noticed him looking. "They will keep anyone out who is not welcome. At least until we know how the monarchy settles out. Come," he said and entered the room.

Kael stepped into the bedroom and winced at the sight before him. The young man on the bed suffered from incredible agony. His body twisted and contorted as it rippled through him. The intense pain bled into his aura like a physical being and Kael knew Zaddyk's life would be measured in months if it continued without reprieve. The prophet opened his eyes, and as if he sensed Kael's thoughts, he turned his head and smiled. The waves of pain melted away.

"You found your way back," Zaddyk said.

"If you say so," Kael answered. "You're not as insane as I was led to believe."

Zaddyk laughed. "We are not talking prophecy, yet, Kael."

"You know me?"

"Of you," the prophet said as he sighed. "At least, I hope I know of you. The currents of time are tricky. You could be one of many yous."

"You know why we're here, then?" Kael asked.

"Do you?" Zaddyk countered.

Kael frowned. "Donis said you might have a way into the dungeons where they're holding King Bale."

Zaddyk glanced past Kael's shoulder and nodded. Brother Donis bowed and left the room. "I cannot tell you how to get there, but I might be able to show you." The prophet offered his hand.

"If you really know what I am, then you know that's a stupid idea," Kael growled. "I cannot control the mind of a prophet. My magic will eat you alive in defense if your magic doesn't swallow my mind first."

"Does it matter?" Zaddyk asked. "I have little time left."

"I sensed that, and I'm sorry," Kael said. "But you cannot fathom how much time I have left. Having my brain scrambled by a prophet—"

"Sorry?" Zaddyk interrupted. "To give your life in the service of your beliefs is what it means to live a full life, Kael. My goddess touched me for the sole purpose of helping Talohna, and together we have. She will not let us down. Your mind will be safe with me. Sit," he said, gesturing to a chair. "Please."

"This is a dumb idea," he repeated as he sat in the chair beside Zaddyk's bed.

"So was fighting your way back to the living." Kael frowned at the prophet, not sure if he heard the young man right, but it did not stop Zaddyk from continuing. "A prophet can also see into the past. It is where I hope to give you the answers you seek."

"What do I do?" Kael asked as he leaned forward.

Zaddyk lifted the amulet from around his neck and held it in his palm. "You are also god-touched, Kael. Hold my amulet with me, and my god will do the rest."

Kael hesitated and Zaddyk placed his other hand on Kael's. "You have every right not to trust anyone in this world, Kael, but sooner or later you will have to," he said. "I have seen things I cannot explain because of the prophet's madness, and before long, it will swallow all of my mind even when I am conscious. It is a price I pay willingly for using my goddess' power because it is the only way that I can help my country. We both know what is coming, I have seen hundreds of futures — you know what will happen if the Blood Kingdoms are not led by a strong Cethosian monarchy in the coming years. The bulk of Talohna's military power lies here in Cethos or else in Ellorya and DormaSai in the south. Ellorya will side with the enemy."

"Just tell me how to get into the dungeons so we can get this over with," he whispered. "My mind is barely my own now. The thought of giving up what little control I have is not a pleasant one."

"I understand," Zaddyk replied, nodding. "But you will never understand what I see if I tell you. You have to see it for yourself."

"Tell me," Kael said. "Tell me what you see."

Zaddyk closed his eyes and sighed as he began. His voice shifted, taking on a monotonous edge. "Surrounded by piles of dusty past, death stalks the long entry forged by wars abandoned…" Zaddyk opened his eyes and coughed to clear his throat. "That is how prophecy and memories of the past are affected by madness, Kael. What I see and what I speak are not the same. Did you understand what I said? Do you know where to go?" Kael shook his head and glanced at his feet as the prophet carried on. The last thing he wanted was to give up control.

"Trust me, please?" Zaddyk offered his hand, again. The amulet sat in his palm. "I can show you where you will find what you need and how to realm jump there safely."

Kael nodded and firmly grabbed Zaddyk's hand, trapping the amulet between their palms. Strange magic rushed upon him, and his mind scattered like leaves on a strong fall wind. What Zaddyk showed him was not a way into the dungeons.

The prophet's voice rolled through his mind as if it were a physical force, and Kael screamed from the pressure inside his head.

I apologize for the pain, but you must see this. After many millennia, the Lost Light prophecy has been revealed in its entirety. The third and final piece has been given to me, and Talohna needs to know the truth. Only a god can reveal the future to the mortal world — you are close enough, my new friend. It won't make sense to you when you see all three pieces now, but it will, soon.

Souls of six collapse the glyph of old magics.. The lone genocide survivor shifts a soul to watch with a single passion... to purge or protect the blackness of aeons ahead.

As Tyr slams his shield upon brother Aegeus's back and rushes to Mylla's rock, three moons invite the Bloods' blackest-born bonds. Revulsion accounts one lost while Dathac reaps the willing. The impending approach will guide reprisal toward both crua as capacity for mercy fades. All last offers live in the dreams of those kept by Dathac. The Bloods' blackest dawns the light's last and will see Black's poured blood, returned to times past:

Dark towers rule over fallen cities. From the sea, from slavery, from magic and death, and from the oldest blood the dogs cry for war. Once united by the birth of blackness, the dogs of war push back against the darkest power. Pray the dogs welcome the blackness before they, too, fall to the darkness while men and gods alike wage war on creation and the darkness, it hides beneath soaring towers.

With darkness covering Talohna, the dogs of war howl as innocent blood flows from mountain rivers. Can a god really die? Pray, Talohna. Pray the blackest god never dies.

CORYNTHIAN MOUNTAIN RANGE
BALE'S FOLLY

FALLEN SEPULCHRE

Kael stepped from the realm jump with Princess Corleya, Lady Alia, and the Pillar, whose name only seemed to be the Spy. He had never been so happy to be out of a city in his entire life. Though it seemed like hours, he and Zaddyk had been under the prophet's magic for a matter of minutes. In that time, Kael quickly learned that Zaddyk's true motives had nothing to do with finding a way in to the secret prison entrance. Although the prophet did eventually show him a way into the dungeon, Kael's sanity felt just as unstable as Zaddyk's.

He shook his head to dispel the thoughts and images taxing his mind from the prophet's dream. He had to focus on the task at hand. They would have to cover six miles of tunnel littered with traps and god knew what else. There was not time to lose his mind. The images he needed finally came back to him as he focused. At the five-mile mark, the tunnel branched with the right leading to certain death and the left leading to their desired destination. Neither Kael nor Zaddyk could see what was on the right path, but Kael's magic told him that if they went that way, they would not get out alive.

The jump magic snapped shut behind him as the last traveler exited the magic and a chorus of moans followed.

"I hate you, wizard. Damn, I hate you," Alia sputtered as she heaved.

"My head hurts," Corleya whined. "Does this ever get any better?"

The fourth Pillar dropped to a knee. "No..."

Though he felt the Pillar was plagued by nausea, Kael was impressed to see her regain her footing so quickly and force the discomfort aside.

"The entryway has to be here," he told them as the memory of the rock-fallen valley Zaddyk showed him flashed through his mind. "Here," he added, pointing to several sets of flat stones stacked over five feet high. *"Piles of dusty past."* The prophet's words began to make sense.

"Behind the stacked rock?" Corleya asked while she stood uneasily.

Kael nodded and shoved the first pile over. The motion took two more towers of stone with it and exposed a partially collapsed tunnel. The fourth Pillar did the same to her right and the tunnel opened completely before them.

"Ready?" he questioned and glanced at the three women. Each nodded, and Alia handed him a lit torch as he went in. Near the entrance, Kael stopped and inspected a massive rusty metal blade lodged between the walls.

"Trap," the Spy stated.

"Yeah. We knew there might be traps. It looks like this one was pressure sensitive," he said while he pressed down on a loose stone with his boot.

"What if some of these are still active?" Corleya asked.

Kael chewed his bottom lip as an idea came to mind. "Plug your ears and use your masks," he said, He lifted the mask attached to his Orotaq cloak and turned to make sure all three women did the same. "You should probably open your mouths as well."

Once they were protected, he stared along the tunnel ahead of him and put his hands together. Opening his arms from wall-to-wall, he unleashed a massive wall of compressed air. It popped his ears as it howled away down the shaft, kicking up a storm of dust. Somewhere up ahead, he heard stone crack and break apart. When the dust settled, and they moved forward, he frowned at the massive hole where the floor had fallen into the earth.

Kael approached the pitfall cautiously, cracking his jaws to relieve the pressure inside his ears. "That is a long way down," he muttered as he stared down the hole.

"At least sixty feet." Alia guessed. She tossed a fist-sized stone into the hole. "Hmm… eighty."

The Spy grunted her agreement. "At least there is a way to cross," she said and pointed to the left side where a foot-wide walkway remained.

"Is it safe?"

"Yes, Princess," the Spy answered. "The walkway along the ledge is carved from the wall's stone. Kael is right. It is a pitfall trap, likely lined with spikes at the bottom."

Corleya stared at the Spy, her eyes wide. "Because a, eighty-foot fall can't kill you dead enough?" she asked in a mutter, and the Spy shrugged.

"I'll go first," Kael offered and crossed over the narrow ledge without incident. The others followed, and they continued onward.

The way ahead was slow going for over two hours. Kael used both his physical magic and esoteric senses to check for more traps. He was forced to trigger one more active pitfall, followed by three bladed traps. A handful of others had been triggered over previous years. One set of crossed spikes had claimed the life of what Corleya called a ruin scavenger. The ages-old skeleton was held together by the corroded spikes and what little rotted cloth and sinew remained.

"*Death stalks the long entry,*" Kael said to himself, shaking his head at the impaled skeleton

"What?" Alia asked and gave him a suspicious stare

"It's what Zaddyk told me he saw. I think I'm starting to understand the way his madness sees things."

"Crazy understands insane," Alia quipped.

Not in the mood to fight, Kael tossed her the finger.

"What?" she asked. "That means what?"

He shrugged and lifted his hands in mock confusion as he turned. Squeezing passed the intersecting blades without disturbing the skeleton, he led the way further into the shaft. Another ten-minute walk and they reached the branch in the tunnel he had seen through Zaddyk's magic.

"You are sure we go left?" Corleya asked while staring to the right.

Kael could sense her uneasiness, and it mimicked his own. "Feel that?" he replied, turning to the others.

"Yes," Corleya answered. She rubbed the back of her neck, clearly nervous .

"Magic," the Spy stated. "Older than that used to create the Pillars of Rule." She turned to Kael. "Do you recognize it?"

"No," he said. "It's not the way forward anyway. Zaddyk was adamant—if we go that way, none of us will get out alive. I have little doubt that what lies that way will be far more than we could handle even if we had an army behind us."

"To the left then?" Corleya asked, though Kael knew the question was rhetorical.

He nodded and led the way forward. "Not much further now," he told them.

REAR ESCAPE TUNNEL
BROKEN BLADE SANCTUARY

Savis Ephemeral released his inherent magic and stepped from the shimmering air with Merethyl Bellas at his side. The two assassins watched silently as the group disappeared into the left tunnel branch.

"They sensed us. It was if the Spy's senses were boosted by his," Merethyl said.

"At least they were smart enough to go the other way."

"And trigger the last of our active traps along the way, Savis," she growled. "Who are they? And how did they know the tunnels were here?"

"You sensed the wizard, too?" he asked. "Wasn't sure at first. Intriguing."

"Barely sensed him," she answered. "Yet he has magic we have not seen before. I'm beginning to wonder if helping Sythrnax was the dumbest thing we could have done. With two seals open, more and more unknown magics seem to be awakening all over Talohna. Who knows what might be next?"

"It would be rather simple to take them from behind. They would never see us coming now that I can cloak both of us both in full invisibility."

Merethyl scoffed. "Has your rashness taught you nothing?" she snapped and tapped his stomach. The massive wound from Kasik's sword had healed with a thick ugly scar. "Sythrnax is not here to put you together this time."

"You don't think... not another one..." he asked, trailing off.

"You know of any other kind of wizard who can hide his magic like that? I can barely tell he is a wizard. If he had not just used his magic, I probably wouldn't have."

"Assani's blades." Savis cursed. "If there is another DeathWizard in Talohna Sythrnax needs to know about it."

"Agreed. Sythrnax will be in Ellorya or else already marching on DormaSai. Go to Soena and take command of the Dyr's Blade. Sail to Avalera and let him know. Hopefully, you can reach him before he attacks DormaSai. I'll let the Ghul know what he's been looking for might just be right under his nose."

"Very well," he said. "Are you gonna let them go?"

Merethyl nodded. "I know Sythrnax wanted the Bales off the throne, but it matters little to us who rules Cethos. If they can find a way into the old dungeons, they will likely never get out alive."

"And if they do?" Savis asked, pressing the issue further.

Merethyl laughed. "Then that will be the Ancients' problem, not ours. I do not believe it is in our best interest for Sythrnax to have his way completely unrestrained anyway. Now, go, and while you are in the Southern Kingdom, keep your ears open about our traitor."

"The one last seen in Northern Ellorya?"

"Yes," Merethyl said, nodding. "Desiree Star has eluded us long enough."

"What of Yrlissa?" he asked. "You wanted me to track down proof that she is alive."

"You are sure you saw her? It was not just the delirium of dying with a sword in your gut?"

"I know what I saw. I talked to her."

"We have no presence in DormaSai, and it is the only place she will go to feel safe. The Whiteblood and Caballa Famlies will know the moment you cross the border. See what Sythrnax says. Perhaps he can shield you from them long enough for you to confirm she is alive and where she might be hiding. But if the White Cabal catches wind of you, get out of DormaSai, immediately. I will not have them resume their vendetta and continue their hunt for our guild, again. Understood?"

"It will be done," Savis said. He bowed and left.

Merethyl stared down the left tunnel for several minutes as if in a curious trance.

"Who are you, wizard? And what powers do you wield?" she whispered aloud. "Intriguing times our world is seeing indeed."

CORYNTH, CETHOS
GUTTERTOWN SLUMS

Journeyman Wizard, Cameron Wik, regained consciousness in a rushed and abrasive way. Surrounded by dark and enveloped by a bone-deep cold, sounds of scuffling and dripping water echoed around him. He tried to move only to discover he was secured to a table of some kind. Fully conscious, it dawned on him what had happened. The Ghul had collected on their contract.

Panicking, Cameron grasped for his magic, but there was nothing. As if he had never been born with Lady Inara's grace, there was an empty pit in his very being where his magic had previously resided. Anxiety overwhelmed him, and he shouted.

"You said thirty days. It's only been twenty-eight. We had a deal!"

Something grazed the bottom of his foot. Glancing down, he regretted doing so in a heartbeat as a sickening pain overtook his neck. Gently tilting his head to the side and down, his chin scraped on what could only be a metal collar.

"You moron," he sneered as loud as he could. "A Poghana collar won't hold a Journeyman Wizard for very long! Even a metal one. Let me go, Ghul, and I might actually forget you tried to do this."

A light rustle by his feet made him glance down only to notice he was stark naked. The collar scraped at his neck, but the pain was tolerable enough for him to investigate. A clenched, pale hand materialized out the gloom. One finger, tipped by a shiny black talon, trailed along the top of his big toe and up to his ankle. A strange tingling sensation followed the path of the razor-sharp nail as it continued moving up his leg. Confused and terrified, he stared, transfixed, as the clawed finger reached his knee. A loud hiss echoed somewhere in the room, and a bright light streaked from outside his vision, sticking to the high ceiling.

Light brightened the room. Without a conscious thought of it, his sight veered to his captor. Cameron screamed with horror as his eyes locked with something.

As a Journeyman Wizard, he had come across every humanoid species known to the world of Talohna. With the creature's face covered by a mask, the eyes were all he could make out.

The eyes looking back at him were of something completely new and very different. They were not Human or Elvehn, and they were not DragonKin. Cameron searched his mind to recall even a small shred of familiarity.

Mahala, no. Troll, no. Toldari, definitely not. Lastly, the cold pale eyes of the Orotaq flashed in his mind. No, thankfully.

More confused, he closed his eyes and hoped his own were failing him or playing tricks somehow. Taking a deep breath, he reopened his eyes slowly, but the strange black gaze was still there. It was not the solid black that scared him — the

Toldari had solid black eyes. He had faced many on the battlefield before.

No, it was the long reptilian red slit of the creature's pupil and the feathered iris of vibrant purple that horrified him. Both eyes blazed with the brilliance of intense power.

Fear unlike any he had felt before flooded his body like a physical entity. His stomach and bowels turned to water as he sobbed uncontrollably.

"You promised... a month..." he stuttered. The black talon stopped its journey up his leg, and a crack split the air as a hand bounced off his head. There was someone else in the room.

"A month you say, Journeyman Wizard?" a familiar voice asked. It was the old homeless man from Corynth's GutterTown—the beggar everyone called the Ghul. He made his way around the table opposite of the purple-eyed creature. The claw dug in a little deeper and carried on its way, slowly crossing over Cameron's knee. This time, however, the tingling was accompanied by a mild sting. He glanced down and to his horror, the finest thread of flesh began to peel from his body as the black talon inched its way along.

"You mundanite bastard! I should have known you weren't the Ghul," Cameron stated, clenching his teeth to control both his irrational fear and the sting of the black talon as the wounds began to burn.

The old man laughed. "You wanted to believe it, just like everyone else. Magic, mundane, shit. Everyone comes to the Ghul eventually, and eventually, they all end up here just like you. Don't make deals you don't intend to keep, wizard, and you wouldn't be here. You could have dealt with the Talo Family yourself. I'm sure they would've let you work off the nine hundred gold pieces you owed them. Gambling is a bad vice for a wizard."

"But, you—"

"But what? I lied? You had thirty days. You started fortifying your home and moving the little gold you had left. Did you believe no one would be watching you when it came to the small fortune we lent you? You even stole an interesting artifact or two from the Eye's vault in preparation of leaving the country. They were Dwarven artifacts I believe, *and* one counters magic."

"I didn't," Cameron whined, shaking his head.

"You'll get your two days, wizard. As it was agreed. But it'll be here, where you can't run and where you can't hide. Besides, there is a very pretty woman coming to see you, Cameron Wik." The old man laughed in earnest. "You do not want to miss that, I promise you. Oh, yeah, go ahead and say hi to the real Ghul," he said, pointing to the creature carving into his leg. "Goodbye, wizard." Though, he could not see him, Cameron felt the air change as the old man left.

GUTTERTOWN
CORYNTH

"There's nothing more I can do for her, Tanner," Siona Vakal told him, turning from the little girl who lay unconscious in her bed. After Kenna woke in the alley behind Sora's, Tanner had helped his sister get to Siona's small hut. He had led her most of the way as she slipped in and out of coherency.

"You have to, Miss Siona. There is no one else."

"Sit down here, Tanner," the alchemist said. She forced the boy to sit and began the arduous process of setting the broken bones in his hand. "How many times have I told you two stay away from the marketplace? Sonny's in charge of the street kids. You have to listen and obey the rules he puts down for you."

Wincing as the old woman pushed his bones into alignment, Tanner sobbed. "We were hungry. Begging in GutterTown gets us a copper a day, Sonny takes five coppers a week. Sometimes we make nothing. We can't steal from the guards! We'll get caught. They beat thieves—worse if they got Kenna. No one from GutterTown gets tested anymore."

Siona frowned at Tanner's observation. Street kids caught stealing were supposed to be taken to Eye for magical testing. The ones who passed the affinity exam were immediately enrolled at the crown's expense. Those who failed most often ended up at one of the pantheon temples under the priestess' care until they were of age. However, only the worst members of the city guard were stationed at the GutterTown barracks. It was a punishment, a dishonorable detail. The guards would sooner torture the street kids than help them, and no one who mattered listened to the grumblings of GutterTown's poor residents.

"I know, kiddo, but because you didn't listen, Kenna is far beyond my help."

"Don't let her die, Miss Siona, please! Who will take care of me if she dies? Help her." Tanner slowly leaned forward, wrapping both his arms around the old woman's waist. The boy's pleading broke Siona's heart. She liked the two mischief makers a lot. However, the girl's internal wounds were far beyond what she could heal with herbs and roots—even the most powerful she could afford.

"I can't help her Tanner. Her only hope is to go see the Ghul if you're willing to pay the price."

Ashamed she had even mentioned such a thing, Siona's heart dropped into her belly when Tanner sat back with a light of hope glinting in his eyes.

Chapter Nineteen

KARIYA

"The country of Kariya is an enigma unto itself. The country produces only one natural resource — trained mercenaries. Every aspect of the country is designed and operated around the birthing, raising, and training of life-long mercenary soldiers. Farmland, lakes, forests, mines, and oceans all are utilized for the sole purpose of supplying the hundreds of training schools through the country. Men, women, and even couples will devote their lives to producing children which will be sold to the schools. This might seem extremely bizarre to people from other countries, but for Kariya, it has always been their way. Once completely trained, the mercenary soldier fetches a large weight of gold and will forever remain loyal to their patron, at least until they are sold or dead. Many of the rich and powerful employ Kariyan mercenaries as bodyguards and personal security. It is a good thing they are so expensive, the thought of an army filled with the ranks of Kariyan mercenaries is enough to strike fear into even the stoutest Northmen warrior, let alone to this simple minstrel."

Garren Sallus,
A Traveler's Codex, Volume 2

CASCADE CITADEL LOWER DUNGEONS
CORYNTH, CETHOS

Kael crouched by the side of the man-sized hole he and the Spy made by carefully removing the stones from the crumbling outer wall. It opened into the lowest and cruelest level of the dungeon. Alia knelt so close to him he could feel her breath on his cheek.

"Those are not King Bale's men," she whispered as six guards stepped into view.

"Mercenaries." He nodded. "It means they're guarding someone."

"Are you sure, Alia?"

"Yes, Princess. They are Kariyan, though, not Salzaran."

Kael frowned. Taking out six Kariyan guards quietly on his own would be impossible even with his abilities. Kariya trained their mercenaries from birth and they were recognized throughout Talohna as the toughest hired swords. Rushing such a group would only result in an alarm being raised. The two closest mercenaries had their backs to them, but the other four faced his group. He was willing to bet that using a short realm jump inside the Cascade Citadel would trip all kinds of alarms at the university of magic across the road.

He turned to Alia and almost bumped noses with her. "The two facing us," he said just loud enough for her to hear. "If I give you a boost," he paused long enough to point toward the upper ledge of cells, "Can you take them with you?" She smiled and nodded. "Corleya, you and your Spy, be ready," he added. The Princess handed Alia the whip she borrowed earlier and eased out her sword while the fourth Pillar removed a dagger from each boot.

"Ready," Alia whispered. He pointed to the heavy shadows to the left, and she crept forward trailing her whips but stayed within the dark. Still nearly twenty feet from the two guards, she stopped as the shadows gave way to torch and lamp light. She glanced back and nodded to him. His hands flared with magic in reply. Alia's whips lashed out, wrapping around two guards' necks. Kael reached out with his magic and tossed her through the air. The agile mercenary landed perfectly on the upper level and jumped over the railing. She ducked under the rail to drop the ground. Her momentum yanked the two guards up into the air by their necks, and she landed safely back on the ground.

Kael wasted no time and released the rest of his magic. It leapt across the closest section of the prison and snared the two closest guards, forcing them to release their swords. The remaining two mercenaries turned and fled. Like a demented marionette, Kael jerked on his magic and pulled the two guards into the tunnel behind him. With no other options, he left them for Corleya and the Spy to deal with so he could vanish into a cloud of black smoke to chase after the two guards fleeing for the alarm bells.

The smaller of the two mercenaries reached for the rope attached to the alarm bell as Kael reappeared trailing black shadows from the Ether. Both short scythes sliced through the mercenaries as if their armor was made of cloth, and the two men fell dead. The alarm never sounded. He leaned over and checked the guards but found nothing that would tell them who they worked for. He let his weapons vanish and returned to the others, passing beneath the men hanging by Alia's whips.

"You good?" he asked and glanced into the tunnel. The Spy wiped her daggers clean and re-sheathed them with a nod.

"They're both dead," Corleya replied quietly as she stepped into the prison.

From her expression, Kael guessed it was probably her first time killing someone. "You all right?" he asked.

"Yes," she answered. "Where would my father be?"

"Down the hall on this level are the only two life signs I can sense," Kael answered.

"Show me, please?" she asked.

"Of course," he said and led her to the only occupied cell in the hidden dungeon while Alia retrieved her whips and the two bodies.

A heavy metal door locked by three bars slid deep into narrow recesses in the wall, sheltered away the life energy of the two people he sensed.

"We will never break through that door. Shit," the Spy hissed.

"We don't have to," Alia said as she nodded to Kael.

He turned to the Spy. "You should probably turn your back," he said. "Plausible deniability and all that."

"Why?"

"Because," he said. "I am going to open this door and free your king if he's in there. I don't want your dagger in my back for using the magic I need to use to do it."

"She won't harm you," Corleya said as she stared at the Spy. "By my order, understand?"

The fourth Pillar nodded. "Of course, Princess."

Kael turned back to the massive metal door and grasped his magic, filling both hands with flaming black and purple magic. The Spy gasped but said nothing as long blades grew from his hands and cut through the metal lock bars smoothly. He pushed the bars back and swung open the large door.

"Father!" Corleya cried and rushed into the cell.

Following her into the cell, Kael frowned as he looked down at the man who had tried so hard to kill him but was now on his own death bed. King Bale's life was likely measured in minutes. The stab wound in the side of his chest was not fatal, but the septic wound had clearly spread toxin through the King's body. He lay on his back in the Queen's lap and writhed in pain. There was nothing Kael could do, so he stepped back into the corner as the Queen took Corleya into her arms.

The King coughed and gasped for air. "I... I knew... you were... alive," he whispered, struggling to speak.

"I'm sorry, Father," Corleya cried.

King Bale shook his head. "You have nothing... to apologize for..." Another racking cough hit the King and it was obvious the wound had damaged the man's lung.

"You are alive," the Queen said. "That is all that matters."

"My apologies, Your Majesty," Alia began as she bowed, "but what happened?"

The Queen offered the mercenary a frown, but Corleya jumped in. "What happened?"

Queen Bale sighed and rubbed her temples. "It took time to sway the other nobles, but after your disappearance, Duchess Vakaran marched her army to our gates. She demanded your father surrender the crown to the grand duke. To try and avoid more fighting, your father invited her into the castle to meet with himself and Grand Duke Sheering. He had been one of the few voices of reason among the nobles since you... left..."

"We have heard no details about who attacked," Corleya prompted.

"Neither your father or I know who did," Queen Bale said. "We were in court with the Grand Duke and the Duchess discussing whether or not an heir had to be in court or dead before the crown could be surrendered when Kariyan mercenaries and assassins attacked. They hit the three Pillars who were present in court. Two died instantly." The Queen paused and put her hand to her mouth. Terror of what she had witnessed crossed her face. "The Priestess was at my side when one of the assassins leapt from the shadows of the court hall and stabbed her in the neck. She fell dead... immediately... so did others in attendance. Your father and the Knight fought until they fell." Again, she went silent.

"Wait?" he prodded. "They died instantly?"

The Queen frowned as if only noticing him for the first time. ""Yes. However, it is proper etiquette to bow before you address your Queen, young man."

Kael frowned and slowly crouched. "You are not my Queen, Miss Bale."

"Kael!" Corleya gasped as he stood back up.

"I am here for you, Princess," he said and purposely bowed in her direction. "I will not kneel or bow before the King and Queen who hunted me to my death. I suggest we return to the problem at hand. May I?" he asked, motioning to the King.

The Queen looked at Corleya and when she nodded, Kael bent over the King and examined his wound.

"This might hurt," he warned. The King shuddered as his fingers slid into the wound and brushed against a piece of wood. "Goddammit. How can an assassin's guild no one knows about be so active?"

"Kael?" Corleya asked.

"Your father's wound isn't fatal. The toxin within the broken blade in his chest is."

"Take it out." Corleya gasped.

Kael shook his head, but it was king Bale who answered her. "It is already too late, is it not?" he asked, staring at Kael.

"I'm not sure," Kael lied.

Corleya turned back to the Queen. "What happened next, Mother?"

The Queen glared at Kael but continued. "Your father and I along with Duchess Vakaran and the Grand Duke were all brought here to the dungeon. Grand Duke Sheering was taken away days ago and they came for the Duchess an hour ago. Neither have been brought back since."

"How many mercenaries in the hall?" Kael asked.

"I could not begin to guess," Queen Bale answered. "There are many throughout the castle."

Suspecting the Queen would not give him the details he needed, Kael turned to King Bale.

"I don't think you have much time left," he started. "You know that, right?"

The King nodded. "I..." He coughed. "Have been wounded... in battle enough to know..."

"I was told the King of Cethos was a warrior, a battle tactician, and a good leader," Kael said. "Tell me what happened. Close your eyes, push the pain aside and tell me what the Cethosian King — the warrior — saw leading up to the attack."

King Bale struggled to breathe as Kael gently lay his right hand on the man's chest. "I can help you see clearer," he offered. "But the blade's toxin might feed on it and speed your passing."

"No, Father," Corleya moaned.

The King took her hand and nodded up at Kael. He trickled the smallest bit of his magic directly into the King's wound and his voice grew in strength. It was a false strength, though, as Kael merely increased the King's heart rate and enhanced the effects of the adrenaline and endorphins already working overtime.

"My time is up... Queen Corleya Bale." King Bale's smile held a joy and sense of pride. "You have to take back our throne..."

"I will, Father. I will."

"Listen child," King Bale said softly. "A monarch listens as much, if not more, than they give orders. It is where I went wrong and why this has happened. I should have listened to Giddeon more," he said.

"You can't begin to comprehend why this happened," Kael quipped. "And listening to that fool wouldn't have helped you at all."

"You would be surprised, young man," the King said. "I am well aware that the Ancients have returned."

Kael scoffed as he spoke over him. "They have, and I highly doubt they'd want a Bale on the Cethosian throne. That is why this happened."

"Perhaps," King Bale agreed as he frowned. "It matters not. The Ancients cannot know about the Citadel's secrets. They were added long after they were gone."

Kael laughed, but kept the magic flowing into the King as he bent closer. "When you assume to know what the Ancients know or how they think, then you have already lost," he hissed.

King Bale held up his arms and motioned to himself. "Perhaps you are right. Again, it matters not." He looked to Corleya. "This castle may have been built by the Ancients,

Corleya, but they were gone thousands of years before the gods granted our family this throne and the Pillars of Rule to protect it. The Pillars will lose their magic the moment I die, and you will have to choose your own." He grabbed the Spy's arm. "Get my wife out of here safely. It will be my last demand of you," he said earning a nod from the fourth Pillar. "You, my dear child. You will have to make this castle accept you as its master. Once you do it will come to your aid in dealing with the traitors above us."

"How, Father?" she asked. "We don't have magic."

"No," King Bale agreed. "But the castle does. The gods made it, so the rightful ruler can bring it to life. The castle will serve your will, daughter. I made them stir once..." His voice trailed off with delirium. The King wheezed, and a rack of coughs rolled through his chest. "Go," he added. "Take back what belongs to our family... Go, please, Corleya."

The Princess stood as the Queen slipped out from under the King and Kael eased the man back on a filthy pile of straw.

Corleya knelt quickly and kissed her father's forehead. "I love you," she whispered. "I am so sorry..."

"I will always love you, child. Never forget that... I am the only... I am... the one who should be sorry." Corleya hugged her father while Kael struggled to keep the man coherent. Alia helped the Princess from the cell, and the Spy left with the Queen, leaving Kael alone with King Bale.

"You are Giddeon's son," he said. "You are not what I expected. They said you were dead. Another thing I am sorry for. Forgive me for what I put you through."

"No," he said. "You drove me into the hands of hell."

The King nodded. "I understand."

"No, you don't, but you will when you get there."

Again, the King nodded. "If you can put her on the throne," he said, his voice failing. "I... I would ask a favor, deserving or not."

"What?"

"Free Giddeon. My daughter will need him."

"Where is he?"

"The DragonKin have him, Saleece, and Kasik imprisoned on the Isle of Ver Karmot... have for over a year now. Free them so they can help her. Please."

"I will do what I can," Kael replied.

"That will have to do. Now, go, so Mistress Spy can get my wife out of here before she loses her Pillar-bond."

Kael nodded and left the cell. Even though the lock bars were cut and it would never pass close scrutiny, he still closed the door behind him so no one would spot the open cell and discover their escape.

"Is he gone?" Corleya asked.

"Not yet," the Spy answered. "But it won't be long."

"We can't leave him, Kael," Corleya said, a she struggled not to cry.

"We'll come back for him," he told her. "I promise. For now, we have to go. The Spy needs what time your father has left to get your mom out of here. You and Alia need to take us to a place where we can see where the new ruler will be holding court." She nodded and turned right, leading the way to the stairs with Alia at her side.

Kael took one last look over his shoulder and shook his head. If King Bale had his way, he would have been held in the very dungeon where the King was about to die alone. Kael sighed and followed the two young women into what he was sure would be another day of pure hell.

GUTTERTOWN
CORYNTH

For the third time in as many hours, Cameron woke to the nauseating rush caused by magic caressing his consciousness awake. After the homeless man everyone believed to be the Ghul had left him alone with the real Ghul, things rapidly became worse. Memories of the black talon digging in deeper flashed in his mind as the pain renewed. Cameron screamed as his skin parted, just deep enough to draw blood.

"P... pl... please stop. S... stop..." he babbled, between screams. For three hours, Ghul had cut into him with his sharp talon. As Cameron glanced down at his sore, naked body. The raised welts all wept a yellow plasma, his body trying its best to scab the wounds to begin healing. However, for some reason it would not dry, it would not scab, and the wounds would not heal.

Not a single word had been uttered from his tormentor.

The Ghul continued peeling Cameron's flesh, tracing lines on his body only the Ghul could see. As the hours passed, Cameron's screams were reduced to an exhausted whimper. The Ghul's black talon cut through the flesh of Cameron's forehead and down to the tip of his nose. With a simple flick, the talon parted from his flesh, taking the last strip of skin with it. A shadow emerged from the darkness and strode to his side.

"Is he ready?" a female voice asked. Cameron struggled against the pain, listening as best he could. The Ghul nodded, and Cameron saw the woman step into view. She was pretty and older, but her bright blue eyes carried the cold horror of no emotion. She was obviously Elvehn.

"Journeyman Wizard Cameron Wik?" she started. It sent a shiver down his spine. The sensation was worse than when he had seen the Ghul for the first time.

"Y... yes, that's me... I—"

"Shhh." The woman touched his lips with her finger so gently he barely felt her. Though it seemed impossible, the fear flooding his veins heightened as if injected into him by her touch. Trembling, he tried to nod, but shook so violently he could not tell if he succeeded.

Without removing her finger, the Elvehn woman began, again. "Let's try this once more, wizard. My name is Merethyl Bellas, and I want the simplest answer to my questions. Clear?" Her finger slipped from his lips.

"Y... yes."

"Much better. Now, pay attention. When you stole that Dwarven charm from the vault below the Eye, you also took a small vile. I need to know if you swallowed it or if you hid it. Which is it?"

"I nev —"

"Stop! I'm going to clarify something for you, wizard. When I said I want the simplest answer from you, a truthful answer should be understood. Do you understand, now?" Too terrified to trust his voice, Cameron nodded — or he hoped he did. He was quaking so hard he had no idea what his body was doing.

"Good. Do I need to ask the question, again?"

Cameron shook his head and took a deep breath. "I didn't take a vial, I swear, just the char —"

The woman placed her finger on his lips, again, harder this time. "Tsk, tsk. I thought you understood." The woman turned to the Ghul and bowed. "He *is* lying."

The Ghul gave her a crooked nod and turned to Cameron. Before he saw the Ghul move, the creature struck. Cameron closed his eyes, waiting for death, but it never arrived. The table he was strapped to popped, and with a dizzying lurch, swung upward to a standing position. For the first time, he got a good look at his captors. It did not help calm his rampaging fear.

The Ghul took a step forward, and Cameron flinched as the creature raised his right hand, palm out, and gently placed it over his pounding heart. The contact added to the burn of dozens of cuts.

"I warned you wizard. No lies," the woman said and turned her back, but not before he caught her grimace of pity.

Cameron locked eyes with the Ghul and braced himself for whatever was coming. He was determined to die with some shred of dignity. The Ghul's mask tugged to the sides as if following a crooked smile. It spoke.

"Foolish boy." The voice washed over Cameron in a mixture of waves of whispers and hisses. The voice seemed to reverberate between reality and the inside of his own mind. It was impossible to tell and it made him nauseous as well as disoriented. "You suffer. Not die." The words crashed into Cameron with enough force to make his head spin. His stomach turned and tossed nothing but bile. Unable to do much else, he groaned. Laughter rolled around inside his head, and for some reason, it helped balance him enough to open his eyes.

"Please," Cameron begged.

But the Ghul shook his head and spoke again. "Truth. *Tornis vagatic.*" Cameron's eyes snapped open, and his breath snagged in his throat as pain overwhelmed his entire being. The Ghul's talons slid into Cameron's flesh, deeper than the previous cuts. This time an ancient magic flooded in with them.

"Truth," the Ghul repeated as the magic drove straight into the Journeyman Wizard like a living entity. The pain doubled. Then, it tripled. With the tiny shred of awareness he held onto, Cameron prayed to the Goddess of Magic with hopes of dying or passing out. His prayers and cries went unanswered. The Lady Inara had long since stopped caring.

Minutes passed, and Cameron lost all control of his body and its functions. Pain ruled his entire being. With no other option, he broke and gave in.

"Stop!" He screamed at the top his lungs, his voice riddled with torment. "P... please, s... stop. Please. I took it. I took it... please, please, just stop," he cried. The Ghul's hand lifted from his chest and the pain vanished. Gone just as fast as it started. The Elvehn woman appeared in front of him.

He panted, shivering from the assault on his body. He was too drained to be embarrassed at the mess dripping down between his legs.

"I warned you, wizard," the woman said, stepping forward, again. "The truth. Or next time it won't stop. Ever. The vial. Where is it?"

Lifting his head and doing his best to keep it from bobbing like an apple in a bucket, he sobbed. "M... my dorm... r... room. At the... Eye. It... it's taped to the inside of the bed frame."

Tilting her head, the woman frowned. "Why not at your home in TinkerTown? Do you need a reminder about telling the truth?" Though futile, Cameron tried to grasp the woman, but his bindings held firm.

"No, please! It's the truth! If my home was searched, it'd be found. The Eye is full of magic! The vial is masked while there. Please…" He cried, sobbing. "It's there, I swear, please. Let me go. You can have it. Please, just let me go. I won't tell anyone. I promise…"

The woman's finger returned to his lips, silencing his weeping and begging. "I can't let you go, wizard. Your deal was with the Ghul. You must settle your end of the bargain."

"Please, I didn't know…"

"If you don't have the gold given to you to clear your debt, wizard, then your agreement states the Ghul gets the use of your magic for one day. Do you have the gold?"

"No, but please…" Having heard enough, the woman grabbed the metal collar around Cameron's neck and pulled. As sparks of deep nerve pain lit up inside his body, he realized the collar was not just for magic silencing. It was for something entirely different. Seconds passed before the fiery electrical signals subsided. He opened his eyes to find the woman nose-to-nose with him.

"Your deal is one day. Should you survive the one day, you will walk from here as if nothing ever happened. Suck it up, and act like a fucking wizard. You spoiled, university-trained brats give all real wizards a bad name." Taking a deep breath, Cameron steeled himself and nodded. Gathering the last of his nerve and what little bravery he had, he turned to the Ghul.

"Do what you're going to do," Cameron said, his voice wavering. Tears ran down both cheeks, but he managed to keep the whimpers suppressed.

The woman gave him a crooked sneer and turned away. "He's all yours." She turned to walk away but stopped as she reached the Ghul. "What you have been looking for is in the city somewhere," she whispered, but the words still reached Cameron's ears.

"You sure?" Ghul asked.

"No. His magic is cloaked, but I know of no other wizard who can do that."

The Ghul scoffed. "You know too little. Find out," he ordered. "And if so bring it to me."

"I thought you wanted me to stay," she replied. The Ghul frowned and grabbed the handle on the table's frame, pulling. With a familiar, sickening lurch, Cameron was flat on his back and staring into the ceiling rafters, again.

"Find it," the Ghul repeated.

The woman stepped back, and the Ghul approached Cameron's other side. Lifting a vial from inside his pocket, the Ghul pulled the stopper and poured the contents into the wound on his big toe. Time passed in a painstakingly slow way as the Ghul poured a fine line of purple liquid into every intricate design cut into Cameron's flesh over. Once complete, the Ghul placed a clear blue crystal on Cameron's chest and began to chant.

Agony ripped through his body as tentacles grew from the crystal and grabbed onto his skin before dragging the crystal into his chest. Cameron screamed while the Ghul stood over him and stared. The pain built to its peak, and he held on for as long as he could before finally losing his grasp on reality.

The Ghul reached across and pressed two fingers to Cameron's throat.

"A survivor," he muttered. Turning to Merethyl, he nodded. "This wizard has passed the first stage. You may begin your search for this possible DeathWizard, as you call him. I need his magic if we hope to create the next line of Vascuul. Find it quickly or else bring me another full binding stone for this fool's second stage."

Merethyl nodded and turned to leave. A young boy stood by the door with the old man who pretended to be the Ghul on the streets. She turned her nose in disgust at the old man. The old man was the true parasite in GutterTown. His reputation as the person who could help anyone preceded him. Unfortunately, as the young boy was about to find out, the price for such a service was immense.

She shrugged and passed by the boy and old man.

The Broken Blades were on the hunt, again, and nothing else mattered to the Queen of Assassins.

Chapter Twenty

"Very few things in life will forge the bond of friendship faster than the rush and heat of battle. When a warrior has bled at your side and witnessed the closeness of death, it creates an unbreakable trust. When we call a 'brother' or 'sister' to battle, this trust is what we call upon. I call you now brothers and sisters. I call you all."

Excerpt from Jarl Drenger Jafnkollr's farewell speech, Bloodbourne Ceremony. 5015 PC

SECOND FLOOR INTERIOR TERRACE
CASCADE CITADEL

Kael knelt behind the railing and gently put his hand on the shoulder of a gargoyle statue. He slowly peeked over the edge and looked down on the meeting hall used by the nobility. Alia crouched on the opposite side of his statue while Corleya sat on her knees by his side. One glance was all it took to clear up what was going on.

"That's Duke Sheering on the throne," Corleya whispered.

"He has been busy," Alia stated. "Two Pillars already."

"Does that mean the Citadel has accepted him?" Corleya asked.

Alia shrugged as she peered around the gargoyle.

Kael nodded absent-mindedly as he focused on the woman tied and bound before the throne.

"Tania Vakaran," the Duke barked. "Swear fealty or die. I will waste no more time with you. A dozen nobles have held out because of you. King Bale is nearly dead, and his daughter has been for months."

"Fool," Corleya muttered.

"There is nothing left to fight for."

"You gods-cursed cowardly grand duke of a shit," the Duchess hissed.

A knight dressed in heavy plated armor stepped forward and lashed out, smacking the duchess. The sheer force drove her to the floor. Blood dripped from her mouth.

"A tyrant from day one," the Duchess said through a mouthful of bloody saliva.

The Duke laughed. "That is no way to speak to your new king. That determination will be needed in the coming months. Talohna is about to change drastically. I could use a strong woman at my side... one who knows her place among Ancient gods."

The Duchess struggled to sit. "You are as stupid as you are fat, Sheering. You think the Ancients will be the godly saviors everyone wishes?"

"Of course, they will be," he answered. He opened his arms wide. "They built all of this—Corynth, Avalera City, Dra'Kahn, Soena, Sao Vatos. The biggest and most wondrous cities in all of Talohna."

"Fool!" Duchess Vakaran shrieked over him. "A race only builds when they are done conquering. The Ancients have no power in Talohna, which means they will conquer it before they bring peace and prosperity back—if those myths are even true. You have done nothing but doom Cethos into slavery."

"We should bow to our superiors, foolish child, like the lesser citizens bow to us nobles when we pass them in the streets. They are the Ancients," he said as his own voice climbed higher. "We bow if they so ask or we will be smitten by their godly hands."

"The Ancients are not gods." Duchess Vakaran sighed. She slumped to the floor, and Kael watched as all the fight had left her body."

"No, they are not," he said, glancing over his shoulder to Corleya, but she was gone. Panicking, he quickly searched for her, but she was nowhere in sight. "Alia!" he whispered. "You see where Corleya went?"

The mercenary shook her head and gasped as she pointed below.

"Grand Duke Sheering." Corleya's voice echoed off the meeting hall walls all the way back to Kael and Alia.

"Ah, shit," Kael muttered and slipped around the gargoyle to Alia. "Get as close as you can to her but stay hidden for now."

"Agreed." She hesitated before moving.

"You'll know it when it happens," he said. She nodded and left while Kael watched the nightmare unfolding below him.

"You will stand down and surrender my father's throne. As heir to the Cethosian monarchy, I demand it," Corleya ordered.

Duke Sheering laughed. "You look like a street rat, young one. I think you will be executed for entering the palace proper without royal consent."

"You know full well who I am, Sheering," Corleya persisted. "Your coup and Duchess Vakaran's rebellion are both irrelevant. I am alive, and I am home. It matters not what either of you believe."

The self-declared king smiled at what could only be his second Pillar. The Wizard nodded to the shadows, and a man dressed in black leather armor, hood, and mask slid through the dark toward Corleya. From what Kael knew, it had to be the Hunter, Sheering's Fifth Pillar of Rule. Lycori told him that the Hunter's black mask was the mark of the royal assassins.

"Shit." Kael cursed a second time while the Hunter closed on the Princess. The man moved almost as fast as he could. Kael readied himself to act when Corleya rubbed her neck and turned toward the Hunter as if she sensed him. The Hunter froze at the edge of the darkening shadows. Kael recognized the magic and knew it gave the Hunter extra cover, like Sephi had done for him in Dasal so long ago.

The stone gargoyle under Kael's hand shivered, and he turned toward it slowly. The statue's eye blinked, and it dawned on him what King Bale meant when he said *I made them stir once.*

Corleya turned back toward King Sheering and the Hunter moved. Kael followed, immediately vanishing in a cloud of black and knowing he would be too late. He stepped through the black and wrapped his arms around Corleya. The Hunter's blade entered his back instead hers. The crack of Alia's whip hit his ears, and he heard the Hunter grunt. Corleya whirled and grabbed him in her arms.

"Kael!"

"The gargoyles," he hissed as his legs gave out. Already, Sheering's Knight was headed their way. "The Citadel's magic are the gargoyles. Call them to help you."

Corleya looked to the second-floor terrace and then back to him. He nodded, and she closed her eyes.

Kael dragged himself aside, letting Alia step in to engage the Knight. Stretching, he grasped the knife in his back and pulled. It snapped in his shoulder, leaving him holding the all too familiar hilt—complete with broken blade.

"You have got to be fucking kidding me," he muttered to himself. Dropping the hilt, he reached back, again, and managed to dig his finger into the wound far enough to hook one of the barbed edges. Pouring magical strength into his hand, he screamed and tore the broken blade free.

"Too close, goddammit." He cursed as the wooden blade fell from his trembling fingers. "Goddamn dirty assassins." A flash caught his attention, and in his peripheral vision, he saw the Hunter struggling on the floor while he choked to death in the wraps of Alia's whip. He grinned at the bastard's predicament, but quickly shifted his attention to the young mercenary. With only one whip, he knew she would never stay ahead of the Knight, and he was right. She was forced to back-peddle toward Kael as she defended against each stroke of the Knight's sword.

It quickly did not matter, and he chuckled as a massive stone claw appeared over the terrace railing. The stone claw cracked apart to reveal shining black skin. Corleya opened her eyes and beamed. Gargoyles all across the Cascade Citadel awoke with one goal in mind: to replace the blood of a Bale to the throne and to keep her there. The magic flowing from the castle into Corleya made him dizzy — or it could have been the loss of blood and Broken Blade toxin, he was not sure. Either way, the Princess was pulling massive amounts of magic from the castle itself.

A dozen black and gray gargoyles dropped to the hall floor. Two landed on the Knight and pummeled the first Pillar. Kael snorted. The two monsters behaved like massive gorillas from Earth, and they fought the same way as they hammered the Knight into the floor with heavy black fists until only a bloody pile of flattened plate armor remained. Black gargoyles rushed the throne and set upon the Duke and his wizard. Both were torn to shreds in the time it took for Kael to blink through the haze working its way over his eyes. Corleya's voice boomed out, cutting through his fog-riddled mind. He did not doubt for a second that every person in the castle could hear her.

"Lay down your weapons and surrender or they will continue to kill. I am Corleya Bale, daughter of King Joran Bale. My father is dead, and I am the rightful ruler of Cethos."

The guards in the meeting hall obeyed instantly, and Kael could sense only a handful of holdouts throughout the room. All were mercenaries, and each of them died in a matter of seconds.

"Kael." Corleya gasped as she ran to his side. "Why didn't your armor stop his blade?"

He held up the broken wooden blade. "Seems Sheering's Hunter was a Broken Blade assassin."

"Will you heal?" she asked.

He shrugged, too exhausted to answer.

"Perhaps I can help," a young woman said as she approached. "I was to be the new Priestess. Let me help you."

Kael nodded as his consciousness fluttered. "The King..." he began, but finally gave up as darkness took over.

ROYAL RESIDENCE WING
CASCADE CITADEL

Kael awoke in a bed far more comfortable than any he could remember. The luxury was short-lived as he opened his eyes and saw a dozen hooded wizards circled the bed. Magic flowed from their hands and enveloped his body and the bed underneath him.

"Wizard's Council. Shit." He groaned and lay back, too exhausted to fight them.

"Yes, Kael," a voice croaked. The voice had a familiar edge to it. "These are the senior members of Talohna's Wizard Council. All are master wizards. Please, do not fight them. It is for your own good."

"Where's Corleya?" he barked.

"That would be Queen Bale, Kael. You are a guest in her castle. I suggest you use a modicum of a respect."

"Guest?" Kael snorted as he glanced at the wizards around him. Considering he was weak and utterly exhausted, he guessed they were suppressing him and his magic somehow.

"Yes. You are a guest. When you are back on your feet, I will take you to her. You have my promise."

Kael scoffed. "The word of any wizard from this country is worthless."

"How about the word of an old friend?" the voice said while he stepped between two of the wizards. He lowered his hood and smiled.

"Galen!" Kael gasped. "I thought you were dead."

"And I, you."

"What about Kalmar? Did he make it, too?"

"Yes," Galen laughed. "We made it together. Took us a long time to get home."

"Where is he? I'll have to see him before I leave."

"You won't," Galen replied. "He's in southern Yusat with the bulk of the royal army. They were watching the peace border from the Wildlanders threatening war. Queen Bale has since called them home."

"Yeah... sorry about that," Kael said as he winced.

"As am I, and I imagine Queen Bale is as well," Galen added.

"Wow," he said. "Guess we all screwed up. You and Kalmar?"

Galen nodded. "We had to... ah... defend ourselves." His voice dropped as he glanced over his shoulder. "Stole some horses, killed a chief's son... took a spear to the throat..." Galen croaked and coughed, again. His finger trailed along a nasty but aged scar.

"Holy shit," Kael whispered. "Your voice? That what happened?"

Galen sighed as he sank to the chair beside Kael's bed. "No. Not so funny enough... that's from the same as you. Though, there weren't two dozen wizards and a Priestess around when I got the blade." Kael frowned, confused. It prompted Galen to pull his robe to the side at his neck. A familiar but very fresh scar marred the opposite side of his throat. Involuntarily, Kael reached for his own as his old friend continued. "I was in court when Sheering made his move on King Bale. Broken Blade assassins took out every Pillar and wizard present." Galen touched his scar, again. "When King Bale's wizard fell, I turned my head the second before a wooden blade entered my neck. Because of that, it missed my spine, but between the blade's toxin and the damage to my throat... well, our new Priestess says Lady Lykke kept me alive."

"Wait," Kael said. "New Priestess? How long have I been out?"

"Three days," Galen answered. "These wizards and the Priestess have been shifting in and out to remove the toxin from your body. Every time we got ahead of it and stopped, it grew in strength and you would fall deeper into a coma. The Priestess said the poison should be purged from your system by morning. It's strange. It's almost as if it were designed specifically to kill you or your kind. They cleared it from my system in just an hour. If King Bale's old Priestess didn't have the knowledge of lost magic she had, we would have died. No one would have even realized the wooden blades carry a toxin—it is a bit unnecessary if you ask me. Apparently, King Bale had a reason to speak with his Priestess about it years ago and she passed it along to all potential candidates for our new queen."

"Fate, maybe, huh?" Kael asked as he laughed.

"I doubt the Ladies of Fate weave so deeply that they pull every single person's strings, but maybe a nudge?"

Galen smiled, and Kael relaxed for the first time in longer than he could remember.

"I am sorry for the scare when you woke. With what we have been hearing, I had to be sure that you... well, that you were still the you I knew," Galen said as his cheeks flushed.

"Probably a good call," Kael muttered. "Cause I'm not."

"I imagine not. Feel well enough to catch me up?"

"Of course. Once your wizards are done, yeah?"

Galen nodded. "Of course. We shall talk in the morning," he said. He got up to leave but stopped. "Kael?"

"Yeah?"

"Would you ask the DragonKin about Giddeon, Saleece, and Kasik, if I asked you to?"

"I promised King Bale I would before he died, so, yes," he replied. He could see Galen wanted to ask him something. He already knew the question, so he shook his head. "I won't promise you anything, Galen. I can't. If I get my hands on Giddeon."

"I understand, Kael. I do. I know he drove you right into Sythrnax. What we went through at Arkum Zul..." Tears welled up in his eyes, and Kael had to look away. "*I understand. We will need them. Giddeon, too. Try to see that far ahead.*"

"You know that Kyah was a Dead Sister?" he asked.

"Heard rumors for a while now, yeah," Galen said, wiping at his eyes.

"I have a hard time seeing that far ahead, Galen," he stated. "It seems like every time I do, those I trust the most reveal their true selves — in a bad way. Giddeon will answer my questions one day and so will Sythrnax. What happens beyond that? I really don't care. Loyalty seems to be a forgotten concept in Talohna."

Galen offered his hand, and Kael took it. "Not for everyone. I will never hold that against you," his old friend said. "You will never have to worry where my loyalty lies. It will never change."

"I know," Kael said and shook Galen's hand. "Now, let me get some rest so we can catch up in the morning, yeah?"

The wizard nodded and left as a young boy entered his room to change Kael's water jug. The boy offered him another pillow, and he nodded while the young servant slid it behind his head. As the boy bent under the bed to check the chamber pot, Kael relaxed and closed his eyes from utter exhaustion.

He was asleep before the boy left his room.

ABANDONED WAREHOUSE
GUTTERTOWN, CORYNTH

"Did you get it?" the old man snarled as Tanner rushed into the abandoned warehouse. He quickly closed his mouth when the terrifying woman walked in behind him. She had escorted Tanner to the castle and helped him get the servant job.

"Of course, he got it," Merethyl snapped. "It was a simple task."

"The boy has returned?" Ghul said.

Tanner nodded and slowly approached both men. He pulled a black crystal from inside his new servant uniform and handed it the Ghul.

"You both may leave. But, Merethyl, stay nearby and let me know when our friends arrive in the city," Ghul ordered. Tanner watched them leave. He relaxed as the woman closed the door behind her, but nearly lost control of his bowels when the Ghul looked down on him.

"Come," he said, leading him into the back room where Kenna lay motionless on a wooden table. "We will try and help your sister."

"She looks dead," Tanner said. His voice trembled, and he wiped tears from his eyes.

The Ghul glanced over his shoulder with his frightening purple eyes and nodded. Tanner had to clench his butt cheeks even tighter.

"She is on the cusp of life," the Ghul answered. "I know of only one way to save her, young one."

"Please," he begged. "She is all I have left."

"She will feel agony unlike any in her life, and she may still die. If she survives, she may be changed. I have never done this before. Would you like me to proceed?"

Tanner nodded. "Please... I cannot..."

"I understand," the Ghul said. "Now come, help me tie her down so she will not hurt herself when the magic begins to work."

Tanner nodded again and grabbed the strap by Kenna's chest. "I am sorry, sister," he said and settled the strap across her chest. "I need you to get better, so we can leave this city someday." He pulled the strap through the buckle, securing her to the table as the Ghul finished her feet and hands.

"Stand back, young one," the creature ordered and eased Tanner backward until he came up against the wall.

Tanner's stomach leapt into this throat as the Ghul drew a wicked hooked dagger from his belt. He took a step forward as the creature placed the knife to his sister's belly, but he quickly stopped as the Ghul cut open Kenna's shirt and exposed her upper body. The Ghul set the black stone Tanner had stolen from the injured man in the castle onto Kenna's chest.

"Remember," the Ghul said. "Do not interrupt the magic — no matter how much your sister screams or what happens. Understand?"

Too terrified to answer, Tanner nodded.

"Then, we shall begin."

The Ghul chanted, and Tanner stared in utter horror as long black tendrils of magic grew from the dark crystal on his sister's chest. Like the fronds on the small dragon lizards outside of the city, the black tendrils moved back and forth. The Ghul's chanting increased in speed as the dark tentacles plunged into Kenna's chest. Tanner slapped both hands to his mouth to avoid crying out while her body jerked and thrashed.

"Help me hold her down, boy!" the Ghul snapped. "Hurry."

Tanner jumped forward and grabbed his sister's arms, pressing his body to hers.

"Watch the magic, dosa!" the Ghul barked and dragged Tanner off his sister by his hair. "Just hold her arms."

"I am sorry!" he cried out as Kenna's body continued to spasm.

"This isn't right. What did you do with the stone?" the Ghul snarled.

"Nothing," he wailed. Tanner jumped back as several silver spikes leapt from the stone and plunged into Kenna. "Help her please!"

"Impossible..." Ghul whispered. He stepped back as a silver-scaled serpent slid from the stone but remained a part of the dark crystal. "It cannot be..." He grabbed Tanner by the neck and lifted from the ground. "The man you took this stone from!

Who was he? What did he look like? A name! Did you get a name?"

"No, no," Tanner begged. "Please —"

The Ghul tossed him to the floor and spun back to Kenna but got too close. The silver serpent lashed out and struck him on the cheek as a detonation exploded outside. The door out in the warehouse opened, and moments later, Merethyl rushed into the small room.

"They're here!" she said. "You have to gain control of them or this will not work."

The Ghul growled. "Stay here with him and stay away from the girl until the process is complete. I'll be back once I calm the Vascuul." He turned and ran from the room. The last thing Tanner saw of him was his long robes as they disappeared out the door.

"Intriguing," Merethyl whispered as the silver serpent lashed at her. She stepped forward for a closer look, but Tanner grasped her hand.

"Stay away," he pleaded.

Merethyl smacked him to the floor. "Do not touch me, cretin! Do you even know what is happening here? I doubt your pathetic little mind could even begin to comprehend it."

Tanner grabbed his face and struggled not to sob. "He is healing her!"

The door out in the warehouse opened again. "Merethyl?" Magkahn Droverson yelled.

"Here, Mags," Merethyl answered.

A mousy haired woman entered the room and smiled. "The attack has begun. The Queen is already pulling back her forces to guard the marketplace."

"Good," Merethyl replied.

"I will not let you take her," Tanner said and stood, ready to protect his sister.

"You pathetic little piece of slim-rot. The Ghul is creating a new life from within the wasted life owned by your sister. A new species of Vascuul, created by using the most powerful dark magic to ever exist. She will belong to my guild."

Merethyl turned to Magkahn and nodded. Both women stepped up to Kenna and unbuckled the straps on her hands. The serpent struck at them repeatedly, but they were faster. As the buckles sprung free, the viper turned and struck Kenna. It burrowed its way into her body and took the black stone with it.

Tanner screamed as black tentacles edged in silver raced through his sister's flesh. Her face, arms, hands and body were covered in black and silver vines. He sobbed as she arched her back and shrieked as more agonizing convulsions ripped through her small body.

"Hurry!" Merethyl barked. "The guild's magic will calm the reaction she's having."

"Talk to her, boy," Magkahn ordered as she stared hard at him and struggled with the buckles at Kenna's feet. "Try to calm her."

He shook his head as Kenna went limp.

"Fuck!" Merethyl cursed and lifted the girl's wrist to check for a pulse.

"Is she dead?" Magkahn asked quietly, placing two fingers on Kenna's throat. "There's no pulse. It didn't work."

"Fuck," Merethyl repeated. "Get out of here, Mags. I'll kill the boy, so he doesn't tell Ghul our plans." The guild council member nodded and quickly left.

"Please," Tanner begged. "I will not tell him."

"Of course, you will," Merethyl answered as she placed the girl's hand at her side and turned to face him. "If it helps, you will feel nothing." The woman's hands filled with blue lightning and Tanner finally lost control of himself as she flung the energy at him. He threw his hands up in a futile gesture to stop the attack. Before he could close his eyes, the magic stopped short and raced away. It struck Kenna and the wooden table.

"Very intriguing," Merethyl snarled. "You have magic." Tanner stared in disbelief at the shimmering wall of blue in front of his hands. "Well done, little one. I've not seen a Puritan's blue shield in centuries," she continued. "That certainly changes things." She approached him and knelt until she was at his eye level. "How would you like to never go hungry, again? You are a gutter rat, right" He nodded and she continued. "So, you must know who the Broken Blades are, child?"

He nodded and nearly lost control of his bladder. Every gutter rat, homeless, and dirt-poor citizen of GutterTown had heard of the magical killers.

"Would you like to become an assassin, boy?" she asked. "We are the most powerful magical killers to ever live. We pay dues to no one, and nobody ever bullies or beats our sisters. It is a one-time offer, child. Yes, or no?"

"No!" Kenna growled as she sat up on the table. Black and silver energy exploded from her body. It lifted Merethyl from her feet and slammed her into the wall. She fell to the floor unconscious.

"Kenna?" Tanner whispered and rushed forward as she fell from the table.

"We have to leave, Tanner," she told him, barely conscious. "It hurts."

He helped her struggle to her feet and she leaned on him while he guided her through the room into the open warehouse. Kenna stumbled, and he nearly fell with her as the door to the outside crumpled. A second impact snapped the door off and it skid across the floor in front of them.

Tanner nearly choked on his own tongue as a massive snake with a woman's body coiled around the door frame and burst into the warehouse. Like some berserker from the Northman stories, the snake-woman attacked the door in a frenzy of slashing claws and spitting venom. He held Kenna tight, too terrified to move. She finally noticed them and slithered over, gently dropping from her tail to her feet.

"Wizard was here, soon ago," she hissed. She cocked her head to the side and reached out her hand to touch Kenna. Tanner shifted his body to protect her and the woman hissed again. "Not hurt," she added and inched closer. The woman gently stroked Kenna's cheek, and Tanner could see her calm.

"Another child of black," the woman said and looked to Tanner. "Flee. You must go."

"Taseeda." A voice barked from the door. "Kill them and move on. The enemy has fortified the market and make their stand there."

Tanner shook at the sight of the bizarre man. Green scales fringed in red covered his body and the leathery wings folded close to his back twitched with annoyance. Slit eyes identical to a lizard's stared at him, and he wondered if he and Kenna would ever get away from the nightmare of the past few days.

The snake woman turned and hissed. "After you," she said.

"After you finish them," he persisted, and he pointed to Tanner and Kenna. "Our orders were a high body count as quickly as possible." Tanner gasped as the man drew a set of blades covering his hands like gloves.

"No!" Taseeda snapped. "Leave them, Kurse. We go."

"Sorry, gorgon," the man said and moved forward. "I do not take orders from you."

The woman slid over to shield Tanner and his sister. She attacked the scaled man in a flash, and Tanner jumped at the stream of hissing venom that shot from her mouth. The smell burned his nose and caught in his throat. The man spun on his foot and jumped into the air, so Tanner shook his sister back to awareness and started dragging her toward the door. The man's wings snapped open, and he slammed into Taseeda. The impact drove her into the far wall. Dropping to his feet, the man turned and headed after Tanner as he tried to escape through the open door.

"Kenna, wake up!" Tanner pleaded and shook her again. "We have to run, I can't carry you! Please!"

"Leave me," she whispered. "It hurts, Tanner."

"Please," he said, trying again. "Please, Kenna..." He stopped short as the winged man crouched in front of them.

"Filthy street rats," he muttered and placed one of his blades to Kenna's throat.

"No," Tanner said and reached for the man, knowing he would be too late. Kenna's hand shot out and latched onto the man's arm. Kurse screamed and Kenna stood under her volition until she hovered over the crumpling man. He was dying slowly, and Tanner knew the winged man had little time left. Tanner stared in awe as a myriad of rippling colours flowed from the man to Kenna.

He struggled with it, but it finally dawned on him that his sister was about to kill this man. He panicked and grabbed her arm.

"Kenna, stop! Please, stop! You will kill him," he said and grabbed her other arm. "We have to run!" With a sharp twist, he tore his sister's grip from the man's arm and dragged her toward the exit. The man panted and groaned on the warehouse floor. Kenna turned and stumbled at Tanner's side, but he sighed with relief. He no longer had to carry her full weight.

In fact, she seemed to be getting stronger with each second that passed. Putting an arm around her waist, he helped support her as they ran from the warehouse without looking back.

Chapter Twenty-One

*"The powerful find more meaning in madness than the weak,
because the weak refuse to see its benefits. The powerful use all the
tools at hand."*

Dead Sister Doctrine

DRAGON ISLES
BLOODKIN CASTLE

Kael glanced back at Galen and the new Queen Bale.
She would always be just Corleya to him, but he understood the
need for etiquette and respect. She had earned his respect. He
put his focus on his spell. They were far from the Kasym, so it
was easier to open a vortex. However, he still found it tricky.
He frowned as he stepped into the swirling magic and jumped
from the Cascade Citadel to Ver Karmot. The magic carried him
away and in seconds the pressure of dragon magic pushed
against his jump, but he shoved back violently, and the
resistance stopped. Their magic would only slow his arrival. He
smiled and watched through the storm of magic as his vortex
began to form on the far side. Queen WhiteScale entered the
throne room and called her honor guard to her side. She eased

into her throne as if waiting for him to arrive. The black and purple snap of immense magical energy exploded around him, and he walked from the white blaze of chaotic energy caused by the Fae realm jump.

Frowning as swords and pikes surrounded him, he said, "I mean you no harm, Your Highness. Your guards can stand down." Shelaryx shook her head. She was perturbed, but clearly intrigued.

"I think not, Kael Symes. Until I know your motives," she purred. "The child of prophecy has finally found his way to another magical race. You should have saved yourself a lifetime and a death by simply coming here first."

"Should have, could have." He shrugged.

"You are right," she replied. "The past is now irrelevant. My spies in Corynth swore you were the DeathWizard who helped Princess Corleya fight her way to the Cethosian throne. I must admit, I am surprised, especially when I was told that you helped her to unlock the Citadel's magic. That magic has been dormant for hundreds of years."

"You offer too much credit," he replied. "Besides, I helped her, not her father. It was he who would have sooner killed me. Or, maybe, you're surprised that I found my way back to the living?"

The Queen laughed. "You act as though forgiving those who wish to kill you and returning from the dead are simple tasks. And, yet, no other of your kind have ever done either."

"I thought I made it clear I'm not here to discuss the decisions of my past, Your Highness."

"No, I don't imagine you are. So, tell me why you are here."

"You have something I want."

"Don't you mean someone, Kael? The only reason you would be here is for a certain ArchWizard."

"Yes," he replied. "We have things to discuss."

"And if I say no? Giddeon Zirakus is here paying for his crimes against you and so many others. It is a miracle granted by the old gods that you stand here before me. It gives me hope. It is most certainly a day I never thought I would see. Giddeon nearly cost this world everything. I am not willing to release a traitor of his magnitude. Ri'Tek warriors walk this world for the first time in over ten thousand years because of him. It is a crime punishable by a very slow and painful death."

Kael snorted, again. "Yet he lives. Maybe instead of you and the Fae hiding behind your ancestors' magic, you both should have come forward and helped. Letting Giddeon and the Wizard Council know the truth would have—"

"What?" the Queen barked, interrupting him. "Saved you? Stopped the seals from opening?"

"To start," Kael quipped as he struggled to hold his tongue.

The Queen rose from her throne and stepped closer. "You are a fool if you believe that. Had the Fae done so and Sythrnax caught even one of them, he would have opened the seal anyway. If he managed to catch a matured Fae, he would have brought down Jasala's Sepulchre and all the Ri'Tek would be free right now as we speak. My Kin and I have been here stuck on these islands for an aeon while protecting this seal."

"Right, so I keep hearing," Kael snapped. "Yet with so much on the line, it still seems like I'm the only goddamn one doing anything about it! I can't fight them alone. Maybe it's time for those with the real power in Talohna to start acting like it. Stand up and help."

The Queen stared at him. Shifting, she eased herself back onto her throne. Her movements reminded him of a slithering, poisonous snake—patient, but deadly.

As he stared, it finally hit him. The way she moved, her entire demeanor—it was not like a snake at all. He blinked to focus his eyes and the Queen's aura lit up like the sky over Sam's Bay on the Fourth of July. He stared, unable to blink, and shock rolled through his very being as the savage and wild mix of colours in her aura revealed her true identity.

"You are right," she said, bringing his attention back to her physical form. "It is time. The Fae and the DragonKin will do what we can to help without risking the Sepulchre. If it does happen to fall, we will commit all we have to the fight."

Kael strongly suspected he was being played long before she opened her mouth.

"Perhaps a deal then?" she offered. "I will give you Giddeon to do with what you will, but I want something from you first."

Kael smirked, he had her. "What could I possibly do for the last Dragon Behemoth?"

Queen WhiteScale glared at him. If looks could kill, he would have been dead on the floor. He began to wonder if he had pushed too far.

"You know?" she growled. Fury marked her frown and pursed lips.

"I didn't believe it until I arrived and saw your presence and mannerisms for myself."

"Rather guarded, are you not, Kael Symes? In reality, I suspect you can read my aura as easily as I can read yours."

Kael chewed his lip and decided insulting a ten-thousand-year-old dragon probably was not his wisest move. "Auras rarely reveal one's race. You are a definite exception," he said, instead. "But in my time here, I have found that guarding one's secrets is the only way to stay alive. And even that doesn't seem to work so well. Trust gets you killed, literally, so just tell me what it will cost me to get Giddeon from you."

Queen WhiteScale bowed slightly and turned to the guard on her right. "Commander Zatassa, tell my daughter to bring them."

"Are you sure, Mistress? He could —"

"He will not. Now, please, Commander." He bowed and left, exiting through a crystal door. He returned with a young woman who carried an ornate wooden box decorated with symbols from corner-to-corner. The carved characters blazed with a kind of magic he had never seen. With his senses wide open, he instinctively shielded his eyes with his hand and forcibly muted his senses before he went blind. As his vision cleared, he recognized the woman Queen WhiteScale had called was her daughter.

"That... just... that makes so much more sense," he mumbled as he stared at the woman he helped save in the Wildlands Forest so long ago.

Queen WhiteScale smirked. "I understand you have already met my daughter, Saleece. It will make your task much easier." Kael raised an eyebrow but didn't answer. "Saleece, my dear, show him."

The young woman stepped closer. Coming to a stop only two feet from him, she slowly opened the wooden case.

Kael gasped as the lid opened completely. "Dragon eggs," he breathed. Six eggs the size of a basketball were surrounded by the box's velvet inlay.

"Yes. One from each of the dragon clans who still have Kin alive on this island. Each the descendant of a clan queen or king. They were all that were saved ten millennia ago when the Ri'Tek Sect priestesses and their Vascuul attacked our nursery."

Kael stared in awe. "Jesus," he said. "I can do a lot of things since I got back, but there is no way my magic can hatch those eggs."

The Queen smiled. "No, it cannot. Only a queen can hatch them and only time — a thousand years or more — will see them begin to mature. Time, we do not have if we are to survive the coming war with the Ri'Tek."

Realizing what she meant, Kael shook his head. "No."

"Then, you will not get Giddeon and the answers you seek. And you will certainly not be able to take him from me by force."

"Then, you can fucking keep him," Kael snapped as he lost his temper. "You're goddamn insane. Just like every other power in this world. Greed and power blind you to the consequences or the sacrifices of what you're asking."

The Dragon Queen remained in her throne, but the threat was clear. "How dare you, Kai'Sar!" she hissed. "You have not earned the right to judge me or my people." A growl emanated from deep within her throat and wisps of gray smoke curled from her nose. "We have sacrificed more in this fight than you can ever imagine! My father knew he would die if he engaged the Vascuul dragons, and still, he gave his life willingly so that your corrupt kind could lock the Ri'Tek away. Vaighar killed five of the seven Vascuul dragons before he fell. We have lived in exile for thousands of years, and the Fae have almost lost the ability to have children because they have been forced to live off-phase from their home dimension. Do not dare speak to me about sacrifice or loss. You will do as I ask, or you will join your father in my dungeon."

Kael's anger jumped to life at the challenge, and he struggled to keep it in control. For the first time since he returned, he did not want to control it. He was tired of being used as a pawn in a war so old no one alive even knew it had ever existed. A voice rolled through his mind as he grabbed for his magic.

Even you cannot win a fight against a white dragon — even one as weak as she is. Secede or die here, Kael.

I thought you'd be drooling over a dragon soul, he snapped inside his head.

By proxy... you'd have to be alive for me to use it, idiot.

I don't care anymore, I am tired of being a goddamn pawn, he growled back. He knew Akai was right, but he could not stop himself from attacking. The long scythe appeared in his hand, and he immediately peeled the shorter scythe from the handle before he leapt at the Queen and swung. Every bit as fast as he was, she slid from her throne, raised her arms, and barked her spell before he reached her. A green shield bloomed from her hands, and his blades slammed into it and stuck. Kael leaned on his blades and the Queen pushed on her shield, but neither gained any ground.

Holy shit! You are as strong as she is.

"Foolish shit," Shelaryx hissed. "You would have been dead long before your vines matured if not for me. How dare you attack!"

"Liar," he snarled. Power surged through him and still he reached for more. Black flames sparked to life along his arms and he pushed his blades further into the shield.

"Dragons cannot lie, little fool, but we can lose our tempers." A blast of energy knocked Kael back as the Queen roared. He stood, panting and looked up into the face of a massive white dragon. "I saved your life in the bottom of the Black Arc over a year ago when a Zakair gutted you like a spring pig." She roared again. "I convinced the DeathGod to heal you. In exchange, I freed him of a favor he owed from over a millennia ago." The dragon stomped and whole throne room shook under her rage. "It was a priceless sacrifice with no equal. Dathac does not grant favor."

I take it back, in this form she is stronger. Akai quipped. *But she is beautiful.*

The spirit and the dragon's words took the fight from his fury as he remembered his first of many horrific nights in Talohna. The foreign entity in his body, the sparkling black magic, the healing—all of it finally made so much more sense on how he had survived.

Akai was right, she was amazingly beautiful.

"Tell me the truth," he panted. "Can one goddamn person in this fucking world tell me the truth." With his anger spent because of the amazing sight in front of him, he released his weapons.

"I am," the dragon growled. "It saved your life, but...I..." He could feel her regret radiate through her aura, and as if her own words had deflated her anger, the dragon calmed. As she shifted back to Human-form, he stared in awe. "You paid a terrible price," she said. "The god's magic left you defenseless for when you encountered Sythrnax. I am sorry for what you suffered. It was not my intention."

Kael shook his head. "I can sense your regret—guilt even—but understand that I have been pulled by strings since the moment I got here. I am tired of it."

"In a way, you have. Unfortunately, it is the way of this world. We are not merely fighting for our lives, but for the existence of our races," she told him. Her determination washed over his senses. "And you are the only weapon we have. I wish to be your ally, Kael, not another enemy."

Finally, he took a deep breath and sighed. "Very well," he said. "What exactly do you want from me?"

The Queen cocked her head and smiled. "Simple, Kael. Take my daughter and these eggs to a dimension where time moves faster—five times faster than it did in the afterlife. Take however long is required to make sure she will be safe while there and then return. After all you could spend a year there and only be gone from here for just over two days. Do so and Giddeon is yours."

"I knew it," he spat and shook his head in disbelief. "Cracking dimensional barriers isn't something I've had a lot of experience with. None, in fact. What you're asking... Free the Northman, Kasik and make sure he is returned to Corynth, and I will consider it."

"Saving your complete goal until an opportunity presents itself. Well done, Kael. Most people would have asked for Giddeon and Kasik at the same time. You have a deal."

"My willingness won't make it any safer," he snorted.

"It is extremely dangerous. Yes. I am well-aware of the dangers of dimensional travel. However, you have already cracked the most difficult dimensional barrier... the one between life and death. Surely, this will be much easier. Besides, Saleece returning in a year's time with seven full grown dragons is well worth the risk, and it will give us an edge against our ancient enemy."

Kael frowned, missing something. "I am not staying in another dimension for a year... wait... seven?" he asked.

"You disappoint me, Kael," Queen WhiteScale said. "I heard that mind of yours was quite sharp and unique."

She had not even finished mocking him before he realized his mistake. The Queen had said earlier that only a queen could hatch the eggs, yet he knew Queen WhiteScale would never leave Talohna. "Of course." He sighed. "Saleece wasn't born, was she?"

"Of course not. She is the heir to the Superior Dragonthrone and only a century away from being mature. A thousand years will make her unstoppable," the Queen answered.

Kael shook his head. "Surely the Fae Matriarch would help you?"

"Of course, she would, but we need to return in a year's time. The Fae will not open a gate twice for anyone. But you can, can't you, Kael?"

"Maybe..." he replied, unable to restrain the disbelief in his voice. "I've never opened a doorway to another dimension before, let alone a specific one. You do know that I didn't open a doorway back to the living. The tree of life brought me here." It was partially true.

"I can give you all the details you will need," the Queen said, smiling.

"Fine," Kael snapped as the Queen returned to her throne. "You have a deal. Just don't bitch about it when I kill us all and I flash cook six dragon omelets."

Chapter Twenty-Two

"Do not engage an enemy more powerful than you and if it is unavoidable and you do have to engage then make sure you engage it on your terms and not on your enemy's terms."

Sun Tzu, The Art of War

VER KARMOT, DRAGON ISLES
BLOODKIN CASTLE

Kael shot from his dimensional vortex as if being launched from a catapult. Unable to control his momentum, he crashed into several DragonKin royal guards, and they all tumbled across the floor before slamming into a crystal wall. He opened his eyes and saw he had made it back to BloodKin Castle alive.

"What happened?" Queen WhiteScale snarled.

Groaning, Kael rolled over onto his stomach. He rose to his knees but knew there was no way he could stand yet. "You'd better hope I get a better handle on this dimensional travel shit over the next year, or your daughter and those eggs are long gone."

"What went wrong?" the Queen demanded a second time.

Struggling to stand, it took him a few tries to reach his feet. "You picked a dimension filled with active magical energies. It reacted with the vortex when I opened the doorway back to here."

"Then you had better practice, Kai'Sar, because I expect you to be back here in Ver Karmot exactly one year from now in compliance with our deal."

"Yeah," he muttered. "Unlike everyone else in this world, I actually keep my bloody word. I'll be here. Now, you have something of mine." He struggled to remain standing, but he finally managed to stabilize himself.

The Queen gave him a quick bow. "I, also, keep my word, Kael. Commander Zatassa, please bring Giddeon up from the dungeon." Turning to Kael, she added, "You are lucky that Giddeon has recovered over the past few months. He is nearly back to full strength. Thanks to my daughter's insistent pleas for his mercy."

"Good," Kael said, frowning as the crystal doors opened. Zatassa led Giddeon into the throne room and pushed the ArchWizard to his knees in front of Queen WhiteScale. Kael stared at the man who had caused him so much pain and just barely managed to suppress the urge to kill him on the spot.

"Giddeon Zirakus," Queen WhiteScale began, "it has been one year since you have been accused of treason against the magical races of Talohna. Under normal circumstances, after the one-year mark, you would be dragged from your cell and executed. You have been spared this sentence because another representative of the magical races has asked that you be placed in their custody."

"Do what you will, Queen WhiteScale," Giddeon said and sighed. The man was a shadow of his former self. Kael almost felt sorry for him… almost.

"I will," she replied. "I have granted his request. You are no longer my problem, Giddeon Zirakus, though you will remain a constant concern for me. May the gods grant your soul mercy. You are now the problem of the only true Kai'Sar to ever live." She extended her clawed hand toward Kael, but Giddeon did not turn.

Kael sensed Giddeon's stomach drop as it were his own and the man's aura flooded with confusion. He did not understand what was happening. The ArchWizard turned slowly and blinked several times as his eyes settled on Kael.

"No," he whispered. "You're dead. You can't be real."

Kael covered the distance between him and Giddeon in less time than it took the old wizard to blink, again.

"I was dead, and I am very real," Kael growled. He grabbed Giddeon by the scruff of his neck and glanced at the Queen. She nodded. Kael pulled Giddeon to his feet and spun, using his free hand to open a vortex. Stepping through, he used the rush of magic to push Giddeon through to the far side and out into the crumbling top floor of Jasala's Black Arc. Using the momentum from the jump, he slammed Giddeon into the stone wall as the magic doorway closed behind them. "Why?"

Giddeon grappled at Kael's hand but could not break himself free. "We didn't know, Kael. I am so sorry."

"Not good enough," Kael growled. He whirled, tossing the wizard across the room into the other wall as he vanished in a cloud of black. Black smoke trailed behind him while he reappeared and snatched Giddeon before he fell over the edge to his death. Kael curled his fingers around the wizard's throat and squeezed.

"How could we... know?" Giddeon spat and gurgled as Kael squeezed harder. "We lost..."

Kael screamed wordlessly and turned Giddeon around. Jasala's memories vibrated inside his head. Her fear, her agony and her exhaustion assaulted his senses. "Look!" he bellowed. Pointing out across the Forsaken Lands battlefield before the Black Arc, he pushed Giddeon further over the edge of the broken wall. "This is where your kind began hunting mine! This is where your kind started killing innocent children! This is where mothers and fathers began murdering their own newborns!"

"We were wrong, Kael!" Spinning again, he pushed Giddeon into another wall. The ancient brick and mortar cracked but held.

"Did you know about the assassin in Kazzador City?" he demanded.

"Of course, not... but I should have known," Giddeon said as he struggled against Kael's grip. "King Bale always had a contingency plan... I should have seen it coming... I didn't want you to die, Kael..."

The urge to snap Giddeon's neck nearly overwhelmed him, and he was shocked when Akai's voice slid into his mind.

Easy, Kael. If you kill Talohna's only ArchWizard, you will be hunted forever. It will distract the world from the true threat.

"I don't care anymore," he growled.

"Who are you talking to, son?" Giddeon asked. "Are you hearing voices? This is why I wanted to talk you when we caught up to you. Let me help you."

Kael laughed. "Always the witless fool, aren't you?"

"Come with me to see King Bale—"

"King Bale is dead," he snapped. "Corleya sits on what is left of the Cethosian throne."

"That can't be true." Giddeon's voice trailed off. "By Inara's grace, what has happened since that day? How long has it been?"

"For you, a year. When you abandoned your search for Corleya and turned it toward me, you drove Cethos into civil war. It opened the door for a coup by the Grand Duke. King Bale died several days ago."

"How?" Giddeon said, frowning in confusion. "Why?"

"Didn't you hear?" Kael mocked. "The Ancients have returned."

"I heard," Giddeon said. "That can only be a good thing."

Kael's anger flared again, and it dawned on him that this idiot in front of him—birth father or not—would only hasten the downfall of Talohna.

"I doubt Joran Bale would agree. That's why you must die, Giddeon." He raised his hand and magic ignited in his palm.

"Don't do this, Kael." Giddeon begged of him, but it only made the magic blaze brighter while Kael struggled to hold on to his anger. "This will eat you alive," Giddeon said quickly.

"No more than crushing an angel like a bug," Kael retorted. The magic in his hand flashed, extending past his fist before solidifying into a black and purple spike. "Good bye, Giddeon," Kael said and swung.

"They're still alive!" Giddeon shrieked. Kael pulled the spike at the last moment, and it exploded against the wall beside his head.

"How dare you?" Kael growled.

"It's true. I swear," Giddeon told him.

"You told me they died." Kael frowned as a storm of emotions rushed over him. "You said—"

"I lied," Giddeon sputtered. "I lied. I'm sorry. I didn't know at that time what I do now."

"Tell me the truth, you goddamn shit," Kael hissed. "Or I will rip your soul from your body and feed it to the WraithLords in this tower."

I'll take it. Akai offered lightly in his head, but quickly retreated as Kael snarled internally.

"They're alive, Kael," Giddeon repeated. "Or they were. I swear, they couldn't have been more than an hour behind us when we found you in Kazzador City. I swear, it is true. Queen WhiteScale told me Ember and Max were with the king and queen of DormaSai. They should be in Drae'Kahn."

"An hour?" he said. "That can't be true. She lied." Kael released Giddeon and stepped back. "She lied. It had to be, had to be... had to be a lie..." Memories true and false rolled through his mind. and none of it made any sense.

"Who, Kael?" Giddeon asked as he approached cautiously. "Who lied?"

"The demon queen," he answered and collapsed to the floor. "She partially lied... but it's true... or did she lie about it all... but why? Why only half truths... it doesn't make any sense," he mumbled and grabbed his head.

"Blessed Lady Inara. What happened to you?" Giddeon asked as he crouched beside him. "Tell me. For once, let me help you, please. Tell me what to do, Kael."

Kael wanted nothing more than to kill the man before him, but his fight and his anger fled as the insipid burn of insanity crept in on him. "The demon queen told me Max and Ember had found me shortly after I died, and that Sythrnax killed them right after," he cried. "But it wasn't real... the Dreamscape. The demon queen, she.... she... it's not real, this can't be real. None of this can be fucking real!" he shouted.

"It's all right, Kael," Giddeon whispered and grabbed him. "Gods, what happened to you?"

"This can... can't be real... not real. More illusions... more dreams... am I back? Really? Really back... am, am, am I even alive Giddeon?" Kael stuttered. Thoughts and images tumbled violently through his head, and reality slipped further away as insanity ate into his mind. "It can't be... r... real, real. Sythrnax knows. Sythrnax... where's Sythrnax?"

Giddeon shook his head. "You are alive, son, I promise you. I don't know about the rest. May I?" he asked, touching Kael's chest. Lost in his swirling thoughts, Kael merely nodded.

Giddeon pulled Kael's armor down a little and gasped. "You were in hell, Kael. You're marked with Reetha's Ichor. How? How are you here in the living world if you were dead?"

"Here?" Kael said. "Killed. Fought... not back yet... this... is not real. DreamScape has... has to be still..."

"Come on, Kael," Giddeon said. "We need to get you back to Corynth. Maybe the Priestess of Rule can help."

"No," he barked. His mind settled the slightest bit, and he focused on the one thing he knew for sure. "DormaSai. If I can't find Sythrnax, then DormaSai... Sephi... real or not, afterlife or not... she will answer my questions. You want to go home?"

"Kael, let me help, please," Giddeon pleaded, again.

"Last chance," Kael barked.

"Yes," Giddeon replied. "Of course, I want to go home."

Kael jumped to his feet and grabbed Giddeon by the scruff of his neck once more as he opened a portal to the Cascade Citadel. He stepped through and let the magic carry him away, but he dragged Giddeon with him for the ride.

EAST OF ACROPOLIS
DORMASAI

Ember stared out across the plain of Peddler's Valley. The expansive mountain valley was DormaSai and Ellorya's most traveled trade route. From the edge of the DormaSain war camp, she could see miles ahead of their location to where the bulk of the Elloryan army remained camped. They were already on DormaSai land. The start of battle was less than an hour away.

"Damn," she whispered. "A lot of people are going to die today." Her stomach twisted, making her groan as her Fae empathy worked overtime at the prospect of the fighting growing closer and of the lives that would be lost. The DeathDogs had been operating hit and run campaigns against the larger army for several days to slow their progress and limit their access to supply lines while Nekrosa marched his army to war. Max led the gorilla-style attacks but was due to return at any time. He was charged with leading the bulk of the DormaSain army against the Ancient-reinforced Elloryan military machine.

"Terrifying sight, isn't it?" Yrlissa asked, stepping up beside her.

"Yes. We're outnumbered at least three to one. I can sense the DeathGod's reapers below us. There are hundreds."

"Any sign of..."

"Dathac?" she asked as Yrlissa's words trailed off. Ember shook her head. "No God of Death roaming the field that I can tell. I doubt he'd care enough to show in person."

"Well, that's a good sign, then. Perhaps we are going to win."

"No, we're not," Max told them as he approached from behind. His voice held a hard edge Ember was unaccustomed to hearing. She turned, and he took her into his arms.

"You made it back in time." She sighed, returning the hug. Her nose twitched, assaulted by the sour stench of blood. The acidic reek of stolen magic burned her nostrils. Pulling back, she questioned, "Magic? The Ri'Tek wasted mystics against hit and run attacks?"

"Yes and no. They wasted nothing. Our last strike nearly cost us an entire unit of DeathDogs. One of the Ancients was wearing Elloryan soldier armor, and we had no idea he was there until it was too late. He killed four soldiers with one attack. We lost another three as we retreated. Please tell me you have a solution to them. Ember? Yrlissa?"

The powerful assassin shook her head. "Now, you know why we nearly lost the war ten thousand years ago. Besides Kael's kind, the Dragon Behemoths were the only thing that even slowed the Ri'Tek and their stolen magic. We are going to risk losing Queen WhiteScale and some of the Fae now. This fight is going to turn into a war of attrition. We'll have to fight them battle-by-battle, town-by-town. Possibly even sacrificing units while we regroup at times."

"God in Heaven, a lot our warriors are going to die fighting that way." Ember sighed. "If our intelligence is right, there are only two seals open. What happens if the Sepulchre falls and the other four open?"

"I don't know, Ember," Yrlissa replied. "I can't see how we win this without the rest of Talohna behind us and without more DeathWizards. It took six of them last time and thousands of fighters were sacrificed to give them the time they needed to complete the Animus Rituals."

"May we intrude?" Nekrosa asked as he limped toward them with Sephi on his arm.

"Always," Ember said and smiled.

"Spies report back yet?" Max asked.

Nekrosa shook his head. "Not the ones we sent to Ellorya, but a spy from the Blood Kingdoms just returned." A dark-haired woman approached as Sephi introduced her.

"This is my sister, Dekayna. She has news from the north you both need to hear."

"Nice to meet you," Ember said, and Max nodded.

"It is a pleasure to meet you, Mistress," Dekayna answered.

"What news?" Max asked.

"I have just returned from Corynth. The civil war is over. King Bale is dead, and Corleya Bale has been crowned the new queen."

"How?" Ember asked. "Last we heard, Duchess Vakaran was on the verge of victory."

"I do not have precise details on the war. However, several weeks ago, a mature DeathWizard helped restore Corleya Bale to the throne, and then, he proceeded to free Giddeon Zirakus and Kasik Blodhjorr from the DragonKin."

"That makes no sense," Ember replied as a frown crawled across her brow.

"We agree," Nekrosa said. "The only DeathWizard who would do such a thing would be—"

"Kael," Ember whispered. Her mind whirled. Kael was dead. There was no doubt about it at all. Unless there was. "Yrlissa," she growled.

"What would I know? I have been here with you."

"Don't play stupid with me," she barked. "The night I found you unconscious by Kael's crypt. What did you do? I could sense the magic you used. It was far from normal, even for you."

"We're going to have to talk about this later." Max interjected, his voice hollow with concern. "The Elloryan army is on the move. We have to engage them now, or we risk losing the high ground to the valley."

"We have a bigger problem," Nekrosa added.

"What?" Ember asked.

"Queen WhiteScale has not arrived and the Fae contingent have not jumped in, yet."

"They promised they'd be here," Ember stated. "My mother promised."

Ember stared back across the valley plains, again. Sure enough, the massive Elloryan army was on the move.

"They must have been engaged elsewhere," Sephi offered. "They are each guarding one seal. Perhaps the Ri'Tek have moved on another seal as well."

"What do we do without them?" Ember gasped.

"We go to war," Yrlissa replied. "War waits on no one—not even a Dragon or the Fae." She turned on her heel and left.

Ember swallowed, hard. "Goddammit, Yrlissa," she snapped, but set it aside to focus on the immediate threat. "Be as safe as you can be."

DORMASAI FORWARD MILITARY CAMP
PEDDLER'S VALLEY

Ember stared out across the valley as the DormaSain ShieldDogs set their feet and pieced their shield wall together to hold back the rush of Elloryan cavalry racing across the valley floor. The bulk of the army ran behind the cavalry. Though frustrated at not being on the front lines, she knew better. Helping from a safe location in the camp was dangerous enough—especially seeing as the Fae and DragonKin were busy elsewhere and could not help.

A flash of magic caught her attention as it rippled through the attacking cavalry. She immediately recognized the adapted Fae shield magic protecting the cavalry's men and horses from the impact with their own shield wall. In a matter of seconds, the shield wall would be obliterated, and the army behind it would be vulnerable to attack.

"Ember!" Nekrosa snapped from her right. "They won't stand a chance. Help them!"

Even as she reached out with her magic, she knew it was hopeless. Her magic faded against the altered shield spell. It was as if she was somehow locked out of being able to affect the enemy's spell.

"I can't," she whispered. "The spell's been changed to keep me out."

"But your reach is that far?" Sephi asked quickly. Ember nodded as the Queen turned to her husband. "That means the Ancient wizards are further back, love. There are no Ancient amulets among the cavalry."

"Right, the White Cabal should be able to use magic," he answered, moving to speak with his runners. "Tell the Whitebloods and the Caballa families to attack — but not at risk to themselves. You carry the attack order to General Soren." He passed the runners a sealed missive each and sent them on their way."

"The shield wall will still collapse," Ember told them as her stomach grew cold.

"My soldiers have trained for that. Perhaps the Cabal can weaken the shield," Nekrosa stated. "Either way, they will hold long enough for the units under Max's command to close the pincher from the northern slopes — especially with the White Cabal and my archers hitting them from the southern edge of the forest."

As if his words were prophetic, magic lit up the southern side of the valley while a storm of arrows whistled through the sky. Ember watched in horror as the magic and the enhanced arrow volley hit the magical shield around the cavalry but did not penetrate.

"Oh no, they —" Her words stopped short as black lightning ripped across the valley. The blast of energy sliced through the adapted Fae shield at the rear of the cavalry just as the first of the charging horses hit the DormaSain shield wall.

"By the Void's holy ass." Nekrosa cursed. "That's DeathWizard magic! Look." Ember followed his finger, looking to the northern cliffs just half a mile from where Max's troops began to charge. A long figure dressed in a black sleeveless robe with a dark hood stood on the cliff's edge. He released another torrent of black and purple lightning. Clearly targeting only the Elloryan forces, the dark wizard's spell tore into the cavalry unit, again. The modified shield winked out of existence as the remaining men and horses collided with men and shields, both exploding along the front line.

The screams of pain from both horse and man made her wince. Another blast of magic from the wizard destroyed most of the remaining cavalry while Max and his units hit the main force of the Elloryan army from the left. Still, a dozen horsemen managed to punch through the front lines. Instead of engaging the main army, they circled to the south and galloped straight for the pass to DormaSai's main camp.

"They're coming our way," Ember whispered. "Why?"

"They would not dare," Sephi began, her voice catching. She stared at Nekrosa with waves of worry radiating off her.

Nekrosa shook his head. "The Ancients have no knowledge of modern warfare. Where's Yrlissa?"

"With Dekayna," Sephi replied.

"Why?" Ember asked.

"Because," he answered. "There's only one reason why those mounts are heading our way."

Ember frowned, still not understanding.

"To kill us," Sephi told her quickly. She scrambled around the command tent, grabbing supplies and two water jugs. "By killing DormaSai's king and queen, the Ancients can place their puppet on our throne."

"Not on my watch," Nekrosa snapped and spat the words to a spell. *"Wings of death's shadow, words of the faithful, speak."* A black shadow bird unfolded from the air in front of him and squawked. The necromancy communication bird dropped to the command table and opened its mouth. The sounds of clashing metal followed on the tail of another screech.

"*Little busy, your majesty,*" Dekayna said as her voice rolled from the undead bird's beak. Three quick strikes of metal on metal rang in the air, and an agonizing cry from a mortal wound chased the words out of the bird.

"I need you and Yrlissa to fall back to the main camp," Nekrosa ordered. "A dozen Elloryan heavy cavalry are on their way. The Ancients are not holding to Talohna's modern warfare etiquette—if they're even aware of it. We may need to retreat, and we'll need you both here."

The clash of more swords came from the bird, and Ember frowned with worry when no answer came.

Several minutes passed and finally a gasp and an answer followed. "*We're on our way, Nekrosa,*" Yrlissa replied. "*Get your ass up, Dekayna—*"

"Dammit." Nekrosa cursed as the connect was severed on the other end and the undead bird vanished. Ember followed him as he hobbled around the command table and approached the cliff overlooking the battlefield. "Ellorya is bringing up a second charge. Our men are going to be hard pressed to hold even though their strategy makes no sense."

"They don't have much choice. They must attack head on. It's why we picked this spot," Ember said.

"Yes," he quipped. "But they're still trying to hammer their way through. There are at least three more units back there, but they're only sending one at a time... why?"

Ember shook her head. "Good question. I'm not a military commander, Nekrosa," she reminded him. She watched helplessly as Max's units were over run only a half mile away. Max would be fine—he always was—she hoped. She swallowed her concern and turned to Nekrosa as a thought jumped to the front of her mind. "This isn't an invasion."

"What do you mean?"

"Think about it, Nekrosa," she said.

"She's right," Max said as he stepped around the side of the command tent, panting.

"Thank god," Ember let out and went to hug him but stopped short. His armor was covered in blood and gore. "Wait, your unit just fell now. We saw it."

"A couple of us came back when we saw the cavalry horses head your way," he explained and stared at Nekrosa. "Ember's right. This attack was just a way to attack this command camp. The Ancients knew you'd be lightly guarded. The Elder Council's war crime commission doesn't allow attacking command tents when royalty or nobility are present, and they're using it to get rid of you both. You have to run. We'll hold them as long as we can—"

"Commander Max, Sir!" Dalen Toth blurted into the conversation as he stumbled over a tent peg and nearly fell. "The horsemen are nearly here!"

"Thank you, Dalen," Max said. "Return to the others and make them ready."

The young DeathDog saluted and left.

"You have to go, Nekrosa," Max insisted. "Take Ember, Cassie, and Aravae. We'll follow when we can. Acropolis is only a dozen miles away. The remainder of the special forces are there."

The King frowned as Sephi approached and nodded. "I can't abandon my men, Max."

"If you don't retreat and regroup, their lives will have meant nothing," Max barked. "Men die in battle, Nekrosa. If you are alive, there is always a chance to regroup and fight another day."

"Come, love," Sephi prompted and finally got a nod from the King.

Ember grabbed Max's arm. "I'll stay," she said. "You'll need to jump out if things go bad."

"And if one of those amulets get too close?" he asked. "Then what? I saw that wizard, Ember. If there is any chance that might be Kael, you must get out of here alive. If you can find him using your magic, then we might have a chance to win this war."

"You really think it could be him?" she began.

"I don't know," he said. "We laid him to rest. He was gone. We know that, Ember. But that DeathWizard up there helped us. His attack seriously weakened the impact of that cavalry charge."

"Okay," she replied. "I'll go, but you'd better follow us, Max. I mean it."

"We will. Now, go."

She nodded and raced after Nekrosa and Sephi.

Max pulled his blood-caked war hammer from his back headed toward the forest. The branches and bushes cracked and crashed as the Elloryan cavalry exploded from the forest line and plowed into the few remaining DeathDogs left.

ACROPA MOUNTAIN PASS
DORMASAI

Ember collapsed, falling to the leaf-mold utterly exhausted. They had been running since the moment the Elloryan Calvary burst into their camp. Dekayna, Yrlissa, and Max—along with the only four surviving DeathDogs—had caught up to Ember and her royal protectors an hour later. Unfortunately, that left the Elloryan royal knights and ground soldiers scouring the forest after their tail. Yrlissa and the four DeadthDogs had dropped back to slow the pursuers.

Aravae and Cassie crashed through the last of the heavy underbrush and fell to the grass just inside a wide clearing, the rest were close behind. Yrlissa burst into the open shortly after. She was alone and shook her head when Max glanced her way to inquire about his men.

"Fuck! Get up! Both of you!" he yelled. Grabbing Ember's arm, he lifted her clean onto her feet.

"Myhnera! I can't, please," Cassie pleaded, dropping back to her knees after only seconds on her feet. "I can't run anymore."

"I'm tired, Max," Ember panted. "Just give us a minute."

Yrlissa bent down beside her daughter. "Come, *mai nohva*. We must keep running."

Cassie started to cry. "I can't..."

"I'll carry you, Cassie. Come on," Max said, turning his back to her. As she climbed up, Max noticed the King leaning heavily on his spear. "Nekrosa? Come on, man. We gotta go."

"He can't. His leg," Sephi replied while she helped her husband remain standing.

"Here, sister." Dekayna handed Sephi a finger-sized rolled leaf filled with turrin moss and returned to her point position out front.

"The feeling in my leg is gone. I'll just slow you down," Nekrosa told them, popping the leaf into his cheek and biting. The leaf would release the resin mix inside the wrapped moss and hopefully, restore function to his leg or deaden some of the pain.

Sephi corrected him in a whisper, "We, love." Turning to Max, she added, "Please, go. We'll earn you some time."

Ember ignored her offer. "I am not leaving you," she barked. "Five minutes. We'll take a five-minute break."

"We can't keep this pace," Aravae added. Bent at the waist, she held her side and gasped for breath.

"We have to and more," Yrlissa snapped. "Acropolis is still three or four miles away and they're gaining on us—"

"Wrong, Guardian," Sythrnax interrupted as he walked from the forest into the clearing. "They've caught you." Over a dozen Elloryan soldiers surrounded them from the rear.

Max crouched, setting Cassie down. He nodded to Yrlissa and left the little girl with Nekrosa and Sephi.

"Yrlissa," Ember said, panicking. "I can't feel my magic."

"Me, either. It's the pendants."

Nekrosa stood straight. "Good thing they don't work on us."

"You're right," Sythrnax replied, stopping less than ten feet away from the DormaSain King. "Normally. But you see, after the last debacle in your castle, the Vikress found this neat little trick to stop your magic as well. Technically, Nekrosa Kohl, bonded or not you are still a wizard, even if you were created within the Void as you claim."

Sythrnax turned back to the forest behind him and waved. Two heavily armored Elloryan knights dragged a woman into the clearing. Dekayna had no choice but to step aside and let them pass.

The Ancient flourished his hand as the knights came closer. "I present to you one Katarina Desolla," Sythrnax said. "This little witch I found has a unique ability. It seems when the Vikress killed Ella the White, this young one took Ella's power for herself." Lifting a small pendant from around the witch's neck, Sythrnax continued. "This pendant will attract any magic. Anything you cast, will be absorbed by her, King Kohl."

He laughed as the knights forced the woman to her knees. Grabbing her hair, the knight to her left yanked her head back. Ancient markings had been carved into her face and forehead. They were healed, but heavily scarred.

"Katarina?" Yrlissa shouted. "Gods, no. I'm sorry."

"I am quite afraid she can't hear you, Guardian. Talohna's new witch of the White does not have much of a mind left I am afraid."

"She will, Sythrnax," Yrlissa challenged. "After you're dead, I will help Ember strip that Ancient script from her mind."

"Ah, now there's the Yrlissa Blackmist I remember. I was afraid you'd lost her after so many years. I remember well the atrocities you committed."

"I committed? You gods-cursed animals were the ones killing innocent people. Most had no magic at all, and still you murdered and slaughtered them," Yrlissa screamed

"Do not speak to me about slaughter, *dosa*! I pulled pieces of your cursed wooden dagger from my daughter's neck before I laid her small body to rest forever within our mother earth. She was nine years old! Your race and every other race deserves every ounce of pain we inflict on you all. You forced us into a war we desperately tried to avoid. After everything we did to help you! I'm tired of having this argument and seeing as how we don't need this young Fae anymore, you can all die here. This rebellion is over!" A six-foot-long staff appeared out of nowhere as Sythrnax breathed life into the weapon with words long forgotten by any living wizard. Lazy wisps of cold air rose along the staff's wicked blades.

"Yrlissa?"

"It's all right, Ember. We'll fight, Sythrnax. Even using mundane weapons," she said, pulling her wooden daggers from the sheathes at the rear of her waistband. Max removed the massive war hammer from his back. Grabbing the neck under the hammer, he set the bladed tip of the handle in the ground.

"It won't be that easy, Sythrnax." Max smiled.

"You will still die, *dosa*, even with a demon hammer."

Yrlissa gasped, and Sythrnax chuckled.

"You didn't know, Guardian?" he asked. "I am truly surprised. The last time I stood across from you in battle, *Assani*, he," Sythrnax pointed at Max, Yrlissa's eyes followed, "fought miles above us. He led your army as you protected that Kai'Sar, Asa N'ahai, while he opened the first dimensional doorway that trapped my people."

"Stop stalling, Sythrnax," Max snapped. "Your stories are nothing but fiction."

"Perhaps," Sythrnax nodded. "But that hammer *was* forged in Hell. Only the purest blood of Hell can wield it, Maxwell Soren." Turning back to Yrlissa, Sythrnax smiled. "What was that DemonKind commander's name, Yrlissa?" he asked coyly. "You remember, the one you loved *so* much that you abandoned your charge when you heard he fell?"

Yrlissa stared at Max and her eyes filled with tears. "Sorynamax."

"Yes, right. Funny, isn't it? This multi-verse really is kinda small at times. I guess it matters little now. You will all still die here. DemonKind, Elvehn, Human, half-breed child," he said, looking at Cassie. "It doesn't matter. You die. It really is simple as—"

A snap of dark energy rocked the clearing, cutting Sythrnax's words short. Both Elloryan knights holding Katarina were yanked backwards by invisible hands, slamming into the trees at the edge of the clearing. Both fell to the grass, the finality of death obvious.

"Not tonight they won't, Ancient." The voice drifted from the forest. Black lightning arced from the north. Four more Elloryan soldiers died instantly.

"Show yourself, Kai'Sar. I saw you on the battlefield earlier today. Using that much magic must have left you tired. Simple black lightning? Is that all you have left? You should have run."

"I am far from tired, Ancient One. Care to see?" the voice taunted as a hooded wizard stepped from the trees. His robe hung open, blowing in the light breeze. Still, it covered the back and sides of the ornate black chain and leather armor worn by the wizard. Moonlight sparkled off the intricate symbols engraved in every link of the chainmail along with the lining of his robe and the tree of life symbol etched into the armor above the heart. The reflecting light stopped only where the mail disappeared under the robe.

The DeathWizard offered no warning and no words as he pushed his hands toward the ground. The tattoo-like black vines with purple thorns pulsated with a strange magic, moving as if alive. Ember's stomach flipped at the sight. They spun and curled their way through the man's flesh. A sickening tear of his skin emanated from around him as the vines vaulted from his hands, hit the ground, and slid into the earth as if they belonged there.

The wizard looked up, but his face remained hidden within his hood. The vines exploded from the ground underneath the remaining Elloryan soldiers' feet and quickly ensnared them. The vines raced around arms and legs, curling their way up the soldier's bodies before wrapping around their throats. Max stepped forward, putting himself between the vine-covered soldiers and Nekrosa and Sephi as they protected Cassie. Despite his defensive stance, Ember sensed the vines would not attack any of their group.

"Impossible," Yrlissa whispered. "It can't be..."

Whether the DeathWizard heard her or not, he did not respond. Instead, he jerked his hands upward. The vines retreated, spinning as thorns cut through Elloryan flesh and armor like flimsy cloth. Legs, arms, and heads rolled to the ground in grotesque piles of gore.

A dozen soldiers died in mere seconds.

"Is that enough power?" the DeathWizard asked, taunting.

The Ancient clapped his hands at a slow rate. "You are much better trained than any of your kind I have faced before. The last one, now he had serious potential... had he not died after bleeding out on the first Animus Seal."

Ember understood Sythrnax meant Kael. Without thinking of the consequences, she pulled a dagger from her rear waist band and hurled it at the monster who had orchestrated Kael's death. Sythrnax's tresa jumped to life, batting the knife away, even though the Ancient never saw her attack. He whirled, his eyes flaring purple in the darkness.

"Be careful, young Fae, if you want to live long enough for this monster to try and save you." Sythrnax turned back. The DeathWizard materialized in front of him and kicked him hard in the stomach. The Ancient warrior flew across the clearing as if launched by a cannon. His staff sputtered and vanished as it spun from his hands. The DeathWizard disappeared in a cloud of black, reappearing off to the side as if knowing Sythrnax would counter the second he landed in the dirt and grass. The Ancient warrior's spell of compressed air cut through four towering trees at the clearing's edge where the DeathWizard had stood only moments before.

"Better worry about living long enough yourself, Ancient," the dark wizard spat. The wizard spread his fingers, and Sythrnax was dragged face first through the clearing by an unseen force. The wizard raised his hand and Sythrnax was jerked up to his knees. Misty black magic fell from the wizard's hands, jumping across the space between them. Curling around the Ancient warrior's throat, it lifted Sythrnax off the ground until his feet dangled in midair.

Yrlissa grabbed Ember's arm, smiling. "It's him. It has to be. No one else has ever..."

"Who? Who is it?" Ember asked as the wizard tossed Sythrnax back to the dirt, but she did not get her answer.

Sythrnax burst out laughing at the manhandling. "Ah, well done," he complemented. "Many millennia have passed since I've had to pick myself up from the ground during battle. But I can feel your strength waning, Kai'Sar. You are almost done."

"Fool!" the wizard snapped. "You think you're a real Ancient? You don't even know the true meaning of that word. If you were a true Ancient, you'd at least know the meaning of their most common words."

"No... no," Yrlissa whispered, trembling. Startled by the sudden change in Yrlissa's behavior, Ember stared hard at the DeathWizard and tried to discern his identity. The man's voice and shape were familiar, but he moved as if he were not completely in the real world. His body shimmered, and there was a slight echo to his voice. Trying to alter his aura, Ember gasped when her magic was swallowed by the swirls of energy surrounding the wizard.

Sythrnax roared with laughter, and Ember returned her attention to the fight.

"I do know what the word means, *dosa*," Sythrnax growled. "We named you. The cursed Kai'Sar: the wizard who

walks with death. A twisted, corrupt failed weapon!"
Sythrnax's bladed staff appeared in his hand, again. It trailed
cold vapor into the humid night air.

"You're wrong." The wizard sighed as if exhausted.
"We had a discussion once, Sythrnax. A very, very long time
ago."

Yrlissa shook her head, and a tear fell from the corner
of her eye. "No. No... please gods, no." Her voice barely
reached Ember beside her. "That's impossible..."

The wizard continued. "At the time, you said you had
hoped I'd see through your illusion. And yet, you can't see
through the reality before you."

Ember could sense fear radiate from Sythrnax as he
answered. "That is not possible. You are dead. I saw you die. I
arranged all of it."

"I did die, you fucking monster!" the wizard bellowed.

"*Mai nahlla,*" Yrlissa whispered, grabbing Ember's arm.
"We need to run. Fast!" she hissed.

"Nobody leaves!" the DeathWizard yelled, throwing
up his hands. Black vines exploded from the ground. The vines
writhed and grew rapidly to heights that rivaled the forest trees.
Surrounding the clearing, the vines completely cut off all escape
routes.

The DeathWizard's focus returned to Sythrnax. "The
Kai'Sar," he said, but paused and slowly circled Sythrnax. He
stopped in front of the Ancient warrior. "The wizard who walks
with death... the wizard who brings death. Half translations
and twisted truths. Propaganda. It never meant a wizard who
walks with death. An angel explained the meaning to me in
detail." Sythrnax snorted and the DeathWizard struck the
Ancient and knocked him to the dirt. The staff vanished, again,
as the savage blow prevented Sythrnax from holding the magic.
"The Arkangel Seraphina told me what the term Kai'Sar truly
means."

Ember could feel Yrlissa shaking as she held her arm
tight. As if lost in a trance, the assassin whispered, her words
identical to the DeathWizard's.

"It means a wizard who walks *from* death!" Kael shouted, lowering his hood. "From! Not with."

"I... I... impossible! It... ca... it cannot be done..." Sythrnax stuttered, his terror obvious. Even with his hood down, Ember could not make out the DeathWizard's identity, but his voice was clearer, his shape familiar — too familiar.

"Kael?" she whispered, and she could believe her eyes, afraid it was a trick or illusion.

"You *are* weak, Kai'Sar," Sythrnax hissed.

"My power is *not* waning," Kael barked. "Like the gods of old, my power has no limit. If one avenue of magic is exhausted, there are many others to tap into. You'll see that as you suffer for everything of mine and of so many others that you have destroyed. I have thought about nothing else for over two hundred years. Every demon I killed, every angel I tore apart, every goddamn soul I stole to get back here, and every single second of every day that I fought and ran and fought and killed — every second of it I saw your face and this moment kept me going. Call your staff back, Sythrnax, and fight. It is more of a chance than you have ever given others."

"Fair enough, *dosa.*" Sythrnax eased himself off the ground, and again, his staff materialized. He muttered a few strange words, and the spell increased the weapon's potency by creating sharp crystals of ice along the bladed edges.

"My turn," Kael said as a smile crept onto his lips. A matching set of short-handled scythes appeared in his hands.

"New weapons?" Sythrnax mocked. "Not skilled enough to handle the double reaper blades anymore?"

Kael grinned as black smoke coiled off the blades and a viscous poison hung from the tips like strings of black goo. "Nah," he replied. "Just upgraded."

"All alone too?" Sythrnax said, continuing to taunt him. "Sure you don't want to summon help, again?" His words were an attempt to unsettle Kael, but Kael calmly shook his head.

"I don't need a demon to help me," he stated. The Ancient warrior frowned, and Kael lunged.

Sythrnax spun his staff and caught Kael's right blade. Three lengths of tresa shot out of his hood and lashed out at Kael's face. The scaled appendages missed, but just barely. Already spinning the weapon in his left hand, Kael slid the short blade past the staff and into Sythrnax's side. Sythrnax countered with a blast of air. Kael dove to the side, and the attack passed by harmlessly.

Coming out of his roll, Kael's hand shot out. Black and purple magic leapt away too fast to follow. Sythrnax stopped dead in his tracks unable to move as a glyph spell formed beneath the Ancient warrior's feet. Chuckling, Kael made a simple gesture with his hand. It silenced the snapping, violently clicking of the tresa.

"My tresa —"

"Not much fun when someone can control your actions, is it?" he barked. In a swirl of black, he vanished, reappearing right in front of Sythrnax's face.

"You recognize that magic under your feet? The Animus Seals have one nearly identical. Do you remember, Sythrnax?"

Getting a slight nod from the Ancient, Kael continued, "It's surprising what you can learn when you spend over two centuries in Hell. Perdition is the worst place I have... you don't sleep, and you don't eat on the other side, Sythrnax — not ever. You run, you hide, and you fight for every second of every minute of every goddamn hour. You feel the exhaustion and the agony of all wounds as real as they are here in the living world, but you never collapse, and you never get to rest. Even in the Paradise realms. For more than two hundred years, that's all I did — every day, of every week, of every fucking year!" Kael screamed in Sythrnax's face as he shook with rage. Taking a breath, he quickly calmed, though Ember understood that a mere thread held Kael's sanity intact as he carried on speaking. "The Lower Brethren spill many secrets along with their blood, and angels spill even more. A few minor changes and that same magic cues to your blood instead of mine."

Kicking out, Kael's foot hammered the Ancient warrior's knee. Bone crunched as the force of the kick spun the Ancient to the ground within the edges of the glyph.

"Get up and fight!" Kael hollered. The Vai'Karth disappeared as Kael stepped back and pulled his hand backward. Vines exploded from the ground, spinning and cutting their way through Sythrnax's armored robe.

"Enough!" the Ancient yelled. Sythrnax slammed his hand on the ground, and the glyph shattered, allowing him to roll out from the vines.

Ember gasped as magic shimmered behind Kael. "Kael, look out!" she screamed, but only managed to distract him.

"Ember?" he let out in shock. He took a step forward, but a blade materialized at his throat. A second blade appeared at the back of his neck along with the man who held both wooden blades.

"Easy, tough guy," Savis Ephemeral growled. "I've never had the joy of killing someone twice."

Chapter Twenty-Three

"If you expect an enemy to act honorable, then you have already lost the fight. Only a brother will act honorably. It is why you should never have an urge to do battle with a brother." Northman Proverb.

"For a society bred and raised to thrive on warfare, I often wonder how the Northmen have produced the legendary philosopher's they have. Their insights toward battle, wars, and even peace have puzzled scholars on mainland Talohna for countless centuries. I had the honor of spending time with several high-ranking Northman military families during my studies at the Skall of Yrstak. A school renowned for training elite Northman military leaders, the school at Yrstak has an impressive library section on philosophy."

Garren Sallus. Tales of Northman Glory

**ACROPA MOUNTAIN PASS
DORMASAI**

Kael's short scythes vanished, and he slowly lifted his hands. "No honor among warriors, huh Sythrnax?" he asked.

"You had help last time, Kael," the Ancient Wizard said as he eased himself from the ground and touched the wound on his side. "It only seemed fair that I bring help this time —

especially considering you are helping an outcast assassin. It is the least I could do for Merethyl."

Savis blew Yrlissa a kiss. "You're next sweetheart," he said and laughed. "Today is *the* day for killing people twice."

Kael snorted, and the wooden blade cut into his neck. "Worrying about the viper two dozen feet away when you already have one in your hands makes no sense, Savis."

Ember winced as the assassin's blade bit deeper.

"I am capable of both," Savis replied. "I assure you."

"We'll see." Kael grinned.

"Long forgotten proverbs won't help you," the Ancient Wizard said and stepped closer. "You should be more worried about the woman being so close to me while you are under the only blade in this world that can kill you. You know that?"

"I doubt she's even real Sythrnax, just more illusions."

"Kael?" Ember said and winced at his reaction.

"I assure you, she is very real. Why else would I be here? Shall I kill her?"

"No," Kael growled and pull against Savis. The wooden blade bit deeper.

"Careful, wizard," the assassin snarled. "If this blade cracks even the slightest bit."

Kael scoffed. "I am well aware what the toxin does when the blade breaks."

"Of course, you do," Savis whispered. "I already killed you once."

Fury built on Kael's face and his body trembled with the desire to attack.

"A mistake I won't make, again. It takes a while sometimes, but I do learn from my mistakes."

Sythrnax leaned in even closer. "Apparently not, or you would know that the people behind me are very real. Though. the demon queen's Ichor must make it difficult for you to see reality clearly. The Ichor is easy for me to manipulate. Perhaps you should calm yourself, Kael." Sythrnax balled his hand into a fist and his magic sparked to life. He opened his fist and touched Kael's shoulder. The swirling magic surrounding Kael vanished.

With Kael subdued, Ember finally sensed more and more of the man she loved. The putrid sensation created by the filth of Reetha's Ichor made her gag as it pulsed in his veins while Sythrnax took control of the Ichor. She felt the waves of images and dark emotions—all too jumbled to understand—as they hit Kael hard. With a confident smile, he shoved the waves of delirium back and reasserted control over his own mind.

"Nice try, bastard. You won't get inside my head so easily," he said.

"I don't really have to, do I?" Sythrnax asked. "Your mind is already scrambled. You can clearly see who is across this field, and yet, I sense you still refuse to believe it."

"Ember and Max are dead," he said. "They're just another illusion."

"No, we're not, Kael," Ember pleaded with him. "We're right here. We survived the cross-over."

"Giddeon told me you survived," he muttered to himself. She could sense his sanity slip further away.

Max pushed past Nekrosa and stepped forward. "Kael? Buddy? We're here, man, and we have been looking for you for so long. I am so sorry we weren't fast enough last time, but we are here, now. Don't let this fucking bastard get away with this!"

Kael frowned and stared at Sythrnax. "They have to be real. Hardly anyone here swears like Max," he stated.

"They are real, Kael. I promise you," Sythrnax answered. "And they will die right after you."

"I won't let that happen, Sythrnax," Kael growled. Ember could sense a vile blackness bloom from deep within his soul. "Not again. I will not die like this, again. Never. And I will never let you hurt them, not as long as I still breathe."

Ember gasped as she felt the dark thing inside of Kael grow rapidly. "Kael!" she screamed. "Be careful."

Sythrnax chuckled. "Kind of hard to not be careful with a Dyr blade at your neck.

"I won't let you hurt them," Kael repeated as tremors shook his body.

In a heartbeat, everything happened at once.

Cassie pushed her way to the front of the group. "Kael, help me!" she cried out.

Ember dropped to her knees while an awful pain built in her stomach. She glanced up at Kael as black mist rose from his flesh and armor. The skin across his cheeks and forehead split with long fissures racing across his face. Wicked thorns burst from the cracks above his eyebrows, and his eyes shone with black. The Kael she knew was gone — swallowed by a dark magic she could not begin to understand.

"Good bye, Kael," Sythrnax said and nodded to Savis.

"No!" Ember screeched. She leapt to her feet and took a step forward but stopped as Savis plunged his blade into Kael's neck. She knew what should have happened, but her eyes showed her something far different.

Savis' blade rushed through Kael's body, and Ember's mouth went dry as Kael's body became immaterial. Like a ghost, he passed through Savis and the assassin stumbled as the force of his attack met no resistance. Kael reappeared in one piece behind Savis, and she immediately knew what happened.

Like the Fae had done to their islands long ago, he had phased right through Savis.

"Holy shit!" she exclaimed. Kael's long scythe shimmered and appeared in his hand. Savis caught himself and quickly stood as Kael swung. The scythe whistled low through the air and easily severed the assassin's right leg below the knee.

Kael's hand shot out and a black cage of sizzling energy enveloped Sythrnax, inhibiting the Ancient from moving. Kael brought his attention back to Savis but said nothing as he dragged the blade of his scythe up Savis' back. Ember winced and covered her ears as the assassin screamed in excruciating pain, but Kael did not stop. Shifting his feet, Kael swung his scythe again and severed Savis' right arm at the shoulder.

Magic flared to life in his hand. He grasped the gushing stump and cauterized the wound, so the assassin would not bleed out.

"God, Kael, stop! If you are really you, please, stop!" she begged, unable to handle the torture anymore. He stared her way and swung the scythe once more, almost defiant to her wishes. Savis' left hand cartwheeled through the air as black mist rose lazily from Kael's eyes. The man she loved was nowhere within the man standing in front of her.

"Kael, stop this!" Max barked and stepped forward with his hammer in hand, but Yrlissa grabbed him by the arm.

"That is not him, Max," she said and held him back. "He will kill you. Let him do whatever it is he needs to do."

"How can you watch this?" he asked.

She shrugged. "It is better than dying."

"Look what it's doing to Ember." He pointed out and leaned down to help the Fae up. "You okay?"

"No," she sobbed. "It can't be him.! I can't watch this!" Max pulled her close and wrapped his arms around, burying her face in his chest. But it did not help. With her magic, she sensed a foot fly through the air while Kael's onslaught continued.

"You have broken the sanctity of life," Kael growled. Ember cringed at the sound. The voice was Kael, but it was scoured by a hollow echo that drove shivers up her spine and agony knotted her stomach. Tearing free of Max, she spun in time to see Kael's scythe vanish. It was replaced with a shorter weapon with a reaper blade at each end—one of the weapons they had buried him with.

Blue magic and strange symbols appeared along the blade of the longer scythe. Ember's piercing screams filled the air as Kael plunged the weapon into Savis's body. Sythrnax smashed his hands against the cage, but it held firm.

"Please, stop, Kael…" Ember whispered. She would have collapsed, but Max's arms held her up tight.

Whether or not he heard her, Kael tore a bright blue essence from Savis' body and the blades devoured it.

Horror drove Ember to the brink of insanity as she understood the blue essence could only be the assassin's soul. The empty shell of Savis' body crumpled to the grass, and Kael's attention rounded back to Sythrnax. All she could do was watch the nightmare unfold.

"The sanctity of death has been restored," Kael told him while the double reaper blade vanished. The shorter scythe appeared in his hand as if it had never left. He lunged and smashed Sythrnax in the mouth with it as the magical cage opened momentarily to let him pass.

"You've had some practice, newborn," Sythrnax spat a mouthful of blood into the grass as he stood, staff-in-hand.

"Newborn?" Kael whispered. "You insult us and the gods with such blasphemy."

"Gods? The only gods who ever mattered are long gone," Sythrnax replied.

"Not any more, Sythrnax," Kael said. Silver and purple metal flowed from his hands like serpents. They snapped at the Ancient, and one struck his mask as Kael pulled the volatile energy back.

The display of magic drove Sythrnax into a rage. "That's impossible!" he shouted and beat on the cage with both fists "That is our magic, our real magic! You dosa bastard! How dare you even touch that magic — let alone use it against me!" His anger faded quickly, and a smile tugged his mask. "But that means..."

Kael shook his head and black magic drifted from his hands like worms. They raced across the short distance between them and twisted around the frosted staff in Sythrnax's hand. As Kael rotated his own hands, Sythrnax's staff twirled, and the ice-covered blades slowly rotated until they hovered over the Ancient's heart.

"You understand now?" Kael asked. Sythrnax nodded and his tresa came back to life. Pushing from his hood, they wrapped themselves around his staff to protect him, but Kael smiled as he continued. "Maybe it would be better if you pulled that staff into yourself?" he offered and stepped forward. Coming to a stop beside the Ancient, Kael frowned. "Agree?"

One of the scaled tresa lashed out at him, but it was too slow. Kael caught it in his hand and tore it from Sythrnax's head. The Ancient roared in agony. Pointing at the rest of the striking tresa with his finger, Kael's magic calmed the agitated appendages, and they laid flat as he tossed the dead tresa to the ground. "Understand now, child?" Kael asked, all traces of emotion were gone from his voice.

"Yes," Sythrnax growled. "Now, finish this, and I'll wait for your mortal soul in Perdition. You won't escape the afterlife a second time, and we can do this over and over for all of eternity."

The Ancient laughed as everyone stared at the revelation. Ember's heart skipped a beat as it hammered against her ribs. She had been right—something or someone had brought him back from the dead. Yet deep inside, she had known all along that the sadistic wizard was really Kael. She was just too afraid to believe it. There was no longer any doubt. He had somehow managed to fight his way back from death. As a true DeathWizard, he had brought back something terrible with him.

"No," Kael said, catching her attention. Slowly pushing his hand forward, the black magic holding Sythrnax's staff over his heart sparked to life. Kael shoved and his magic pounded the blades deep into Sythrnax's chest. The black cage evaporated, and he continued in a monotonous tone. "You will not go to the afterlife, Ri'Tek. The gods designed your people to pass their energy to those who are worthy. Your power will be given to the spirit, and you will cease to exist."

As he stopped short, Kael shook his head and glanced around as if confused. He nodded to himself, and the expression passed as he stared back at Sythrnax.

The hollow echo around his voice vanished as he spoke. "I promised a Dwarven General that I'd pass along his message," he said. "He survived the siege."

Sythrnax shook his head in disbelief and Kael changed, again. The echo in his voice returned, and any emotion fled from the words of the spell that came out of him. *"Sai Vai' Karth Kull' Vai!"*

"No, Kael! Don't," Yrlissa yelled.

"Please, Kael!" Ember added, trying to save her husband one last time.

Both were too late. The Vai'Karth appeared in Kael's hands. He gently slid the scythe-blades over Sythrnax's shoulders and guided him closer. One blade rested gently on each side as the hooked blades slid into the Ancient's flesh and drew blood. Kael slid his thumbs along the bottom sides of his weapons, and he held Sythrnax close. Their blood mixed, and the Vai'Karth pulsated with life.

"You are not a simple mortal," Kael said. "I take back the life that was given by the true gods of Talohna." As the staff stole the Ancient's life, Kael's blood-fueled blades tore Sythrnax's soul from his body and pulled it inside the weapons. The blades pulsed one last time as the last traces of Sythrnax's soul were consumed.

Shocked at the display of such cruel and volatile magic, Ember gaped at Kael's back as he stared down at the vacant body of the Ancient.

"Kael?" She swallowed hard, her voice barely a whisper.

"No," Yrlissa said, quietly, grabbing her arm. "We need to leave, *nahlla*, you don't understand."

"I will not leave him, Yrlissa! Jesus Christ, Kael. It's me. It's me, Ember," she yelled. Her heart broke as he continued to ignore her.

"Ember, now," Yrlissa snapped. "We must leave. He's not the same—"

Ember tore her arm free from the assassin's grasp. "Never!" she shouted and ran to Kael. Grabbing his cloak, Ember turned him to look at her. Her breath caught as his blades appeared and slid easily into her sides.

"Leave me be, mortal!" he snarled and pulled her close.

Ember touched Kael's cheek and smiled softly. The fury and madness fled his eyes. "You... found me." She sighed. The blades vanished in a puff of black smoke, and he caught her as pain overwhelmed her senses.

Blinking, he gasped. "Em... Ember? What happened? Who, no...no!"

With her consciousness fading, she heard Yrlissa scream a spell through a haze of pain and felt magic slam into her and Kael. Both were knocked to the ground.

"Yrlissa... don't hurt him," she moaned while Kael stumbled to his feet. He stepped over her, his hands flared with black and purple magic. The energy grew quickly as it surrounded them in a shield of smoky black and purple mist.

Yrlissa moved closer. "It's my responsibility to stop him, Ember. I'm sorry."

"It's all right, he knows..." She gasped in agony. The assassin's aura vanished, replaced by black and purple swirls of a Guardian. Yrlissa closed her eyes as if to focus, and the pounding chaos of Kael's magic increased. Surrounding him in wavering layers of smoky-black magic, he called back his hand scythes.

Yrlissa's eyes snapped open, and her spell leapt from her tongue. "*Ivey Vanahr Saleesta.*"

Like a switch had been thrown, Kael collapsed to the ground, lifeless. With no link to his power, the magical shield dissipated on the dying winds, and the wall of thorns circling the clearing retreated into the earth.

Chapter Twenty-Four

"Reality. What is reality? Is it what we know? What we feel or experience? Or simply what we see and comprehend? I know not and for some reason it troubles my mind more than ever. I do know that my reality slips from my grasp more rapidly now. Those who write my thoughts will continue to record them until my last breath. Perhaps as these few coherent moments become even more scarce and only prophecy rolls from my tongue will the definition of true reality become clear. It gives my weakening mind something to hope for while in the throes of complete and utter insanity. The approach of it comes frightening close most d… da… daysss…"

The prophet Zaddyk's journal entry
has been cut short by an unsolicited prophecy-Brother Donis Kincaid.
Prophecy was recorded
and handed to the TimeKeepers, 5026 PC

DORMASAI
ACROPA MOUNTAIN PASS

Even severely wounded, Ember's only concern was Kael's well-being as she crawled to him. "Is he… alive? Yrlissa? I… is he alive?" she asked, struggling to catch her breath.

Yrlissa went to Kael's side to check on him while Max hurried to help Ember, opening her cloak. The pain told her long before Max's expression that Kael's blades had almost torn her apart. The two garish wounds had opened her sides wide. Max pressed her cloak tight against the wounds and applied pressure. Ember bit her bottom lip as the savage agony swelled

She coughed, and blood dripped from her lips. "Max, I... I... can't... not heal... I..."

"Yrlissa!" Max yelled. "Christ. She's not healing!"

Yrlissa left Kael unconscious where he fell, going to Ember. "Let me see," she said, opening the cloak back up. "It's the Vai'Karth—his scythes."

"Gods." Aravae sighed, kneeling at Ember's side to help. "Who would make such weapons?"

"You don't want to know," Yrlissa said, looking to Max. "Bring me them, but don't touch them bare-handed."

Max quickly moved to Kael's side, searching for the Vai'Karth. "Sorry buddy, but we need these." he said, sighing as his friend's chest rose and fell. "He's alive, but ah... there's no weapons here, Yrlissa."

"Impossible," Yrlissa whispered, looking back in Kael's direction.

"The blades are gone," Max offered. "They must have vanished."

"Good riddance," Yrlissa spat out. "Tie him up. I'll do a spell to collar him once we do what we can for Ember." Turning to Aravae, she asked, "Are you ready? We have to do one side at a time. Kael's blades slid along the outside of her ribs, but the hooks rode along the bottom of her rib cage and went deeper."

"I see them," Aravae answered, nodding with a frown. "We have to stitch her inside and out to stop the bleeding. I'm ready. Thank you, child," she replied, taking one of Ember's med kits from Cassie as the young girl handed a second to her mother.

Max tied Kael securely while the two women stitched the ugly wounds on Ember's sides. "Boy, are you gonna have some apologizing to do, buddy," he muttered. Turning Kael gently on to his side, he finished the hog tie. "What the hell happened to you on the other side, Kael?"

Snapping branches and the clunk of loose armor from within the forest caught everyone's attention.

"I got it," Max growled and grabbed his hammer. "I need to kill something anyway." He turned to face whomever was crashing through the forest.

A young man exploded into the clearing. "Commander, Sir!" Dalen Toth shouted. "I found you."

"Dalen?" Max demanded, frowning in shock. "Jesus, man! You got more goddamned lives than a cat! I thought you were dead."

"You and me both, Sir! I've been killing Elloryans the whole way here. The cowards abandoned the battle. They fled the field like cowards as soon as they realized King Kohl and the Queen had retreated. But we got undead birds from Drae'Kahn, several Elloryan knights and Ancient wizards have been spotted near Garrett's Vale. I followed after you as soon as the messages were read."

"Garrett's Vale?" Nekrosa repeated as he approached. "You're sure the messages said Garrett's Vale?"

"Yes, Your Majesty," Dalen said, and he bowed, only just seeing the King.

"Nekrosa?" Max asked, letting his hammer rest on the ground.

"It's the location of the Human Animus Seal. The invasion was a feint."

"Of course, it was." Max sighed. "What do we do, Yrlissa? Ember is no shape to jump us, and the Vale is three days hard ride on horseback."

Yrlissa shook her head as she tied off the last stitch and applied a clean cloth to the wounds.

"I'll live," Ember assured them quietly.

"Good," Yrlissa said. "Then, we need to bring Kael around and convince him we are who we say we are. He's the only one who can get us there in time."

Max smiled at Yrlissa. "Easy enough."

"No, Max. It won't be."

"That's why you wanted to run," Ember whispered. "You knew he'd be different. You said, he was corrupted."

Yrlissa piled a couple travel bags behind Ember's back and helped her to sit up. "Yes. Kael has spent the last year to us in the afterlife — most of it was probably in the Nine Hells. The corruption that runs through his kind will have had no tempering in the afterlife. I imagine it will have run abundant. He clearly has no problem killing anymore."

"Wait," Aravae said. "The last year to us? What do you mean?"

Yrlissa sighed as she sank back and used a clean cloth to wipe Ember's blood from her hands. "Time passes differently in other dimensions. Earth is the only dimension I have ever heard of where time passes the same as ours, only on the opposite clock. Night-to-day and vice versa. But the afterlife? People, regardless of race or magic, are not supposed to come back from there. Period. One year here was probably hundreds of years or more to Kael. Ember, Max... he may not understand that only a year has passed here. Even if he does, his mind is likely twisted up from his trials in Heaven and Hell. He called you a mortal, Ember. I can't understand that, unless he has been affected by Reetha's Ichor or the gods' only know what else."

Max jogged over to Kael and yanked his armor aside. "You're right. That's Kroa magic," Max said and spat to the side. "Nastiest shit found in any dimension. He'll be detached from reality."

"Yes," Yrlissa said as she glared at Max. "We are going to discuss your knowledge of that and a great many other things as well."

"Fine," Max agreed. "When there is time. First, we need to bring him back to reality."

Ember shook her head. "Everyone he's ever trusted in Talohna either died or betrayed him." She struggled to regain her composure but continued. "The Kael we knew would never hurt us, but I can still reach him I saw it in his eyes right before you knocked us down."

Lying his hammer on the grass, Max knelt at her side. "Yes, you can. You and I will show him the way back. Like we did after he killed that punk back home. All right?"

Ember nodded, smiling. "Okay."

"Then, we'd better move and fast," Yrlissa said. "Dalen? You said our main camp and the battlefield were deserted?"

"Yes, Mistress."

"The blacksmiths — did they pack up and leave?"

"No. Those who survived the attack on the camp are still awaiting orders."

"Good," Yrlissa said. "We'll need them to forge chains that I can spell in order to hold Kael."

"Is that a good idea?" Aravae asked, still sitting beside Ember and watching her close. "After what the Dead Sisters did to him —"

"We have no choice," Yrlissa argued. "We have to collar his magic, or he will kill us all the moment he wakes."

Sephi, guarding the clearing's eastern approach, called over her shoulder. "How do we get back to camp without him waking?"

"I'll jump us," Ember said softly. "It's only a few miles."

"You can't," Max argued. "You're too weak to risk it."

"She'll be all right," Yrlissa offered. "The Vai'Karth didn't have a chance to drain her soul. She'll be exhausted, but it's the only way to get Kael secured safely — for us and him."

"All right, everyone," Nekrosa yelled. "Settle in close to Ember." Magic swirled around Sephi and she lifted Katarina over her shoulder, turned, and walked back, taking Cassie's hand.

"You've done this before, Cassie," Yrlissa said softly. "Close your eyes and hold my hand tight."

"Yes, *Mynerha*," she replied, cuddling in close.

"Max, drag Sythrnax and his assassin over here before you get Kael," Yrlissa added quickly. "I'll destroy their pendants. We cannot risk leaving them here for someone to find or revive them. The way this day is going, nothing would surprise me."

He nodded his agreement and brought the dead bodies first. As Max dragged Kael closer, Yrlissa smashed the amulets. While she did, Cassie put her other hand on Kael's shoulder.

"It will be all right, Kael," she whispered. "I will help you. It's my turn."

"Ember," Yrlissa said. "Only account for Sythrnax and Savis' weight. Their magical energy will be inert."

"Are we ready?" Ember asked. A round of nods was all she needed. A blaze of white lit up the clearing, and they were gone, whisked away by Fae magic.

DORMASAIN MILITARY CAMP
PEDDLER'S VALLEY, DORMASAI

As Kael fought his way back to consciousness, he was not sure what hurt more—his face or every nerve ending in his entire body. He sat on a dirt floor with a row of wooden desks at his back and his esoteric senses told him he was in a cloth tent. It was not much of a leap to assume he was on the Elloryan side of the battlefield. From what he had heard, even the DormaSain king would never welcome the Dead Sisters to his country or be in league with demons. It was the only explanation for the blank in his memory.

Realizing he was secured by heavy metal chains, he opened his eyes and examined the ornate symbols forged into the metal cuffs and along the lengths of chain trailing to the collar around his neck. He flexed his neck muscles but felt no pain from a Gyhurra collar. It mattered little. He recognized the symbols burned into the cuffs. Ancient magic. Ri'Tek magic. It had to be the Dead Sisters, then. He snorted. It would not hold him for long.

"You find something funny?" a voice demanded behind his back.

"Was she real? I'm surprised Sythrnax left me alive. Or was it just more Dead Sister or demon illusions?" he asked

"It was real, Kael. Ember is resting a few tents over. She can't heal, and the jump back here wiped the rest of her strength. Though, I'm not a Dead Sister. I promise you that much."

Lifting his chains, Kael laughed. "This is Ancient magical script invented by the Ri'Tek. Only a Dead Sister or an Ancient would have access to this magic and seeing as Ember would never side with either of them..."

His voice trailed off.

"True on all counts, but a Guardian would also know Ancient magic. It was their responsibility to kill your kind when you succumbed to the corruption after all."

"Of course," Kael mocked. "The corruption — more proof you know nothing about my kind."

"More proof?"

"What you call corruption is merely magic you don't understand, and were you yourself a real Guardian, your spell back in the forest would have killed me."

"It should have. Believe me, I put everything I had into it. You are different, though, aren't you? The Guardian spell was designed to kill a living DeathWizard. Not one like you."

He slid his chains so his captor would not hear the sizzle as he fried the script from the links using the little bit of magic he could access. Kael smiled as two of the symbols melted back into the metal and the smallest amount of his magic returned.

"You have no idea."

The voice hesitated for only a second. "I'm pretty sure I know better than anyone what you are."

Kael frowned. "Yeah, everyone keeps saying that. Then, they find out they're wrong, I lose my memory, and lots of people die. You don't know shit about the magic in my blood.

If you knew the truth, the word *corruption* would never leave your goddamn lips. Blasphemy."

"I have seen it first hand," she replied, "hundreds of times over more years than you can imagine. I know exactly what that corruption can do."

"It is not a magical corruption!" he bellowed. "It is a magic you cannot begin to understand. I am not going to waste my breath explaining what little of it I understand—and I discussed it at great lengths with an entity you cannot imagine as well as one of my own kind."

"Did you see her on the other side?" Her voice trembled with suppressed emotion.

"Who?" He gasped.

"Jasala Vyshaan." the woman asked. "Did you see her?"

Kael's heart jumped and took off as he tried to keep himself from falling into the flashback magic that was always so close to the surface. "I did." The woman sighed, but she coughed immediately to cover. "Why would you care?"

"I already told you. I am a Guardian. I was her Guardian."

"You lie, witch! A fallen god protected Jasala."

"Do you know who Assani is, Kael?"

He smiled. "Nice try."

"She wasn't always the goddess of assassins you know."

"I know that," Kael replied softly, his mind starting to whirl. "But do you? Because no Dead Sister would. From what Jasala told me, no one alive in the last five thousand years knows that story."

"Assani was once the Elvehn Goddess of the Hunt. It was why the Dyrannai Elvehn were chosen as the first Guardians, and it is how we became the Broken Blades."

Kael's mind whirled at the possibility—if it were true. "And then the gods demanded you kill all of my kind," he stated. "Those alive after the war and any born thereafter, including Jasala."

"Yes. And for disagreeing with my brothers and sisters, my godhood was stripped."

"Assani, the fallen god." Kael sighed. "If you are really her, then tell me why Jasala was so hard to kill. There were several Guardians loyal to the gods at that time. The spell you used on me would have killed her otherwise. She didn't have the protection I do."

"She was protected in another way."

"Obviously." He snorted. "Answer the question, or we're done talking.

"Assani… I protected her from the Guardian death spells."

"How?" he snapped.

"You have come across the Orotaq in your time here? You know of them and their shamans?" she asked.

"They're damn hard to kill."

"The branding on the shamans is more than just scarring. The warriors wear theirs as a sign of battle feats or honor, but the shamans... it is what makes them — combined with their natural defenses — it makes them completely immune to most types of magic."

"Including the death spell?" he asked.

"Yes. Jasala's brand was placed at the back of her neck when she was a child by a shaman who was indebted to a certain goddess of assassins."

"Assani. Of course," he replied.

"When you have lived as long as I have, you earn favors and procure debts."

"You don't need to live a long life for that," he stated and paused for several minutes. "I have a message from Jasala, but it is not for Assani."

"I may have been Assani once, but it was a very long time ago, Kael. I don't even know whether another has taken up my — Assani's mantle. I am Yrlissa Blackmist now, and that is all that matters."

"Let me see your face," he said. Shifting his weight made the chains rattle, again, and three more Ancient symbols vanished from the cuffs. More magic trickled back into him. Yrlissa stepped around him and knelt, looking him straight in the eyes. "I saw her," he said. "Jasala... she wanted me to tell you something. Would you like to know?"

"Yes."

"She knows who killed her." Kael watched closely her reaction. Only the real Yrlissa would be affected by what Jasala had told him to say. "She said, it wasn't your fault, that she doesn't blame you."

Her eyes glossed over with moisture, and she nervously chewed her bottom lip. "Thank you. I tried to stop her."

"I know," Kael said quietly. "I have her memories, now. All of them, the good..."

"And the bad," Yrlissa finished for him. "A god's genetic memory is tough to handle at times, isn't it?"

"Yeah, but not as bad as a scrambled mind. You should let me go, Goddess. I can't tell reality from illusion half the time—not after months with the Dead Sisters. Then two hundred years in the afterlife—decades of those with the demon queen. You can't help me."

"Reetha's Ichor..."

"You know there's no cure," Kael said, nodding. "So, set me free and let me continue doing what I was. Let me kill as many Ancients as I can before the day comes when you or someone else will have to hunt me down to kill me."

"You believe now?" Yrlissa asked.

He nodded, again. "You spent the last five millennia thinking Jasala blamed you for her death. She knew it was your sister and never doubted you for a minute. Jasala was loyal to a fault." She sighed and collapsed on her backside, so he carried on. "Dead Sisters can do a lot of things, but they can't feign empathy or regret, and demons can only use your own memories against you. I hope this means I'm actually back."

"You are, Kael. We have heard what you did in the north for Queen Bale and even for Giddeon. You are here in the

living world, but you can't leave us now. What about Ember —
"

"Is she really alive? What about Max?" he interrupted.

"They are both alive and here, but —"

"Then, that is exactly why you have to let me go. I'll be nothing but a danger to her and to Max. Akai will remove the magic stopping you from healing her."

Yrlissa sighed, but it quickly turned into a laugh. "Ah, Kael. There is so much you don't know. Let me bring Ember to you. Remove the Vai'Karth's magic, and you will see for yourself. Ember and Max have done well here since they arrived after you. You'll understand so much, finally. Please, you are everything we have been fighting for. Reetha's Ichor can be balanced with help from —"

"No!" he barked. The mere thought of facing Ember or what he might to do her in the throes of a bad flashback turned his stomach to ice. "I'm not safe to be around even on a good day. Even after more than two hundred years, I cannot control the magic I was born with. I can't control the power that came back with me from the other side. Mix the Ichor into that and… no. Remove these chains, and I'll summon my blades. Akai can remove the silence magic in Ember, so you can heal her and then I'll leave. Tell her… tell her… I…"

"Tell her what?" Ember whispered as the tent flap eased to the side, and Sephi helped her inside. "After everything we've gone through over the last year and the year prior as we tried to find you… tell me your goddamn self instead of running."

Kael averted his eyes but said nothing.

Sephi supported her as she sat across from him. Slowly, he looked back up at her, ashamed of all the things he had done He was far more afraid she would be torn from his sight or killed like the millions of times he had envisioned it happening before. He caught his mistake too late as his mind slipped back into his memories. Grabbing his head, he screamed at the pain hammering the inside of his skull.

Ember grabbed his face between her hands and pulled him close. "Push it back, Kael," she ordered him. Her words barely registered with him before the memory swallowed him whole.

"What's wrong with him?" Sephi asked. Moving to Ember's aid, she slid behind Kael and held him tight.

"His eyes are black and silver." Yrlissa gasped. "Is it Fae remembrance magic? Ember? Or?"

"It's not prophecy," Ember hissed through clenched teeth. "Fae magic is pulling him back into his memories, but he doesn't know how to move away from or control the bad images, the nightmares."

Kael's hands shot up and both cuffs snapped. "I can't hold him for long!" Sephi growled as magic flared around her and she wrestled his arms back down.

"Quick, Ember!" Yrlissa barked.

"I'm thinking," she snapped back. "It's an inherent magical ability and part of who he is! I can't just shut it off!"

Black and purple magic sparked to life in Kael's right hand while his left snapped outward, grasping Ember by the throat.

"Kael, listen," she began as Sephi struggled to hold Kael's magic-filled hand down. Yrlissa grabbed his hand and tried to pry his fingers from Ember's throat.

"*Naolass Sai'eed!*" Ember finally gasped.

The spell slammed into Kael's mind and yanked him from the dark before hurling him through a flashing tunnel of lights. Seconds passed before his mind burst from the far end. The DormaSain tent and Ember materialized out of the silver and black covering his eyes.

He released the only woman he had ever loved and pulled his magic back from his right hand. More magic invaded his mind and did nothing to affect his thoughts, but calmed the caustic images struggling to surface. "I'm sorry... I'm sorry," he whispered. "You are not safe around me."

Instead of being repulsed, she wrapped her arms around him and whispered in his ear. "I thought I lost you. We will get through this, love. There's so much you don't understand."

Kael closed his eyes, terrified that the incredible feeling would not last long enough for him to draw a single breath — or worse, it would last only to be torn away weeks or months later, again. "I'm sorry," he breathed. "I am so sorry." She let go and leaned away, wincing from pain.

"Take this collar off," Kael ordered.

"Is that wise —"

"I need my blades to remove the magic stopping you from healing her." Kael interrupted Sephi mid-sentence, the urgency in his voice bordered on anger. He scoffed and used his magic to melt the last of the Ancient symbols from the collar. A pop of underworld power echoed in the tent, and the collar and chains fell to the floor.

"Never mind," he muttered as the Vai'Karth appeared in both hands. Sephi stepped back and drew her blue daggers. "I remember you, Sephi of DormaSai," Kael added. "You told me a long time ago that I was welcome in your country."

"You are."

"Then, put your blades away, Your Highness, so I can remove the magic affecting her. The spirit in the blades will attack anyone with a weapon drawn."

Yrlissa gasped, and Sephi did as he requested. "Are you talking about Kin Akai? The entity created during the weapon's creation?"

"Yes and no," Kael answered and refocused his attention to the weapons. "Akai is the spirit who possesses the blades, but he was not created at their forging." Placing one handle over the other, he flexed his wrist and forced them together. With a grunt of effort, he drove the blades into the dirt between him and Ember.

"*Vai'Karth Aytto. Kin Akai T'Seanah,*" Kael whispered. The cracks along the top of the handle separated and smoky gray magic flowed out before coalescing into the form of a man. "Akai. *Tai Seanah. Ayttosah megin.*" Kael nodded as the spirit hesitated. Finally, it huffed and turned. Kael watched Akai closely as he fell into Ember's body. When, he rose back out again, he pulled strings of pure black magic with him. Akai took the magic into himself and spun back to Kael. Bowing, the smoky man slipped soundlessly into the handles of his weapons, and the blades disappeared.

Kael looked back down Ember with shock. He could sense her wounds healing and rapidly.

"How?" he asked. Bending forward, he slowly lifted her shirt and peeled back her bandages as the wounds in her sides closed. They healed even ten times faster than he did. The stitches fell from her skin without leaving a scar. "Fae accelerated healing... has to be," he muttered. Her eyes glowed a celestial green as he stared at her. She smiled back. "You're..."

Ember nodded. "Fae. Yes. It seems you and I were born to help save this world, or to at least try and stop it from being destroyed."

Kael shook his head. The absurdity of her words almost broke him. "You sound like there is no apocalypse coming, Ember. All of you," he said and looked around the tent. "The Ri'Tek will not destroy this world — not in the way you are all thinking. Instead, they will bring everyone in it to their knees in subjugation. We can't stop it because most people will do it willingly — happily even." A silence followed his words.

He pushed his hands through his hair in frustration and a hiss rushed passed his lips. "Shit. All we can do is kill as many of them as possible before —"

"Kael," Yrlissa said. "We *can* stop this. If we can unite Talohna."

"You're insane." He snorted. "Do you not understand that we are the bad guys here? Who are you going to unite? Huh? Cethos won't be able to help anyone — including themselves — and for some time. The civil war just ended and most Cethosian citizens have idolized the Ancients to the point of nearly worshiping them as gods. The Wildlands natives will be into Ynasu before the year is out — especially seeing how Queen Bale has now called back her army from the peace border. The Yusatan army is the only presence on the border, and they can't cover more than a quarter of it."

"We can fight, love," Ember said. He could tell she was shocked at his response, but she had no idea what had been happening elsewhere in Talohna. "We have to fight," she persisted. "This is our world now, our home."

Kael shook his head, again. "I will fight to my very last breath — for a second time — but the Ri'Tek are after something, and I'm not talking about freeing their people or returning to their former glory. They will open every seal, yes, but Talohna will return to times past. A time when the Ri'Tek ruled Talohna as the lone supreme race."

"You understand the prophecy..." Yrlissa stammered.

"I understand it," he replied. "I've seen it through the eyes of a prophet. I know it can't be stopped. Sythrnax's death will buy us some time."

"Afraid not," Sephi added. "I imagine they are marching on the Human seal right now. The Elloryan invasion was a feint."

"Of course, it was," Kael spat. "This is what I'm talking about. They are more advanced than us in every way. Smarter, faster, stronger. They don't even think like we do. They can use normal magic in ways you could never dream of." Standing, he stretched and forced back a wave of dizziness. "Where's the Human seal? I can't stop them, but I can take out some of their wizards, perhaps even the Vikress if she's there."

"Listen to Yrlissa, Kael. Please," Ember begged.

"And unite Talohna?" He scoffed. "Do you even realize what has happened in the north?"

"Our spies have reported in, but most only relayed what we thought were rumors. They mentioned descriptions that fit you, but we knew you were dead. We all interred you," Sephi replied.

Kael shook his head. "Then, let me explain it to you, so there is no misunderstanding. King Bale is dead. Princess Corleya is the new queen. I made sure of it, but they are in no shape to fight another war, especially against the Ancients.

Ellorya is already under Ancient control as you have seen, so Talohna's two biggest military powers are with the Ri'Tek. I returned Giddeon Zirakus to Corynth, and Kasik should be there by now if Queen WhiteScale kept her word. The DragonKin and the Fae will help us, but it will be very limited help for now."

"Ta'Ceryss will help too. My family... our family are well respected there," Aravae stated as she entered the tent.

Kael chuckled and shook his head. "I don't know who you are, but sure. Their forces are about the same as those who were freed from the first seal. The Dwarven Seal opened months ago, and the Human seal will open soon if they are in the general vicinity already. Jasala's Sepulchre should hold until a fourth seal opens, but I doubt if it will hold for a fifth. The Ancients have all the time in the world, and there is no one left in Talohna to unite. Salzara and Kariya will side with the Ri'Tek if they can pay the mercenary price. If not, they will stay neutral especially now that Joran Bale is dead. His alliance with King Vhorez died when he did. I am telling you that the only hope we have is to either kill as many Ancients as we can or venture into their kingdom to find help there because there is no help south of the Kasym."

"Kael, this is Aravae, you —" Ember started to say, but the Elvehn woman cut her off with a hand up.

"Now is not the time," she said, and she stepped forward to shake Kael's hand. "My family are Ta'Ceryss nobility. They will help."

Kael shook her hand in return but sighed. "Then, they will be in the minority, I promise you."

Ember cleared her throat. "Getting across that Kasym isn't an option either. It's nearly impossible," she said. "I don't know how your jump back here was, but ours was devastating. It nearly killed us all, and those of us with magic took months to recover. I'm still nowhere near full strength."

Kael shook his head, yet again. It was becoming a regular reaction for him. "I had to jump us. We were surrounded. Had they caught us... we were already dead. It was jump, be mauled by dogs, or swing from a hangman's noose. It was our only very faint hope. I won't do it, again."

"Us. Our?" Yrlissa asked.

"Princess Corleya and her merc — her lady-in-waiting were with me."

"That is how you helped her reclaim the throne," Yrlissa stated.

Kael nodded, but did not offer anything further.

"There has to be another answer," Ember persisted.

The colour was slowly returning to her features and her hair sparkled with the vitality he remembered.

"If there is another answer to this," he said, "I don't have it. But for now, I can get to that seal and do whatever possible to disrupt their plans."

"Agreed, but you're not going alone," Yrlissa said.

"I can't take any of you with me when I jump," he said. "You won't survive, and Ember's in no shape to jump a large group that far." Turning her way, he added, "You're far weaker than you're letting on. You can't fool me."

"I can come with you if you skirt the afterlife during the jump," Yrlissa told him.

"I don't jump that way anymore, not after Cassie..." he stopped and shook his head, again. Yrlissa frowned, but he was glad when she did not push.

"Then, I can bring a smaller group with Max," Ember offered.

"Max is here?" Kael asked.

She nodded.

"You're sure you can jump a small group?" he demanded.

"Yes," she said. "As long as we find the ancient charm that's affecting our magic. We destroyed the ones Sythrnax and Savis had before we jumped, but there must be another on one of the dead enemies nearby. Our magic hasn't worked since we returned, and our landing was rough. The soldiers are searching the bodies, but..."

"There's a lot of dead to check," he finished for her. "I know. I killed them. Most Ri'Tek magic doesn't work on me. Their charms and glyphs don't either, not anymore," Kael said and closed his eyes. He reached out with his senses. The Ancient relic lit up inside his mind in a beacon of blazing silver. Adjusting the magic, he pulled his view wider and the DormaSain camp appeared in his mind as if he were floating above it. After a moment, he opened his eyes. "There's a dead Ri'Tek wizard just inside the tree line behind this camp. The amulet is with him. There's no other life nearby."

"I'll take care of it," Sephi offered and quickly ducked out of the tent.

Kael glanced back over his shoulder to Yrlissa and seriously took her in for the first time. Startlingly familiar amber eyes stared back. "Your death flower always been that size?" he asked.

She shook her head. "It was much larger up until you died."

"Hasn't grown since I've been back?" he asked.

"No."

"That deserves some research at the appropriate time," he stated and turned to Ember. "Did you bring back Sythrnax's body?"

"On a cart in the center of camp," she replied. "The Broken Blade is there, too."

"He has something of mine. May I?" he asked.

"I'm going to go lay down until we're ready to leave, love," she said. "Come join me when you're done or ready."

He nodded and helped her up. She left the tent with Aravae's assistance, and he rounded on Yrlissa.

"I'll show you where," she offered.

Kael followed her out to the middle of camp and slowly approached the cart.

You actually did it.

"Accomplished nothing," he answered aloud, no longer caring what people thought.

"Kael?"

"Akai," he said as he pointed to his head.

"He speaks to you?" she questioned.

He nodded but offered nothing more.

"I would like to discuss *that* with you at the appropriate time," she said, smiled and walked away.

He did not bother with a reply. Instead, he focused his attention on Sythrnax's body.

You proved it can be done. If nothing else, those who end up following you will believe… will know that it can be.

"I am not looking to lead anyone, Akai," he replied, and removed both gloves from Sythrnax's hands.

You do not and will not have a choice in that. Those who oppose the Ri'Tek will flock to you.

"Then, they will flock to their deaths."

Many will. That is the nature of war.

"I like it better when you're not chatty," Kael quipped as he took out the two binding stones in the armored gloves. One was black, and one was a pale blue.

Those stones could be passed along and put to good use.

"The black one is likely mine," Kael answered. "But the blue one probably cost a good wizard their life."

"Then, make that life lost worth the sacrifice."

"Max," Kael said and grinned, but did not turn around.

The big man came up beside him and dragged him into a massive bear hug. "It is good to see you, brother," he said and put Kael down.

"Yeah, it is," he said. Tears welled up in his eyes, and Max grabbed him, again.

"I am sorry, brother. I should have been there with you."

"Not your fault," Kael replied. Max let him go, again, and he took a deep breath.

"Yes, it is," his friend said, and he could see the agony of failure written all over Max's face.

"Never."

"Look closer, Kael," Max demanded. "It was my job to protect you."

He shook his head, unable to comprehend what Max was saying.

"Look closer."

Kael added more power behind his senses. Magic swirled through his oldest and closest friend, and he startled when his own power peeled the magic away. "Holy shit," he whispered. "You're pure of DemonKind blood. KiPara and DragonKin soul."

Max nodded but said nothing.

Kael frowned. "You're the watcher from the beginning of the prophecy... *to purge or protect...* Why would you not say anything to us?" he asked, as his voice trembled.

"The truth?" Kael nodded. "After so many countless centuries, I had begun to question my own reality, so how could I tell you?" he replied, but Kael knew it was not a question. "I knew the moment I first laid eyes on you and Ember together... you were just children. I knew in my very soul you would never destroy any world. I believed that you were in no danger at all. I'm not even sure I... what I believed was true anymore. Can you even imagine?"

"I have an idea," he answered.

"How long were you there?" Max asked.

"Over two hundred years," he muttered. "I can't imagine several millennia."

"We good?"

"Yeah, brother," Kael said and smiled. "I get it."

Kael stared at the stones in his hand and slid the blue stone into his Orotaq cloak as he held up the black.

"What are you going to do with them?"

"Returning this one where it belongs," he said. His friend watched in awe as Kael grasped the black stone in his left hand and forced the dark energy out with his right. The thorn-covered vines on his fingers grew and lifted from his skin.

"Jesus," Max breathed.

The dark magic touched the vines gently and slowly slid inside as if the vines were pulling nourishment from the magic. The vines thickened, and the thorns grew longer. As the stone's power drained away, it paled in colour and revealed a white crystal — an empty binding stone.

"I'll give it to the DragonKin the next time we come across them," he said, and Max nodded his agreement.

"That is going to be hard to get used to," Max stated.

"The feeling is mutual," Kael said. "So, how about we ignore this weird shit we're both mixed up in?"

Max laughed. "I can do that, brother," he said and draped an arm around Kael's shoulder. "Now, let's go get ready for this jump to the Human seal."

"Yeah."

"Kael?" The voice came from behind him and he recognized it long before he turned to face it.

"Cassie!" he said and grinned. As he dropped to one knee, she ran to him and launched herself into his arms.

"I missed you," she whispered.

"Me, too," he replied and gently eased her back. "How did you end up here?"

"I followed Ember after you... you... her magic took me with to the forest. Yrlissa is my *mynerha*."

"Your mother?" he repeated. She nodded as he touched her chin. "May I?" Waiting until she nodded, again, he gently turned her head. Sure enough, a tiny deathflower marked her temple. To anyone else in the world, it was nothing more than a small birth mark or mole. He smiled. "I'm glad you found them."

Cassie reached out and gave him another hug. He laughed as she squeezed her arms together hard.

"I'm happy for you," he whispered.

"Are you all right?" she asked, stepping back

"I will be."

"You scared me," she said.

The sentiment nearly broke his heart. "I'm sorry, sweetheart. This world is scary enough already, isn't it?" She nodded as he continued. "I promise, I'll try not to scare you again, okay? But try to understand I'm not well right now."

"You died," she stated. "Of course, you're not feeling well. I'll help you get better, I promise," she said and hugged him one more time.

"Ah, I know you will," he laughed lightly as tears welled up in his eyes, again. "Now, let's go get ready. We have a lot to do, little Guardian."

Cassie beamed with pride and happiness, and for the first time since he arrived back in the world of the living, he began to believe he might really be back.

At least he hoped so.

Chapter Twenty-Five

"Time passes through the hourglass like sands pass by the sun. Neither touch reality because they are forgotten as quickly as they are remembered. A father's love is felt only when it has nothing to feel itself. Donis forever plies to write unable to see the words on the paper at hand..."

The Prophet Zaddyk's Final Journal Entry,
penned by Brother Donis Kincaid.

"I hope your mind finds peace some day, son. For I have always considered you one. I have never been prouder to write such words about any of the faithful I have raised, taught, and known."

BDK

CORYNTH MARKETPLACE
GRADUATION DAY

Weeks had passed since Kael had brought him home, and as Giddeon stared out across Corynth, he almost wished he had not. The university's biggest graduation day in years had become a total disaster. It was exactly as the prophet Zaddyk had predicted before his slide into complete madness. Giddeon shook his head as he stared at the destruction surrounding him. Wizards, warriors, and archers of all skill levels fought desperately against hordes of monsters from a deep forgotten hell.

Giddeon sighed. He had been so wrong about so many things, and now, his beloved city was paying the price. Zaddyk had tried, relentlessly, to tell Giddeon that a DeathWizard was not responsible for the coming attacks on Corynth and many other cities throughout Talohna. However, he ignored the prophet's warnings and dismissed them as visions tainted by madness.

Newly christened Master Wizard, Galen Vihr, knelt at Giddeon's side, too exhausted from fighting to stand. He could sense no magical reserves remaining in the young man's body, and his life force fluttered unsteadily from using it to power his magic once his cruus was depleted. Every wizard, warrior, and archer in Corynth had given everything they had to slow the monstrosities ravaging the city—all in vain. As Galen looked up at him with blood-shot eyes, he smiled even though the massive black dragon and its smaller creatures continued to make their way deeper into the marketplace.

Galen did not buy his bravado. "We must flee, Giddeon. We can't fight it."

"Go," he said. "I'll buy you the time you need to escape. Go to the Southern Kingdoms and find Ember and Yrlissa—beg the Dead King if you must and find Kael. Warn them of what's coming, and then, help them track down the two DeathWizards you told me of after Kael brought me back here. They must be kept safe. Go! Now!"

"I will not leave you to fight that thing alone."

"He won't be alone."

"Xallis?" Galen let out, struggling to rise. "You're back."

"I am," he said, wrapping him in a hug. "Kiirein and I snuck into the city through the slums' west side gate. He is helping the city guard and several Fae women evacuate civilians. Fae, Giddeon. The gods-blessed Fae are here helping. I came looking for you straight away."

"It is so good to see you, again, my young friend, and I know. The Fae Matriarch was here a half hour ago." Giddeon laughed and gave the young man a hug. "I missed you, boy. But go with Galen. Don't throw your life away on a hopeless fight."

"Hopeless?" the young wizard said, grinning. "Not yet. It is long past time for me to repay the kindness you showed me as a child and the support you gave as a wizard —" All three ducked as a winged aberration swooped down at them and flew back into the air toward the Cascade Citadel. Giddeon let loose three fireballs in rapid succession, but the creature was too fast and spun through the magic unharmed.

"The small ones are too fast to track," Giddeon began

Xallis chuckled. "We'll see." Two books hung from his belt, and with a quick flick of his wrist, both books jumped to life and floated in midair before him. "You gave me these, but you had no idea what they really were," he said, winking at the ArchWizard.

Giddeon immediately recognized the two books from the set of five he gave Xallis years prior before he left to study with Ta'Ceryss' most prominent Elvehn Elementalists from Aravae's family in Kyll'Darhen.

"The Elemental Grimoires."

"Yes," Xallis replied. "I memorized the first three, but these two. Oh, believe me, these two —"

The flying creature turned from the castle and dove again as a long spear appeared in its hands. Banking to the left, it dropped from the sky while Xallis amplified the stiff breeze blowing through the city. Throwing his hand out, the young Elementalist released a wave of volatile air with his magic. The creature's attack ended, and it was tossed back into the sky, buffeted back and forth under Xallis' continued manipulation of the wind.

"Flame, Giddeon," Xallis shouted. Giddeon never hesitated, forming a fireball in his left hand as the spell leapt from his mouth. Xallis snatched the fire as he pulled silver magic from the books in front of him. The flames raced side-by-side with the silver energy and both surged across the sky. The wind fueled the temperature of the wizard's fire until it exploded and engulfed the flying creature in midair well above their heads. Xallis continued feeding the silver magic to the flames and used one hand to spin the fire magic into a swirling hell-storm of wind and heat. Overwhelmed, the flying creature fell from the sky, burning to ash before its charred bones clattered as they struck the ground. The elemental magic winked out just as fast as Xallis had brought it to life.

"Well done," Giddeon complemented. The large dragon grabbed onto the wall and scaled up the side of Cora's Den at the edge of GutterTown. It shrieked and headed to the marketplace. Turning to Galen he nodded. "Go, now. Xallis and I will slow the dragon. Go!" Galen bowed to them before he turned and ran toward the slum's far gate.

The black dragon took flight, diving and landing only a short distance from where they stood. The impact shook the ground and nearly knocked both wizards off their feet. Giddeon stared up at the massive Behemoth, but for the first time realized it was not a true Dragon. A putrid energy rose from the being like greasy smoke as if a vile magic had corrupted the creature, leaving it in a constant state of decay. Its tattered wings should not have been able to support flight, were clearly enhanced by magic to give it the skyward advantage. Rotting scales the size of tower shields dripped with the same corruption. Veins of black and purple coursed through the creature's flesh, and vibrant silver marred the edges of each scale, leading Giddeon to have once believed a DeathWizard was responsible for its creation. Now, he was not so sure.

He frowned, trying to imagine what possible vile magic had been used to create such an abomination. A bright light snapped behind him and caught his attention. He whirled, the words of magic forming rapidly on his tongue. Stopping short as he recognized the man behind him, Giddeon shook his head in disbelief.

"What's the matter, ArchWizard? Never seen a Vascuul before?"

"Commander Zatassa? What are you doing here?"

"Your city has been attacked by one of my corrupted forefathers and several of my mutated Kin along with hordes of other Vascuul," he stated, pointing to the flying creatures as two other DragonKin Zephyrs raced to engage the flying creatures. A lone female Zephyr stayed beside Zatassa.

"This is ancient magic, ArchWizard Zirakus. It is what your *Ancients* do best," she said.

"The Ancients didn't do this," Giddeon replied. "They haven't even made an appearance here."

"Yet they are not present to help when their creations attack your city," Zatassa said, pushing past Giddeon. The black dragon roared as the DragonKin commander stepped forward, challenging it. "My mistress will deal with you creature," he shouted, pointing at the corrupted dragon. "Leave this city or fall here, breathing your last among those you hate."

"Shelaryx is a Dragon, then," Giddeon said, awestruck.

"Yes," Zatassa said. "But she is weak from suppressing our magic over the numerous millennia. We may have to help her fight the *alakvalto*."

Giddeon frowned at the strange word. "It is Dragon-tongue," Xallis told him, quickly translating. "It means changeling of evil."

"Made good use of your time in Ta'Caeryss," Giddeon muttered, and Xallis shrugged. Both ducked as the dragon roared a second time and opened its rotting jaws. Sinister black fire spewed out, and Commander Zatassa threw his arms wide. The green, flame tattoos covering his body pulsed with energy. It activated a shimmering shield of emerald fire to cover himself, Giddeon, and Xallis. The poisonous black fire hit the shield hard, forcing Zatassa to his knees, but his shield held. The attack rolled up over the shield and struck a building behind them. Giddeon paled as he watched the black flames eat into the building like acid. Whatever the sticky fire did not eat immediately, the flames' outer edges consumed. The hairs on the back of his neck stood on end at the thought of what the vile magic would do to armored or unprotected flesh.

From out of nowhere, a second impact smashed into the ground, staggering the three men and cutting off the noxious dragon-fire. Giddeon glanced up to see a white dragon grappling on top of the black. With its jaws locked tight behind the black's head, the white used its front claws to push the black dragon's wings flat. Bone popped as the white Dragon shook its head, peeling putrid scales and flesh from the black's neck.

Turning to Giddeon, Zatassa smiled. "My queen will deal with the *alakvalto* for now. We must stop the flying Kin from distracting her as she fights, and we must assist her when we can by distracting it."

Giddeon did not answer. He could not tear his eyes from the incredible sight of the two majestic creatures battling. The white Dragon stabbed the black with her tail spur, and it screamed in agony as the bladed tailbone punched through its belly and into the dirt underneath. On the verge of losing the fight, the black shook its body, kicking up dust around its claws. The vibrations rolled through the ground and tickled the soles of Giddeon's feet. He gasped as a dozen long spikes along the black dragon's back snapped upward, piercing through the scales on Shelaryx's shiny white belly. Blood poured from the wounds, and she cried out in pain as her jaws released the black's neck. The intense shaking tore the wounds wide, and finally, she jumped from its back before she was completely disemboweled by the vibrating spines.

Shelaryx stumbled as she landed and exposed her side. The black dragon lunged. The female Zephyr rushed forward and sticky emerald fire leapt from both her hands. The green fire splashed against the black's side, up its neck, and across its face. The distraction drove it back several steps and gave the vulnerable queen time to recover. Shelaryx shook her head as her tail coiled up and shot out, striking the black's shoulder. Leaping ahead, she slammed into the black, knocking it from its feet and onto its back. Stomping and slashing with her back claws, Shelaryx lunged at the black's throat, her jaws clacking as she missed time and again. Three mutated DragonKin swooped down to help their fellow Vascuul, but both Zatassa and the female Zephyr unleashed more magic to draw their attention away.

Sparkling emerald fireballs and dark green spears of ice rocketed away at staggered intervals. Two of the flying DragonKin rolled through the fireballs but were impaled by the spears of ice as Xallis distorted the air around them. They dropped from the sky and hit the ground with a solid crunch. The third flying Kin swooped low, and it dodged both attacks as it headed straight for Zatassa. Xallis stepped up and pulled more magic from his grimoires while Giddeon barked the words to Gabriel Alatar's lightning spell. The mutated Kin was far faster than the others, and it landed among Zatassa and his companion unharmed by their magic. It lashed out with a set of wicked blades that surprised Giddeon. He had not seen anyone use a bladed hand-glaive in over a century.

Zatassa and the female Zephyr drew their green swords to defend themselves as Shelaryx continued her frenzied assault against the black. Scales and rotten flesh flew from her back claws, but finally, the black got its back legs under it and flung her into the sky. Shelaryx dove back down and crashed into the black. The two dragons rolled across the marketplace, slashing and hissing as they crushed vendor stalls and a store. Giddeon and Xallis dove behind a stone wall as a spiked black tail whipped past their heads and leveled the burning building behind them.

Shelaryx pushed off the black Vascuul dragon, belching a stream of searing flame as her wings carried her higher into the air and out of range of the black's spiked tail. Instead, its tail crashed into the second floor of the Merchant's Inn and swept through to the other side. The Dragon Queen did not hesitate. Folding her wings, she plummeted the forty feet back to the earth and landed amidst the burning magic atop the black dragon.

The black Vascuul was ready for her and grabbed Shelaryx. Both rolled into the building and the inn collapsed while the two dragons fell through the floor into the large basement. Giddeon watched on in horror as a roar of defiance shrieked out of the rubble, followed by the muffled explosion of whiskey barrels and more noxious black flame. He heard Shelaryx bellow in agony as the black dragon burst backward from the wreckage with a torrent of acidic black fire spilling from its mouth. For a full twenty seconds the black dragon saturated the destroyed inn with its vile dragon-breath. Commander Zatassa and the female Zephyr fought desperately to reach the inn, but the lone mutated DragonKin was more than a match for them.

"ArchWizard!" Zatassa yelled. "Help my queen n —" His words were cut short by a frenzied attack of flashing glaives.

Giddeon attacked the black dragon without thinking twice on it. As Xallis crept through the rubble with his grimoires in hand, the ArchWizard continued his assault, chanting the words to several spells one after the other.

"*Kveysa drepa,*" he barked. Lightning leapt from his hands, sparking across the black dragon's chest but failing to penetrate the heavy scales. Without missing his chant cadence, a second spell followed on the heels of the first.

"*Leysa Svell.*" Spinning blades of intense cold whistled away. Smashing into the dragon's chest, the cold cracked numerous scales. Giddeon planted both feet, trembling from the immense strain caused by the third spell leaving his lips.

"*Kippa bjarga —*" The spell's first words pulled large slivers of stone from the ground beneath his feet and nearly drained Giddeon's magical reserves. Still, he continued casting. "*Hvessa'...*" The large spear-like shards of rock floated into the air and spun, humming with intensity. Blood dripped from his nose as he pushed himself harder, forcing the spell's final words from his mouth. "*Foss hrinda!*" The Shards of Hell Mountain rocketed away at subsonic speeds, smashing into the black dragon's chest. Frozen scales cracked and peeled away, staggering the great beast and bringing it to its front knees. A roar of defiance bellowed from its throat, and it quickly regained its feet.

From the inn's far side, Xallis attacked. Pulling water from the river winding through the center of Corynth, he sprayed the inn, dousing the flames with one hand while the other sent jets of thin water stitching up the monster's neck and split a horn on its head. The dragon spun toward him, roaring with rage as the broken horn spun into the ruined buildings. Dropping his connection to the water, Xallis raised his arms and pulled magic from his grimoires as well as the earth below the dragon's claws. Giant spires of rock exploded from the ground beneath the black dragon. A sharp spire of stone pierced each shoulder, and two more punched through the black monster's tattered wings. A final pillar of rock burst from the earth and punctured its tail.

Growling, the dragon fought to tear itself free of the stone spikes, but Xallis held the stone together, refusing to release his magic. The dragon heaved itself to the right and cracked several of the stone pillars. Xallis reinforced the rock from within, forcing more magic into the spires. Giddeon paled. He could see Xallis tremble as he continuously reformed the stone holding the impaled black dragon. The ArchWizard drew his staff from his back and used the enchanted magic inside to attack the dragon from the rear. Energy bolts jumped from the staff but did little damage. With his own magic depleted, the distraction was all he could do to help the young Elementalist.

Tremors raced through Xallis, and his whole body shook from the stress of taxing the Archaic Grimoires and himself. No longer able to hold on, he collapsed to his knees when Shelaryx WhiteScale burst from the smoldering rubble of the inn. Belching flames at the black dragon, she crawled her way out of the hole. Her spurred tail lashed out, knocking the black sideways and cracking three of the massive stone spikes. Giddeon stared in awe openly before having to dive behind a rock wall as chunks of stone and dragon flesh bounced around him.

Shelaryx attacked relentlessly, curling her tail and spewing more flames. Still pinned in place, the black dragon lowered its head and exhaled more acidic black fire. The Dragon Queen unfurled her tail. It snapped forward, striking the black's chest. With little protection left after Giddeon's shard spell, her spur slid past the few cracked scales deep into its body and came out between its hips. Forcing her tail spikes to stand, Shelaryx ripped her tail free on an angle meant to shred the black dragon's insides. The black fire winked out as the dragon collapsed in the dirt. One last bellow of defiance ripped from the black's throat as the Dragon Queen's tail spur slammed into its head. Not satisfied, the white Dragon leapt forward, sinking her teeth into her enemy's throat. With a growl and a savage twist from her powerful neck, she tore the Vascuul's head off and dropped it on the ground. She fell to her knees already transforming into Human-form.

Giddeon glanced over the wall and saw Zatassa and the female Zephyr still fighting against their winged Kin. Both DragonKin warriors attacked relentlessly and fought as one, but the mutated Vascuul was too fast. His long-bladed glaives blocked every swing of their glass swords. Turning toward Giddeon as he danced around the attacking blades, the winged Vascuul saw the dead dragon. Lunging at Zatassa, the creature knocked him to the earth and jumped into the sky while his wings opened. Looking back for a second, the creature grinned and wheeled away and was out of sight in a heartbeat.

Zatassa sheathed his swords and rushed to his queen. He helped her to her feet as the female Zephyr draped a robe over her naked body. Giddeon approached cautiously.

"You finally decided to help," he stated, but quickly changed his tone. "Thank you for coming."

Queen WhiteScale nodded. "I promised your son we would help as much as we could. Even this is a risk for the Fae that are at the GutterTown gates helping with the evacuation. Such a huge risk is… my apologies, Giddeon, but we could not let Corynth fall. We will need it in the days and months to come."

"Thank you," he repeated and offered a respectful bow. "We should—"

He was interrupted by a blaze of white magic from the market's far side. A strange woman dressed in a white hooded and masked robe stepped out from the Fae realm jump magic, but she was not Fae. Giddeon recognized her vibrant purple eyes as identical to Sythrnax's.

"My queen," Zatassa hissed. "That is the Vikress. We do not have the numbers to fight them without the Fae. We must leave, now."

As the realm jump magic faded, Giddeon's caught sight of two more flying Vascuul diving toward them from the sky. The Vikress reached out with both her hands and black magic flared to life. It raced away, snaring the two Vascuul. As if pulling a rope, the Vikress dragged them from the sky with a force unlike anything Giddeon had ever seen. The two mutated DragonKin smashed into the earth and died instantly, crushed on impact.

Another snap of Fae magic cracked beside him, and Giddeon turned as a young Fae woman stepped from the light. The light did not fade as she kept the doorway active.

"We have to leave! Now!" she barked. "Ri'Tek have entered the city at numerous locations, and I can't find Matriarch Thornwing."

"Kyr, what happened" Shelaryx demanded.

Kyr Meadow shook her head. "The gate where we were helping… the enemy controls it. We had to flee."

"Mistress," Zatassa said and extended his hand out toward the Fae portal. "Please."

The Queen nodded and stepped into the bright vortex, followed by Zatassa and the female Zephyr.

"Good luck, ArchWizard," Kyr said and followed the DragonKin. Giddeon frowned as the vortex collapsed behind the Fae's second-in-command.

"ArchWizard Giddeon Zirakus?"

Giddeon turned and took a deep breath as the purple eyed woman approached, accompanied by two others. One was dressed in a heavy robe, and the other was in armor unlike any Giddeon had seen in Talohna before. Both wore masks but had the same purple star-burst eyes. "Yes?"

"My name is Illara D'Artagen. I am the Vikress of the race you call the Ancients. This is one of my military leaders, Commander Tuz." The Vikress gestured to the woman in the robe. "And my priestess, Lady Kaheen. Can my people and I offer you assistance in dealing with the monsters destroying your city?"

Giddeon gaped, too stunned to answer.

"ArchWizard?" The Vikress prompted him, again. "While you still have a city standing, may we offer our help?"

Giddeon nodded at the absurd request but could not get his tongue to work.

The Vikress nodded to the warriors, and they each opened a realm jump vortex and left to the distinct crack of Fae magic.

The Vikress offered him a slight bow and offered him her arm. "My people will destroy or drive the creatures from your city. You and I have much to discuss, and I have little time. My people are needed at other locations across Talohna. I would like to inform you of our intentions and for you to arrange an official meeting with your new queen for when we return in a few days' time. Shall we?" she asked and pointed across the market to the Cascade Citadel and Giddeon's wizard tower.

Giddeon forced himself to smile and nodded, again. There was little else he could do.

WESTERN GATE
GUTTERTOWN

"Slowly, people, please," Eva Thornwing yelled across the mass of panicked people as she helped guide Corynth's citizens through the gate in the western wall. The terrified atmosphere calmed almost immediately. The poor helped carry the injured rich and the rich not injured helped carry street orphans, merchants, noblemen, and city guards helped the Fae defend both—whether they were from their own social status or not. Eva smiled even in the heat and panic of the attack. It gave her hope to see such unity, and it added to the guilt she already felt for pulling the Fae off-phase from Talohna so long ago.

Several children ran past. The fear in their auras caught her off guard and nearly made her sick to her stomach. A young teenage girl ran by but stumbled as she struggled to carry her injured brother—at least that was Eva's guess. She rushed forward to help and brushed against the girl. It sent a shiver down her spine. The young girl—no older than thirteen—carried no fear in her aura, but there was something else she could not identify. It was something powerful. With no time to waste, she helped the girl to her feet and sent them toward the gate. As the two vanished into the crowd of escaping citizens, she frowned and wondered who the young girl was.

"Mistress!" a voice yelled. Eva turned in time to see a storm of blue lightning hurdling for her. She sidestepped the attack, and the magic tore into a Vascuul creeper as it jaws snapped shut in the space she had just occupied. The massive mutated millipede fell back dead, its shell cracked wide open.

Looking to the wizard who saved her, she saw Master Wizard Galen Vihr drop to his knees exhausted. His life force fluttered dangerously, and she realized he had been powering his magic with his life energy.

"Fool!" she snapped and hurried in time to catch him before he fell on his face. "Humans! Foolish!" she muttered and grasped at her magic. "*Amaeh Sianas Afaney.*" The ageless Fae's spell bloomed into a myriad of bright colours and entered Galen's body. Shallow wounds healed instantly, and magical energy surged through him.

She helped him back to his feet. "Thank you, Mistress Eva."

"Thank you, Master Wizard. Your spell saved my life —"

"A very small price to pay," he interrupted.

"Foolish," she argued. "Your life holds as much value as mine. You Humans do not value it enough."

A series of bright flashes echoed around them. Eva stared on as a dozen Ri'Tek wizards and two warriors each walked from the blazing jump magic.

"Mistress ThornWing," Ghul began. "How nice to see you, again."

Eva glanced around and frowned. They were outnumbered almost six to one. "Are you sure you brought enough help with you, Ghul? You could have just asked nicely. You are here for me, I assume?"

The Syddic priest laughed. "I am. But experience has taught me to never underestimate your people, let alone you, Eva. Though, with all the fodder trying to escape, I could have come alone. You will surrender to me to save them. You cannot help yourself."

Eva nodded and stepped forward.

Galen moved in front of her with his back to the new arrivals. "He would not dare kill innocent people just to take you."

"Kill innocent people?' Ghul asked. "My, my, wizard. You do understand we are here to help stop the creatures destroying this city, do you not? My Vikress merely wishes to resume contact with the Fae. I have come to collect her for our first official contact."

Eva leaned closer to Galen. "We are outnumbered and have been out-maneuvered, Master Wizard," she told him. "Let it be a lesson to you going forward. You cannot predict what they *will* do, you can only try to be ready for whatever they *may* do, and hope the sacrifice required to live another day is not too heavy."

Galen's voice lowered to a whisper. "I cannot just stand here and let them take you."

"You have to," she replied. "Go along with whatever they want until you can get to my daughter and our allies in DormaSai. We may have lost today, but this will be a war of attrition unlike any your race has fought before."

"No... I—"

"I am waiting patiently, Eva," Ghul interjected.

"Listen to me," Eva snapped and grabbed Galen's chin. "When you fight this race, your only goal is to survive for one more day, for one more week, and then for one more battle— until the puzzle comes together."

"What does that mean?" he asked.

"DormaSai," she said quickly as Ghul's warriors moved. Eva put up her hands as Galen and several other defenders were forced to their knees. "Your word, Ghul," Eva snapped testily. "Or this gate will not just run with red blood."

"You have it. Our Vikress should already have requested a meeting with Queen Bale to take place in the coming days," he barked. "Come now. No one else will be harmed. My orders were clear. Cethos is to be considered an ally."

Eva nodded and stepped forward. With a simple wave of his hand, the wizard with Ghul opened a jump doorway.

"After you, Mistress," Ghul mocked.

A bright light snapped around them, and they were gone.

Chapter Twenty-Six

Kael walked from the swirling maelstrom amid the vortex of his jump spell to see Ember and her group had already arrived. There was no sign of the Ancients or their army. The ruins where the Human Animus seal were located in the open plain next to them. Before them, the enchanted dark forest spread as he could see. His heart hammered with excitement as he stared at the gnarled, mutated trees. The distorted cries of wildlife drifted from the forest on the early evening's gentle breeze, and it filled him with vigor.

Max stepped up beside him and huffed as if disappointed. "We're sure this is the place?" he asked.

"It is," Yrlissa answered. Max nodded, and Kael watched quietly as he moved out to scout the area. The assassin glanced between the ruins and the tree line at the start of the dark forest. Turning toward Kael, she frowned and pointed to her right. "DormaSai weathered the Cataclysm without any changes to its landmass. That forest was the battlefield for this seal. It had to be opened on the surface over on the southern rise. There," she said, pointing back to her left, "because there's no Deep Earth caverns below us."

At the mention of the forest, Ember groaned. "That place makes me ill." She moaned a second time but quickly covered her uneasiness. "This forest grew out of the bodies that fell in battle here. So many violent deaths — I can feel them, feel their spirits. This whole place grew twisted and wrong as if their magic rotted with them. They're angry, very angry."

Yrlissa nodded in agreement. "I told you years ago when we were on Ver Karmot, Nahlla. This enchanted forest is not like the others we have been to. The number of lives lost here were so high they were just left to decay. Those of us left were devastated after the war. Races were extinct, or nearly so. There was no one to put these souls to rest. Every vile creature dwells in there. Feral weres, harpies, succubi, and feral DemonKind vampires, too — and many that are a far worse."

"And quite possible some creatures we have never seen," Sephi added, pointing to show them. "Drexa Bakar found my sister and I a couple days west and north of here, within The Tail of the forest."

"There is no doubt about it. That explains a lot actually," Yrlissa offered, though no malice or sarcasm marred her voice. "This forest's magic will seep into us if we stay for any longer than a single day. It is likely what happened to your sister and yourself. Your unique skills may be from your time here."

Nekrosa laughed and kissed Sephi's forehead. "And that is why you are my heart," he said.

Kael snorted and turned from the forest. "Magic gone wrong, nothing more."

Yrlissa frowned and stepped in front of him. "You must stop shunning what you are and embrace it, instead. Feel the energy — that magic which is around us. What happened here and the magic that remains within it acts like a living entity. Connect with it, Kael. Dark or Light, enchanted forests channel magic like this into this world and — with a blessing from Lady Lykke — perhaps even into you."

"You sound like her," Kael said, calming.

"Jasala?" Yrlissa asked. He nodded as she continued, "Good. You should listen to us both."

"Embrace the corruption, right?" he quipped.

"Yes," Yrlissa answered.

He turned to her and frowned, lowering his voice. "Except it is not a corruption. It is a power no mortal was ever supposed to handle let alone be imbued with at the conception of life."

"Does it really matter?" she asked. "Accept what you are, so you can be who you are meant to be."

"Yeah, suck it up, right?" he snapped. She nodded but offered nothing more. Yrlissa might have said the words, but it was Lycori's voice he heard. Like a ghost from the past, a shiver ran up his spine and compelled him to turn toward the forest. The familiar feeling calmed his nerves and allowed him to shift his focus back to their present situation. "Nekrosa?" he barked.

"Yes?"

"Where's this seal? We need a plan. With Queen WhiteScale not receiving our messages, we need a good plan. This place is too open to defend effectively, and the Ancients can't be far behind us."

"This way," the King said. Kael followed him until they came upon a pile of rocks.

"The seal is under ground," Nekrosa told him. "But only about fifteen feet or so."

"We dug a narrow shaft wide enough for one person to get down and verify what was there," Sephi added. "It confirmed the seal is there without exposing it to any spies who might have been watching."

"Max?" Kael yelled over his shoulder. Max appeared at the forest's edge. Kael was not surprised to see his old friend had nearly completed his reconnaissance. "This pile of rocks is what they'll want." Max waved his recognition.

"Yrlissa," Kael said. "How will they come at us?"

"It depends how many the Vikress brings. The Syphoners of the Syddic order are on the far side of this seal. We need to be ready, Kael. She could bring everything she has.

If even a handful of those leeches survived the fighting all those millennia ago and were pulled into this seal... the Vikress will risk everything she has and all of her best people to free them."

"Why?" he asked, shaking his head with confusion. "Why put a majority of your strongest magic users at this battle and not at the seal where Asa was fighting? He was the one who cracked the Still Dimension. The other five seals would never have opened if not for him."

Yrlissa frowned, rubbing her forehead in frustration. "No one battle was more important than the others in the minds of the Ri'Tek. They didn't believe we could pull off using such powerful magic, let alone have the power required to succeed. We were the Lesser races for a reason, Kael. DormaSai has always been Talohna's magical powerhouse. Most Human and Elvehn wizards studied in Drae'Kahn before the Eye was created, and the largest wizard family known is the White Cabal, they lived here. Fae and Dragon Behemoths studied or taught here before the war. The Syphoners were best utilized fighting the massive number of wizards in this country. It was nothing more than that. The Ri'Tek were merely balancing the battle at this location."

As Max returned to the rock pile, it was clear he had overheard them. "What makes them so dangerous?" he asked

"The Syphoners?" Yrlissa replied, getting a nod from him.

A crack of magic rocked the ruins behind them and a white light flooded over the small clearing. Emerging from the light, several newcomers put everyone on edge.

"Because without them," Vikress Illara began, "we cannot use your magic. But, more importantly, we cannot make new Vascuul unless they are freed. My apologies for the delay in our arrival, but we had to make a detour."

"Mom!" Ember screamed as two of Illara's Sect Priestesses and a male wizard pushed Eva Thornwing forward, forcing her to her knees. Kael gasped, and his heart fluttered as the wizard stared at him.

"I am all right, daughter," the Fae Matriarch assured her and smiled up at Ember.

"Well, well," Illara smiled. "Interesting, surely, but ultimately irrelevant."

Ember grabbed his arm. "Help her, Kael, please!"

"Let her go," Kael barked. Calling forth his reaper blades from the Ether, he quickly closed the distance to Illara's group. The others followed him while Ember remained tight at his side.

"Of course, I will let her go," the Vikress said, gesturing with her hands. It prompted a priestess to place a dagger at Eva's throat, and Kael stopped. He held out his hands for the others to stop as well.

"You don't need a Fae Matriarch to open this seal," he snapped. "Even your kind doesn't believe in senseless killing."

"True," the Vikress replied. "Though, this really would not be a senseless killing. Far from it, in fact."

Yrlissa gasped and Kael sensed real fear in her voice. "No! You can't!" she practically shouted.

"Of course, I can, Yrlissa Blackmist. The blood of a matured Fae would bring down Jasala's Sepulchre in a matter of hours, and the remaining four seals would all open at once. The blood of the High Matriarch will destroy the Sepulchre in seconds and will free my people from the living hell you trapped us in for over ten millennia. Though, I must admit it is a shame that our first meeting will be our last. Sythrnax has told me plenty about you." The Vikress closed her eyes and sighed. "I have not killed a Guardian in so very long."

Kael scoffed. "You're crazy if you think we'll let you do that. You made a mistake, Illara. You didn't bring enough fighters."

The Vikress laughed. "Of course, I did, Kael. You have spent too much time focused on me and not nearly enough on your surroundings."

"Kael," Max mumbled. "We have a problem."

As Kael glanced around, he saw Nekrosa and Sephi had joined Ember by his side. Max, however, had hung back and was the only one protecting their rear flank from attack.

Kael turned in time to see two dozen warriors surrounding a Ri'Tek wizard. The Ancient wizard slammed his staff into the rocks protecting the seal's entrance.

An explosion of rock and dirt tossed Kael and the others through the air as if they weighed nothing. His shield flared to life when he hit the ground, but it did little to cushion the blow. The dust cleared slowly, and he groaned as he rose to his feet with the others doing the same. The pile of rocks was gone, leaving an amphitheater-sized crater in their wake.

The Human Animus seal was fully exposed for all to see. Twenty or more Ancient warriors and wizards made it their duty to guard it.

Illara's voice penetrated the ringing inside his head. "It is a shame you will all die here today. If you had accepted us like the rest of Talohna, you would have lived to see this world returned to its former glory."

Yrlissa pulled a chunk of sharp rock from her shoulder and spat a mouthful of blood toward the Vikress. "Return to oppression under Ri'Tek rule?" she said, spitting more blood from her crushed lips and torn mouth. "I'd rather die here before becoming a Lesser race, again."

"Come now, Yrlissa," Illara cooed. "We both know you were never part of the Lesser races. A Lost race, perhaps — and they certainly never lived on their knees under our rule. Now, sit down and watch while I tear down your prodigy's magic and free my people from a fate worse than death."

Unable to move, Kael and those with him watched helplessly as the Vikress' Sect priestesses dragged Eva onto the seal and shoved her to her knees. Images of Kazzador City flooded his mind, and he struggled desperately not to fall into the Fae memory magic.

"Please, stop," Ember begged. "You don't need to do this —"

A Ri'Tek warrior lunged forward and smashed the pommel of his sword into her mouth. Kael quickly stepped in front of her as she crashed to the ground, protecting her body with his. The warrior's second swing struck the left chain mail bracer of his enchanted armor.

Catching the pommel in his left hand, Kael angled the blade upwards with his right and drove the sword straight into the warrior's chest. A moment passed and his short scythes appeared in his hands. He rushed Illara.

Side-stepping with ease, she barked orders for her people to stand down. "I have killed more of your kind than any of my people — dead or alive, Kael. If you insist on fighting, I will add your life to that number."

Catching his breath, Kael settled his feet and grinned. "I promise you have never killed one my kind. I am nothing like the Kai'Sar you faced so many years ago."

"Good," she said, returning his smile with a short bow. "Then, perhaps you will live longer than the rest of the abominations spawned before you."

Kael mocked her bow and attacked. Three fast strikes missed as the Vikress twisted her feet and dodged each swing. Her hand shot out and hammered his chest, forcing him backward. Driving his blades into the ground helped hold his footing, and he glanced up to see a massive glaive appeared in the Vikress' hands. An ugly bladed head edged in serrated barbs had been seamlessly forged into the spear's handle. The blade extended the glaive's reach to extensively in a way that made her practically untouchable. The weapon's defense alone was tremendous.

"I am impressed," she said, titling her head. "Your chest should have collapsed under the pressure of that spell."

Kael snorted. "Several species of demon hit far harder than you do." He knew he would never get inside the glaive's reach with his shorter blades, and he struggled to see a way to defeat the Ancient warrior.

Akai's voice rolled through his mind.

A double fanged scythe will give you the reach. You must free me to make the first change of a new weapon. Only then can you summon it at will.

The second Akai offered it, Kael took a step back and twisted the handles of his shorter blades together cracking the dragonbone handles. White fog rolled out, lengthening the weapon. A wicked scythe blade shifted to the end while a shorter second blade followed underneath. As the handle curved and twisted to fit his grip, he watched the shock come to life in Illara's eyes.

"Your time was well spent in the afterlife, I see. We heard rumors during the war that the Dwarves were trying to forge a sentient weapon—they succeeded. I am surprised."

"Funny thing about rumors, Illara. They're seldom true," he said.

"Says the man at the heart of two very true rumors," she replied. "I might have been mildly concerned there for a moment."

Kael did not bother to respond. He knew from experience the Ri'Tek liked to play verbal mind games when they fought. Smiling, he vanished in a cloud of black smoke. Illara spun immediately, prepared for the attack from behind, but he emerged at her front and swung his scythe when he stepped from the Ether. Realizing her mistake, Illara spun on her heel and drove her glaive into the ground. Kael's scythe cut through its handle as she leapt backward, spinning through the air only to land on her feet a dozen feet away. The broken glaive vanished. Though surprised by the phenomenal acrobatics, he still smiled. The top blade of his scythe was lined with purple-red blood. He smiled wider.

She was not quite fast enough.

Illara gasped at Kael as she touched her fingers to the gash across her stomach. "You are an enigma, Kael Symes. We should not be fighting. We should be bringing peace to Talohna together and repairing the damage done by the Lesser dosa."

Knowing how dangerous she was, Kael played along. He refused to attack the unarmed woman to avoid falling into another Ancient's trap.

"Not interested," he hissed. "Sythrnax already gave me the sales pitch. I gave him the same answer right before I tore his soul from his body."

"Impossible," she snapped. Even still, Kael heard the disbelief in her voice.

"I may be a lot of things," he replied, "but a liar isn't one of them." He placed the butt of his scythe on the ground and called to the ancient spirit inside it. *Akai.*

Show her?

Yes, she likes to play mind games. It's our turn, he said inside his head.

You will need the double reapers, you can only pull a soul from its original form.

Kael let the double-fanged scythe vanish and instantly called forth the Vai'Karth in the form he had found them. One of the double reaper blades appeared in his left hand, and he slid his finger along the scythe's short blade to draw his own blood. The longer blade flared with power as vibrant blue glyphs sizzled and appeared along the scythe's dark surface. As he pulled his hand back slowly, a screaming soul was drawn out from the metal. The distorted ethereal face materialized before them, and its identity unmistakable.

The Vikress shrieked with rage as he let the weapon re-absorb the soul. "How dare you! You verminous dosa," she spat. "How dare you defile the soul from one of my people? My brother!"

"Simple, really," he barked. "Because it makes me stronger. The stronger I get, the more of you I can kill until there are none of you left."

Illara cocked her head to the side, and a smile tugged at her mask. "With a thousand years of training and experience fighting my people, I believe you would accomplish that goal. I do. But most of your power is far beyond your ken, and it will remain so. Those who could teach you are long dead, and you will follow them today. I will not permit you to leave here alive." Her glaive reappeared intact in her hand.

Kael lifted his scythe and attacked. Using the outer edge of the Void as a conduit, he lunged forward without the cover of black smoke. His scythe slammed into Illara's glaive and locked tight. The Vikress pushed back on the entangled blades. Even using all his strength, he still slid backwards on his heels as she forced him back.

Akai?

On it.

White smoke poured from the handle of his weapon. A sharp crack echoed as the handle snapped, freeing the bottom half. Spinning the half in his right hand, Kael grinned as two blades jumped from the broken end. With her glaive still locked tight to the scythe, the Ancient warrior was defenseless as his short-handled scythe raced for her exposed rib cage. Her glaive vanished in a puff of white smoke.

Losing his balance, he was not fast enough to recover. Illara's right hand hammered the inside of his right elbow and changed his weapons trajectory. His own blade sank into his stomach as Illara snatched him by the throat. With no other choice, he released the hold on his weapons and they vanished. He was left with a garish wound in his lower abdomen while at her mercy.

"Kael!" Ember cried out as he dropped to his knees.

The Vikress pulled him sideways by his throat and dragged him closer to the seal. "You were right about one thing," she said. "We don't kill unless it serves our needs, so why don't we test my theory? Lady Mosen?" Turning to one of her priestesses, she nodded. The Sect priestess drew a thin blade.

"Leave her alone!" Ember yelled, rushing forward. Two warriors caught her before she could get close.

Again, the Vikress' smile pulled at her mask. "Easy, my dear," she said. "Lady Mosen? I will not ask, again."

The priestess dragged the point of her dagger across Eva's cheek, drawing a thin line of blood. "*Sja megin,*" she whispered, flicking the blood from her blade onto the seal in front of Eva. The Fae Matriarch's blood reacted with the seal's magic instantaneously. A shadow matching the seal's size appeared. It quickly grew straight into the air, where it branched off in three different directions. One headed toward the Forsaken Lands, the one went toward the Dragon Isles, and one far beyond the Cauldron's Teeth mountain range where the Sea of Storms lie.

"Amazing." The Vikress laughed. "For those of you who do not know — I give you Jasala Vyshaan's Sepulchre Prison. The magical lock that kept the Ancients away from Talohna for an extra five thousand years. The first seal was already crumbling when she died, and her life force created this monstrosity." Turning to Yrlissa, she continued. "Very good. You taught her to use the dimensional bleed from the seal to power the Sepulchre continuously. Had Sythrnax not escaped the seal before her death, we would never have gotten out. Even in death, he will be a hero to our people forever."

The Vikress turned to her priestess and nodded her directive once more.

"Take me!" Kael screamed. "Use me!"

"No, Kael," Ember begged.

The Vikress glanced between him and Ember. "You must think I am stupid beyond the dimmest dosa to ever live," she snapped. "I would never give you the chance to walk from death a second time. You are already far more powerful than any Kai'Sar before you. You will die, Kael, but it will not be on that seal where its magic can create a way back." The Vikress pulled him close until they were nose-to-nose. She winked at him, clearly taunting, before turning to Lady Mosen and gesturing for her to continue.

The priestess slid her dagger into Eva's throat and let her drop her face down on the seal.

Ember's scream pierced through the fog of agony and red buzz of suffocation plaguing his mind. He watched helplessly as she was forced to the ground along with Max and DormaSai's king and queen. The Ancient wizards chanted as the world heaved and split open around the seal. The dark Sepulchre groaned and fell, fading as if it had never existed. The wizards completed their spells. More than a dozen shields sprung to life, covering everyone including Kael and those with him. The earth twisted and tore itself apart. Large cracks exploded outward from the seal, rocketing across the ruins and into the dark forest as they widened.

A scream of savage agony rolled through Kael's mind. It took him a moment to register that it was the forest itself crying out. The scream lessened and an intense feeling—a plea for help—followed, but there was nothing he could do. His heart clogged his throat as he looked to where the door to the Still Dimension was open.

A giant horned warrior jumped through the breach and landed on his left knee. The massive sword in his hand slammed into the ground, cracking the earth around him. Slowly rising, he snorted and stared around the field as two dozen others walked from the dimensional rift. Ten Ri'Tek wizards dressed in black followed, and the large warriors stepped to the side, bowing as they passed. Ember's sobbing was drowned out by the sound of hundreds more Ri'Tek warriors rushing through the breach. In seconds, they were outnumbered several hundred to one. The earth trembled one last time as the dimensional doorway collapsed, and the wizard's shields disappeared.

The Sepulchre had fallen.

Staring over her shoulder, the Vikress winked as Ghul joined her, and they both turned towards what could only be the head wizard from the Animus seal.

The wizard bowed low at Ghul and Illara's feet. "Vikress. Master Ghul. You are alive!" he said and looked around. "And we are free."

"Tehk, my apprentice. It is good to see you once more, boy."

"You now have your Syddic priests back, Ghul," the Vikress said, giving him a slight bow.

The young wizard and the others from the breach dropped to a knee. Their heads nearly touched the ground. "You have our thanks, Vikress Illara," Tehk said.

Ghul nodded. "I feared they would never be free."

She gestured for them to rise and examined the freed wizards. "Ten from your order? That is it?"

"Yes, Your Holiness, along with a few young novices," the Ghul's apprentice told her. "Most of the Syddic Order perished in the battle before we were pulled in. Twelve of the Syddic Guard also survived. It is a start," the young wizard replied, but clearly something was bothering him.

"Yes, Apprentice Tehk?" the Vikress asked.

"Forgive me, Vikress, but why are we speaking the dosa tongue?"

Illara sighed. "Because we have been gone a very long time, and it is now the common tongue everywhere in Talohna. It is a change we must suffer through."

The mask on Ghul's face scrunched in what could only be a frown. "I agree, but change is... good. Now, come There is someone I would like you to meet. Say hello to the most powerful Kai'Sar ever born and the reason we are free — as well as the reason my father is dead."

The young wizard stepped closer and leaned over, gently touching Kael's cheek. "May I?" he asked.

"Of course," the Vikress replied. "He is to be a dead man, anyway."

The wizard knelt beside him. "I am known as Tehk. Do you know what I am? What my master is?"

Nodding, Kael struggled to speak. "You're—" he coughed, and the Vikress released her grip on his throat a bit. He coughed as air rushed in for relief. He continued, "You're a parasite. No magic of your own, so you steal power from others."

The apprentice smiled but said nothing. Stepping back, he let Ghul take over.

"We have no magic of our own," Ghul said. "Because it was stolen by those who created us and swore to protect us. Now, I steal magic. It is balance, as all magic must."

Tehk slid his hand inside his robe and pulled out a binding stone with faint traces of black inside it. "I fought one of your kind here on this battlefield. See the traces of black in the stone? I had him, but the fool opened his seal before I finished. Perhaps we should see how powerful you really are?" he asked but looked at the Vikress for consent.

Getting a nod, he began. Tehk spoke in a strange language. The words assaulted Kael's senses. Waves of vertigo washed over him, and he crashed to the ground, screaming. Punishing blasts of dark power gushed from Kael and even the Vikress stumbled. Ghul merely smiled as the energy flowed into him, his apprentice, and the black stone. The stone filled with an inky black mist.

"Very good, Tehk," Ghul complemented.

"Fight it, Kael!" Ember yelled. "Fight them!"

"Yrlissa, Sephi," Max called out. "We have to do something. I won't let him die, again—not without doing something this time."

"Neither will I," Ember snapped. "I may not be able to cast a jump spell, but I'll fight."

As fast as it began, Tehk was finished. He stood, turning to the Vikress. "For my Vikress," he said handing the Ancient warrior a solid black stone. "Pure as they come."

"It will be days before he recovers," Ghul added.

Vikress Illara grabbed Kael by the throat again and lifted him back to his knees. "That is why you will always lose," she told him softly. "The seals are all open now and time is up for your disgusting race of monsters."

Kael chuckled.

"I doubt you will find your death humorous this time, Kael. Even you will not return a second time. It is all that is left to be done here."

"Go ahead." He wheezed, laughing. "Killing me will either return me to the afterlife as a god or merely just grant me the eternal peace of nothingness. Either way, I will never have to see *your* race, again."

"You can have the world of death, Kael, or you can cease to exist." she said, the mask tugging up in a smile, again. "I will take this land and the living world with all it has to offer. Last words?" Her hand tightened around his neck. He knew without his magic he would never break free of her grip.

"We need to move, Yrlissa. Now, for fuck's sake," Max hissed.

"Wait," the assassin said. "What she said about the world of death—that's the answer. Kael! The for—"

A sword pommel to the back of the head cut her words short and he watched helplessly as Max grabbed his hammer from the ground and exploded with violence. He punched the guard in the jaw and swung his demon hammer. It caved in the second guard's chest, and he whirled to help Kael. Six of the massive Syddic Guard warriors stood between him and his best friend.

Max's huge smile was the last thing Kael saw as the throbbing red in his eyes turned black.

In the darkest corners of his mind, flashes of memory jumbled together one right after another: him and Ember playing in the creek by her father's house as kids... arriving in Sam's Bay... the dance floor on the patio of Tinker's Bar where he gave her the ring he had made... waking up in Talohna... being tortured for months by the Dead Sisters... dying...

The flashes came faster and faster. He saw his years in the afterlife in what he thought was Paradise... he saw the first time he met Jasala—Jasala!

The flashes came to a screeching halt as her voice hollered inside his head.

Embrace the corruption, Kael! Make it serve your will!

At the time, she was talking about the corruption of death. His time in the Ether had taught him the corruption of death was not an insidious entity or even a corruption at all but simply the energy—the magic of the Ether. But he access to another type of magic, the magic of death itself and it could only be embraced and controlled — used by one who had conquered it.

It had made no sense to him before.

Kael's eyes shot open and filled with the black power of the staggering amount of death around him: the Midnight Canopy Forest.

The last time such magic filled his soul, he had lost all control and an entire witch ternion had died in Arkum Zul. He was careful this time. This time, he was fully aware. The Midnight Canopy, a dark forest of death, offered him all its power freely. He felt it in his very core. Monsters and nightmare creatures shrieked and growled from deep within the forest, and hundreds of eyes along the tree line glowed in the failing light. The roots running beneath the ground hummed with energy as creatures beyond all nightmares begged for their release. It was a release he granted.

"Thanks, Jasala," he croaked aloud, unfurling the Vikress' hand from his throat. "You'd better run, Ancient," he barked, climbing slowly to his feet.

"You are still outnumbered, fool," she snapped.

Kael smiled. "Not for long." Glancing to forest, he smiled as a pack of massive two-legged wolves burst from the trees and hordes of flying monsters swarmed in from the tree tops. A blonde vampire led the way. "Let's try this again, shall we?" he said. Mimicking the Vikress' earlier spell, he blasted her with compressed air that would have killed a Dragon. His smile vanished as she spun through the air, coming to her feet with her glaive staff in hand.

"Let us," she said. "Attack!" The Ancients' army responded, rushing for the forest monsters with no visible signs of fear.

Ignoring the large battle, Kael lunged, skirting the outer edges of the Ether. Nearly invisible, the Vikress saw him too late, and his scythe passed through her magical shield before it formed. Shattering her glaive, his blade cut deep into her shoulder. Spinning on his heel, he saw Ghul syphoning magic from him. Kael released his control over the forest's power and dumped more magic into the syphon than the Ghul could handle. The intense blast of energy hit the Ri'Tek wizard and exploded. He flew back in the rubble and dust of the ruins and did not move.

Turning back to the Vikress, energy burned along the back of his armor. The heat seared the skin on his back, and it sizzled as if under a branding iron. The pain merely fueled his next spell. Black roots leapt from the earth and snaked around the Vikress' legs, pinning her the ground. With a simple twist of his wrist, the roots writhed and twisted their way up the Vikress' waist and her chest. When they encircled her neck, Kael closed his fist and the roots tightened until she could no longer move.

He played it safe, carefully approaching her. With his magical senses spread as far as he could, Kael sensed no threat. He smiled. "Say hi to Sythrnax, Vikress, if you end up wherever he is."

The Vikress laughed as he flipped his scythe back to strike. "Ah, Kael, I already told you. You lose."

As he powered his weapon, a bright white light exploded from where the Vikress had been ensnared in the forest's root system. His scythe crashed into the vines and sunk deep into the dirt. Max's demon hammer slammed into the ground beside his scythe.

"No, goddammit! No!" Kael yelled. Looking up, he watched helpless as the stolen Fae magic activated across the ruins.

The Ancients were gone.

"Fuck! That's twice I missed her!" Max grumbled.

Kael sighed with frustration. "They got what they wanted. Her people are free, and we're no threat to them. Getting away was their only goal. It was simple, whereas we expected something complicated." He watched on as Ember fell to her knees beside her mother. He gave her some well-needed space before finally going to her.

"I'll check on everyone and get them ready to go," Max said.

Kael nodded to him and knelt beside the woman he loved but no longer knew. "I was told she was your mother. You got to know her?" he asked.

"Yes. She stayed with us in Drae'Kahn—even took me to Vaenaria..." She gasped as she sucked in quick breaths of grief. Her heartache radiated in her aura, washing over him painfully.

"Your real father?" he asked.

"He was the commander of the Dwarven Host. He died a few months ago, defending their seal. I'm not sure what is more insane... the fact that I really did have a mother and father who cared about me or that they're both dead."

Kael smiled and pulled her close. "I can promise you that Dravik BloodPounder didn't die in the siege. I don't think that grumpy bastard can die. I spent a few minutes with him when I returned."

Ember glanced at him. "You sure?" she asked.

"Commander of the Dwarven Host, yes. And probably the only person alive who hated Sythrnax as much as I did. You'll see him again, Ember. I'd bet on it."

"I hope so," she said and rested her hand on Eva's shoulder. "Help me with her, please?"

Kael gently slid his arm under Eva's shoulders, but the ground heaved as he did, throwing him onto her body.

"Go!" he yelled. "I'll bring her."

The earth shook a second time, and the Animus seal cracked down the middle. As he struggled to get his footing, another heave split the seal wide in the opposite direction. Grabbing Eva's legs, he lifted her clear of the seal and scrambled after Ember. The seal crumbled under his feet as he ran and black smoke poured from the hole. He recognized the essence pouring from the hole. —

It was the Ether.

Kael stopped and watched as the dark smoke slowly faded. A black surface formed over the hole. As it did, the figure of a man lay unconscious on the remains of the Animus seal.

Kael carefully placed Eva's body on the grass and went with Ember to the seal.

"He's still alive," she gasped.

"Where did he come from, Kael?" Max asked. "You know, don't you?"

"Yeah," he replied. "That was the Ether."

Yrlissa limped to the seal, shaking her head. "That is not possible. Is it?"

"It would seem so," Kael mumbled, taking a closer look at the new arrival.

Ember rubbed her head. It was obvious the frustration was getting to her. "But you said the Ether was a place beyond our multi-verse."

"It is," he agreed.

Yrlissa's expression turned flabbergasted as she visibly processed what he had said. "That means..." she began but could not seem to finish. The man moaned as he regained consciousness.

"Yeah," Kael answered, agreeing. "It means he might be an old god."

Rolling onto his back the new arrival groaned a second time. "*Kai no vai*," the man said. "*Kai no vai*."

"That's a dialect of Ancient that the Lost used," Yrlissa said. Disbelief rode her every word.

"It is." Kael nodded. "It means death of the soul."

"Not quite." Yrlissa corrected him. "He's asking if he's alive or a ghost." Slowly bending over, she held up her hand and the man placed his against it.

"Kin?" he asked, nodding as if he already knew the answer.

"Yes," she said smiling. Using her other hand to gently touch his chest she added, "You, alive."

"You?" he repeated. Putting his hand to his mouth and opening it palm out, he repeated, "You? Alive?"

"Fast learner," Nekrosa muttered under his breath.

Tapping the man's chest, Yrlissa tried, again. "Kin? Old god?"

"Old god?"

"He is learning," Ember offered. Bending closer she smiled and put her hand on her chest. "Ember." Touching the assassin beside her, she said, "Yrlissa," she continued pointing to the others, "Kael. Max. Sephi. Nekrosa."

At the end, she touched the man's shoulder, prompting an understanding frown.

The man tapped his own chest. "Treach. Kin gone." He stopped, clearly frustrated. Again, he put his hand to his mouth and opened it.

"Holy fuck." Kael gasped as the reality of who and what the man was hit home. "Did he say Treach?"

"Treach!" the man exclaimed and repeatedly tapped his chest.

Kael shook his head as his mind itched with disbelief. He turned to Yrlissa. If the situation had not been so bizarre, he would have laughed at her bug-eyed stare of incredulity.

"Th... that's... holy... shit" she stuttered. "Holy shit..."

"What?" Ember demanded.

"Fuck me..." Max let out. "Treach was the father of the old gods. The creator of this world."

Chapter Twenty-Seven

"Changes in the world happen often, as with people. Being able to deal with change as it happens is what creates a strength in people that we will need in the coming years. Talohna is on the verge of one of its biggest changes ever in history. The race of beings credited with all we are have returned and instead of inciting war over lost territories, or demanding cities and lands be returned, they have instead offered to risk everything by attempting to cross the Black Kasym. Their only desire is to settle within the lands north of the magical scar and then hopefully heal the Kasym from their side. It is as if everything in the myths and legends that refer to them is true. As an experienced world traveler and celebrated minstrel, this concerns me greatly. Truth is rarely found in the days of yester-year and I firmly believe that to worship these returning 'heroes' is to court disaster for the entire known world and perhaps even beyond."

Garren Sallus, Memoirs of a Hidden Past.
Year One of the Ancients' Return, AR

MIDNIGHT CANOPY FOREST
GARETT'S VALE, DORMASAI

"I will never get used to that," Kael muttered, referring to Max's wealth of information about Talohna and true past.

"I know, brother," Max replied softly.

Treach had been following the conversation and quickly seemed to be absorbing every word they said.

"He watches us talk," Max stated. "That must be how he learns."

Treach pointed his index finger at Max and nodded.

"Good," Kael said. "He can listen to us, and hopefully, he can pick up the common tongue... but what now? What the hell do we do now?"

Nekrosa cleared his throat. "I vote we head back to Drae'Kahn. We can do little here. We need to contact Queen WhiteScale and find out what happened to the DragonKin..."

"But," Kael prompted when the King stopped mid-sentence.

"If this really is an old god, then perhaps taking him with us is not the wisest decision," Nekrosa told them. "We are in a country full of magic."

"I agree," Yrlissa said. "But we also need to know how the Ri'Tek plan to get home. It will be their primary goal now, and he might be able to help us."

"It's actually irrelevant. Only one man *can* get them home. We just have to find him," Kael replied.

"Of course. It has to be him." Yrlissa nodded her agreement, but her voice held an edge of pain Kael recognized. "No one else has sailed the Jaws and returned except Dominique Havarrow and Cassel Morena. And Cass died years ago."

"I don't like either idea."

"Yeah, I get it Nekrosa." Kael sighed. "But we need to find one of Talohna's most notorious pirates, and soon. Maybe sooner with Treach's help. Besides," Kael added as he glanced around the battlefield, "we cannot let him fall into the hands of the enemy."

"Gods, no," Sephi snapped. She quickly apologized for her tone, "Sorry."

"Settled?" Nekrosa asked, eliciting a smile from his wife.

"Home, then?" she asked and earned a nod from Kael. Leaning over, she hugged Ember, adding, "You, my friend, need some time to relax, and you both need to find out who you have become. My and Nekrosa's home is the best and safest place for you to do that while we locate Captain Havarrow."

"I will meet you there," Kael told them, kissing Ember on the cheek. Turning to the blonde vampire waiting patiently at the forest's edge, he smiled. "I have to say hi to an old friend first."

"You good alone, brother?" Max asked. "There is a whole lot of ass-nasty standing behind that 'friend' of yours. You sure?"

"No worries," Kael replied, laughing. "I promise you I'm in no danger here. It's the opposite in fact."

"Don't be long," Max said, slapping his shoulder.

"See you soon, love," Ember quipped as her realm jump activated behind him.

The vampire walked toward him and he could hardly believe his eyes.

"You are a hard man to find, Kael Symes."

"Yeah," he said. "I just got back, you could say."

"I heard," she replied, coming to a stop just outside of arm's reach.

"You died," he whispered, trying not to choke on the lump in his throat. "I couldn't find you on the other side."

She laughed. It was a laugh that always seemed to calm him. "Ah, Kael. You can't kill true DemonKind with silver," Lycori reminded him as she grabbed him in a hug.

"I thought I'd never see you again, sister."

"Me neither, brother. When Havarrow told me you had been killed."

"I know," he said. He felt her struggle to let go of him as if it took all her will power to do so. To help, he eased her away. "I need your help, Lycori."

"I know. I didn't know if I'd find you here or not. Galen told me to come here and use the forest to help you. I'm sorry they got away."

"It doesn't matter now. We have to focus on finding Dominique."

"Havarrow? The pirate?" she asked. He gave her a nod. "He'll be taking the Ancients home, eventually. Now that they are free, they will be home long before we could travel to Havarrow's hideout."

"Maybe not," he said, laughing. "We travel a bit differently now."

"You found Ember and Max?" she asked.

He nodded and could not stop the smile from creeping onto his face.

"It really is time you introduced me to them, no?" she asked

"Yeah," he agreed, pulling her closer. "Hang on tight, and I'll show you that travel by magic thing we do."

Her arm wrapped around his waist, and he tightened his own grip on her as he stepped into the blaze of white from the jump. Clouds of black and purple swirled into the brightness, and they vanished.

CASCADE CITADEL
CORYNTH, 2 DAYS LATER

Queen Corleya Bale sat on her throne and took several deep breaths. Her Knight stood to her right and the new Wizard of Rule stood to her left. Taking one last breath, she nodded to her wizard.

"Kalmar, please, show them in," she ordered.

Kalmar Ibess had volunteered to attempt the ritual to become the Third Pillar after two others had died during the process. Corleya knew he offered in the hope that what Kael had done to him at Arkum Zul would keep him alive. He was right to hope, and he would stand as the Queen's Third Pillar until one of them died. Corleya could not help but wonder why anyone would volunteer for the positions of Pillar. However, there never seemed to be a shortage.

Seconds passed before Kalmar returned with the Ancient contingent sent to make the first official contact. Even though she was ready, her stomach still went cold at the sight of the Vikress and her retinue. It was difficult for her to sit still and play the diplomat when she knew the vile truth about those she was meeting.

"Vikress Illara," she said, feigning a smile. "Welcome to the Cascade Citadel. I hope your accommodations are suitable."

"Of course, they are, my dear," the Vikress purred. "You surrendered the royal bed chamber to myself and the royal wing to my fellow Ancients." Corleya failed to stop her cheek from twitching with irritation at the deliberate use of the word surrender.

"They were once my quarters, you know," the Vikress continued, "at a time when I sat on a throne very different than the one you now occupy."

"I am glad it pleased you," Corleya offered.

"I would imagine you are, my dear, seeing as how my people rid your city of the pests that nearly destroyed it. I have heard that your citizens have been singing praises to my people for two days."

"Most are, yes," Corleya quipped. 'However, there are those who steadfastly believe that you turned those creatures loose on our city for the sole purpose of coming to the rescue. I must wonder myself. I have inspected the bodies of the dead and nothing like them have ever been seen in Talohna."

The Vikress laughed lightly. "Conspiracy theories always run amok among the rich and powerful," she answered. "For they are at risk to lose the most. Do you not agree, Queen Bale?"

Corleya nodded and changed the subject. "I was told you wish to make an official declaration now that you've returned."

The Vikress titled her head but said nothing. It irritated Corleya and some of those who stood with her. With the Cascade Citadel fully awakened, she could feel her Pillars emotions and intentions. Four of the five had an insane urge to attack. Her mental restraint was the only thing holding them back. Only Kalmar remained calm. Along with the anger of her Pillars, hundreds of stone gargoyles growled inside her head as they, too, itched to neutralize the threat. It was as if the stone effigies and the Pillars mirrored her own hatred of the woman standing before her.

"I must make my people's intentions known to all of Talohna," Vikress Illara finally said. "I merely desired to begin here. You need not worry, Queen Bale. We will not be making demands for any lands south of the magical nightmare to the north. We will be returning to our own homelands as soon as we are able and once settled, *we* will heal the disastrous wound *your* kind have made to *our* world. I do have two concessions to ask, however."

"And they are?" Corleya demanded, barely managing to avoid scoffing at the boast.

"My people and I ask for official sanctuary here in Corynth for the next two or three weeks. It is the seat of our old capitol, and its name has remained the same since our time. My people are scattered throughout Talohna. They will be confused and disoriented by the land shifts. Once they learn Corynth still exists, they will make the pilgrimage here. I ask that you make them welcome at the first gate they come across and protect us all until we are ready to depart for Tai Se Neban—our true home far north of the magical breach you call the Black Kasym."

Corleya coughed to cover her indignant snort at the near demand for protection. Unfortunately, with nearly all of Cethos praising the Ancients as returning heroes, she had no choice.

"Of course," she replied. "Until such time as you are ready to return home, your people are welcome to gather in Corynth. I warn you, though, Vikress Illara, the behavior of your people while in my city will be your responsibility. They will be subject to our laws." The Vikress' cheek twitched with anger, and Corleya offered her a cool smile.

"Agreed, Queen Bale," Illara answered. "I promise you, that after so long, the only thing my people are concerned about will be finding family and friends who may still live."

"Perhaps so," Corleya said. "But your previous representative touched the lives of many people, Vikress. I suggest your people stay on the castle grounds while you are here. I cannot promise you that those who suffered at Sythrnax's hands will not attempt retribution. Any crimes committed by my people will be punished accordingly, but your people will also be subject to the laws of this land as if they were citizens."

Again, the Vikress' cheek tugged at her mask in irritation. "My people and I are not responsible for my brother's actions, Queen Bale. As our military commander, Sythrnax did what he thought was right—to free our people. I do not agree with his methods, and he paid the price with his very soul at the hands of a magical war criminal that should have been executed at birth, by the decree of your own laws. Yet I do not stand before you demanding retribution for his life. Perhaps the people of Talohna are not as enlightened as I had hoped."

Corleya sat taller in her throne and took a breath. "If you give them a chance, Vikress, you will find the people of Talohna are very open and accepting to those who offer the hand of friendship. But when that hand is slapped away or bit... well, let's just say nothing brings people together faster than a common enemy."

The Vikress smiled. "Then Talohna and the Ancients will become the closest of allies," she said. "I promise you, Queen Bale, my people and I are of one mind. We want nothing more than to recover our home, and then, we want to heal the Black Kasym. It is an affront to the memory of this world's creators and doing so will open new trade routes to our lands."

"Fair enough," Corleya replied. "We are in agreement. If your people can heal the Kasym, then Cethos will be happy to arrange and facilitate trade, if you so desire. And your second concession?" The Vikress offered a slight bow, an action that drove a cold shiver up Corleya's spine.

"An easy concession," Vikress Illara said. "We ask that you continue to execute any and all of the creatures you call DeathWizards at birth or at the first possible chance."

"Why?" Corleya asked as her ears burned with fury.

"In my time they were called the Kai'Sar and were the scourge of our world," she offered. "Death walked behind them, and everything they touched suffered or died. Your scholars are very intuitive. A wizard of death is a proper name."

Corleya shook her head. "I am not in the position to make that promise, Vikress," she said. "Countries like DormaSai in the south rule their countries as they see fit."

"I understand the idea of independent rule, Queen Bale," Vikress Illara said, nearly snapping at her. "It is already law. I only ask that is enforced. Once the Kasym is healed or we find a secure route across, we will be more than happy to enforce this law ourselves. In fact, I will insist upon it during our first round of trade talks with every country we deal with."

On the verge of losing her temper and the castle resources at her disposal, Corleya smiled tightly at the Vikress and nodded. "As will be your right, Vikress," she answered. "Now, I must deal with several matters of state. I look forward to dining with you tonight."

"Thank you, Queen Bale," The Vikress replied and offered the slightest bow.

"Kalmar," Corleya said. "Please, show our guests to their accommodations." As he led the Ancient contingent away, she exhaled slowly.

"Patience," the Priestess stated as she offered her council. "You did well."

"For now," Corleya whispered. "Summon Giddeon and Galen, please." The Priestess bowed and left as she continued. "It is time Cethos and DormaSai set aside our differences."

"You're to send Giddeon to King Kohl?" Alia asked. "He will not survive this, Your Highness. The Dead King's intentions have been clear for years."

"Noted," Corleya quipped and nodded to the guards at her left. They stepped out the door and returned several seconds later with a thin grimy man. "This time, we have a peace offering. But if he dies, then Galen will be there, and Kael will never harm him."

"Your Highness," the guard started, "the prisoner you ordered released from the dungeon."

"Thank you," she replied. "You may go." As the guard walked away, Corleya's face flushed with embarrassment. "Tallin Kohl, I am Queen Corleya Bale, and I would like to offer you my sincerest apologies. As the Queen of Cethos, I hereby pardon you from all crimes you have been accused of by my father, and I declare you innocent of all said crimes. Though I honor him, my father was a close minded-person with many faults. You are free to go, but please, avail yourself of my hospitality for a day or two until you are stronger. You need only ask and anything you desire will be provided."

Tallin looked up at her and shook his head. "I guess I should be grateful you are the new queen, but you are not your father. I have heard it many times over—even among the guards who patrol the dungeons."

"I am glad." She sighed. "I cannot express how sorry I am. I freed you the moment I discovered your name in the dungeon records. I apologize that my guards didn't at least offer you a heated bath."

"If I am free to go, I only ask for enough coin to get home. My brother must think I am dead for… I don't even know for how long now."

Corleya blinked back the dampness in her eyes and swallowed the lump in her throat. "Absolutely. I do ask that you please allow two of my most trusted wizards to escort you."

"Do I have a choice?"

"You do. I meant what I said," she replied.

"Then, no offense, Your Highness, but I will take my coin and take my leave."

"I understand," Corleya said and nodded to the Corsair.

He stepped forward and offered Tallin a bag of coin. "Do not trust my queen, that is fine. But many of my men sail under the Suns' flag," he said and offered Tallin a whalebone amulet. "You know what this is?"

"Yes," Tallin answered. "It will get me home safely without having to worry about a knife in the back." The Corsair nodded and returned to his place. "Thank you," Queen Bale," he added.

Corleya nodded to the Corsair. He and the Hunter escorted King Kohl's brother from the room before clearing the hall as Kalmar returned with the Priestess, Giddeon, and Galen.

All bowed, and the Priestess and Kalmar returned to their normal places in court.

"Your Highness."

"Thank you for coming, Giddeon."

"Of course, Your Highness."

"I have a task for you and Master Vihr," she began, "Tallin Kohl has been freed from the dungeon and released — all charges dropped. He has a written declaration of innocence and free travel throughout Cethos."

"Are you sure that is wise, Your Highness?" Giddeon asked as Galen frowned at his side.

"Something to offer, Master Wizard?" she asked.

"No. Your Highness."

"We are in closed court, Master Wizard. Please, speak your mind."

Galen shook his head. "My apologies, Your Highness," he said. "It is just that I argued against his imprisonment at the time he arrived. I am glad he was finally released."

"I agree," she answered.

"I certainly am not in agreement," Giddeon snapped. He quickly calmed under her stern glare.

"ArchWizard," Corleya said. "You have been at the top of Talohna's magical hierarchy for too long, I believe. An ArchWizard is not an all-powerful, all-knowing title. I saw more humility from your son in the few days I traveled with him than I have seen you display since your return — with his help, I might add. It is the reason why I am tasking Master Vihr with the ArchWizard trials upon your return from DormaSai."

"Yes, Your Highness," Galen said as he bowed.

She waved for him to rise. "I am elated that my father's Spy has passed the rituals to become my fourth Pillar of Rule. Therefore, you and Giddeon will accompany her to Drae'Kahn to inform King Kohl that Tallin is alive and has been set free. With luck, he may even be there before you."

"That is a death sentence for Giddeon, Your Highness!" Galen protested.

"We will have to hope that King Kohl's Fae advisor is in court," she replied. Her voice never wavered as she continued, "Either way, Master Wizard, you will command this mission. Besides notifying and apologizing to King Kohl, your main goal is to find Kael."

"Your Highness," Giddeon sputtered. "I must protest—"

"You can protest all you like, Giddeon," Corleya snapped. "I spent months suffering at the hands of these so-called Ancients. They instigated and organized the downfall of my father, and I will have peace with DormaSai if it is the last damn act of my life. We need to be united with the only country left that has access to so much magical knowledge and who are opposed to the Ancients. Am I understood?" Giddeon bowed as he nodded. "You will go with the Spy to DormaSai via the Royal Fleet, and you will fly the Cethosian democratic flag as you dock in the mouth of the Kraken's Tail at the city of Eraleen. You will declare yourself to DormaSain authorities and obey every command made of you while there. All of you, your sole purpose of this mission is make peace with King Kohl, to let him know we are of like minds — even if my hands are tied right now. Your secondary objective is to find Kael and support him in any way he needs. Am I clear?"

Galen and Giddeon nodded then bowed. The Spy stepped forward and the three left the room.

Corleya sighed with relief as the magic imbued in the castle told her where every Ancient being was currently located. If the Ri'Tek stayed within the castle grounds, she could keep track of them using the citadel's magic.

She relaxed, finally.

BLACKVOID CASTLE, 3 WEEKS LATER
DRAE'KAHN, DORMASAI

"There is no way to get into Arkum Zul!" Kael yelled and smashed his hand on the map spread across the table. "Period." He stared at the people in Nekrosa's war room. Even with nearly a dozen bodies present, there was plenty of room, but he still felt confined and irritable. His thoughts still reeled after Kyr Meadow had insisted on arguing with him about whether Ember should have returned Katarina Desolla to Dasal or not after her mind had been healed. Kyr might be Eva Thornwing's sister, but she had none of the elder Matriarchs manners or understanding—none of what had made Ember's mother amazing. The Fae woman wanted Kat brought to Vaenaria where the magic of the White would be under their control. Naturally suspicious of everyone, Kael refused to budge, and when Kyr demanded he jump to Dasal to retrieve Kat, he made it very clear what would happen if she tried it at all. Ember had openly supported him, and her aunt had left in a huff. While she was likely harmless, he planned to warn Seifer Locke the first chance he got.

"It was Sythrnax's stronghold and where he operated from," Sephi added. Kael set his thoughts aside and focused on the problem at hand.

"The Vikress probably... she has to be there along with most of the Ri'Tek," Nekrosa offered. "It's our chance to do some serious damage to them *if* they are still there. Don't forget Lycori said Havarrow would take them home when they are ready to go."

"It is what he told us, but he did not say when or by what route," Lycori clarified.

"You'd think they'd head home immediately," Aravae replied.

"Not necessarily," Yrlissa corrected, finally saying something. So far Kael wasn't impressed with the Guardian aside from her martial skills but shook the thoughts of their training sessions from his mind as she continued. "The Sepulchre fell and all the seals opened at once—seals that are located across the breadth of Talohna. The Vikress will not leave for Tai Sa Neban until most of her people have been recovered. We need to find out where she is waiting for them—whether it is Arkum Zul or not and we need to be sure before we move. We will only get one chance, and they will likely still be waiting for us."

Kael sighed with frustration and shook his head while Max cleared his throat. "Why can't we get in?" he asked and placed a hand on Kael's shoulder. "You and Lycori both got out which means we can get in."

"We had a lot of help." The vampire countered him as she raised her fingers. "And the Mahala dogged us most of the way."

"I still say we try jumping in," Ember suggested.

Kael shook his head. "We can't jump in. There are spells and wards throughout Arkum Zul. The Dwarves designed it as a research city devoted to countering and destroying magic. The Arterius device is there, for Christ's sake. If we fail, we would be dooming Talohna to life under Ri'Tek rule for an eternity because all our magic would be in their hands. The other two ways in—the way Lycori escaped—" he rubbed his throbbing head and continued— "taking a large force through there would be like ringing the Mahalan dinner bell. There are tunnels to the sides, in the floors, and above. Our fighters would be swarmed long before we got close to Arkum Zul. The way I escaped... I collapsed the only exit I know about while we were—are you all listening to me?" he barked and pointed at Lycori. "Running for our goddamned lives from the Mahala." She nodded her agreement.

"Easy, love," Ember whispered, but it only irritated him more. She gently caressed his cheek and the headache vanished.

"Thank you," he said and sighed. "This is a waste of time."

"I agree," Max said. "We need more information before we do anything. Acting without all the facts is what has been fucking us over every time we deal with the Ri'Tek. It was the same during the first war. Yrlissa, you remember what Asa used to say? I don't remember the words exactly."

"I'll never forget them," she replied slowly and quoted, *"Before moving against the Ri'Tek, think twice, and act not. Think twice more, and then think again before making your move. They will still outsmart you or be ready for you, but you might cover how, allowing you to adapt to win or to retreat and fight another day."*

Kael snorted. "Every time I turn around people want to plan to fight another day. You will not win this goddamned war by planning to lose or by minimizing losses. A war of attrition does not mean running when the losses get heavy. It means fighting, man-to-man, woman-to-woman, or wizard-to-wizard in the cities, the towns, the streets, and even from building to building if need be."

"Kael," Ember began, but he ignored her and carried on.

"We get the bloody intelligence we need, and then, we attack them mercilessly and to hell with the losses. I'd rather die fighting them than live under them. Magic users like Ember and I will be nothing but magical milk cows if we are caught. I will not spend the rest of my life letting the Ri'Tek drain my or Ember's magic over and over, so they can use it to make others suffer—"

"Perhaps you won't have to. We—" Kael recognized the voice instantly and immediately disappeared into the Ether for a fraction of a moment before materializing with his short reaper pick at Giddeon's throat. Nekrosa's DeathDogs reacted slower, but still surrounded the Cethosian retinue with their swords drawn.

"Wait! Please, Kael," Giddeon pleaded quickly. "I have the information you need."

"Your Majesty!" the guard captain blurted out. "I am so sorry! He stepped ahead before I could announce them!"

While he could sense Giddeon, Galen, and several others entering the war room, Kael's only concern was securing the ArchWizard. He had to protect the King and Queen in case Giddeon's intentions were to harm them. King Bale's Spy of Rule smiled at him, but he could not sense her Pillar magic—though he knew the woman had become Corleya's Fourth Pillar. When he frowned in return, she merely held her smile.

"It's all right, Captain," Nekrosa said and grinned. "There is no harm done. You may go." The captain nodded and led his guards from the room, but the King's DeathDogs remained. "Well, Giddeon Zirakus and Galen Vihr in my castle. The gods have shone on me this morning."

"Why didn't I feel them?" Yrlissa barked.

"Because of this," Kael snarled as he yanked a Ri'Tek charm from the ArchWizard's neck. He tossed it to Ember.

"Why would you come here, Giddeon?" she asked. "You had to know it was a death sentence."

"Because my queen ordered me," he replied. She lifted the charm and held it in front of him.

"Watch close, *father*," Kael growled while Ember's magic pulled a soul from within the charm. With a whisper, she set it free. It rushed away, and Kael flicked his fingers. Black misty magic enveloped it as it vanished.

"Now, the soul that powered this disgusting charm will go to the afterlife as it was intended to aeons ago," she said.

Giddeon swallowed. "You..."

"My mother showed me how to do that, Giddeon. I believe you met Eva Thornwing while on Ver Karmot," Ember spoke over him, and the ArchWizard winced. "Kael's magic will protect the soul from the eternal fight in the afterlife so it arrives safely where the gods intended. My mother showed him how to do that, too. Your country sided with the wrong race, and my mother paid for it with her life."

"We... we... we didn't," he stuttered.

"He's right, Kael," Galen added as he calmly took a step forward. "Queen Bale sent us with that charm in the hopes that King Kohl or someone loyal to him could help us counter its magic. I apologize for Giddeon's outburst. He is having a hard time adjusting to the fact that this mission is not his to command, but rather is mine."

"Always the pompous prick," Max quipped. "Even when you've been demoted."

Galen prodded Giddeon. "My apologies," the ArchWizard let out.

"What can we do for you, Master Wizard Vihr?" Nekrosa asked.

"Your information is up-to-date," Galen stated. "I'm impressed."

"It was," Kael corrected.

"My spies returned several weeks ago," Nekrosa offered. "But the new ones have yet to report back."

"And they won't," Galen said. "The Ancients have most of Cethos on magical lock-down with charms like these and other devices much larger. Your undead birds won't help you contact your spies. Their magic will not connect now that the Vikress has worked White magic into the pendants."

"Why would you allow that?"

"We didn't, King Kohl," Galen responded as he faced Nekrosa. "Queen Bale was forced to offer the Ancients sanctuary after they helped us defeat the Vascuul."

"We know," Ember replied. Her sorrow seeped into Kael as she continued, "They used the attack to draw the Fae and DragonKin to Corynth while the Elloryan army invaded

DormaSai. It was all designed as a way for the Ri'Tek to kidnap my mother—the Fae Matriarch. It is how they brought down the Sepulchre."

"I know," Galen said. "I was with her when they took her. I am so sorry, Mistress Ember. Eva refused to let me help her. I would have proudly taken her place had they allowed it. The cost to civilian lives was all she cared about."

"My mother did what she thought was right," Ember said and then went quiet.

"What happened next?" Kael prompted as his blade against Giddeon's neck never wavered.

"Like I said. We had to agree to let them stay. By the time we realized our magic had been shut down, it was too late to object. Vikress Illara claims it is for the safety of her people. I only found out about it the morning we left to travel here, and by the time we reached Soena, magic was shut down there too."

"What does Queen Bale want from us?" Sephi asked.

Galen sighed. "I was given two mission directives, and one was to find Kael. Thank Mother Inara he is here. It makes my job easier. The second objective is to inform you that Queen Bale has freed Tallin from the dungeon. Your brother is alive, King Kohl." Galen stepped forward with his hand in his pocket, but Max put a hand to his chest to cut him off. The Master Wizard carefully removed a letter from his pocket and held it up.

"This from Queen Bale," he told them. "I grant your brother uninterrupted movement throughout Cethos if you would like Tallin to be your official ambassador to Cethos—or someone else of your choosing. It also contains a written apology for his treatment at her father's hands. She is offering peace, King Kohl, at any cost or reparations you deem fair."

Nekrosa accepted the letter, opened it, and read it. Finally, he nodded. "Fair enough," he said aloud. "The cost is Giddeon's life. You should have brought my brother with you, Master Wizard."

Galen held up both his hands. "We tried, Your Majesty," he said. "He refused to accept our help. Queen Bale gave him sufficient funds to get here, but he refused all other help."

"Can you blame him, you shit?" Sephi hissed. "He was sent under the banner of peace, and you imprisoned him. We ought to execute your entire entourage."

"That won't be necessary," the Spy said as she winked at Kael. The green leather armor melted away and Kael turned Giddeon to face the Spy. His second small scythe appeared in his other hand as the Spy's facial features dissolved until nothing remained but a grime-covered man in tattered rags.

"Tallin?" Sephi whispered.

Nekrosa gasped. "Brother? Is that really you?"

"Yes," he said. "I needed their protection to get home, but I could only trust Queen Bale."

"Goddamn, it's good to see you," Nekrosa said as he limped forward and wrapped his arms around his younger brother.

Kael chuckled. "No wonder I couldn't sense the Pillar's magic," he said. "I can't sense anything on you."

"Of course not!" Nekrosa roared with humor as Sephi joined the hug. "That is what allows a doppler to do what they do! Damn, brother! I thought Bale had you killed."

"Near enough," Tallin replied as he stepped back. "Half the man I was."

"Weight can be regained, Tal," Sephi added. "Death is permanent."

"I would have been dead, had it not been for these two," Tallin said and pointed to Giddeon and Galen. "This one even argued with King Bale against my imprisonment."

Galen nodded. "It was not right," he said. "Your Majesty, my queen knows what these gods-cursed Ancients are. Her hands might be tied by the citizens of Talohna right now, but she is on your side. Help her get into a position to help you. I give you my word that you can trust her."

Nekrosa glanced at Kael, and he nodded. "Galen's word is as good to you as mine," Kael assured him. The King nodded and pushed his hands to the side. The DeathDogs backed down and sheathed their weapons.

"Fair enough," Nekrosa said. "At least we know where the Ri'Tek are."

"Yeah," Max added. "Out of our reach. If we attack Cethos, Queen Bale will be forced to defend them."

"We can't jump into a magical dead zone anyway," Ember said. "And moving troops by land will take too long. Most of the Ri'Tek will have made the pilgrimage to Corynth by now. They could leave at any time."

"You can't jump to a dead zone," Kael replied. "But I can."

"So, can I, Kael," Lycori pointed out to them.

"Not this time," he said and shook his head. Lycori knew him better than anyone else including Ember and merely nodded her agreement. It was why he loved her so much. She always had his back, and her support was guaranteed. His blade vanished, and he released Giddeon. "Do what you want with this fool, Nekrosa. I'm going to Corynth."

"Kael!" Aravae snapped. "He is still your father."

Ember flashed him a frown, but he ignored them both.

"This is exactly the point I have been trying to make for weeks," he told them. "We can't take them head on, but we can pick them off one or two at a time."

"You cannot go alone," Ember argued. "I can't balance Reetha's Ichor unless I am near you. It must be done daily. If you leave, you will have a hard time telling what's real, again."

"Don't care." He shrugged. "If I can get to the Vikress, you will have the advantage down the road—even if I lose my mind."

Yrlissa shook her head. "You forget that we will have to be the ones to hunt you down," she said. 'You really want to put that on Ember?"

He shrugged, again, but Nekrosa spoke before he could answer.

"I say we let him go," the King suggested. "Even if for no other reason than to know when the Ri'Tek leave Corynth and become vulnerable to attack. We could sink Havarrow's entire fleet if we have prior knowledge of the route and some time to prepare."

"Good," Kael said. "It's settled then."

Nekrosa cleared his throat. "I agree with the others, though, Kael," he said. "The intelligence is far more important than killing an Ancient or two. Think about that while you are there."

Kael nodded, and Ember frowned but did not argue with him further. "You had better jump back here the moment you start to slip from this reality, Kael," she ordered, instead. He offered her a slight bow and a grin.

"I could probably go with you," Max offered as he stared at Kael. "You'd have to jump with death magic."

"Not this time, brother," he said. "I rarely use the afterlife to jump anymore, and I can't risk any of your lives by jumping into a Ri'Tek dead zone. Treach hasn't recovered enough to help, it'll be days before I can understand him well enough to talk with him about magic."

"All right, all right," Max grumbled. "I get it."

"We have the start of a plan, then?" Nekrosa asked as he glanced around the room at everyone. Getting only nods of agreement, he added, "Guards, take Giddeon to the dungeon until I decide his death sentence. Master Wizard Vihr, if you have a DeathDog escort, you may have free reign of my castle. Do not make a liar of Kael."

Galen nodded then bowed. "As you wish, Your Majesty," he replied.

Tallin coughed, deliberately trying to attract the attention.

"Yes, brother?" Nekrosa asked.

"I ask you to spare Giddeon's life, Nekrosa. I've seen enough to know he doesn't deserve to die."

"I will consider your words," the King said. "Now, let's get Kael ready. Galen, any information you can give him would be greatly appreciated."

Again, Galen nodded. Kael wrapped an arm around his shoulder. "Come on," he said. "You have to see this."

He laughed when Galen gave him a frown. The Master Wizard would be spending most of his time in Drae'Kahn deep in the Arcane Library's Catacombs, Kael would bet on it. He figured the Master Wizard might as well start as soon as possible.

CASCADE CITADEL
ROYAL QUARTERS

Kael groaned as he stepped from his realm jump magic onto the balcony of Corleya's private quarters. With all magic shut down by the Ri'Tek charms and devices, there was no concern the Wizard's Council would detect his jump. To be sure that the Vikress would not catch him, either, he purposely jumped using magic drawn from the Ether. It was unstable, but the magic was foreign to Talohna and hopefully undetectable by the Ancients.

"*Na gravasay shadus mal,*" he whispered. Shadows enveloped his body and feathered out around him. He laughed lightly. "Thanks, Nekrosa." The necromancer had taught him several spells over the previous weeks, but it was the first chance he had to use one. If Yrlissa was right, he would be able to access each race's magic. The thought was a startling one, and he pushed it aside as he peered into the large room outside the Queen's bedchamber. He could sense it was unoccupied, but he checked anyway. Corleya was the only one who could tell him where in the castle the Ancients were or when they might be leaving.

Voices at the door caught his attention, and he stepped back out onto the balcony to hide until he knew the Queen was alone. The chamber door opened, and he peered around the corner. A sharp breath caught in his throat as the Vikress walked into the room and stopped by the massive fireplace. A knock on the door made her turn, but he knew immediately from her demeanor that she was expecting someone.

Kael cursed under his breath as Ghul walked into the room. He had hoped the leech had died at Garret's Vale when Kael had overloaded the bastard's syphon spell.

"My Vikress." Ghul bowed. They were not speaking the common tongue, and Kael nearly gasped out loud when he realized he understood what they were saying.

"Is everything ready?" Vikress Illara asked.

"Yes. Only one action remains for the plan to work." Kael sensed a slight amount of sarcasm in the man's voice that bordered on disrespect.

"Worry not, Ghul. We have gone over every detail. The plan is a good one. The last few details will come together and soon. I have a distinct feeling it'll be even sooner than we expected. Just make sure the dosa dekai devices will shut off when we jump to Havarrow's fleet."

"They will," he answered. "All the dekai are tethered to you and they will stop working when we leave."

"And the other?" she asked.

"Should stay active for a few hours after we leave, but it will have no effect on the lesser or the mundane."

"Good," Illara said. "Then Cethos will know that we have kept our word and that we mean them no harm. You will know when the time has come to jump to the fleet. We have done all we can for the day, you may go."

"Yes, Vikress. Sleep well."

Kael watched as Ghul left the room and the lock slid home behind him. The urge to attack the Vikress nearly overwhelmed him. If not for the traces of Fae magic in his blood, he would have. He had decided he was going to gather information and then leave if he could not figure out a way to kill several Ri'Tek at once. It was not worth the risk for just the two.

The Vikress sighed loudly, and Kael glanced back around the corner. She was staring directly at him from across the large room.

"You do realize, Kael," she said. "Though it might have taken a while for me to sense your filthy blood, you cannot hide right under my nose."

He stepped into the room. "Sooner or later, your oversized brain will fail to cover every possible detail."

"Come now, Kael," she replied. "Magic is currently not working in Cethos. None of your other *dosa* could come. Oh my, I do hope you came alone. Anyone with you… well, I am sure you know what would happen to them."

"I came alone, Illara. The plan was not to kill you."

"No, I suppose not." She smiled. "I imagine you wanted to know how close we are to leaving with Havarrow's fleet."

Kael frowned.

"Please, dear," she continued. "You cannot attack Cethos. We are protected here. The only chance you have is to intercept Havarrow's fleet as he takes us home."

Not knowing what to say, he grinned and winked at her. Ghul's big mouth let him know they were nearly ready.

"Thanks to my ever so trusty, big mouthed Syddic priest, you now know."

He shrugged. "And seeing as how you have to jump to the fleet," he added. "That means you are leaving from Arkum Zul."

"Well," she quipped. "Here my scholars believe the Kai'Sar are all insanity and killing. You actually have a brain under that vile blasphemy you call magic."

"I have what I need, Illara," Kael replied. "Be seeing you. Likely on one of Dominique's ships." Knowing the balcony was probably covered in archers, he reached out and opened an Ether portal behind the Vikress. The Ether's magic roared through him, and he rushed forward as time drastically slowed around him. As he passed Illara, her arms slowly raised and filled with magic. Wrapped in the speed of the Ether, he knew she would be too slow to stop him. He hit the portal entrance and the oxygen evaporated from his lungs. Energy exploded around him and flung him backward into the wall by the balcony entrance. Pain thundered through every molecule of his body as time sped back up.

"No," she said calmly. "I think you will die with that information, and my people will be home before your fellow *dosa* in DormaSai even know you are dead."

"How?" he groaned and rolled onto his back. It had been decades since he had felt such agony.

"You honestly thought you could steal what belongs to my people and use it against us?" she asked as she approached him. Profound disbelief riddled every word. "The magic you brought back with you is the magic our true gods granted us countless aeons ago. I may not have caressed it in a score of millennium, but I certainly have not forgotten how to deal with our magic while it is in the hands of a mentally-deficient child."

He stumbled to his feet and forced the throbbing ache aside. "Then, I guess we'll get to see who is stronger right now," he said and pulled his long scythe from the Ether.

"Dosa!" she snapped. "I look forward to killing you. It is what I have always done best."

"Yeah, yeah," he muttered. "You've killed more of my kind than any other, blah, blah. Can your race even fight without talking? I've heard it all before."

"Yes," she answered. "We can." Her glaive appeared in her hands, and with a whispered word, it flashed with magic. Flames danced to life along the blade.

Split the scythes, Kael. That flame is alive! Akai screamed in his head, and Kael nearly panicked as the spirit's fear hit him like a hurricane.

Dammit, Akai. What the hell? he asked inside his head.

Be goddamned careful. The spirit answered him and then fled to furthest reaches of Kael's mind. It was what Akai did to not distract him in battle. He did so just in time.

The Vikress lashed out and the glaive came with her. Kael jumped back, but the flames roared off the end of her glaive and raced toward his face like a flamethrower. On instinct, he raised his hand and pushed the magic aside as he stepped in the opposite direction. The flames struck the balcony entrance, and a vibrant red shield flared to life. The red glyph magic was all too familiar, and the Vikress had somehow turned it into a shield to block his escape.

The thoughts flashed through his head in less than second, but it was enough of a distraction. Again, the glaive shot his way. Out of instinct, he stepped into the Ether, but realized his mistake too late.

Another explosion rocked his body and tossed him across the room. His Ether magic was booby-trapped and not just when he used it to realm jump.

"You are a slow learner, Kael," the Vikress snapped. In several strides, she stood over him. The glaive's flames vanished, and she prodded his back. He rolled over and she stepped on his scythe with her left boot. "The shield over this room reacts to a god's magic. It really is a shame it only works on such a small scale and only with you inside it, but it serves its purpose for this night." The spear's wide blade touched his chin, and his goatee and skin sizzled from the hot metal.

"*Mutto Soulai, dosa*," she demanded.

Kael knew the term well—*bow or die*. "I will never bow," he snarled.

"Then *Soulai*, pest," she barked.

Kael grabbed his shorter reaper scythe as it phased from the long-handled weapon. The glaive sliced into his throat as he swung. The short scythe cut through her glaive, and he drove it into her side with every ounce of strength he had. The Vikress fell to the floor grabbing her ribs and her weapon vanished. Kael bound to his feet and clutched his neck. Blood pulsed through his fingers, and he pressed harder to compress the torn artery.

The Vikress laughed. "Well done," she moaned. "Looks like you have a nicked artery, Kael. Even with pressure, you have less than five minutes."

"And you have even less," he growled, and he pointed to her side. Illara pulled her robe apart and revealed the wound from his curved blade. Putrid black ooze wept from the wound mingling with the purple-red blood. Veins of black corruption raced through her bloodstream and marred the surface of her flesh.

"The DeathGod's ooze," she whispered. "Well done, *dosa*. Unfortunately for you, I have a Sect priestess on the fleet who will heal me sixty seconds after I arrive. But you will bleed out long before anyone can help you." She laughed.

"Wait," he said, and stumbled as dizziness washed over him. "You said *on* the fleet."

Illara laughed again. But it turned into a groan as she held her side. "You *dosa* fool," she growled. "My people are nearly home. I knew you'd show the moment I realized those two wizards left for the Southern Kingdoms. This was a trap to catch you alive or kill you if not. I call it a success. No one can save you. This shield will stop you from jumping out, and no one will find you in time. Goodbye, Kael." White light blazed around her, and he collapsed as she vanished.

Kael

"Nnn… not know, Akai."

Get up.

"Can't jump." His mind tumbled through thoughts, but he could not grasp a single one. He was too tired to try.

Kael! Try. Akai bellowed, and he twitched as the words frightened him.

"Ghul said… said…"

The dekai devices. They're down now that she's gone, use your Fae magic. Jump goddammit!

Kael laughed, mostly from the delirium of blood loss. "You lose, Vikress."

Fae magic laced with energy from the underworld lit up around him as he cast the same spell that had taken him to Giddeon in the DragonKin's island. He thought of Ember, so the spell would take him straight to her, and he rolled into the magic.

Black and white light crackled through the room as he, too, vanished within the Fae realm jump.

Chapter Twenty-Eight

"Peace is a rare commodity in our world today. With so many countries at risk of war and with even more borders being threatened as well as our own war having just ended, we must appreciate the peace we have gained through the coronation of our new queen. I never wanted a civil war, but merely a strong Cethos to see us through the trials ahead. With no desires for the throne myself, I am happy to see our former princess and current queen firmly seated on the throne. The lands and banners of the Vakaran nobility reaffirm our oath to the Cethosian crown. May we pray her reign is long!"

Duchess Tania Vakaran's Toast, Queen Corleya Bale's inauguration dinner.

GODSTONE PILLARS
BLACK HOLLOW PENINSULA

A blaze of white surrounded by a cloud of black exploded out of nowhere on the steep cliffs high above the Jaws of Rock and Ice deep within Orotaq controlled territory. Kael walked from the black smoke and touched his neck as he turned to Lycori, She came out of the jump with him, and in one piece. Her smile let him know she was all right. Knowing the others would be seconds behind him, he stared out across the ocean that no longer had a real name as he gently massaged the wound on his throat. Ember had managed to heal him before it was too late, but he was still a long way from being healed fully from the near fatal attack. Time was not on their side, and they had lost more than a full day by the time he regained consciousness.

"Shit," he whispered.

"You were right," Lycori said. "If nothing else."

A much stronger white light followed by a deafening crack of energy announced the arrival of those he had been waiting for. Ember, Yrlissa, Giddeon, Galen, and Treach materialized from inside the light.

"Look," Kael told them, pointing across the Black Kasym's western edge. "We're too late. Those are Havarrow's ships."

Yrlissa groaned and stepped up beside him and Lycori. "The Vikress told you the truth. They did leave earlier. The rowboats have already made land, Kael. The Ancients are home."

"What does that mean, Yrlissa?" Giddeon asked.

"I'm... I'm not sure," she answered honestly. "We might not have arrived in time to sink Havarrow's fleet in the Jaws, but we do have some time at least."

Kael could sense Ember's trepidation and knew what was coming before she even asked. "Time for what?" she snapped. "What will they do now that they're home?"

"Yrlissa?" Kael prompted when no one offered an answer.

The assassin rubbed her forehead. "I imagine the Vikress will order the Ri'Tek to head north to Tai Sa Neban — the old seat of their power. If it wasn't destroyed in the Cataclysm, it should be to the far north of the land mass across the ocean. Months' worth of travel at least. It bordered the Glacial Mountain Range as far north as you can go."

Kael struggled to control his anger when he understood the Ancients were already far out of reach. "What will they do after that?" he asked through clenched teeth.

"After what?" Yrlissa asked. "After they establish themselves as Talohna's living gods? I would imagine the Syddic Order and the Sect Priestesses will try to find a way to cross the Kasym safely. Once they do..."

Kael shook his head. "Treach? You're awful quiet."

Scratching his jaw, the newcomer winced. "Ancients. Ri'Tek. Matter not what you call them. For years of thousands, they had one goal: free what was taken from them by me and Niis."

Kael lifted his hand and muttered, "This." Silver and purple magic blazed to life in his hands and turned on him, snapping and lashing like an angry viper. Banishing the volatile magic, he shook his head, again. "They want their magic back."

"All they care about," Treach added.

"Then, we need to find the Lost," Kael said. "If anyone will know how to stop them—"

"And to teach you to use yours," Treach added. "Without mine, I cannot."

"Yeah." Kael sighed. "So you said. We have to find them, which means we have to cross the Kasym one more time and without magic."

"I disagree—" Giddeon began, but Ember cut him off.

"What a surprise," she quipped.

Kael turned, disgusted. "Let me guess? Talohna's only ArchWizard thinks he has a better idea."

Giddeon stood his ground. "I know I've made mistakes, Kael, but this is different. We need to unite Talohna and convince them the threat is real. Look," he said, gesturing across the sea. "Havarrow has at least three dozen longboats heading back to his ships for a second load."

Yrlissa shook her head. "I never imagined so many Ri'Tek would survive the far side of the Animus seals."

"You not see the full force of the Vascuul yet, either," Treach added. "Kael see what they left of Dal Dagore. Dwarves had no chance. Vascuul travel underground to Tai Sa Neban."

"Through the Kasym?" Ember asked.

Treach cocked his head to the side. "Vog tell Kael there is way through with magic. He do it. I not recommend you try jumping through Kasym, again," he said, glaring at Kael.

"Agreed," Yrlissa said. "Jasala's Sepulchre fell, Kael. The magic within the Kasym will be more volatile than ever. We can't fight them without more numbers. Soldiers, warriors, wizards, even kings and queens... we need everyone who will listen. We need an army—a real army."

"Not this shit again," Kael scoffed. "We've been over this. You will *never* unite these countries when most worship these bastards. Or worse, like in Cethos, where Queen Bale knows exactly who and what the Ancients are, but can't do anything because ninety-nine percent of the population consider them their saviors."

"I can't believe I am going to say this," Yrlissa said, "but I agree with Giddeon."

Kael slapped his forehead. "Giddeon's stupidity is not supposed to be contagious. What the hell is wrong with you two? Corynth burned for two days because of that thinking. Had Queen WhiteScale not arrived in time, I bet my life the Ri'Tek would have let Corynth burn instead of showing up to play the heroes by killing the so-called renegade Vascuul. They would have taken Eva either way. They only saved Corynth, so they could be heroes. The entire Elder and Wizard's Councils along with all the nobility swallowed the Ancients' charade hook, line, and sinker, Giddeon. You will never raise an army big enough in time without their support."

Ember gently touched Kael's arm. "We have to try," she told him. He could hear the determination in her voice. "It'll take months to find a way into the Ancients' Kingdom, and you have no idea where to look for the Lost."

Treach raised his right hand. "Not precisely accurate," he said. "Kael know from time north. The Lost be found in northwest of Ancient Kingdom. Perhaps."

Kael frowned. He was starting to think the old god could read his mind.

"What are you thinking, Kael?" Ember asked.

"How long will Havarrow stay, Yrlissa?" he asked, still frowning.

"Not long, I would expect," she replied. "Only a fool would trust the Ri'Tek, and Dominique is no fool."

Kael chuckled. "No, he's not, and the man does owe me a favor."

Yrlissa moved closer and took the length of braid hanging in front of his ear. "This is not yours," she said, dumbfounded. Pulling the braid aside she leaned closer. "It's threaded… a kreeda? Havarrow's kreeda?"

Kael nodded. "Yeah, it is." He reached inside his travel pack and pulled out the scrimshaw charm Dominique had given him so many years ago. He handed it to Yrlissa. "I imagine Dominique will cool his sails at Rejtett Island after they leave. The islands location is on the back of the scrimshaw charm," he said and pointed to the pirate's fleet. "Go see if he'll help us against the Ri'Tek. If you believe building an army is the answer, then at least start with the people who might agree to help us. Treach, Ember, and I will go look for the Lost."

Ember shook her head. "I can't go with you, babe. If we're going to build our army this way, then I know the first place to start."

"Of course," Kael said, pushing his long hair from his eyes as Ember smiled. "Seifer Locke and Kyro Yorcali are sitting on the largest standing army in the northern half of Talohna."

"Elderblood wizard, gladiators, and Witch of White," Treach said, nodding. "He owes you debt, too, Kael. Not refuse."

"Especially since Ember and Yrlissa saved his wife and returned her to him," Kael said.

"We are going to do this, then?" Giddeon asked, getting only nods. "Then, I will travel with you, Ember, if you don't mind. I have an apology to offer a… friend… in Dasal."

Quiet up until that point, Lycori finally joined in the conversation. "You know I am with you," she said as she stared at Kael.

"Never a doubt," he agreed. "Treach, I know you came with Ember this time, but are you sure you can travel with me when I jump?"

"Worry not me. Demons not grab."

Kael snorted. "I was more worried about the Ether keeping your ass on the way through than actually hurting you. It is your home. I only use the underworld now to move during combat, and you wouldn't be with me." Kael laughed.

For the first time in the weeks since they had met, Treach laughed, but for another reason. "Even so, your demons irrelevant. Ether hold no power over me like Talohna not hold you."

"I hope so, my friend. It has been nice having you along, especially now that your grasp of the common tongue is getting better."

"Take time," Treach replied. "It be good be here. When we lock Ri'Tek magic away—not foresee nightmare they become. Even old god make mistake. We chance make right or die to try."

"Good enough then," Kael said. "We have a plan, or at least the start of one. Let's hope we have the time needed to complete it all. Thank you, all of you, for everything."

Getting a round of nods, he turned and walked to the far side of the towering stone pillars to look out at the ocean. It had been many years since he had trusted anyone that he had forgotten how good it felt. Sensing Ember behind him, he smiled.

"You owe me a dance, handsome," she said.

He chuckled. "Those very words started this mess," he said. "You realize that, right?"

"Tinkers' Bar, three years ago. Yes."

She slid her arm around his waist, and he sighed. "It's been a lot longer for me. I'm sorry for being distant since..."

"I know, babe," she whispered, resting her head against his shoulder. "I just found you, and again, we have to go separate ways. Promise me it won't end the same way this time."

"You know I can't," he told her. "But I can promise to do everything I can to get back alive."

"And I will do the same. But for now, let's go home. We haven't stopped to rest since this all started—the glade where we found you, the fight at the Human seal, the past few weeks trying to find out when Havarrow would move, healing your throat after you jumped into my bed bleeding out, the race here... taking a day or two—or even ten—before we start will make no difference in time, but it will mean a world to us. I'll also need that time to help you heal fully and to find a better solution to balance Reethor's Ichor if we are going separate ways."

"Home." He laughed, again. "Where is that? I never had a home here."

"My home will always be yours, Kael. Come with me to DormaSai. We will be safe there ,and I have begun building a life there. We can rebuild *our* life there."

"That sounds like Heaven—or Hell maybe." He sighed.

"Hell?" Ember asked.

"The closest I got to a real heaven was in Hell—in the DreamScape. It was missing something, though."

"I don't understand," she replied. "The DreamScape is supposed to be perfect. What was missing?"

"The real you," he said, smiling. "Let's go, love. We have several years, at least, before the chaos in Talohna begins."

A snap of stunning white light cut his words short, and a woman stepped from the Fae realm jump.

"That is not true," Kyr Meadow barked as the light faded behind her. "The Ancients are wreaking havoc in Vaenaria, now. We need you home, niece. The family Matriarchs have voted."

"On what?" Kael demanded.

Kyr shot him a dirty look, and he knew her hatred of him was stronger than ever. "On the new leader of the Fae people... you, Ember."

"Holy shit," Ember whispered.

"That's ridiculous," Kael said. "Her magic is not even close to being mature."

"It matters not," Kyr replied. "The Matriarchs were unanimous. Ember will assume the role of High Matriarch as her mother desired, and I will act as her advisor and mentor as my sister… as her mother should have been. We must leave now. The Fae Animus seal is located within Vaenaria's main island. Ri'Tek wizards and warriors from the broken seal are attacking the main city from the inside. We are losing the city."

"What took so long?" Giddeon asked. "The Sepulchre fell weeks ago."

Kyr pinched her nose in frustration and sighed. "When Eva died and the Sepulchre magic failed, it forced Vaenaria back into phase with Talohna. We think it may have caused a delay in the seal's opening."

"Or, is it possible the Ri'Tek remained hidden for two weeks while they recovered," Kael offered. "If they are recon units, the moment they learned where they were and what happened, they would've gathered intel before they attacked."

Ember's face went white. "If they have had three weeks of undetected reconnaissance in Vaenaria, the Fae are in serious trouble, Kael."

"We'll come with you," he offered.

"By the grace of the Ladies, you will not!" Kyr snapped. "Even the High Matriarch cannot allow a Kai'Sar to enter the holy lands. Wife or not, it is forbidden."

"What are going to do? You need help," he insisted.

"That is why Ember must return with me, now," Kyr stated. "Fae Matriarchs are born, not made. They think different from other Fae. She will have the answers we need—not magic that will destroy more than it will help."

Kael turned toward Ember and she kissed him. "I have to go, babe."

"I know, and I am very much not welcome there," he said.

"In time, I promise." She kissed him, again, and added, "Go with Nekrosa and Sephi. Stay and rest until I get there, please?" He nodded. "I trust them with my life, Kael. So, can you. I will be there as soon as I possibly can."

She kissed him a third time and held it longer. It was real, and no nightmare magic swarmed his mind. As Treach coughed to politely interrupt, he smiled and released her

"Go," he told her. "I'll jump to Ver Karmot and tell Shelaryx what's happening, so she can send you help. From there, I'll wait for you in Drae'Kahn."

She kissed him a fourth time. "We will drop everyone off," she said and turned to gather those she had brought with her. He watched them leave and the vivid magic of the two jumps faded away. Only Treach and Lycori remained.

"You did not tell her," Treach said. "Wise?"

"I don't know," Kael replied.

"She will sense it sooner before later. Perhaps before we leave to find Vog," Lycori suggested. "You should have told her that, too."

"I know," Kael said, almost snapping. He took a breath and held up his hand as an apology. "How do I tell the only woman I've ever loved we are planning to ask a Mahalan scout—who by the way, is not a murderous frenzy killer like all the rest—to help us cross the Kasym by using his magic? But oh, yeah, it's completely all right. Everything should be fine because I might be a god? How exactly do you two recommend I bring that up? What time do you two think is the right time to have that conversation with the Fae's new High Matriarch?"

"Good point," Lycori replied and offered a slight bow of apology.

Treach was a lot less tactful. "Know not, Kael," he answered. "She need know. More now because who she is. Cannot keep such from allies."

"I know," he said and shook his head.

Treach clasped his shoulder. "The truth, always," he said. "You... I... stand here, alive today because only gods survive death. That is truth, friend."

The End

Epilogue

NORTHERN ICE AND ROCK OCEAN
ANCIENT KINGDOM

"Are you sure, brother?" Shasta Trey asked quietly. Havarrow nodded and calmly pointed to the eleven other ships that sailed in their wake.

"Get it done, first mate," he said. "Only eight of our ships are equipped with cannons. We are beyond the spires of ice and rock, and the beasts have given up. We will reach land this time. I want the Ancients off my ships and then the easy winds out of here."

She nodded and left to speak with the flagman on their ship.

Dominique frowned. The way through the spires had been easy — just like the last time — but the beasts had been far more aggressive as if something had thrown them into a fury long before his ships arrived. The ships' cannons and Ancient wizards had made a world of difference in dealing with the magically deranged wildlife, and it allowed his ships to reach the edge of the deep water in a matter of minutes.

"You did it, Captain," Vikress Illara said as she approached the helm. "You brought my people home."

"Not all of them," he answered.

"Sythrnax willingly gave his life for his people. My brother was a hero, and those freed from the Fae seal will fight or sneak their way to the mainland eventually. The Fae seal held our counter intelligence, reconnaissance, and sabotage units. They might even annex a new set of islands to our lands. When you hear of them, you can offer to do the same as you have done for me—bring them home. From what we have been able to ascertain, those beyond the Dragon seal have been lost to us. The reptiles always were stubborn and conniving animals. Once we are whole, we will investigate why the Dragon seal did not open."

"I will have my crews on alert for news of your people," he told her. "Wherever they may come from."

"I appreciate that, Captain. Have you given any thought to my proposal?"

He shrugged and instantly recognized that she was vetting him in the same way he or his crew vetted a contact aboard a merchant ship.

"My brother's death frees you from the oath you had to kill him, does it not?" she asked. He nodded as she carried on, "I have already told you that had I been the one freed from the seal during the Cataclysm, I would not have followed the same path and made the same decisions he did. I meant your friend Kael no harm. I would like for our people to be allies."

"So, would I, Vikress," he answered, offering a smile. "But I haven't changed my mind. For now, I must sail south to consolidate the Suns under my banner. Bauro had over sixty or seventy ships under his command. Even with the upgrades done on the first eight ships, I cannot hope to hold off an armada if they or another of your enemies should decide to come your way. If you want me to defend your waters, I need as many of those ships as I can get."

"Understandable," she replied. "I admire a man who thinks with his brain and not his emotions."

Dominique chuckled. "I think with the chests of gold in my hold, Vikress. If the gold and gems flow steadily, I will gladly sail with your flag above mine."

"Ah…" The Vikress sighed and eyed him closely. Having been under worse scrutiny, he did not flinch. "The simplicity of a pirate's loyalty — a gold coin. As you have already been, you will be paid well to patrol our seas, I promise you," she added and seemed convinced of his sincerity. "Very well. Consolidate what forces you can and return. From what I can see of the landmass ahead of us, our old lands are mostly intact. However, they do seem to have shifted as if peeled apart from the middle like one eats a kona fruit. If so, several miles to the west you should see a river that you can follow inland until you find what is left of an old dam sight we created a dozen millennia ago. I will lead my people overland to the dam first. A detachment will remain there once we move on. They will send word to Tai Sa Neban upon your return, and hopefully, by that time we will have found a way for your ships to dock at our capitol city. Our kingdoms river system was once intricately convenient. I hope it has remained so."

"Fair enough, Vikress," Dominique said. "Now, let's get your people to land. Prepare the rowboats!" he yelled to his crew. His flagman signaled behind them to the other ships as their anchor plunged into the deep water. The other seven cannon heavy ships turned to the side and lined up bow to stern across the entrance to the deeply inset bay before them. Havarrow's ship remained at the back of the line. The remaining four ships not outfitted with cannons dropped anchor behind the row of eight.

"I will prepare my people, Captain," the Vikress told him.

Havarrow nodded and waved to Shasta. "My first mate will oversee the loading. Each boat will need two of my men and can fit twenty of yours, but we should still be able to offload all your people with two trips."

"That sounds fine, Captain," she said. "I will remain aboard your ship until the last rowboat leaves."

"Would you not rather be the first of your kind to step foot on the soil of your homeland?" he asked.

"On the contrary, Captain Havarrow," she replied. "My people believe in never leaving anyone behind unless it absolutely necessary. Had the units beyond the Fae seal been normal warriors, you would have sailed us to the Fae islands now that they are back in-phase with Talohna. Your cannons would have leveled Vaenaria to get our people out. As it is, the Arna Kem will wreak havoc for the Fae until they can get to the mainland."

"Fair enough," he said as Shasta stopped at his side. "Oversee the loading, first mate."

"Yes, Captain," she replied. "This way, if you would like to join me, Vikress Illara."

Illara nodded and began to follow Shasta but turned back. "Thank you, Captain," she said. "For everything."

He offered a slight bow, and Shasta winked at him, letting him know that his message had been passed among the other ships.

Relaxing against the helm, he sighed. It would take a couple of hours to offload the Ancients and there was nothing more to do until they were gone from his ships.

UNNAMED BEACH
ANCIENT KINGDOM

Vikress Illara stepped from the water onto the soil of her homeland for the first time in thousands of years.

"Welcome home, Vikress," Commander Tuz said.

"Are they ready?" she asked.

"Archers and magic users are both ready for you to give the order. Dominique Havarrow and all of his ships will be on the ocean floor before the longboats return."

"It is a shame," she said and turned to the bay full of pirate ships. "His armada would have been nice."

"I agree," Tuz said. "But those weapons... the cannons. He is also a Northman. Wherever they came from is irrelevant. I understand they are loyal to a fault."

"And his loyalty does not lie with us," Ghul reminded them as he approached. "He may not be aware that Kael is alive yet, but when he finds he is, that armada will turn on us when he finds out what actually happened."

"True," Illara agreed. "And we will need years to deal with the Kasym—even longer to heal it. We are safe up here from Kael's wrath if Havarrow is not alive to bring him here and hopefully our own armada remains safe in dry-dock storage. Give the order, Commander." Illara turned on her heel and headed over the ridge of sand to help her people prepare for their long journey ahead.

"What is Havarrow doing?" Ghul barked as the returning longboats lurched ahead and raced across the bay. They were back to Havarrow's ships in only seconds.

Commander Tuz shielded his eyes from the sun. "Niis' curse," he swore. "The longboats were tied to the anchor winches..."

"The formation of the cannon ships..." Ghul began.

"Signal the retreat!" Tuz shrieked as he and Ghul rushed for the far side of the sand ridge on the beach, but it was already too late

The beach erupted with explosions and roaring thunder.

"Our men are aboard, Captain," Shasta hollered.

"Fire, Eamon!" Dominique roared. "Every gods-damned cannon we have!"

Cannon fire from his own and the seven other ships rocked his vessel. The concussion of so many cannons lighting off around them nearly brought him to his knees.

Prepared for the betrayal, Havarrow's ships unleashed a hell-storm of cannon fire. All eight ships' sixteen broadside cannons belched flame and cannonballs peppered the beach full of Ancient warriors and wizards. A dozen wild spells arched away harmlessly as the few Ancient wizards already casting magic died screaming among the explosions.

"Cut the fucking anchors and get us out of here!" Shasta yelled. "Move it men! Before they recover! Talvira, you know what to do!"

The four ships without cannons crossed the western point of the bay and reached safety while Havarrow's ship brought up the rear. Talvira tapped into her abnormal magic and unleashed a massive wall of wind. It blew across all eight ships. Shasta took over the helm, and Dominique stepped to the stern to stand beside his new sorceress. He stared at the carnage on the beach. The surviving Ancients scrambled to get away from another volley. Because the distance had been too far to effectively aim the cannons, he doubted more than a handful died in his initial attack. He snorted and turned back to the helm as all his ships lurched ahead, powered by Talvira's magic.

Havarrow knew the moment Ghul and Tuz remained on the beach that the Ancients would attack his fleet. He had not just expected it but planned for it.

"Good thing we were ready," Shasta stated as if reading his mind.

"Never doubted for a moment they'd betray us — whether or not we had discovered they killed Kael."

A second ship slowed and came alongside. "Where now, boss?" Cassel Morena shouted from the second ship's railing.

"Any leads on Yrlissa?" Dominique yelled back.

"If the Blades believe she is dead or if they are actively hunting her, she will be where they have the least influence."

"Cass!" Shasta shouted. "That is in DormaSai now. The White Cabal has made it their mission to wipe the Blades from existence." She glanced at Dominique. "We'll have to dock at Fathom's Deep. We cannot begin to guess the influence the Ancients might have in the Twin Cities and even Cormack WhiteFrost may not be able to help us."

"I agree." Dominique nodded. "We will have to get to DormaSai by land until we know that a headman's axe is not waiting for us in Alegra or Argela."

"To Fathom's Deep?" Cass hollered.

Dominique nodded to Shasta at the helm. "To Fathom's Deep, first mate. The Reaver's Curse is yours."

"Yes, brother."

"I'll be in my cabin if you need me."

A blaze of white magic rocked the main deck as the Vikress, Ghul, and an Ancient wizard stepped from the realm jump.

"You are a fool pirate," Illara growled as the wizard held the realm jump open. Without warning, she leapt forward and grabbed Eamon by the throat. "You should have just died," she added and dragged the alchemist backwards through the portal.

"No!" Shasta yelled as she vaulted the railing and dove for the Vikress a second too late.

The Vikress, Ghul and Eamon O'Leary vanished into the white light as the wizard followed them. The portal snapped shut.

"By the gods," Shasta whispered. She turned and stared at Dominique, helpless. "What have we done, brother?"

Unable to find the words, Dominique shook his head and stared at the blackened smoking beach.

The Ancients had one of Talohna's deadliest weapons, and they had all the time they needed to exploit him.

Also available from JD Franx:

The Darkness Within Saga
Book 1 The Legacy
Book 2 Blood of the Lost
Book 3 Fallen Sepulchre

A Darkness Within Novella
Sins of the Past

Talohna Origins: The Northmen

Coming Soon:
The Darkness Within Saga
Book 4 The Curse of Home Fall
Book 5 Of Gods and Men Spring
Book 6 The Chaos of Ancient Magic

Talohna Origins: The Northmen

Author JD Franx

Copyright (c) JD Franx

Registered Copyright 2019

Cover Illustration and Design (c) Amalia Chitulescu

www.amaliach.com

Editing by Bitter Brownie Books

Kindle design and formatting by Rachel Bostwick

All rights reserved

ISBN 978-0-9953363-4-6

Dedication

For my readers and fans:

Many of you have been with me from the beginning when The Legacy was first published nearly three ago now. A lot of you will also pick up this Northmen book as your first introduction to the world of Talohna. To all of you who have shown me your amazing support over the last few years, and for those who have decided to just recently give my books a chance, I thank you. As a way of showing my gratitude, I have compiled a list of Origin stories that many of you are asking to see. Seeing as how the Northmen's arrival to Talohna ties directly to the events in Kael's next book, and it was the most asked for origin story, I wrote it first. So, whether you are a new reader, or a devoted fan, these Talohna Origins novels are for all of you who helped make it possible for me to write these stories. Thank you all.

Chapter One

"Talohna is only one of many dimensions. It has evolved with the help of magic in a similar fashion to the way technology has affected my Earth. This has made for some interesting similarities and more than a few curious differences, including the events throughout the histories of both Earth and Talohna."

--Kael Symes, 6 Years After the Ancients' Return

Steinn Fortress, Sokn
Northman Homeland, Hours Before The
Cataclysm

War, death, and rot hung heavy in the air, but a dozen other problems rested firmly in the front of Engier's mind. Jarl Engier Striith-Blodd let his hands rest easily on the head of his sheathed war axe and stared out across the valley situated on the northeastern edge of Sokn's mainland. From the upper ramparts of the fortress below his feet, on this clear, early morning he could see for miles. Though the decrepit state of the buildings and barricades surrounding him scarcely qualified as a fortress, it was the only place to make their stand. Engier snorted at the stupidity of defending the old fort. Even though the people working in the mines far below had spent years trying to make it a home, the fortress was just that. A home, it was no longer a secure fortress. He needed more men to mount a solid defense and whether or not more clans arrived in time to help remained a major concern at the fore front of his mind.

Shaking his head to clear it merely opened the door for other problems to quickly invade his thoughts. It dawned on him that with the death of the High King and his family several weeks ago, Engier's Striith-Blodd clan, as it was traditionally known, now held the responsibility of being the oldest and most respected family in all of the Northmen lands. Engier himself wasn't a traditionalist and most often referred to his own clan as most other Northmen did: The War-Blood clan. It was something that might have to change in the coming days should the clans choose to vote on a new high king. Tradition or not, he would be the favored noble for Sokn's highest throne. The thought made his head hurt. He prided himself on living up to his family's namesake for every one of his sixty years, and he still had well over half his life to live, if the gods deemed it so. Having fought in wars and battles since the age of fourteen, he earned a respect from the other clans that bordered on awe.

It was a good thing too, because he needed to use that influence to call all the northern clans to his command in order to deal with the threat facing his people from across the valley. The threat of rogue magic gone unchecked in Sokn loomed yet again. Engier had fought many rebel magic users over the years, but the fetid approach of death from across the valley was the only threat large enough to warrant uniting all the clans. New and unknown magic had a way of forcing such alliances to be made. With no other choice, he would continue to command the clans until the threat was over and the new magic was understood and controlled, or preferably destroyed, but Engier had no interest in becoming High King. He was a warrior and the High King only fought during times of danger or threat to all Northman people, not in times of trouble for individual clans.

The Ama Taugr wizard at his side coughed, bringing his mind back to the immediate threat yet again. Drengr Stone-Wise was a loyal friend and the only magic user he would ever trust completely. "I never dreamt the Ama Taugr rebels could raise so many dead in such a short time, especially with so few of the bloodstone runes," he said, pulling his long blonde hair back into a high ponytail and checking his rune sack in preparation for the upcoming battle.

Jarl Engier scoffed but deep down he agreed with his clan wizard, the enemy forces had to number close to a thousand. He continued to stare across the valley where the four outcast rebels who controlled the hordes of walking dead were encamped. Thankfully, the large, undead horde was still several hours from the fortress where Sokn's largest source of bloodstone now resided. Bloodstone the necromancers camped across the valley wanted very badly.

Like most Jarls in Sokn, Engier was a battle-hardened and grizzled man who had earned and kept his lands through the support and love of his people, his mental and physical prowess, as well as that of his men and women. Deep in thought, he tugged at his braided black beard. Streaks of silver marked the braids, something that only came with the experience of age.

"Ama Taugr..." Engier snorted at the words even as they left his brain and finished rolling over his tongue. "Magic users cause more trouble than they are worth. The current state of the North is just another example."

"Agreed. *Taela*, all of them." Though blonde and nearly a foot shorter when standing at Engier's side, Jarl Brenna Kaesia's presence was just as prominent as his own, and a matching grunt followed her agreement about the four *taela*, traitors, each and every one. Such agreements were a rarity between them.

"Traitors, of that there's no doubt. They shall be dealt with as such. Jarl Brenna, you have my thanks for answering the call. How many warriors came with you?"

"Eighty, plus twenty of my High Guard," she replied. "I sent a missive to the mines at Dragon's Breath calling for all five hundred men, but it will be at least a week before they arrive. You have my apologies, Jarl Engier. Until we received correspondence from our nobles who survived the attack at the High King's castle, I believed your missive might have been a battle tactic. A way of drawing my army from the mines."

He scoffed at the low number and at the unintended slight. One hundred warriors doubled his forces but still left them seriously outnumbered against an enemy who proved damn hard to kill during their first engagement. A week would mean a world of difference as almost a thousand of his own men would also arrive by then. "I would never call for your clan to support a Northmen threat as a ruse to take back the opal mines that rightfully belong to my clan. There is no honor in it. Our differences must be set aside for the good of all the Northmen now. We can return to our war later."

"That is why I apologized." she said.

"Your men are ready?" he asked, changing the subject.

"They are," she answered. "But that southwestern wall remains a weak spot."

"We have as many men as we can spare standing guard there. Should it collapse, others, including myself, will reinforce their position."

"Good," she said. "Hopefully it won't come to that. These runecasters seem to cause more trouble for the people of Sokn than any other clan, but this particular group of outcasts are far more insidious. After discovering that the bloodstone gem could be runed for more than just talking to the ancestors..." Brenna paused as a frustrated frown crept across her features. "They killed that boy, Engier, like true cowards. Then they took the stones and papers he was working on for themselves," she said. Like most young Northmen, Brenna's emotions were more volatile and much closer to the surface.

Though she was decades younger and they had been fighting against each other for possession of the fire opal mines below the Dragon's Breath Keep for months, Engier respected the female Jarl as he would any other noble or warrior. He carefully considered her council on matters of war or politics and not so long ago, when they were rivals, he evaluated every move she made before acting against her.

"It is certainly possible that they are responsible for his death," he replied.

Jarl Brenna persisted with her argument. "A strong Northman, even a boy, does not die from illness. The Ama Taugr at the school have offered us nothing but wizard lies when it comes to his death. The boy was training to learn the creation of runes so he could become a Rynstar, like his father. That placed him in their protection. It is no coincidence that he died shortly after he discovered that bloodstone can be runed to raise the dead." When the young Jarl lowered her voice, Engier leaned closer. "We rely on those rune stones and the Rynstar smiths to repair the ancestor weapons, as well as to forge anew," she said. "The wizards' lies make this problem more complicated than the undead army that gathers below us. You've heard the rumors, Engier. We cannot trust the Ama Taugr any longer. They must be dealt with as soon as the undead and the rebels are no longer a concern."

Engier glanced down at his axe. It was a true ancestor weapon passed down through his family for many generations. The silver blade coursed with throbbing red and pearl veins of fire opal that gave the weapon a searing hot edge. So much so, that his sheath was also runed in order to protect the axe-blade from harming its owner and those who might brush up against it in passing. But the valuable runestones had another use, it was true. Like Brenna and almost all Northmen, he disliked the Ama Taugr still having access to the runes that wizards used to unleash hellstorms of savage magic like the Skeyth of old. For several hundred years since the Rune Wars and subsequent banishment of the Skeyth that resulted in the creation of the Ama Taugr, wizards were given limited access to the gemstones or completed runes that were needed to harness their magic. Since the murder of the High King and his family, most Northmen now agreed that even this limited access should be revoked.

Whenever the wizards rebelled or were given free rein, the world of Sokn found itself in the state it was in now, with the united clans fighting against the wizards and the deadly magic they controlled. This time it was four necromancers and their army of walking dead that marched on Sokn's lone bloodstone mine.

A chunk the size of a merchant's cart had been extracted less than a week ago in the hope of destroying all of the supply within the mine. However, without the research from the young Rynstar, Engier's own wizard and others who made the attempt were unable to damage, let alone destroy the massive stone.

Engier rubbed his throbbing temples and shook the pointless thoughts from his mind. "Agreed. They will be dealt with in time," he finally muttered. "The young Rynstar was from my village, Jarl Brenna. I know his family well, especially his father. Aro is one of Sokn's most experienced Rynstars and he has kept my axe whole during many a war, but ultimately his child's death does not matter to us in the here and now."

"No?"

"No," he insisted. "We will investigate the boy's death later but for now, his discovery is all that matters. All we know for sure is that when properly marked, the bloodstone rune also raises the dead. When the High King called the Jarls to vote on the matter, we agreed unanimously that all of our current bloodstone supply and any found in the future must be destroyed. That means the *KunSkyn'A* Festival will no longer be celebrated by our people. Never again will we able to seek wisdom from those who came before us. These rebels have cost us the means to summon our ancestors, and it is a part of the Festival of Knowledge many of our people celebrate, whether high noble and royalty or commoner. Having the ability to commune with our ancestors has kept the knowledge and history of our people alive, up until these events. The Ama Taugr will be taught a lesson for that, I promise you, but after the dead have been returned to their eternal rest and these wizards brought to justice."

"My lord," Drengr interrupted. "It was a small group of Ama Taugr wizards, *taela*, rebels, who took the last of the bloodstone and the young Rynstar's research before they fled the Ama Taugr school at Kastali Fortress and perpetrated the attack on the King's family. I beg you not to punish all of the Ama Taugr at the Skall for the actions of a select few. The Skall is a school, my lords, a safe place for learning and research, but it is also the only home many of those young wizards have ever known. Most are shunned by their own clans and are not welcomed elsewhere in Sokn."

Engier studied the man hard. Drengr had served him faithfully for many decades and was the only Ama Taugr he would ever trust completely. Drengr was a son of clan War-Blood first and an Ama Taugr wizard second.

"We know beyond a doubt that they are responsible for what happened at Savingar Castle, but are you sure that the four acted alone?" Engier asked. "We have to be sure."

The wizard nodded with a sigh. "I am. The four acted for their own selfish reasons and definitely not with the Skall Council's blessing. The attack on the king happened less than two weeks after they fled the school with the last of the bloodstone. That was... What? A week after the vote to destroy all the bloodstone," Drengr stated. Getting nods from the Jarls, he continued unabated. "They waited long enough after the vote to make sure most of the Jarls and Thanes had left before attacking the High King. They are responsible for all of it, I am certain. This has been many months, if not years in the planning, my lord. The new knowledge of the bloodstone merely gave this particular group of rebels the confidence to put their plans into action. I would think that the attack on Savingar Castle was the easiest way to seed discord among the nobility —"

Jarl Brenna grunted in agreement. Cutting the wizard short, she turned to Engier. "Anarchy was their goal. It took two days for you and your warriors to fight through the living corpses only to find the High King, his family, and all the castle servants among the ranks of the raised dead. It could have been planned as a diversion, or simply as a way for them to test the rune magic before beginning to grow their numbers of undead in earnest. Ultimately it gave them the time to organize, and to raise their undead army, that is what they needed most. The proof wanders aimlessly across the valley."

Engier nodded his head and looked out across the valley from the fortress' upper catwalk. Though the lowlands were clear of the walking dead that morning, the arrival of the dead and the filthy red mist emanating from them had already begun to poison the land. Blackened grass and patches of darkened brush dotted the valley floor and larger trees held the brown shade of impending death. Standing between Engier and the overabundance of corrupted earth miles away, were acres of fertile, cropped farmland and fruit orchards. Abandoned by the farmers a day or two earlier for the safety of the fortress, the land was slowly falling victim to the insidious approach of death. Frowning at the devastation already wrought on the valley's far side, Engier was glad he ordered everyone to pull back to the mine's fortress in order to protect the citizens of the valley along with the block of bloodstone. It was the only practical choice, leaving the farmers outside the fortress walls would simply add to the army of undead.

"Dammit," Brenna cursed lightly. "We had a tough time with the small group we encountered on the way here. It's going to be hard to win this war when the enemy's soldiers are incredibly hard to kill and those who do fall are replenished and reinforced by our own fallen after each battle. During the battle, for that matter." It was a lesson they both learned the hard way during their first, but separate engagements with the rebel necromancers.

"As did we at Savingar Castle, and that is the crux of the problem, Jarl Brenna," Drengr Stone-Wise added. Though the wizard was in the employ of Jarl War-Blood, he openly offered advice to both of the allied Jarls. "We experienced the same difficulties at the High King's castle. The rebels might have been gone, but their lingering magic raised the dead bodies of our own warriors faster than the priests could consecrate the dead."

"Yet we cannot afford to lose more warriors while fighting over the bodies of our dead. We need more Ama Taugr,

Drengr," Engier growled. "The few who are loyal to the Northmen. I hate to admit it, but nothing works against the walking dead better than a fire opal in the hands of a runecaster. How long before they arrive?"

Drengr shook his head. "It will be close, Jarl. They should begin arriving tonight, depending on how many missives made it through the rebel line."

"We have retreated as far as we can without giving up the fortress, and because of the peninsula behind us, there is no worry of attack from our rear, but the necromancer's forward line is awful tight because of it," Jarl Brenna reminded them. "I wouldn't count on many of your missive scouts getting through. At least it means the rebels cannot get their hands on the block of bloodstone unless we fail. We will stand our ground here, even if it means we don't get reinforcements. We do not want to be fighting the dead inside the mine."

Engier nodded his agreement. "A few stones the size of my thumb has allowed them to raise hundreds of corpses each. The block we protect is the size of a mule cart. Losing it to these rebels would be catastrophic for all of Sokn."

"That is why the other clans march day and night to get here, my lord," Hamay Nordstrom answered as he climbed off the ladder onto the rampart. "We merely need to delay the battle if possible."

"You have information about their arrival then, Housekarl?" Engier asked.

Hamay bowed to the Jarls. The Housekarl was a highly respected position. As one of Engier's best warriors and his right hand, Hamay oversaw all of Clan War-Blood's affairs including acting as overseer for the *Temja*, clan War-Blood's young warriors-to-be. Hamay quickly stood before he answered. "Two scouts made it through the rebel's forward line..."

"Only two?" Engier asked in disbelief.

"Yes, my lord. The first from one of the mountain clans, they have already arrived with fifty men, and will remain hidden within the slopes of the western hills outside the valley, moving closer would reveal their presence and prompt an attack from the rebels. The other scout is from Thane Rollik. He leads close to fifty Riddari horsemen and has agreed to attack from the valley's eastern lowlands should he arrive in time. The messenger says they are still a few hours away though."

"That is still good to hear," Jarl Brenna said. "We only need another hundred men on the western flank in order to surround the rebels from three sides. The Riddari clans can lead the charge and grind the undead into the dirt under the hooves of their war horses, hopefully they arrive in time."

"Last we heard, the Sea Lords might be here by then also, but they are coming from the south," Hamay offered, earning a nod from Jarl Brenna.

"Good," she replied. "Send three of our fastest outriders to intercept the Lords and steer them more to the west. Inform them of the new battle strategy. One should get through." Even though he was Engier's right hand man, he bowed and in turn received an immediate nod of approval from Engier before leaving.

"With the ability to attack from two sides, we do have the military advantage, even if it is only just," Drengr mumbled. "They still outnumber us better than three to one with the forces we currently have."

"True," Engier agreed. "And I would back any Northman warrior against a shambling dead man even if two on one. We cannot rely on the Sea Lords or the Riddari, and the walking dead cannot use runed weapons. Besides, all the Rynstar have been accounted for so they will not be making any more runes for the rebels, bloodstone or otherwise. They have to be nearly out of the rune stones they stole from the school at Kastali Fortress by now. The High King's court wizards put up a serious fight against the rebels in the outer courtyard during the attack so I doubt they acquired a lot of runestones from Savingar."

"Thank Tyr's bloody blades and pray you're right. The damage they've done with the little they've had..."

"I know, Brenna," Engier agreed.

"I cannot imagine the chaos they will create should they get their hands on the stone we protect," Drengr offered.

"Then perhaps you should continue trying to find a way to destroy it," Brenna snapped.

"I will do so," Drengr said, and bowed. "Jarls."

Engier watched the wizard leave and wondered if their friendship would ever be the same. Drengr was an Ama Taugr wizard, he just happened to be a member of the War-Blood clan as well. He had no doubt where the wizard's loyalty lied, but nevertheless, he knew Drengr struggled with the idea of destroying the bloodstone and that he might have to face his fellow wizards on the battlefield.

"Magic," Engier spat. "More trouble than it's bastard worth."

Jarl Brenna snorted. "Something to be discussed at the next council of Jarls without doubt. Preferably before the moot when we vote for a new High King."

"Agreed," he said.

Brenna bumped him gently and pointed forward across the valley. "But for now," she said. "It looks like our rebels want to talk."

Sure enough, as Engier glanced back out across the valley, the Ama Taugr rebels moved to the front of the shuffling mass of walking dead. The first of the four wizards carried a flag inscribed with the symbol of peace. The three offset triangles on the unbroken line was one of the symbols known throughout Sokn as the universal sign to speak during times of war, especially when scrawled on a flag of white cloth. Even the indigenous peoples of the south acknowledged it. He had hoped for the crossed spears instead. It meant all would be allowed to leave the parlay unhindered. Without it, there were no promises if talks broke down.

"Well," Engier said as the Ama Tagur rebels advanced to within a half mile of the fortress and then stopped, while leaving all of the walking dead behind. "I guess we go talk with the wizards before we fight. I'll get Hamay to find Drengr and send him to meet the rebels, then bring ten of my high guard to the front gate."

"Have him roust the same number of my own guard," Jarl Brenna said. "If it's a trick and these wizards want a fight then our high guard will get us back inside the fortress with the most lives intact."

Engier nodded his approval and waved at one of the rampart guards to notify Hamay, she quickly slid down the ladder, out of sight. The clan's heavily armored high guardsmen wore solid plate armor and would fight to the death in order to protect their Jarls. They were big, strong men, even compared to Engier's large frame, and all were fanatically loyal.

"A moment?"

"Of course, Jarl Brenna," Engier replied.

"I know we are going to try stalling the battle, but if we do, have you considered ghostwalking the rebels tonight? You carry the hooked blade, as do I and many of my scouts."

"Entering an enemy camp and killing everyone in their sleep is a battle tactic reserved only for invading foreign armies or for those clans or individuals who do not respect the Northmen ways of life or war," he explained.

"You mean like *taela* Ama Taugr wizards who have rebelled against the Skall Council like spoiled little shits?" she hissed.

"It would make a point wouldn't it?" he asked, scratching his beard in thought.

"A damn clear point in my opinion," she stated.

"Perhaps it will be worth considering," he said. "Let's see if we can convince them to hold off attacking for a night. If possible, I'd rather fight once we have more numbers, or they have less."

"Very well."

"Shall we go, Jarl Brenna?" he asked holding his hand out towards the rampart ladder. "The traitors walked the road to parley without guards or living dead, so I do not believe it to be a trick. Drengr can ascertain the likelihood of treachery, he will arrive ahead of us."

"After you," she said. "But if it all goes to shit down there, don't die too easily, Jarl Engier. I'd hate for the Valkyries to pass you by." She laughed and a slight bow was all he received before Brenna disappeared down the ladder.

Southeastern Plains Of Austain

"Jarl Engier, Jarl Brenna," Drengr said. "May I present Sabjorn Toll. He speaks for the Ama Taugr leading this undead army."

Engier snorted when the weasel-nosed man stepped forward. An instant dislike of the older wizard overwhelmed him. From his high ponytail of mousy black hair to his scarred hands and wrinkled, beady eyes, every part of the wizard emanated mistrust.

"Jarl Engier," Sabjorn said, offering a bow. "I am disappointed to see you here, but not surprised. The clans *would* only unite under your leadership."

Jarl Brenna scoffed and twisted the handle on her sword. "Disappointed because you must face Sokn's best warriors on the battlefield, coward? After your treachery at Savingar Castle? What did you expect, wizard? A welcome party and a celebratory banquet?"

"Jarl Brenna, always quick with the tongue," Sabjorn chided. "I am disappointed because I would hate to take the lives of such warriors."

"Watch yourself, *taela*," Brenna snapped. "Or my blade will have *your* tongue right now and we can get on with the reason we are here."

Engier raised his hand to calm her down. "Speak your peace, wizard, if there are no terms to delay battle then we can commence with war."

"So hasty and so quick to fight. There does not have to be a war, Jarl Engier," he answered. "Surrender the stone of blood and we will leave peacefully, taking the dead with us."

"Give us one night to consider your request?" Engier asked.

"No," Sabjorn said, shaking his head. "One night means several more clans arrive and our victory may not be as assured as it is now. Your messenger scouts are not getting through my forward line, Jarl Engier."

"You're awful confident of that," Drengr suggested.

The rebel wizard smirked back. "You cannot communicate with your reinforcements, and we outnumber you, three to one, or better," he said confidently. "Though it is getting hard to tell exactly how many dead men are tethered to our magic now when new undead soldiers rise without our command. The magic just does it on its own. Remarkable, really." The necromancer shook his head as if slightly puzzled by his own words, but quickly added, "Just surrender the stone," he said.

"That is not an option," Engier said, spitting at the wizard's feet.

"And giving you another night to reinforce your position while you wait for reinforcements is not an option either," one of the other rebel wizards said.

"You've raised half the souls of Niflheim with the little you have," Engier growled. "No more will come your way, so if that is all you've come to bargain with, then leave and prepare your mockeries of Northmen warriors. They will not save you from a true Northman's blade."

"You would have Sokn lose its two most powerful clans just to keep the bloodstone from our hands, Jarl Engier? You're outnumbered and the bulk of both your armies are a week away. You can't have more than two hundred men between you including your high guard, and I doubt the battle-lacking population of the mine will tip the balance in your favor, even should they be brave enough to pick up a spear and fight. Are you sure you can win when we merely want to continue to study the stone's new properties in peace? I can promise you that even though we now have the knowledge to do so, we will not cut the large block to make individual runes that could raise thousands... hundreds of thousands of undead. We mean no harm to the clans and certainly not to the people of Sokn."

Engier nodded when Drengr glanced his way in the hope his wizard could get through to his own kind.

"Sabjorn," Drengr began. "You speak of only study, yet you killed the High King and his family with this pestilence the bloodstone produces. The traces of it are seeping into every living thing in this valley, just look at the area around your camp. Everything has died. We are taught to preserve the grace of Freyja's beauty. The Earth-mother is weeping for what you have done."

"The gods are long past concerning themselves with the happenings of mortals, brother," Sabjorn replied. "Most Northman no longer worship Odin and Freyja. Tyr has taken the throne of Asgard as our people have come to worship war far more than anything else."

"Sacrilege..." Jarl Brenna snarled, but Sabjorn quickly interrupted her.

"Is it?" the wizard barked back. "How many years of peace have you known, Jarl Brenna? You have been Jarl for only ten years, and you inherited nothing but war from your father. Before we caught your attention, you and Jarl Engier were at each other's throats over the Dragon's Breath opal mines at the feet of Freyja's Grace. You fought over stones in a mountain and now you only unite to fight against us over stones from the earth. Should you defeat our army here today you would return to your own wars where more sons and daughters of Sokn will die for the glory of the war god. It is time this changed. Sokn and our way of life must change."

Drengr gasped. "You speak dangerous words, brother."

"Perhaps," Sabjorn agreed. "But the ancient writings at the Skall tell of a time when war did not dominate Northman life. The school built for our kind has many such writings."

"Careful, brother," Drengr said, repeating his warning.

Jarl Brenna stepped forward. Clearly having heard enough, she grabbed Sabjorn by his collar. "You speak with a traitor's tongue, wizard! The dark times should be left in the past."

"Why?" Sabjorn asked. "Because the Skeyth—magic users—ruled Sokn? Because there was peace and prosperity for all Northmen, whether slave, serf, wizard, or noble? This world, our world, it knew peace for hundreds of generations under the Skeyth."

"No," Drengr spat. "You speak of peace during that time, but you must also speak of the Rune Wars if you do so. There is a damn good reason why the Skeyth no longer rule and why they do not leave their exile from the heights of Freyja's Grace, Sabjorn. The Rune Wars nearly destroyed Sokn and everything we are as a people."

The wizard jerked himself free of Brenna's grasp and shook his head. "In the hundreds of years since then, the Jarls have done far worse, to our people and to our young, whether Northmen or Ama Taugr. They have led us nowhere but down the path of war," he argued. "Think about it Drengr Stone-Wise. You yourself would never cast a single rune, never use your natural gifts, if you were not in the service of a Jarl who is more of a warlord than a ruler. You are one of the very few Ama Taugr allowed to freely do what we do best. Sokn needs to change, before we destroy ourselves."

"So that is your plan then?" Drengr asked, clearly stunned by Sabjorn's words. Engier frowned at the tension in his wizard's voice but held his tongue as the man continued. "To raise an army of dead, only to force Sokn to its knees under your rule?"

Sabjorn nodded. "I am not interested in being High King, but it is an option we are willing to explore if necessary. The large block of bloodstone can be marked with runes that will change it into a... a kind of forge, if you will. One that will not just create limitless numbers of undead soldiers, but may also prolong life, cure diseases. And if not, at least it will create a disposable army and provide us with a means to end the current hierarchy," he said. "It will be a far better end than watching the Jarls tear Sokn apart over who will become the next high king. Because I assure you, brother, that is what comes next regardless of Engier War-Blood's popularity. The ice clans will put forth their ancient claim to the high throne."

Engier scoffed at the asinine remark. "You will address me directly while I am standing in front of you, wizard, and I assure you that the men and women from the northern ice shelves will never bend the knee to a wizard," he barked. "The southern clans will also call for unity and then they will grind every wizard into dust at the first sign of a full Ama Taugr rebellion. You will die or be forced to kill all of Sokn's people, and you will be left to rule over absolutely nothing and no one."

Sabjorn replied with a crooked smile. "Don't fool yourself, Jarl Engier, the common people care not who rules over them. Certainly not enough to fight back as you claim. Which leaves only the clans' warriors. And yes, we will fight willingly, even if it means rebuilding our society in the process."

"No," Jarl Brenna growled as her sword rasped from its sheath. "You will not!" Without warning, she swung at the wizard's head. He ducked easily and stepped back to the snap of breaking runes. Engier stepped in front of Brenna with his shield raised as the wizard tossed the broken runes at her feet. An explosion of bright white light lit up the area but immediately subsided without doing any harm and Engier knew instantly that Drengr had countered and collapsed the explosion with his own set of runes.

Blinking the glare from his eyes, he lunged forward with his shield but quickly stopped short when he saw the bright swirls of blood red magic surging from the broken runes lining the knuckles of the four rebel wizards. The ground shook under his feet and he glanced down in time to see a skeletal hand burst from the earth.

"Retreat!" Drengr shouted. "There are dead in the ground below us, it's a trap."

"It wasn't meant to be a trap, Brother Drengr," Sabjorn yelled over the hiss of rune magic. "But the Jarls will never see reason through parlay and so, we must force them to see it." With one last crack of broken bloodstone, the rebels tossed more runes on to the ground.

A dark red mist permeated the soil and grass at Engier's feet as more earth stirred over the waking corpses buried below. Both Engier and Brenna's high guard acted immediately, closing around the Jarls, while leaving them room to fight as the group backed away from the remains of at least a dozen undead bodies rising from the dirt. The walking corpses steamed in the cool morning air and Engier roared before rushing ahead with his high guardsmen.

He slammed into an animated skeleton, pushing at it with his shield. The skeleton shattered under the tremendous blow and he swung his axe at a corpse with more rotting flesh than not. The hot blade sizzled when it struck the dead man's chest. Engier planted his feet and tore the blade up through the creature's skull. Seared by the runes forged into his axe, the scent of fried, rotting flesh hit his nostrils and he growled, ripping the blade free in time to see their superior numbers had already won the fight.

Jarl Brenna slashed at the last raised corpse. Her double swords flashed repeatedly until the rotting body fell, unable to move without limbs. Engier wiped the dark ash from his own blade with a heavy cloth as Brenna's razor-runed weapons pierced the dead man's skull and the creature finally quit moving.

"Let's move, quickly," he said. "Back to the fortress and get everyone ready." He grunted. "It seems ghosting their camp is not an option. This battle begins today and it has just become the fight for Sokn's future."

Made in the USA
Columbia, SC
27 July 2020